BEHIND THE REVOLVING DOOR,
AN ANTHOLOGY OF CHOICES

VOLUME I

BEHIND THE REVOLVING DOOR,
AN ANTHOLOGY OF CHOICES

VOLUME I

Edited by
Ann Stolinsky and Ruth Littner

CELESTIAL ECHO PRESS
ROSLYN, PA, USA
2025

Celestial Echo Press
An imprint of Gemini Wordsmiths, LLC
P.O. Box 1191
Roslyn, PA 19001
celestialechopress.com

Cover art and design: **Miss Elaneous Arts, LLC**

Acquisitions and editing: Gemini Wordsmiths, LLC

Illustration by WikimediaImages 

Contents

Praise for
Behind the Revolving Door, an Anthology of Choices, Volume I

"Behind the Revolving Door, an Anthology of Choices, Volume I, is a collection of stories bursting with strong writing, riveting imagination, and above all, the kind of humanity we don't see enough of these days. This anthology will intrigue and inspire."
- *Christopher Ryan, editor/publisher,* Soul Scream Antholozine

~~~~~~

"One of the most eclectic and enjoyable anthologies I've read in years. Finishing each story and starting the next is like stepping through a revolving door from one exhilarating universe to another!"
- *Phil Giunta , Award-winning author of* Testing the Prisoner *and* By Your Side, *www.philgiunta.com*

~~~~~~

"This thought-provoking collection of finely crafted tales runs the gamut from humorous to chilling. The stories, spanning the fiction genres, show you 29 ways in which one simple choice can rewrite a person's life. Open your mind and dig into this literary treat!"
- *Austin S. Camacho, author of the Hannibal Jones mystery series*

Foreword

Decisions, decisions… every day, so many decisions. From the moment we wake up in the morning: What to eat? What to wear? Should you have a second cup of coffee? How about a sixth?

And each one of them can be life-changing (especially that sixth cup of coffee).

It is often said that you are what you eat. Biochemically, that may be true, but in a deeper sense, you are what you *choose*. The things we decide to say or do and sometimes more importantly, the things we decide *not* to say or do—this is what defines us.

In *Behind the Revolving Door: An Anthology of Choices, Volume I*, Celestial Echo Press has assembled for its fifth anthology twenty-nine choice tales from thirty talented authors. The stories span a range of genres and styles, but all have one thing in common.

Each story has at its core a decision, from the mundane to the bizarre to the downright existential. To be or not to be. To kill or not to kill. And they are all important. After all, even the most routine decisions can have massive repercussions, both for the decider and for the world around them. Before the flap of a butterfly's wings can have profound, distant, and unexpected consequences, that butterfly must choose whether or not to flap its wings, must decide when to fly and where.

The protagonists of these stories aren't the only ones facing such momentous decisions. You, dear reader, face decisions of your own. Hopefully, the decision to buy or borrow this book has already been made (Good one, you!). But now you must choose where to start, which story to read first. Start at the beginning? Or skip around based on some arcane system based on criteria only you are privy to? So many decisions…

Jon McGoran is an editor and the author of eleven novels, including his latest thriller, *The Price of Everything*. He can be found at www.jonmcgoran.com.

Nocturna à l'Orange Sanguine in Five Easy Steps
Joachim Heijndermans

"You ready, Ter?"

"Yeah. I'm great. I'm ready."

"All right. Recording in three, two, one--action!"

"Hello, hello, hello! Welcome, all you daredevils of the kitchen. I'm chef Terry McKellard, and welcome to '*The Razor's Edge*,' the life-hack/cooking course on how to prep dishes with special and bizarre ingredients. Boy, I tell you what, I'm right excited for what's in store today. This is the tenth, yes, tenth, week of my 'Risky Tastes' series, where I try my hand at all the top recipes collected from around the world that call for hazardous to life-threatening ingredients, poisonous herbs, and the most lethal of flavor-enhancers, which I'll be making into perfectly safe to eat dishes that you can make at home. As they say, 'what might kill you has to be delicious', am I right?

"On last week's episode, when we discussed cooking with contaminated and spoiled meats, I brought up beef and pork that has been affected by HFMD and how we can still make a decent rare steak or pork belly with it. Click the link up here to see or rewatch that video. Now, today I'll be continuing this theme with what has to be *the* most requested dish by our lovely and wonderful supporters on Fund-Folk. Special shoutout to all of you. I love you guys, and we couldn't do this show without your support. If you want to see more of the behind-the-scenes stuff and our pre-show prep, please consider signing up and subscribing to our Fund-Folk exclusive channel and see all the exclusive content we daren't show here. I will get into this again at the end of the video. For now, we'll move on to today's recipe. Yes, I've caved in to your pleas and your wonderful donations, so I'm finally doing that insane dish made with the rarest and most dangerous of all meats: *Nocturna à l'Orange Sanguine*, or: vampire filet with blood orange!"

The silver links cut into my wrists. Trapped, like a rabbit in a snare, while the chains that hold me slice into my flesh with all the ease of a knife through butter, halted only by the bone. I go limp, but even without struggling, I am left with searing marks on my skin courtesy of these chains. Maddening. Were these made from anything other than silver, I would've been free in a prey's heartbeat. Or so I tell myself, had my captors not also pointed harsh bright lights on me to diminish my stamina, and put that mister laced with garlic extract to numb my senses, in this cell.

Sloppy. I was so fucking careless. Years prior, I would have never fallen for such a simple trap. An obvious one, really. Promises of an eager woman to service me with sex and blood in some back alley hovel? They must have been just as shocked as I that I fell for such a ruse. My recent life without a familiar to fetch food for me has made me a careless dunce. Lust, loneliness, and laziness led me right into the palm of their hands. Seven hundred years, living as counts and warlords and imperators, and now I dangle here like a gutted sow whose fate is to feed these mongrels. Shits who aren't fit to lick the dirt from my heels. So damned sloppy.

Regardless of the details of my capture, my stupidity and my current predicament, I am getting the fuck out of here. And once I do, I will kill every bastard in this place. They will curse their wretched God for bringing them into this world only to feel the agony that I shall unleash on them. They came into life screaming, and they'll scream far louder as I wring that very life out of them with my bare hands. They will howl for death as I drain their blood, feast on their hearts and snack on their tendons whilst they live. I will get out. I will swim in blood. Paint the world red with their innards and force their families to wear their skins.

Speaking of blood, what little I still have in me has gone to my head. The room spins. The world spins. Endless vertigo, embraced in silver chains.

Bastards.

"Now, don't let the scary name fool you, folks. It's not really a filet. It's actually more of a sirloin cut, if you'll pardon the comparison with actual beef. Yes, yes. I know. It's not the same. We've had some trouble with the beef industry folks before, so the filet thing is just shorthand.

"Before we start, I need to reiterate that if you're brave enough and want to give vampire steak a shot, you should make the proper arrangements before trying this recipe. I'm not kidding here folks. This is one of the big ones. With most toxic or spoiled products, it just takes a lot of heat, spices to counteract toxins and a squirt of lemon to get it all cleared out. Vampire meat? The word is that if you don't prep it the right way, you could end up as one of these bloodsuckers yourself. Or worse! Better to be safe than sorry. So follow my instructions well, and you can safely dine on a piece of meat unlike any other.

"All right, now that we've got that out of the way, let's begin!

"First, we'll need our ingredients: One and a quarter pounds of vampire meat, preferably cut from the stomach or thighs. A tablespoon of salt, Himalayan preferred. One tablespoon of extra virgin olive oil. One peeled blood orange. Half a teaspoon of minced shallots, or do a whole teaspoon if you want a bit more of a kick to it. And finally, a tablespoon of minced fresh herbs to your liking. I suggest thyme or parsley, but that really comes down to personal taste.

"What we're doing here is similar to a garlic sirloin steak, minus the actual garlic. We wouldn't have much left to work with if we used it. But that little contrast is just the thing that makes this dish so special. And with the added blood orange slices, it will create that clash of flavors that comes together so well in a perfect blend of sweet and spicy.

"Once you've gotten all the ingredients, we can start.

"First off; the meat. Now, here's the thing about vampire meat: it's alive. Yes, even after cutting the meat from its source, the cut piece continues to technically be alive. That means it still thinks and feels, and if you don't cook it the right way, the sucker will try and choke you by clogging your throat once it goes down.

"And secondly; utensils. You'll also need a pestle and mortar, which we'll use to tackle the herbs later, which most seasoned chefs should have in their homes. The most important tools you'll need are fine-grade cutting materials if you want to cut yourself a slab of vampire in a way that won't take hours since the flesh regenerates quickly if you're using basic tools. I myself use silver-embedded cooking knives from Hidotachi (link to their store here and in the video description below). These are worth every penny when it comes to preparing…unusual meats. We'll be using them again once we tackle the topic of Lycan roast. I do need to warn you that the silver could disintegrate the meat if not used carefully, so try to stick to determined quick slices.

"Now, vampire meat has both a downside and an upside when measured against normal bad meats. It is a far better-quality cut of meat that stays good much longer than any beef or pork. But on the other hand, the chance of infection spreading when eating is far greater if you don't prep it right. While vampirism through a bite is one of the most contagious afflictions in the world, consuming vampire flesh is not as bad and usually leads to only minor infections. But even that can be prevented by doing the proper work on the meat beforehand. The threat of infection is the reason why the FDA has banned its consumption in legal circles. That's also the reason why I can't divulge the identity of my supplier, but trust me, they are the best in their field. I mean, look at this piece on the platter. Juicy. Fresh. Exquisite meat, if I may say so. In my experience, a lot of the so-called dangers are overblown. Direct contact with vampire blood can lead to some anemic symptoms, but nothing a good walk in the sun won't cure. Their flesh is also devoid of other parasites, so it's technically cleaner than most meats. The only surefire way to be transformed into a vampire directly is still through a bite, so if your sucker is muzzled and tied up all right, you should be fine.

"Anyway, if you follow these simple steps for vampire meat prep, you shouldn't have any trouble at all, and you'll be chowing down on a nice, juicy vamp steak in no time."

The chains sap every ounce of strength from within me. Clever shits. This operation of theirs must have cost them a lot of time to plan and quite a penny in resources. They got me good. But I have time. No matter how much of my flesh they take from my body, I've got all the time in the world.

They won't kill me. They need me for my flesh. Lunatics that feast on me for…sport I would suppose. Madness, as my flesh and blood could turn them into one of my kind. Worse, actually. They could become the misshapen, the ghouls that serve me blindly. All my strength, but no will of their own but to serve me. I could simply wait until they slip up.

Then again, I could be left waiting quite a while.

I flex my muscles as much as I can. The silver shoots lightning through my dried-out veins. I'd hack up my guts if I had the strength in my throat to do so. I catch my breath, but that just causes me to inhale their damned garlic fumes that they keep misting the room with. Just enough to incapacitate my senses, but not so much to burn my skin. The itch in my eyes grows worse with every passing moment. These ones, these mercenaries and their cook, are far better equipped than the average hunters.

But that doesn't mean I'm not without a plan of my own.

"So let's get started with step one: the prep of the steak itself. As I mentioned earlier, you'll need your tools. Get your knife and get ready to prick some small holes into the meat. This'll allow the juices to seep out better once the steak is in the pan. You can try it with a fork or toothpicks, but in my experience that usually doesn't work. The flesh heals too quickly. I would use something sharp and silver, but again, don't let it touch the meat too long.

"Now that you have your cut, we move on to the prep for flavor. First, we apply a dry rub with the salt. Rub it in well, but not so much that it damages the cut. For safety reasons, I'd suggest you wear plastic gloves. While you should be okay, the vampiric bacteria could enter your bloodstream through small cuts or scrapes on the knuckles, which might increase the risk of a minor infection, so treat the meat with caution.

"After you've rubbed the salt in, it needs to sit for about four to six hours for the flavor to seep into it. Put it somewhere dark, always out of the sunlight. We all know why, but you wouldn't believe how often I need to reiterate this.

"Once the meat has sat long enough, it's time to move onto step two: prepping and seasoning the pan. Pour in the olive oil and gently heat it up on a low flame. You can take your time here, as it doesn't take much to heat up vampire meat. What we're doing here is making our 'garlic' flavor with the shallots. Chuck them in and give them a gentle stir until they get that beautiful caramelized look. Look at that. Lovely. You can add some more salt or other seasonings if you'd like. If you have faith in your cooking skills, you could even add a pinch of real garlic. Just be sure not to overdo it.

"I do think it's time to move on to step three: cooking the steak. Take the meat out—and make sure not to expose it to any UV-based light sources—and place it on a plate near the flame. Now, here's a little extra tip from Chef Terry. Before you put the steak in the pan, you can sear it with the silver. What does that mean? Simple; you take your silver knife and gently press it down on one side for about ten seconds, then flip it over and do the same with the other side. Make sure not to leave the silver on too long, so you don't blacken it. You want it at a nice, almost caramel color. Once you've done that, lay it gently in the pan.

"Mmm, do you hear that sizzling sound? That hissing? That's the vampire still trying to fight back. See, the thing with meat like this is that you're actually eating it alive. The cooking is really just numbing the flesh while adding a bit of kick to it with flavor and spices. Wild, am I right?

"See that? The way it wriggles? That's it fighting back. It hasn't realized yet that it's already lost the battle."

Plots have I laid. A plan of escape. It might not work on the first try, and it will leave me in more agony each time I try it again. But like I said, I have all the time in the world. Performing the first step hurts, but it was but a minor pain compared to my regular flaying at the hands of my butcher. Nearly five times they cut strips of meat from my torso, each time patiently waiting for it to grow back so they can take more. My regenerative abilities, once my saving grace, are now the reason I have been hunted and chained. A ready supply of regrowing meat. Beastly.

But that does not mean I cannot still use my regrowing skills for my own benefit. They feed me from time to time with just enough for me to stay alive. Just enough to regrow.

I move. I clench. I break what needs to be broken. What little blood remains in me fills my mouth. With great pain and effort, I swallow and push it down, letting it find its place within me. The pain in my intestines shoots through me like lightning. But if this gambit of mine works, my state of bondage will come to an end soon enough.

"All right, time for step four: the blood orange. What you need to do is take the orange and slice it into six to eight slices. Take two slices and put the rest aside. Now, what you'll do is give the two slices a good squeeze over the pan. Push out all the sap in it and let it fall over the meat. The holes we poked earlier will allow the sap to really get in there.

"Next, take two more slices of the blood orange and place them gently on top of the meat. Once you've done that, turn up the heat. We're going to start cooking with fire here for a moment, but be sure not to burn your steak. Look at that. The orange slices are slowly leaking out onto the meat. Give it a good blast of heat, then turn it down. We're going to let the meat simmer in the orange juices while we move on to step five: the additional seasoning.

"Take all the herbs you have, the thyme and what have you, and mix them together in your mortar. Crush them down with your pestle and keep mixing them. You can use a bullet blender, but I prefer to get in there myself, if you know what I mean. Once the whole concoction is made into a nice powder, we should be far enough along with the meat. Take the blood oranges in the pan off the steaks, remove the meat from the pan and place it on the plate. If you like, give it another sear with the silver knife to brown it a little. Then, sprinkle your seasoning over it. As a final garnish, place the last of your blood orange slices on top to bring the whole thing together.

"Voila! Look at that. Simple. Delicious. Absolutely out of this world. All that's left is to sit down and enjoy this lovely, truly unique meal. Look at that! Look how the knife just glides through the meat. Beautiful *Nocturna à l'Orange Sanguine*. I am going to enjoy this.

"That's our show for today. This was '*The Razor's Edge*'. Sign up and support our Fund-Folk for exclusive content, tips, behind-the-scenes footage of this video, and previews of upcoming episodes and more.

"Next week, we'll be tackling a special dish with ingredients from our friends at Base S4. Something a bit greyer of a cut, if you can catch my drift. Be sure to watch that, because it'll be wild. With that, I bid you adieu, so I can enjoy some of the sweetest of meats imaginable. So, bon appétit and-

"Ow! Son of a bitch. That hurt. Goddamn!"

"You all right there, Ter?"

"Yeah…no. Shit, I bit into something hard. Goddammit, did you guys cut too close to the bone?"

"No, man. Stomach, like before. Why?"

"There's something in this. Jesus, it's hard and sharp. Is…is that a tooth? Is that a tooth, Jason? How'd a tooth get in the…in…the…the--"

"Ter? You all right?"

"…no."

And there it is. Screams of the unprepared. Panicked gunfire. Bone shatters and meat is torn to shreds. I can hear him weep as he rips his way through his former compatriots. Strength of the newborn, but without any self-control when faced with viable meat in front of him.

The screams stop. No more violence. Steps approach my cell. The doors open with a rusty creak, and not a second later a bullet shreds the lamp in my cell to pieces. A second shot kills the mister. Finally, I am in darkness once more, and my skin, eyes and nostrils are no longer defiled by the scent of garlic.

"Muh-master-" the chef, the man they called 'Terry,' mutters. Gargled words manage to escape past the pool of blood in his mouth. "Y-you suh-su-summoned me?"

"I did, little mouse. I did. Be a dear, and undo these chains," I hiss. I lick my lips, tasting the freedom that will soon be mine. I smell the blood on the chef's clothes and the cold sweat underneath his pits. "Oh, and would you be a dear and fetch me something to drink? In a cup, please. I seem to have lost my teeth."

Joachim Heijndermans is a writer, artist, filmmaker, and SFWA member from the Netherlands. His work has been published in a great number of publications, featured on podcasts and adapted to television and film, including the Netflix animated series "Love, Death & Robots."

Invasive Species
Jonathan Maberry

We stood outside and none of us wanted to go in.

The choices were obvious–turn and go, and write the whole thing off as another tragedy, another loss in the long list of losses on the slate of space travel. The long list of failures in humanity's struggle to not destroy itself. Leaving was the easy choice.

The harder choice was to do what we'd come to do. Find, investigate, salvage, and rescue. That was the job and that was the noble choice. The better choice.

Better doesn't always mean the *right* choice, though.

No, it damn well does not.

The ship was one of those old-school colony things. Ponderously slow, built when we all thought Einstein was right about the possibility of faster-than-light travel. Dumond and Chung tore holes through that maybe sixteen years after the last colony ship was launched. Somewhere way out in the black are forty-three tubs as big as the one we found on Elliot's Moon. Six earlier ships have been found, either crashed somewhere or drifting.

This one, *The Anthem,* was the seventeenth to launch. No one heard either jack or squat about it since the 2130s, and that was a long time ago. Way before my grandfather was born.

Now here it was.

Nudged up against a slope on Lemuria—formerly Kepler 62e—a super-Earth exo-planet 330 parsecs from what remained of Earth. Big, blue, with a heavy cloud cover that hid most of the land masses scattered throughout its vast oceans. We didn't know Lemuria even *had* land masses, and sure as hell didn't know some of them were forested. Now we do.

Our bird, a VB-530 tunnel rat doing long-range recon for rare minerals, squatted just outside of *Anthem's* shadow, looking like a ladybug next to a beached sperm whale. The scale was about right. We'd drilled through the dark matter gateways, riding one of the less-explored routes in the galactic network, following data interpretations from the astronomical spectroscopy to what we hoped would be sizeable deposits of palladium, rhenium, molybdenum, and tungsten.

Instead we found this big son of a bitch of a colony ship.

It lay there, its back broken from a bad landing. The hull pitted and rusted from its travels.

"How?" asked Collins, my copilot.

"I don't know."

He'd asked that question at least fifty times. *Anthem* and ships of its class could not—absolutely could not—have come this far out. There was no way. Before the first transduction tunnels were built it was a laughable concept. *Anthem* was fast, but she was sublight. At top speed she should just now be closing in on Alpha Centauri, which is only 2.4 light years from Sol. There's simply no way she could have crossed *990* light years. Not without a tunnel. It's folded space or it's centuries of travel, that's the new math. It's the core of what we know about FTL travel.

And yet.

"I don't know," I said again.

-2-

The screen display inside my helmet kept trying to convince me that the atmo was 87.2 percent of Earth normal.

That, at least, made some sense. Kind of.

The colony ships were built to land on alien exoplanets in the goldilocks zones of star systems. More than ninety percent of the ship was a terraforming processing plant. We could hear the hum of machinery. We could feel it beneath our feet. All of the scanners told us that, damaged as she was, *Anthem's* machineries were running full-tilt to transform the planet. We'd seen evidence of it while we descended from our ship, *Hera IV,* which was orbiting at seven hundred klicks. We saw vast stretches of forest that had withered and died as the mixture of gasses changed. And we saw huge new forests growing outward from the wreck site—forests with genetically-modified Earthlike pine trees, cereal grasses, fruit trees, hardwoods, and shrubberies.

There were insects in the air all around us—modified honeybees, beetles, even a species of leather-winged butterflies. Scanners told us that there were worms and spiders and other animals in the soil beneath our boots. We were even picking up thermal signatures of small rodents, squirrels, birds, and a kind of deer adapted to this kind of world.

Since we'd cracked the science of folding space, Earth had terraformed just shy of three hundred moons and seventeen planets. There were some so far along that the colonists didn't need to wear pressure suits.

None of the colony ships had done that, though, because until now we thought that none of them had been out there long enough to set up shop.

Anthem proved all that wrong.

Don't ask me how, because I simply do not know.

"This is freaking me out, Dix," said Collins as we walked slowly toward the ship. The sun was rolling toward the horizon and darkness was coming. "This looks like they've been running the processor for at least fifty years. Given how big this planet is, they've already impacted it. The old biosphere is in active collapse and the new one is spreading fast as hell. How?"

"You keep asking me as if I could know," I said. "Only thing that makes even a little sense is somehow they jumped way out here and got the terraforming going as soon as they crashed. If that happened sooner than later, it means this could have been running for better than ninety years."

It was true enough. Just from the size of some of the towering hardwood trees this had to be in motion for better than half a century, and the ninety-year mark seemed likely.

"Bottom line is," I said, "we may never know how they got all the way out here."

Collins held a scanner up and moved it from end to end along *Anthem's* hull. "Picking up thermal signatures," he said, but then paused, his lips pursed.

"You mean there are survivors?" I asked. For some reason I had been expecting the processor to be running on automatic. There were no shelters, no signs of orderly cultivation. No recent signs, at least. The fruit trees had clearly been hand planted, but everything around them was overgrown. Same with the smaller crops. On the way from our bird we walked through planted fields of some rough-looking gray cabbages, pumpkins, potatoes that—when pulled from the soil—looked stunted and mushroomy. There were other crops, too—salad greens, herbs of many kinds, and long rows of radishes and garlic.

Lots of garlic.

Collins had knelt to study one of the cloves. "Pretty pure," he said. "Close to Earth normal. And they have a lot of it." Then he added, "That makes sense. Garlic has lots of healing qualities, and it's a blood purifier. Useful in any new or modified biosphere."

We took samples, but I tapped Collins and nodded to the sky. "Computer model says twilight is short here. Tilt of the planet and orbital analysis says the days are short and the nights are long. So, let's get this done while we have some light left."

He moved closer to the ship. It was massive. 1677 meters long, vaguely arrow-shaped, with all sorts of fins and flaps for reducing speed and friction during a slow planetfall. The hull was ringed with flexible sections to allow it to settle onto uneven planet surfaces without breaking apart. That design philosophy worked pretty well, but there was an obvious fracture nearly amidships.

"They did a lot of repair work," said Collins, pointing to sections where plating from less important parts of the ship had been carefully welding over the break. "Must have been a bitch, doing all that while wearing those old-fashioned suits."

Our new pressure suits were like a second skin, allowing max flexibility and range of motion. The old ones were clunky, awful things.

We walked through the camp, looking for some sign of recent human activity. But everything we saw was overgrown and damaged by weather. It was a clear purple-blue sky now, but it was an ocean world, so there was a lot of rain and likely a lot of heavy storms.

Then we saw it.

Saw *them*.

It had been hidden by a copse of pines and some kind of rhododendron-looking shrub.

They were made from all kinds of materials. Plastic, thin sheets of metal, wood, and even stone. They formed their own grove, though nothing was ever going to grow there except weeds. Collins and I walked over and stood looking at them. Most were too poorly made and too badly abused by the weather to be legible. Others were in better shape. We read some of them. The names. The cities where they had been born. The ages they had been when they died.

We read the names of the dead colonists, and when we ran out of markers we could read we just counted them.

The oldest markers were in the back, and all of them had the same date.

"When they crashed?" mused Collins, and I nodded.

There were many hundreds of them. Maybe thousands, because we stopped counting.

The newer markers were a mix of dates, but the entire span—from first post-crash death to the most recent—covered a span of just under forty years.

And then nothing. No new markers. No new graves.

"Was that it, then?" Collins asked. "Did they all just die out?"

"Seems like it," I said.

"How? Why?"

"We'll have to do tests to figure it out, but if I had to guess…it was some kind of infection. Terraforming changes a world, but you know as well as I do that worlds fight back. Bacteria, viruses…stuff humans don't have any resistance to. Or maybe some Earth bug hitched along and mutated here. Or…"

I trailed off because I noticed something written in small letters across the bottom of the closest marker. Twilight was deepening, so I aimed my light on it. We both read it.

I am sorry.

I had to.

God forgive me.

Collins tapped my arm and pointed to the marker closest to it. The same words were written there.

We looked closer at all of them.

Except for the headstones for the people who probably died in the crash, every other marker—hundreds and hundreds of them—bore the same three lines.

Collins and I exchanged a long look.

"What do you think happened here?" he asked, his voice hushed. "Maybe the pilot who crashed the ship?"

I shook my head. "He'd have written that on the oldest markers."

"Then what? Some biologist who let the wrong bug out of a jar?"

"Maybe."

"Or," continued Collins, "maybe it was something else. Maybe the soil here didn't generate the right kind of bacteria and the food became toxic."

I said nothing, but instead spotted a second, smaller cluster of markers forty meters beyond the big cemetery, and then headed in that direction. Collins trailed along.

"What is it?" he called, but I didn't answer.

The second graveyard was less orderly, a few dozen graves in a vastly more overgrown field. Oddly, the plants that choked this space were all of the same kind. There were thousands of meter-high stalks, some capped with pink or purple flowers. I squatted down and pulled on one thick stem, and the soil yielded a fat, pale bulb. The smell was strong and familiar.

"More garlic," I said. Then qualified it. "Only garlic. And see? It's not wild. These were planted here. There's some around each grave."

"Garlic? Why? Oh, I remember," said Collins. "It chases off rabbits and moles and…"

"Do you see any leaves that look chewed?" I asked.

He did not.

"Look at the markers," I said. "Tell me what's different about them."

Collins frowned again, then looked around.

"None of them have that apology. No *I'm sorry* stuff."

I gave him a long, hard look. "And…?"

"And what?"

"*Look,*" I snapped.

He studied my expression for a moment, then looked. I saw his face when he realized the other difference.

"These markers…they…."

He didn't need to say it. Every grave marker in that field had symbols for whatever religion the people had believed in.

I got to my feet.

"Why'd they plant garlic on *these* graves?" asked Collins, a note of unease clear in his tone. "There's none on the other graves."

"No," I said. "There's no garlic over there, either."

We stood there in the gathering gloom and stared at the ship. I felt a slow, cold dread creep into my flesh. My blood turned to ice water.

"What did they *bring with them* from Earth?" I asked.

Collins could not answer. He couldn't speak. He stood there shaking his head as the sunlight thinned and faded and finally died over the rim of this world.

We did not see the hatch open. It was too dark.

We heard it, though.

Yeah, we heard it. Old hinges screeched in weary protest as a door somewhere opened. But by then we were running.

Running.

Our ship was one kilometer away, beyond the overgrown fields. Beyond the cemeteries.

We ran.

God damn it to hell, how we ran.

Jonathan Maberry is a NY Times bestseller, 5-time Bram Stoker Award-winner, 4-time Scribe Award winner, Inkpot Award winner, and author of over fifty novels. He is also a comic book writer, poet, executive producer, and writing teacher. He's president of the International Association of Media Tie-in Writers, and the editor of *Weird Tales Magazine*.

This story originally appeared in the *Philcon Souvenir Book 2023*.

Maggie
Charley Heenan

Maggie chose not to choose.

Every day, she ordered the same thing for lunch at the cafeteria. For dinner, she ate the first thing she saw in the fridge. What to wear to work? She let her fingers run over the hangers, eyes closed, and randomly selected her outfit. That's where she was in life – not deciding. There was too much room for failure. Her boyfriend had made every decision in her life over the last two years, including the one to end their relationship. He knew things she didn't and was so much more experienced in life. It was why he could point out her mistakes – purchasing the wrong toothpaste, loading the dishwasher, or adding mushrooms to a sauce when she should have known he didn't like them. Without him, how would she ever know the right thing to do?

Making decisions was a funny thing. Someone's choices were good or bad depending on the outcomes, but outcomes were unknowable. Maybe predictable or likely, but not knowable. An outcome was the big plop in the lake, but there were all these ripple effects of a choice. If an outcome was unknowable, the ripples could be unfathomable. Who determined bad or good? The decider or everyone impacted by the choice? Was there some aggregation of opinions? And just to complicate things, a bad outcome could be good in the long run, but sometimes hard to see. A good outcome might be short-lived. Different for every person impacted. Adding to the anxiety of decision-making, some choices can't be undone. Not choosing gave her peace.

Choosing randomly worked well until the arrival of a new office supply catalog. It took time to write all the catalog numbers of potential items on Post-its, drop them into an empty trash can, and then select the winners. Complaints that Maggie's delayed ordering caused lost discounts, along with concerns about the hot pink caftan she wore into the office on that snowy December day, resulted in a mandatory visit to HR. The counselor there suggested she attend the "Super U" conference hosted by the famed one-named motivational speaker, Sage. Maggie explained that getting to the event meant deciding whether to go by bus or car, which route to take if she drove, where to park, and ...

The HR man interrupted her. "Just take an Uber, for god's sake."

On the day of the conference, the Uber driver dropped her at a downtown Holiday Inn. Dressed in a flowy sleeveless chiffon dress in bright yellow and snow boots, she entered the small event room and stood, looking around at everyone, not talking to anyone, and feeling less-than. Everyone else was so together, so obviously in-the-know. She felt their judgment and pitying looks. Mercifully, an emcee took the stage and encouraged the crowd to take a seat, "Anywhere, anywhere is fine, really. Just sit in the closest open chair." She and everyone else sat. The lights soon dimmed except for the stage area at the front of the room. A banner with the motto, "Super U makes you super," hung as the backdrop. The attendees tittered in anticipation, and then *he* appeared.

Sage, dressed in a neon blue suit with a red "S" on his chest, strode onto the stage wearing his shiny shoes. He pointed randomly to the crowd. "How many here today do not feel super?"

Most of the crowd raised their hands, which surprised her. Huh...

With his hand on his chest, he said, "That breaks my heart. I will tell you something, and you will think I'm...mistaken... untruthful. I am not. Do you hear me? I am not. Here's what I want to tell you…You are capable. You are amazing. You have skills. Everyone brings something to the table. Everyone. If you came here and don't feel super, you will before you leave today."

It was like he was reading her mind. Maggie did think he was mistaken. How could she be amazing when she was always messing up? He wouldn't be able to change that.

"Does that little voice in your head tell you that everyone else is better? That you are too short, fat, tall, thin, young, old, poor, weird, inept, too whatever? Does it?"

"Yes," Maggie screamed in her head.

"That voice is wrong!" Sage pleaded. "Your issue is that you have no confidence. You have to believe in yourself. Somewhere along your life, people have knocked you down and shredded your confidence."

Could it be that maybe… she was sort of, kind of okay? No, but…

"Tell me if this sounds familiar," Sage said. "I feel intimidated in social situations. I avoid taking risks that might enhance my life. My mistakes prove I'm inadequate."

Yes, it's familiar, she thought. It's the mantra of my life.

Sage asked, "Who here has trouble making decisions? Maybe you worry you'll make the wrong one."

Despite the crowd, it was as if he were talking only to her, one-on-one, like he knew everything about her, cared, and wanted to help.

He continued. "Free yourself! When you're indecisive, you are a stone lodged in the current of life – you won't move forward, you'll only be battered. Do you feel battered? All of these feelings you have come from a lack of confidence. Today, we will start the process of building back your self-confidence. This is your first and most critical step to being a Super U. Once confident, you will be ready for our discounted follow-on program, Success U."

He had the crowd break into smaller groups to run through various exercises based on themes like making mistakes is okay and a way to learn, winning depends on trying, and the importance of challenging negative thoughts. She felt less than super and was holding back, but she knew she had to let go. Sage wanted that for her. Listing her six positive traits seemed insurmountable, but she plugged away–obedient, loyal, and honest. She was stuck at three when the break was announced. Disappointed that she could not complete the assignment, she was the last to leave the event room.

In the anteroom, the attendees milled about a buffet table lined with snacks and beverages. Without looking, she randomly selected one of each and ended up with a grape soda and a bag of cheesy curls that created orange dust on her face and hands that wiping only smeared. As Maggie stood alone at a pub table, still wiping her fingers, a woman approached and introduced herself. The woman was stunning with long, shampoo-commercial shiny hair and bright blue eyes that almost matched the cobalt blouse she wore with jeans.

"I'm sorry to interrupt, but I'm working on my confidence. My name is Debra Webb."

Maggie found it hard to believe Debra needed confidence. If this woman doubted herself, it only proved Sage's truism–that our inner voice and others' opinions can destroy our belief in ourselves. "I'm Maggie. Pleased to meet you."

"I saw you inside, and I just wanted to say how much I like your dress. It's beautiful," said Debra.

Maggie hadn't noticed Debra, but the event room was crowded. "Thank you." She couldn't think of what else to say.

Everything she thought of sounded stupid or weird. Surely, Debra expected her to say something, anything. The thirty-second silence felt hours long.

Debra asked, "What kind of work do you do, Maggie?"

"I'm an admin. I do filing stuff." She shrugged. With Debra's prodding, Maggie explained that she worked for an attorney, Ken Harris.

"That's impressive. He's always in the news. He handles all those high-profile civil cases–big tobacco, opioids. He's suing the fracking companies…something about contaminating the water supply, am I right? Wow. I just work in a bank," said Debra.

Maggie raised her chin and puffed her chest. "Remember what Sage says, all our work has dignity. Don't sell yourself short." She added, "Banking is important."

The two women smiled. Debra suggested they sit together in the afternoon session, but then realized she'd have to miss it to be on a Zoom call. She proposed they meet after the conference and grab a bite. Maggie thought it was odd that Debra's company paid for the session and then had her miss half of it, but Maggie was happy to meet one of Sage's goals, which was to get out of her comfort zone, and boy was she out of her comfort zone. She had spent the last years going to work and keeping house for her boyfriend. Meeting up for a bite with a relative stranger was something other people did. It seemed so cool and sophisticated, which she was not. Despite the afternoon's lectures focused on being positive and surrounding oneself with positive people, her anxiety grew, and she hoped Debra had gotten tied up with her call and would postpone. But no, at the end of the day, there she was, waiting in the lobby.

"Hi," Debra said with a wave. "Should we start with a drink and a chat at the hotel bar?"

Maggie wasn't a drinker and couldn't remember the last time she'd been in a bar, but she couldn't say no. When the bartender asked what she was drinking, Maggie said, "I'll have what she's having."

Debra ordered a double vodka and cranberry. Maggie had never had one, but it went down very easily. She ordered another and became positively chatty, talking with Debra. That Sage was truly amazing. Before Super U, she could never have conversed comfortably with someone she'd just met. She and Debra had much in common–both lived alone after recent breakups, both were working on their confidence, and both thought Sage was the best. Debra kept the conversation going by asking about Maggie's work.

"The secretary runs the office," said Maggie. "I'm like her assistant. I list and keep the depositions and science reports organized and secured, then after the trial, I ensure all the documents are included in the file folders before sending them to our library."

"That's probably the most important job in the office besides Harris's. Are they difficult to work for? My bosses are super-condescending."

Maggie paused. Sage had emphasized being positive, but she also wanted to empathize with Debra. "Well, they were kind to send me to Super U. They pay me well, and they're pleasant. One thing, though, is that the secretary leaves at four p.m., so I have to do her job and mine until five p.m. It's quiet then, but still…"

"I wonder if the lack of respect we get in our jobs is what hurts our confidence."

During Sage's session, when she considered those who tore down her self-confidence, Maggie thought about her overly strict parents, even more stringent private school, and her boyfriend, who she now realized might have been a bit controlling…she'd never thought about work. Her job was easy. All she had to do was follow procedures.

When Maggie stayed quiet, Debra said, "I imagine after a big case, you get a big bonus and are taken out for a fancy lunch." Maggie shook her head.

"Have they offered you any promotion opportunities?"

"No, but…" Maggie had no desire to take on more responsibility, but Debra made it sound like the offices of Ken Harris, Esquire, were taking advantage of her. Maybe they were? "It's something to think about."

Over the next several weeks, the women met for lunch for what the two called their "Super Us" sessions, where each practiced positive self-talk and offered each other compliments and praise. At Debra's suggestion, Maggie sorted her closet by season so she could randomly select weather-appropriate outfits. Both thought they were progressing, but Debra remained concerned that Maggie's work environment was holding her back. "I'm probably self-projecting, but maybe if I saw for myself? How about I swing by at the end of the day?"

Maggie never felt constrained or diminished at work, but Debra had gotten to know her in the Super Us sessions, so maybe she was picking up on something. Most of her co-workers would be on their way out the door then, or still at the courthouse, so Maggie wasn't sure what there was to see, but she valued Debra's support and, hoping to allay her friend's concern, she said, "Okay, I'd like that."

Just after five p.m., the front desk alerted Maggie that her guest had arrived. Debra looked different from the way she had at lunch. Her hair was up in a pencil bun. She wore oversized eyeglasses, and her cute sweater dress was hidden behind a baggy trench coat. Maggie was curious, but she said nothing, to avoid any hint of criticism or make Debra feel less-than.

Maggie had never had a friend visit the office. Most areas were off-limits, so she could only point to them. They started in reception, then moved to the junior attorney offices, the break room, the library, and ended in Mr. Harris's suite, where Maggie worked. Debra gazed around the admin area, then sat at Maggie's desk and surveyed the room again.

"You know you have the smallest desk in the place," said Debra. "And your lighting is horrible. How do you see?" She leaned back, crossed her arms, and said, "I'm buying you a lamp."

"I never really noticed a problem. It's not necessary, Debra, honest. Plus, the secretary has to approve that kind of thing."

"You'll see. You'll thank me. I'll get one in the same style as the secretary's. She can't complain if it's aesthetically comparable. You need it for your eyesight. You have value. You're worth it, Maggie. They can't deny you that." She added, smiling, "I'll even get a smaller one, because of your tiny desk."

The next day, at closing time, Debra appeared in reception with a mini executive desk lamp wrapped in cellophane and a big bow. Beaming, she couldn't wait to see it on Maggie's desk. She set it up, wiped it down, then had Maggie open an empty work file, so that Debra could position the lamp and ensure Maggie had "optimal lighting."

Maggie thanked her profusely, not so much for the lamp, which she still wasn't sure she needed, but for the kindness. "I'd like to return the favor," but Debra waved her off, insisting that Maggie's friendship was reward enough; still, she made a mental note to think of something special for Debra.

In the morning, the sight of the lamp on her desk made her smile inside. Her friend had given that to her because Maggie was valued. When the secretary entered, Maggie mentally dared her to say something, but she only lifted an eyebrow, letting Maggie know that it was seen. Maggie was prepared to use her Sage-isms to argue her worth and justify it, but nothing was said, probably because the fracking case was ramping up.

The office tempo had gone from calm to frenetic in days. Maggie was too busy to meet up with Debra for "Super Us" sessions, but her friend said she understood. People were in and out of Mr. Harris's office. Documents hit her desk. She gathered, sorted, and indexed witness statements, whistleblower statements, lab reports, and engineering reports. Having the lamp seemed to have eased the task of assembling the massive document tranche. Usually, her eyes would be strained and tired, but she told herself they were less so because of the lamp. She was so thankful for Debra's thoughtfulness. The lamp reminded Maggie to treat herself well because she deserved to be treated well.

When the trial date arrived and Maggie's workload eased, she called Debra to arrange a meet-up, but got voicemail. She left a message, but got no return call. She called the next day, and the next day, and the next day–nothing. Was Debra mad?

Maggie should have found time for her friend before this instead of cutting her off because work was busy. She needed to be a better friend. Debra had gotten her a gift, but she never gave her anything. Maybe something happened to Debra? Should she go to the police? Women had to look out for each other's safety. But what if Debra stopped taking Maggie's calls because she was tired of her? Maggie would look foolish if she went to the police, and that was the case. She only had Debra's phone number. She didn't know her address; only that she lived in town. She didn't know exactly where she worked; only that she worked for a bank. All the time they spent together, their conversations were always about Maggie. What a selfish, needy, ego-centric person she was.

Maggie considered asking Mr. Harris about contacting the police, but he was never approachable during a trial. He stormed around the office even more than usual because the case was not going well. The attorney for the fracking companies rebutted every expert's testimony. The two whistleblowers were no-shows. It was almost like the opposing counsel anticipated his every move. Maggie even said so to the secretary.

The verdict came in on a Thursday. Mr. Harris lost–a first. All those homeowners whose wells were destroyed by methane and toxic chemicals were left without recourse. Their life savings poured into houses and mortgages that were now worthless and uninhabitable without access to safe water. Most would have to declare bankruptcy, and their credit would be ruined. The television news showed whole families crying. Mr. Harris closed the office for the rest of the day.

When she entered the office on Friday, detectives of some kind, suited men with badges and guns, were gathered around her desk. Maggie slow-walked. Was it Debra? Something had happened. Oh God! Her heart weighed heavily in her chest. She couldn't form the words to ask the questions for fear of the answers. It must be Debra. Mr. Harris asked her into his office, invited her to sit in the client chair, and then ushered in the detectives before he closed the door.

"Maggie, we sent you to a Super U conference, if I remember? Did you like that?"

Shaking, she answered, "Yes, very much so. I learned so much about being confident, speaking up for myself, and I met..." A sob caught in her throat.

"Are you happy here? Is there anything that makes you unhappy?"

She was thrown, expecting a question about Debra, but to stay positive and be her own advocate, honoring Sage, she said, "I'm very happy here. I have to cover for the secretary for an hour every day, and I have the smallest desk and don't get invited to the fancy lunches, but overall..."

The frown on Mr. Harris's reddening face deepened. "LUNCHES! You eat the same thing every day." He exhaled long and loud. "Tell me about the lamp."

He couldn't be mad about that, could he? "It provides good task lighting. It really helped with all of my fracking workload. I don't think it's a big ask to have it. It was a gift from my friend, Debra Webb." He held up his hand to stop her from continuing.

The detectives pounded on their phones, seeking any information, warrants, or wants on Debra Webb. Mr. Harris explained, "The gift you accepted was from a fracking company operative. A camera in the lampshade provided our opposition with our entire case."

He was obviously mistaken. "Debra's no operative. She works in a bank. I met her at Super U. Like me, she is developing her confidence. I haven't been able to get in touch with her, though. I'm worried something's happened."

Mr. Harris leaned in and spoke slowly. "Yeah, she's working on her confidence, all right, because she's a con woman. She's ghosting you. She's probably on a beach in Belize with a big fat load of cash. If she works for a bank, it's the Bank of Debra Webb."

The detectives reported that no Debra Webb was registered at the Super U conference, and no one by that name lived in the tristate area. They showed her a video from the outside security cameras, and Maggie identified Debra, who was wearing a mask as she approached the building, preventing facial recognition searches. The lamp had none of Debra's fingerprints.

"I didn't know," Maggie sputtered through tears.

Mr. Harris pointed at her. "Think about it. You did."

The detectives handcuffed Maggie and formally arrested her on the charge of conspiracy and took her to the station for booking. At her arraignment, the assistant district attorney said that she had admitted accepting a gift, the lamp, that provided privileged information on a multi-million-dollar lawsuit, and she had provided no helpful information on her co-conspirator. "For all we know, she's going to meet up with her friend or get a big payout at some later date."

She was not that person, but Maggie told her Public Defender she wished to plead guilty. A guilty plea would allow Mr. Harris to refile the lawsuit, albeit with a much weaker case. The plea might help atone for all the damage she did.

At sentencing, the judge appreciated her not contesting the charges, but said, "The decisions you made undermined the justice system, and, as a result, you hurt families, causing homelessness and financial ruin. It is beyond my imagination how you could inflict such harm on your neighbors. What do you have to say for yourself?"

"Your Honor, that was not my intent at all. I was feeling low and met someone who showed genuine interest in me. She listened to me, encouraged me, and made me feel like I mattered. The bottom line is that I befriended someone I shouldn't have, someone who manipulated me. Everything else that happened, all those terrible things, were only ripples of that one bad decision. That's what I'm truly guilty of."

The judge gave her 23 months, and prison gave her time to think about her one big, bad decision and the follow-on choices that led to this moment. Whether it was just loneliness or self-doubt, Maggie gratefully chose to accept Debra's friendship, ignoring questions and red flags. She never saw Debra in the Super U conference room, but believed her when she said she was an attendee. Debra's outfit with the pencil bun and heavy glasses, intended to disguise her appearance, seemed odd, but Maggie ignored it. She never questioned the lighting at her desk, but she accepted the lamp because Debra was nice. She ignored company policy on décor for the same reason. Was she a manipulated victim of a con or someone incredibly desperate for friendship and connection? For all her quoting of Sage, she hadn't learned the lessons. If she'd only worried less about being accepted. If she'd only seen what was right before her, trusted herself, and mustered the courage to go it alone. Because of her lack of confidence, she abdicated her judgment, and her world exploded. She'd have to do better and be more discerning. The prison library had all of Sage's books. She planned to read and re-read them until his way of thinking was hers. In the meantime, prison wasn't so bad. They told you what to wear, what to eat, and when to sleep. It was nice not to have to make choices. She lay on her cot, reading, thinking, and waiting to be told what to do.

Charley Heenan worked a variety of jobs before graduating from St. Joseph's University and having a successful career in military finance and logistics. Her experiences and the people she's met along the way inspire her. Heenan's first novel, *Danny's Boys*, is on sale now. She can be found at: https://www.charleyheenan.com/

The Flight of the Skylarks
Don Reilly

It was half five. The sun was just after rising. Meaghan was standing over the sink, having her tea and brown bread, so she could hear the knock when it came. She stopped mid-bite and listened. That was a knock for sure. She ran to the door for the third time that morning. As she reached for the brass handle, her hand froze. Was she having a stroke? She wiggled her fingers. Urged them forward. On the other side of the door, there could be no one else but Mrs. Quinn, a neighbor from two doors down. A second urgent knock broke the spell.

"I saw your sitting room light on," she said when Meaghan opened the door.

"I couldn't sleep, Mrs. Quinn." Meaghan reached for her throat and struggled to catch her breath. "Did the hospital ward call?"

"Aye," the older woman said, reaching out to hold Meaghan's hand. "Liam's taken a turn for the worse. The doctors want you there now."

The word "now" cramped Meaghan's stomach, like she was about to vomit. She swallowed hard. Breathed deeply. "Thanks, Mrs. Quinn."

"Be strong, dear," Mrs. Quinn said.

Meaghan closed the door. Be strong? So easy for people to say. Her mother-in-law had been spewing those miserable words at her for weeks. From her, it felt like an indictment. "Be strong, love. Honor Liam's wishes." What about Meaghan's wishes? The children's? She was sick of people telling her that there was strength in letting him go.

She felt dizzy. Her thoughts whirled. She had to get ready. Feed the children. Get them off to school. They couldn't go with her. Couldn't see their father . . . Her throat tightened again. She ran to the kitchen window and wrenched it open. Maybe the earthy smell of the Bog Meadows Reserve would calm her. The cool air. The lush green landscape. Breathe, she commanded. She reached for the sill to steady herself, stared at the treetops and the dim red glow behind the dull pewter sky. A flock of brown skylarks pumped their frenetic wings as they flew toward the outskirts of town. How odd that their flight should bring her peace.

She spun away from the window when her mother-in-law's bedroom door screeched open from above. After five heavy steps, Geraldine's feet thumped down the stairs. "Was that Mrs. Quinn? Did she get the call?"

"Aye," Meaghan said, looking down at Geraldine's thick calves. "Her phone's a blessing for sure." She paused. "Liam's in a bad way. Can Patrick drive me to Long Kesh?"

"He'll be driving us both," Geraldine said. "I'll not be left behind. He's my son, you know."

Geraldine had often repeated this regrettable biological fact during the last fifty-nine days. She always added, *And I'll see to it that his wishes are honored.* Liam expected them to let him die. Daily, Meaghan and Geraldine argued about this. "Liam's chosen his path," she said. "We can't interfere." For weeks, Meaghan fought back, asserting her right as Liam's wife to make the decision when the time came. She wanted her children to grow up with a father. Her father-in-law, Patrick, was on her side.

"But the children," Meaghan said to Geraldine when she insisted on going to Long Kesh that morning. She fought the urge to push her mother-in-law. "We can't take them with us. If this is the end, I don't want them there." She paused and hugged herself. "They must go to school."

"And what am I? The bus driver? Fiona Quinn will take them to school, for sure. You know how she likes to rub her nose in everybody's business."

They were in the car now, heading to Long Kesh. Patrick was at the wheel, muttering under his breath, his knuckles white, as they raced along the A55 in Belfast. Their normal route was under construction. Geraldine was in the back seat. There was traffic ahead. The car slowed. "Nothing's ever easy," he said aloud.

Neither Meaghan nor Geraldine responded.

There was even more traffic at the first roundabout. Patrick took long deep breaths. Banged his thick fingers on the steering wheel. He rolled down his window, stuck his head out, and craned his neck to see how far ahead the backup extended. Over the next ten minutes, they inched forward. Patrick kept shaking his head. "I hope he holds on." The women were silent. "You'll sign when we arrive, won't you?" he asked, turning to Meaghan.

"We'll see what the doctor says."

"We'll see?" Patrick stuttered. He clamped his lips shut and exhaled. In a moment he said, "What do you mean we'll see? I thought that was the plan."

"That's not Liam's plan." Geraldine said. She clawed at Meaghan's headrest and pulled herself forward. "It's not what he wants."

"I don't care what he wants. He's not in his right mind." Patrick twisted to see her. His big belly pressed against the steering wheel. The car swerved.

"Da," Meaghan screamed.

Patrick spun as quickly as his large body allowed. Steered the car back into the lane. He looked at Geraldine in the rearview mirror. "He's been without food for two months. How can he know what he wants? We have to save him!"

"I'm so tired of your holier-than-though attitude," Geraldine said as she pulled even closer to the front seat. Her breath was hot on Meaghan's neck, the smell of tea still on it. "You were in the IRA. You know how this works," Geraldine added.

This was the screw that Geraldine often turned. Patrick grew quiet, slouched in his seat. Sighed deeply. "I was a different person, then," Patrick said.

Meaghan slid her hands under her blonde hair and massaged her neck. They had been having the same argument since Liam was arrested. She was tired of it, especially how Geraldine kept throwing Patrick's former membership in the Irish Republican Army back into his face. She turned away from them and watched the Black Mountains pass. During better times, she and Liam hiked there with the children. On their last outing, Meaghan had twisted her ankle. Liam, ever the hero, carried her piggyback down to his father's car. Three miles! The children were star-eyed. "Da could carry all of us if he wanted," her son screamed as he skipped after his father, pulling his sister behind him, her arm trailing behind her like a tail. The children giggled as Meaghan kissed Liam's neck, complaining that he tasted of salt. "Let me taste," her daughter said. Liam spun around and swept the girl up with his left arm. Meaghan wrapped her legs around his torso to stay on his back. Her son grabbed Liam's other arm. "Me too," he chanted as he bounced on his toes. That was the life she wanted: the life Liam had promised her before they were married.

The traffic cleared. Patrick put his foot to the floor and raced onto the southbound ramp of the M1 Motorway. The sign said, "To Lisburn," where Long Kesh Prison was located.

At the first security stop, prison guards in bomb suits interrogated them about their business at "Her Majesty's Prison Maze," their name for Long Kesh. They pushed mirrors on long poles under their car to check for explosives. The guards made Patrick unlock the boot of his car and demanded to see inside the suitcases. Patrick opened them and removed each garment, one by one. Meaghan was embarrassed for him as tried to avoid holding up her panties. The guards hooted. At times like this, Meaghan felt Liam's rage at the way the British Army treated Catholics in Northern Ireland. She had the urge to grab one of them by the neck and squeeze.

At the next security stop, the guards demanded identification even though they knew Meaghan. They ordered her out of the car. As they frisked Meaghan, Geraldine shouted, "Now why would she be carrying a weapon with my son lying on his death bed. Have you no heart?"

"Maybe the Mrs. would like to remain outside," the guard said to Patrick.

If only, Meaghan thought.

Once inside, they were escorted through the cement halls and iron bars of H Block. Irish Republican Army prisoners screamed their support for Liam. "God love him. Tell Liam to hang on. We're right behind him." Some said, "Be strong, Meaghan!"

She entered the hospital ward with its beige walls and subdued lighting. Heart monitors and IV stands stood unused. At the nurse's station, two women recorded their notes. They looked up when Meaghan entered. It all seemed so normal, like any hospital in Northern Ireland save the bars. Liam was in bed, lying on a sheepskin blanket. There was a metal frame over his body. The nurses used it to support a pile of woolen blankets that were too heavy for his thinning skin. Even with this tent over his body, Liam was shivering. How could he look so much worse than he did just a day before, Meaghan thought? His eyes had sunken in his balding head; the skin of his face was pulled taut. Every breath was a struggle. He looked three times his thirty-one years.

Liam's body was the last weapon he had left in his protest to force the British government to treat Irish Republican Army soldiers as prisoners of war who had fought to liberate Ireland from colonial rule and not as common criminals. Today was the fifty-ninth day of his hunger strike. Four other men had already died in the same protest.

Meaghan followed Liam's gaze. His head was turned toward a barred window where a skylark was perched on the ledge, pecking at the cloudy plexiglass. "What's that?" he asked.

"'Tis only a skylark," Meaghan said. Liam jumped at the sound of her voice as if he were pulled back from another world.

"Aye," he said. "'Tis only yourself." He swallowed. Took a shallow breath. Seemed to be gathering strength. "It won't . . . be long now."

"Don't talk like that, Liam."

"We're behind you," Geraldine said.

Patrick shook his head.

Liam reached out. "Ma," he said.

Geraldine lunged to his bedside. Her green and white polka-dotted dress rose up on her calves, revealing a cobweb of varicose veins. Her gray hair fell onto Liam's face. She caressed his chafing skin and kissed his cracked and bloody lips. "My brave son," she whispered. Geraldine had deep Republican roots. Her father was an IRA soldier as was his father before him. But she was proudest of her own membership in the women's branch of the Irish Republican Army.

Geraldine pushed a straw into Liam's mouth. He took long sips of water, the only thing he'd ingest. Until a week ago, he'd insisted on watching the nurse fill water pitchers from the tap so he'd be sure she didn't add any nourishment. Almost immediately after his sips, Liam wretched. Meaghan elbowed Geraldine out of the way. "He has to take water in small sips." A nurse rushed over. Together, Meaghan and the nurse rolled Liam over. He cried out when they touched him. Meaghan jerked her hand away as if his body was a raging flame. His skin was so thin she could have pushed her fingers through it. He heaved into the pot at the side of his bed.

When he was done, Liam reached for Geraldine again and whispered, "Don't let her." His voice trailed off, too weak to say more.

By this point, Meaghan knew better than to be insulted by the alliance Liam had formed with his mother. It's what four mothers and sons had done during the last few months. Four mothers had allowed their sons to die on this hunger strike. Eulogists at their funerals called these mothers the backbone of the revolutionary movement. But those men were unmarried. Meaghan was Liam's next-of-kin. The law was on her side. She'd make the decision about life-saving intervention.

Before the strike, Meaghan fantasized about what life could be like after Liam's release. He had less than three years left in his sentence. They'd have another chance. Maybe move to Sligo, where Meaghan was born. They'd escape the war-torn north, the Troubles. Thirteen years ago, that had been their plan. It was what Liam had promised when he proposed, but Meaghan was hesitant. "Being an IRA wife's not for me," she told him. If that was the life he was offering, she couldn't do it. But Liam begged her. Promised that he'd leave the IRA, wildly nodding his head up and down when she asked, "You'd do that for me?"

She turned away from Liam and Geraldine, grabbed her suitcase, and walked out of the ward. The medical staff had arranged for family members to stay in vacant cells so they could be there when the end was near. The strikers were against this. With family members nearby, there was a chance that someone would break and sign the affidavit that would enable doctors to provide life-saving measures if a striker lapsed into a coma before death. Then the strike would be over. And the British would have won. Again.

Alone in her cell, Meaghan sat on the bed. The bars of the bedframe bled through the thin mattress, and she twisted her hips to find comfort. She unpacked her clothes, some toiletries, and placed them on a metal nightstand. She looked around. The walls were bare. A bulb, encased in a small, barred dome, forced a bright light upon her. There was a single window, barely one square meter in size, a thick sheet of plexiglass behind the bars. It was so scratched she could barely see the sky outside. When she stretched out her arms, only a short distance separated her fingertips from the nearest wall. They began to close in on her. She shut her eyes. Shook her head. This must have been awful for Liam. And for what? To get a bunch of concessions from the Brits? Without warning, tears streamed down her face. This had been happening more and more, like she had no control of her body.

She needed to be held. Liam was too weak. Geraldine's embraces felt like death. Patrick was down the corridor in his cell. Maybe a hug from him would help. He had been supportive when the strike began. Whenever Geraldine cornered Meaghan to "try to talk sense into her," Patrick appeared. "I won't let my son die like the others," he screamed. "We won't," he added, wrapping his big arm around Meaghan's narrow shoulders. She was strong then, ready to stand up to Geraldine. To assert her rights as Liam's wife.

Recently, though, Patrick came to her rescue less when Geraldine tried to turn her. Was he giving up on Liam? On her? Meaghan shifted her weight on the mattress and wrapped her thin, freckled arms around her body. An irresistible urge to see her mother gripped her. But just as quickly, she felt guilt.

Meaghan's mother had begged her not to marry Liam. But Meaghan followed her heart. After a small ceremony, no fanfare, just the two families, the newlywed couple settled into a Belfast flat. "Temporarily," Liam said, so he could tie up loose ends. Soon, Meaghan was pregnant. As her belly swelled, she hoped it would push away the bombings and the killings of the Troubles, the fire and death that was all around her. The baby felt like a contract. Liam would leave the IRA. Give up on the revolution. Settle down. The news of her pregnancy turned her father soft. He offered them a plot of land in Sligo, so Liam could have a start in life. Raise sheep. Maybe dairy cows. Chickens even. But most of all, they'd be safe.

But the Troubles worsened. Catholics were burned out of their homes by Protestants who feared the IRA. Pubs were attacked and Catholic churches set afire. The IRA retaliated with ambushes and car bombs. Liam got sucked in. Thirty thousand British troops arrived to 'keep the peace' and encircled Catholic neighborhoods in open-air prisons. Checkpoints and watch towers grew all over Belfast like weeds. The British Army arrested hundreds of men and women suspected of IRA activity. No charges. No juries. No justice.

When Liam was arrested, Meaghan prayed that it was all a mistake. His sentence shattered her dreams. At first, she refused to visit him in prison, but the children wanted to see their father. She took them until the protest grew radical. When Liam started his sentence, he refused to wear a prison uniform.

It would confirm his status as a common criminal and would recognize the authority of the British government. Instead, he wrapped his naked body in a gray woolen blanket, like hundreds of other IRA prisoners. When prison guards refused to let Liam wear his blanket as he walked barefoot down the long cold corridor to the freezing bathrooms to shower, Liam, like his comrades, refused to wash. The guards retaliated by refusing to empty his chamber pot, so Liam spread his feces on the walls of his cell when the pot filled. His visiting privileges were reduced to thirty minutes every month. Meaghan was relieved. Visits were unbearable. He looked like a caveman with his long and tangled hair. A scraggly beard covered his face. His smell was awful. How could the man she loved live like this? With each monthly visit, he became more and more unrecognizable. Like she was unknowing him.

As Meaghan sat in her cell, under the glare of the naked bulb, she had the urge to pray. She lifted her skirt. The cement floor was hard and cold on her knees. Again, Meaghan thought of Liam, who was forced to sleep on the floor after he destroyed his cell furniture, enraged by how the guards dragged naked men out of their cells and into bathrooms where they were sprayed with liquid disinfectant and hurtled backward into tile walls by the force of firehose water.

She made the sign of the cross and tried to pray. "Lord, I know it's been a while since I've been to church." He knows that she thought. Doesn't he? She started again: "It doesn't seem right of me to ask you . . . after all this time . . . when I could have asked . . ." That didn't work either. She tried an "Our Father." That got her lips moving, at least. She knew those words. But when she tried to use her own words, to ask for something, she couldn't.

Meaghan rose from her knees, pushed her arms into a black sweater, and returned to the ward. The head doctor stopped her and led her back outside, his hand gently cupping her elbow. His touch scared her.

"Your husband doesn't have long," the doctor said. His voice was sympathetic.

Meaghan nodded. Tears welling up in her eyes. "His breathing," she said.

"His heart is failing." He pointed to the nurses' station across the room. "The affidavit is there." He paused. "If you want us to intervene." Another uncomfortable silence. "His life is in your hands."

She was silent for so long, the doctor stiffened and turned to walk away. Meaghan grabbed his arm. Surprise flashed into his face. "Can he be saved?" She paused, not really wanting to ask the next question. She pulled a tissue from her sweater pocket. Dabbed at her dull blue eyes. Pushed her tangled blonde hair away from her face. Swallowed hard. "And be normal again?" she added.

The doctor shook his head. His voice now professional. "Liam's organs are badly damaged. Some, like his kidneys and liver, might never fully heal. His muscles have atrophied. And the blindness in his right eye. That's permanent. The other one could get worse, too."

Meaghan nodded. Tears spilled down her face.

The doctor touched her shoulder. "Look," he said. "We saved a striker before. Do you remember Declan McKenna?"

Meaghan gasped. Brought her hands to her mouth like she was about to vomit. Backed away.

A year ago, in 1980, there had been another hunger strike. Another attempt, in a list of many, to pressure the British into granting prisoner-of-war status to IRA soldiers. When Declan was near death, and the prisoners thought they had a deal with the British government, they authorized the doctor to save him. But in the end, there was no deal. Just another betrayal.

"What is it?" the doctor asked.

"You haven't heard?' Meaghan said.

"Heard what?"

"Declan's gone mad," she said. "His family put him away."

Early the next morning, just as the sun was rising, a nurse woke Meaghan. Liam was in a coma. The doctor was on his way. Meaghan walked toward the ward. Wringing her hands. His parents must have heard. Geraldine ran past her, wrapping a bathrobe around herself. Patrick grabbed Meaghan's arm and dragged her to Liam's bedside.

Meaghan opened her mouth, and stared at the nurse, but said nothing. Geraldine pushed forward. "What happens now?" she asked.

"We'll monitor his vitals. If they deteriorate, Mrs. Maguire will have to decide if she wants to sign the affidavit."

"I'm Mrs. Maguire," Geraldine said.

"I mean Liam's wife," the nurse said, looking at Meaghan.

Patrick was still holding Meaghan's arm. He shook it. "Sign the affidavit, now," he urged. "He's in a coma. This is what we've been waiting for."

Geraldine said, "You can't. You know what'll happen."

Meaghan turned to the nurse. "Is there a chance he'll wake?" she asked.

"The doctor will be here in less than five minutes."

Patrick grabbed the clipboard from the nurse's station and held it out to Meaghan.

"I have to think," she said, backing away. He held the clipboard so tightly, she expected it to snap.

Geraldine pulled a chair to Liam's bedside and sang an old Irish lullaby into his ear.

"What good will that do?" Patrick snarled.

"This song's always brought him peace," she said.

Geraldine continued to hum. Meaghan collapsed onto a vacant bed opposite Liam's. Patrick paced, clutching the clipboard. When the doctor arrived, he asked for a fresh set of vitals and studied Liam's chart. "His blood pressure and respiration are dangerously low. It's time."

Patrick grabbed Meaghan's hand and pulled her up. Forced the clipboard into her grasp. She pretended to read the words as Patrick hovered, her mind racing.

The two of them stood there in silence, linked by the clipboard. Geraldine was still humming. But then she stopped. Meaghan turned. Followed her mother-in-law's gaze. A skylark was at the window, pecking at the plexiglass. It began singing.

Meaghan turned to Patrick. He was crying. "Please," he said. "He's my only son."

She looked at Geraldine. At the skylark. Then down at Liam.

The skylark's singing stopped. Its pecking grew insistent. Meaghan stared into its eyes. They seemed to grow wide. After a few more pecks, it pumped its wings and flew away. Meaghan recalled the skylarks that she had seen the previous morning, on their flight toward the outskirts of Belfast. Where Milltown Cemetery was located. Where IRA soldiers were buried.

Meaghan released the clipboard and Patrick swayed. He took a step to steady himself.

She turned and ran out of the room. Patrick screamed, but she didn't stop.

Don Reilly is a writer and a professor of English at Bergen Community College in NJ. His work has appeared in *Apricity, Chewers by Masticadores, Mr. Beller's Neighborhood, Promethean,* and several anthologies. He earned his MA from University College Dublin and his MFA from the City College of NY.

This story previously appeared in *Chewers by Masticadores* in August, 2025.

Revolving Door
Rik Hoskin

"Admit it. We *do* make mistakes," Cooper said as he hauled a woman through the door into the safe area.

"Is this the Hitler thing again?" Wang, Cooper's partner, asked. She held the woman's other arm tightly, eyes never leaving her bent-over form.

Cooper nodded. Like Wang, he was good-looking in a forgettable kind of way, with a winning smile that oozed charisma. It was the ideal look for field agents, who had to both blend in and engage with many different groups through the timestream. Wang and Cooper handled the twentieth century. "We put Hitler in power, it was awful," he bemoaned.

"It was better than the alternative," Wang told him. "You remember the alternative, right, Coop? What was his name? Wagner? Werner? Something."

"Werner von Wagner," Cooper confirmed. "Well, yeah, he was a madman."

"He executed anyone who didn't have blue eyes," Wang said, "and once he was done then he moved onto the mass execution of all women. That would have been the end of the human race. He'd have done it. We computer-modelled it!"

Cooper sighed, accepting her point. "Yeah, we did. I just can't help wondering why we couldn't find someone better than old Adolf to take his place."

"The timestream adjusts," Wang reminded him. "Can't do more than that."

As they spoke, the agents walked their charge along the corridor, past Nolan working at one of the doors with a screwdriver. They were the field agents; Nolan was just a normal guy who maintained the doors.

Nolan eyed their captive as they passed. Her brown hair was cut into a long, shaggy bob, and she had the docile appearance of someone who had been tranqed. "Who's your friend?" he asked.

"Cindy 'Sin Killer' Snyder," Wang replied. "She's psychotic."

"She was destined to be the most prolific serial killer of the twentieth century," Cooper added.

Was. That was the key. The Agency were social workers, only they worked on problems at a societal scale, using the doors to shuffle men and women into new configurations like pieces on a chess board until they hit on the ideal timeline.

The Agency was not perfect. Just as Cooper had said, they made mistakes. Their job was to try to fix the big messes in human history, find the best course to proceed toward a utopian ideal, utilizing the time drift technology at their disposal here. It was like painting the Golden Gate Bridge--by the time you'd fixed all the shit that had piled up in the twentieth century, you had to go back and rework a whole lot of mess that was breaking out in the Middle Ages.

Nolan watched as the agents escorted Cindy "the Sin Killer" toward the holding pens. She stirred in her docile way, eyeing him with what he imagined were the cruel, cold eyes of a killer, and for a moment Nolan was transfixed. Then Wang's voice intruded on his thoughts:

"Hey, Nolan. I know you're busy ..."

"Always," Nolan said with a sigh.

"... but can you take a look at '63 on your next check? Door keeps sticking."

"'63, what is that?" Nolan asked. "Moon landing?"

"Kennedy," Wang said.

Nolan nodded. "Oh yeah, now I remember."

Nolan was left watching as the trio disappeared. His mind returned to the thoughts that had been churning there before the door had opened. He had his annual appraisal coming up later that day and it was giving him all kinds of stomach cramps.

Why am I dreading this damn review? he asked himself as he secured a replacement plate in place. *I haven't done anything wrong. I just do my job, fixing the doors. It's agents like Wang and Cooper who get the real shit thrown at them.*

He admired his work. *1971.* Always a problem door. It got overused.

Later, Nolan was sitting before the review board with all the enthusiasm of a man attending his own wake. There were three people seated across from him in the brightly lit room, one man and two women, led by Amanda "Don't ever call me Mandy" Rourke. Rourke was a hard ass, she had worked her way to the top by a combination of hard graft and utter ruthlessness. One rumor said she had once used a door when she was a field agent to go find her first husband at the moment he had cheated on her in 1999, killing him as he left the motel room. Another rumor said she had gone back into that motel room and bludgeoned his mistress, blotting her out of history, too.

"How do you think this year has gone, Phil?" Amanda Rourke asked.

Nolan looked at her blankly, trying to figure out what the question meant. "This year?" he asked.

"The one just gone," Rourke confirmed.

"I mean … yes, we've had some ups and downs," Nolan said. *What do you want me to say?* he wondered.

"You could certainly say that," Rourke said. Nolan detected a note of judgement in her voice; she was looking down on him. "Performance has dropped by two percent all across the board, but it's statistically closer to six percent in your area. The doors you maintain frequently fail to open and there's often a problem in retrieving our field agents."

"It's old technology, ma'am," Nolan said. "I do what I can to keep it running, but--"

"But it doesn't run," Rourke interrupted him.

"I was going to say," Nolan said, "that this old tech takes a little goosing sometimes. There're patches there that go back fifteen, twenty years. I'm doing what I can to keep every one of those doors working smoothly, but there are only so many hours in the day."

"So you're telling me you're not up to the job?" Rourke questioned.

"No, ma'am, I ... no," Nolan said. "It's just, I'm one guy and this is technology that could use an upgrade like the sixteenth century doors got last year. You send people through time on a daily basis, it wears these portals down and we don't get the breathing space needed to give them a proper clean and service."

Rourke nodded, showing a smile that reminded Nolan of a shark--one that had just smelled blood. "Would you prefer that we slow down our operations, is that it? Would that give you the time to maintain the doors in proper working order?"

"That would be ... uh ..." Nolan thought for a moment. *It's a trap*, he realized. *I say I need more time and she'll get someone younger and faster to do the job, if I say I don't need more time she'll ask why I haven't been able to keep up with the repairs up to now.*

It was ageism, he knew it. He was fifty-two, same as her, and he worked the doors, spending at least an hour a day tooling custom parts, while she sat in a private damn office on the fifth floor whose windows looked out on the river. But he was old in her eyes and she wanted to be rid of him, even though he had more knowledge concerning the operating of the doors than any three other engineers in the building put together.

"Mister Nolan?" Rourke prompted. "Phil?"

"I don't need more time," Nolan said. "Just need to prioritize better, I guess."

Rourke and her cronies nodded like they were all operated by the same string.

"That's refreshing to hear," Rourke said. "It's good for a man to know his limitations."

Emasculated, Nolan was dismissed, and any hope of a raise, let alone a performance-related bonus, evaporated.

Nolan went back to work with a heavy heart. He could read Rourke's mind without needing to ask. He wasn't simply not getting a pay raise this year but, as far as she was concerned, he was teetering on the edge of losing his job entirely.

It wasn't fair. It wasn't his fault that the doors were glitchy. Like he had told her, they were old, overused and the tech had always been glitchy. He remembered when it was installed and it was glitchy even then, and that was way before Rourke had even come to work in this department. That tech was becoming outdated now and was harder to repair. What did she know about doors? She'd screwed over everyone around her and landed as top dog before she even turned fifty, while guys like him worked long hours and all they ever got was grief. Top dog--that was a laugh. "That woman ain't a dog, she's a bitch," Nolan muttered as he opened up his toolbox and started working on the door for 1963.

After removing the fascia along '63's edge, Nolan identified a line of burned-out wiring, stripped it back and replaced it with new, like for like. He was just soldering a last connector in place when Cooper and Wang emerged from 1971, bounding back into the safe area. They came alone this time, just the two of them, no captives.

"How was '71?" Nolan asked as they strode toward him.

"Door's working," Cooper said. "Doors not so good."

Wang smiled.

"Whuzzat?" Nolan asked.

"The Doors," Cooper said. "The band. Their frontman, Jim Morrison, just died. Again."

"Couldn't stop it," Wang explained. "Hell of a scene."

"Right," Nolan said. He didn't know Jim Morrison or the Doors or anything the agents were talking about, he only knew the heavy hitters--Hitler, Stalin, Lennon, McCartney, Ali.

"But look at you, man," Cooper said. "You're still working. You were here when we came in and that's, like, nine hours ago."

Nolan checked his wristwatch. "Yeah, I lost track of time. So many little jobs to get done."

"How's '63?" Wang asked.

"It's getting there," Nolan said. "You can go try to sort out the Kennedy thing again tomorrow."

"Nice," Cooper said, flashing his brilliant smile.

"Don't work too hard, Nolan," Wang added as she and Cooper headed to the staff room to clock off.

In good spirits, the two agents passed him, smelling of patchouli and rock-and-roll, discussing the best way to set some fella called Eddie Quicksilver up to deal with a famine in Africa.

Their words ran around Nolan's head like cyclists in a velodrome long after the two agents had departed--

You were here when we came in and that's, like, nine hours ago.

Don't work too hard, Nolan.

They were right. He worked long hours and he worked hard, and that bitch Rourke had just walked all over him in his annual appraisal and made him feel small and worthless. "Damn, I have got to get a better job," he muttered. Maggie would be at home, and she'd be waiting for him to tell her the lousy news that he wasn't getting a pay raise or a bonus this year. That was another reason he worked those long hours--he just couldn't face Maggie's disappointment these days, coupled with her sermon outlining all the ways he was failing in his life, their marriage, and his duties as a man. It was easy for her, she didn't have Amanda Rourke riding her over every screw *she* replaced and every wire *she* soldered.

It was gone ten when Nolan finally clocked off and took the elevator down to the parking lot to go home. He unlocked his *Sca Phoenix*, a tired-looking car he'd owned since new and that now passed for vintage, put his hands on the wheel and sighed.

"Okay, Maggie, you see, it's like this," he murmured to himself as he drove toward the exit of the parking lot, trying to figure out what he was going to tell his wife.

He turned toward the barricade and slammed on his brakes as a figure walked out right in front of him.

"Hey!" Nolan shouted, jamming the heel of his hand down on the horn. "Hey! What are you--?"

The surprised face looking back at him in the brilliant beams of the headlamps was Amanda Rourke's. She saw him, scowled, and said something he couldn't hear over the sound of his horn, before striding off to where her own car was parked. *Working late. Like him.*

"Shit," Nolan muttered. "Shit, that's great. I coulda killed her. My boss." And now, she'd no doubt kill him tomorrow when he got to work.

He might as well just tell Maggie he'd quit, because there was no way he was going to recover from this. "Maybe if I had killed her I'd be in better shape," he muttered, chuckling at his own grim humor.

The thought nagged at him all the way home. Nolan lived twenty minutes from work, twelve if traffic was light the way it was this late into the evening. He watched in the rearview as Rourke's car--the latest *Sca Roc* sedan--followed him for the first three miles of the highway before finally pulling off. Just coincidence, he knew, it wasn't like Rourke cared two shits about him.

He laughed then. To think, he really could have killed her. Run her down, just like that, ending the life of his *bête noire* in a parking lot accident. Could have got away with it too, maybe. She wasn't looking where she was going, it would have just been an accident. He might have lost his license, but that would have been an insignificant nuisance in the grand scheme of things.

But he wasn't a killer. And, anyway, it wouldn't help, his annual appraisal would still be sitting on her desktop, approved by those two asshole yes men from senior management who had nodded in time with Rourke when she interrogated him.

Two minutes from home, caught by his sixth stoplight in three miles, Nolan turned his car around, struck by something that hadn't occurred to him until then. He pressed down on the accelerator pad and sped back to work.

The Agency building was eerily empty at night, just the security guard--Patel--sitting at his desk in the lobby watching the game on his *i-handy*. Nolan often worked late; Patel didn't even look up when he came back through the lobby and headed inside.

"You forget something, Phil?"

"Every day," Nolan replied, and the security guard laughed.

The holding pens were low lit and modern, strips of light running along the floor in a diffuse manner designed to soothe their occupants. Nolan paced along them until he found the pen he was after--the one containing Cindy Snyder. He ran his pass key over the lock, and when it failed to open because his security clearance was not sufficient, he tapped in his override code, the same code that allowed him to work on restricted doors like 1941 and 1962.

The door opened and the serial killer looked up. She had been sleeping, the room pumped with tranq at a ratio of five parts per thousand of air.

"Hey," Nolan said, not knowing what to ask. "You okay here? They treating you all right?"

Cindy sneered. "Better than some have," she said. "Better than my pa."

Nolan nodded. "Yeah," he said. "I didn't get on with my old man so good either."

"He beat the sin out of me," Cindy said coldly, bereft of emotion.

Nolan stood there, watching her eyes; a killer's eyes. *Could you tell?* he wondered. "You want to get out of here, go for a little vacation, a day out kinda thing?"

Cindy eyed Nolan up and down like he was a frozen shank of meat she was considering thawing to throw on a barbecue. Or maybe she'd eat him cold. "What's in it for me?" she asked, a challenge in her voice.

Nolan made a show of looking around the eight-by-ten holding pen. "You get out of this," he said. "And you get to kill someone. That's what you do, ain't it?"

Cindy smiled. "I think that is right," she said. "It's getting hard to remember."

Nolan nodded. "Yeah, they ... er ..." He stopped, realizing what he was about to tell her. The Agency used a combination of meditation drugs and subliminal messaging to rehabilitate people, but only enough so they could transfer them to a permanent secure facility. "Dociling them," they called it.

And then he remembered how Wang had described this woman: "psychotic," that was the word she used. This from Wang who had argued to keep Hitler in power as the lesser of two evils. Oh, yes, Cindy "Sin Killer" was exactly the tool he needed for this repair. He just had to open the door.

Nolan unsealed the door to 1999, looked out on the motel where its neon sign hummed under a darkened sky.

"Where are we?" Cindy asked from his side.

"Here?" Nolan said. "Maine. Nice place." A man in suit pants and shirtsleeves, jacket over his shoulder, was just coming out of one of the rooms, heading for a Lincoln Continental parked in the lot. Nolan turned away, pulling a screwdriver out from his pocket. "I figure you'll need this," he said, and he handed it to Cindy.

Cindy took it, looking it over for a few seconds. "What for?"

"To fix something," Nolan said.

She kept looking at the screwdriver, confused. "Things need fixing sometimes," she said. Then she looked up at Nolan. "Sometimes pa got his friends over to help make sure all the sin got beat out."

They both turned then at the sound of the gunshot. A woman had emerged from where she had been hiding close to the Continental, and she was holding a pistol in her hand. The man in the shirtsleeves was kneeling before her, hands pressed against his chest as he tried to hold in the blood before he breathed his last breath. Then, he was dead.

Cindy smiled. "Did she just murder that man?"

Nolan nodded. "Yes."

"That's a sin."

Nolan smiled as he watched Cindy stalk into the parking lot, away from the shelter of the open door they had both stood in, wielding the screwdriver like a knife. It was like setting a bird free, he thought; a beautiful bird of prey.

And after she had done Amanda Rourke, Cindy would realize the woman in the motel room was an adulteress and that was a sin too, so maybe she'd get a couple more kills on her tally. At the end of the day it was all about choices, wasn't it? And the timestream--well, that would adjust, it always did.

He turned away from the scene and closed the door to 1999, leaving Cindy to do her favorite thing in all the world.

The next day, nobody noticed anything different. The first thing Nolan did when he got into work was check the holding pens, searching for Cindy Snyder. She wasn't there.

"Hey, Nolan," a voice called from behind him. It was Wang, a cup of coffee in her hand. "You know Rourke's looking for you?"

Rourke? Shit.

Wang saw the look in his eyes and she laughed. "Yeah, fifth floor, what a chore."

Nolan caught the elevator up to fifth and did the death row march to Rourke's office. An intern with too much hair and too many teeth sat at the desk outside the office. His hair looked like a dandelion in bloom.

"Phil Nolan," Nolan said.

The intern spoke into his head-rig, then told Nolan to go in, all without ever changing his expression.

Inside, Rourke's chair was empty and for a moment Nolan felt deeply unsettled. Then someone cleared their throat from over by the window with its impressive view of the river, and Nolan turned to see a man standing there, his back to him.

"Quite a view," the man said, "I never get tired of it. Always something happening on the water."

"There is ..." Nolan began hesitantly, "... sir."

The man turned, and flashed a warm smile at Nolan. He looked to be about fifty, and in good shape. You could tell he lived well. "'Sir'?" the man said, chuckling. "Come on, Phil! How long have we known each other? We apprenticed here together. I might be your boss, but we're still just Phil and Jason, there's no pretense here." He shook his head as if he still couldn't quite believe how Nolan had addressed him. "'Sir'! You want to know the truth, Phil-meister? You were always the better engineer. I went into management because I knew my skills would never stack up to yours. And here I am."

"And here you are," Nolan agreed, bemused.

"I admit I had some lucky breaks along the way," Jason Rourke continued, pacing over to his desk. "Anyway, have a seat. I need to talk about this performance-related bonus I want to get locked down into your contract on top of that pay raise we discussed yesterday."

Nolan took a seat. On reflection, he thought, maybe he just got along better with a male boss.

Rik Hoskin is a multi-award winning, New York Times bestselling writer of novels, graphic novels, video games and animation. He's written comics for Star Wars, Superman and various other properties, and won the Dragon Award for Best Graphic Novel. He writes SF and horror novels and short stories under his own name and as "James Axler."

Sentient Castles of the January Islands
Beth Goder

Pennelop's boat brushed against the shore of the January Islands. She shucked off her shoes before dipping her feet into the purple sea. The sand of the islands was waxy and smooth, like sheets of umber paper.

It had been days since Pennelop had seen anyone but crabs and sea stars, so when the Castle of Life asked her, gently, why she was there, Pennelop had to clear her voice to answer.

"I would like to know the manner of my death."

Pennelop had premonitions of beetles stinging her. Of breads containing poisons, death rushing through her veins. Her sleep was haunted by hulking granite columns and delicate lace shawls.

These were not mere dreams, but possible futures.

The Castle of Life had all her possible deaths.

There were other castles on the islands. The Castle of Death held all her possible lives. And the Castle of Waking held her dreams. But she had not come here for them.

She would travel the Castle of Life's breathing halls. She would find the death she liked best, and she would tuck it under her cloak to save for its right moment, and the dreams would stop.

The Castle of Life towered above the beach. Crenelations swayed to the rhythm of the Castle's soft breath.

"May I enter?" asked Pennelop.

"Only if you are prepared for what I will show you," answered the Castle of Life.

Pennelop brushed the waxy sand from her feet and donned her sturdy shoes. She tied the cord of her cloak in a double knot.

The Castle's gnarled entrance dilated.

Inside, doors stretched out to forever.

The first room was covered in beetles, their blue bodies shining starlike from the walls. Before Pennelop could flee, the beetles descended, swarming her arms and legs, her back, the soft underside of her knees.

She did not like this death, not the crawl of beetle legs upon her neck, not the whisper of their jaws.

She brushed the beetles from her. "I will not take this death."

In the hallway, the doors no longer stretched to forever. There were more doors than she could count, but they had become finite.

"What have you done with my deaths?" she asked.

"Be careful of your choices," said the Castle of Life. "Not all of these doors will remain available to you."

The next room smelled like a bakery. Loaves of golden bread gleamed on wood-woven tables.

The bread smelled so good that Pennelop thought this death would not be difficult, but she was wrong. Poison poured like fire through her, congealing in a dense knot in her middle.

"Not this one," she gasped.

When she emerged into the hallway, there were fewer doors.

She tried to peek into the next room, but as soon as she touched the doorknob, the door swung open and a granite column engulfed her, trapping her like a bug in amber.

"Please, no," she said.

As the column dissipated, the hallway shifted around her, contracting and spinning.

Only three doors remained.

Although she had not made a choice, lace shawls crawled from beneath one door and wrapped themselves around her.

"This doesn't seem fair," said Pennelop.

"Your choices are narrowing," said the Castle of Life, still in a gentle voice.

"I don't want this one," said Pennelop. Her face was covered in layers of shawl. Through the fabric, the ceiling looked like shattered hexagons.

"Are you sure?" asked the Castle.

"No shawls." She could barely speak because loose threads had worked their way down her throat.

The shawls curled around her, then flowed away.

The hallway had only one door left.

"What's in there?" she asked.

"Your true death," said the Castle of Life.

She opened the door and the Castle of Life closed in on her, digesting her, swallowing her into the infinity of its maw.

Unlike the other deaths, this one she could not tuck under her cloak for later.

Pennelop awoke in the Castle of Death, which was situated on the other side of the January Islands, away from her little boat, away from the gentle-voiced Castle of Life.

She had lost her cloak and one shoe. Her hair was covered in white threads layered like beetle wings. Her skin smelled like freshly baked bread, masking some sweeter, more dangerous scent. Her eyes had morphed to the color of granite, speckled and wide.

"You're here again?" said the Castle of Death, who held all her lives.

"What do you mean?" asked Pennelop. She brushed dust from her calves. She could not remember visiting the Castle of Death. She had never before been to the January Islands.

The Castle of Death breathed in and out. A sigh. A sign.

Around Pennelop, the walls shivered.

"Which door will you choose this time?" asked the Castle of Death, in a voice like stones rubbing together. "Which life?"

A hallway stretched before her, rows of doors reaching to forever.

"What do you mean, again?" asked Pennelop. Had she been here before?

The walls breathed in and out.

Pennelop held her hand against one door, then the next. She saw lives thick with oceans and sea stars and wave-tossed lullabies, where she would learn the songs of whales and name her own constellations. She saw lives of queens and courtiers, gem-sewn gowns and ghostly galas, sweetmeats and silk stockings, betrayal, redemption. She saw lives that ran woven like tapestries, which threaded through forests and flying machines and the snowy, silent mountains of Eln and gleaming cities of tangled keys. Hundreds of lives she saw. Thousands.

"I always come back here," she said. "No matter the life."

How many of these lives had she already lived?

"I know which one I want," she said. She searched until she found the right door.

"Are you sure?" asked the Castle of Death.

A new castle erupted from the umber sands of the January Islands. Pennelop breathed, the walls of her new body pushing in and out. Within her, doors stretched out to infinity.

Beth Goder is an archivist and author. Her stories have appeared in *Escape Pod*, *Clarkesworld*, *Lightspeed*, *Flash Fiction Online*, and *Horton's The Year's Best Science Fiction & Fantasy*, among others. She loves chocolate, hiking, and checking out too many books from the library. You can find her online at http://www.bethgoder.com.

Face It
Carol Gyzander

Connor drove down the two-lane highway, heading to their country house after their latest visit to the hospital. Amy, his wife, sat dozing in the seat next to him. It was late at night, and she was exhausted from the rounds of medical testing she had undergone. Again. None of it had shown any difference.

No good news.

He sighed and rubbed his face to try and wake up, his blue eyes bleary with fatigue. Wouldn't do to run off the road. *I'm just so tired — tired of it all.*

His glance flickered over to his wife. The side of her face that was toward him was smooth and unlined, but he knew what the other side looked like. Had been staring at it over breakfast every day for the past two years. Creased and full of pus-filled blisters—and part of the cheekbone eaten away. Her eye was sunken into her face.

It was just a matter of time until it spread to the side nearest him. Or her brain. For now, in this moment, he could almost pretend she was not affected by the terrible disease.

But deep down in his heart, he knew she was dying. Knew what the doctors told them every time—there was no cure, no way of arresting the progress of the flesh-eating disease. They even had a name for it—ETR—that made his fists clench and his stomach roil. He knew the letters stood for some technical terms but could never make himself remember the acronym. He couldn't get past the idea that the damn disease was eating his wife alive and just called it EATER.

Her head lolled a little as she slept, turning toward him, and when he glanced over the next time, he saw the ravage of the other side of her face, which extended down her neck and shoulder into her arm. Her hand was clenched and twisted in her lap.

EATER? Fuck me.

He replayed in his mind the reaction of the people at the hospital as he'd brought her in. The way even the medical professionals had pulled back from her. Not to mention the way ordinary people reacted to the two of them. It'd gotten difficult for them to go out in public anymore—people feared she was contagious, which she wasn't, and countless times they'd been refused service at a restaurant or asked to leave a cocktail lounge.

People wouldn't even shake his hand.

Connor and Amy had been the "it" couple for years, with money, prestige, society connections. Then their busy social life, once so bright and vibrant, had slipped away as her EATER disease progressed. They spent most of the time alone. Friends no longer stopped by to visit. *What kind of life is this— for either of us?*

She had pleaded with him to help finish her struggle. "I just can't do it myself," she'd whispered. "But I can't stand what this is doing to you. To us. But mostly to you. I know I'm going to die. Where's the quality of life anymore?" Her one good eye had searched his bright blue ones, looking for some kind of a response.

He had refused, of course. How could he kill his wife? Even if she begged him. In a stunning display of the power that desperation and anxiety could have over a strong person, she had let her normally capable veneer slip to show her inner fear.

And he had turned her down. *What does that make me?*

Don't I love her anymore? Or maybe I'm just afraid of going to jail.

Of course, he already felt like he *was* in jail. No friends, no life, just stay home and watch Netflix while he took care of his sick wife. She didn't deserve it, but then again, he didn't, either.

Only one part of his mind was on the driving. They were the only car on the road at that late hour. He took a corner on the rural road a bit too fast, and the vehicle swerved along the shoulder. He gave himself a scare as he yanked the wheel to pull the car back into the lane.

Wow. Almost drove right off the road there. Would've hit the trees ... and at this speed. Damn. Well, if it killed us, at least she would've gotten her wish.

He mulled this thought as he drove along at a more sedate speed. She had not even woken up when the car swerved. Had no idea of the danger they had just averted. The steady consumption of painkillers her condition required left her mostly absent from his world.

But if I do that, it kills us both. Is that what she wants? I don't think so. She just wants to end her suffering and therefore end mine. She doesn't wish for me to die, too.

Right?

He looked over at her again and then reached out to hold her hand where it lay on her lap. *I love you, darling. But maybe you are right. This is no life for you.*

Or for me.

He released her hand and slid his fingers down to the buckle of her seatbelt. Pushed in the button. Released the belt, controlling it to let it retract quietly into the door.

Okay. I'm not really going to do it. But if I did fall asleep on the road, she wouldn't have wanted to walk away from the accident.

Right? She wouldn't.

Of course, I would be okay. Oodles of airbags in this car. I mean, with my seatbelt on and the airbags, I'm sure I'd be fine. What about her? He looked over at the dashboard on her side of the car. Saw the button for the passenger airbag. Idly reached up a hand and stroked the button. Pushed it in. It lit up.

Passenger airbag *OFF*.

Well, that would probably make a difference, wouldn't it? I mean, if I actually fall asleep on the road. It's not like I'm planning to, or anything. But if I did.

She did ask me to. She begged me. She's had enough.

I'd be doing her a favor. It's not just for me, so that people stop identifying me with … with … this horror that is eating my wife. Fucking EATER.

No, it's not just for me.

His hands tightened on the wheel, and his foot pressed harder on the accelerator. The car leapt forward, barreling down the deserted two-lane highway through the woods at breakneck speed. He had trouble making one curve, the tires screeching as he went around it. Her head lolled back and forth, but she didn't wake. Too many pain meds.

He saw the perfect situation up ahead. The road curved to the left with a large clump of trees on the right—her side. He took a deep breath and settled himself in the driver's seat. Moved one hand off the wheel—they said that airbags going off commonly pushed the driver's hand into their face, breaking their arm and smashing their teeth. *No point in messing up my own face, is there?*

He kept going toward the corner. The road banked slightly to the left, but he steered straight ahead, not following the curve. As he drove off the road, heading for the trees, his breath caught in his throat.

I love you, honey.

But I love myself more. Then all went black.

He awoke to an overwhelming combination of lights, both in his eyes and in his memory. Blinking red lights of the emergency vehicles. The EMT shining one in his eyes. The brightness of fluorescent lights overhead alternated between bright and then dim as he was rolled down the hallway on a gurney.

And then the pervasive brightness of the operating room.

He kept his eyes closed now, starting to hear the sounds of the hustle and bustle of the hospital around him — just lying quietly and soaking it in. *What happened? Why am I here?*

The car. The road.

Amy.

He remembered the curve and the gut-wrenching collision that had smashed his wife against the dashboard — where he had turned off the airbag. *Is she gone? She has to be gone.* His eyes fluttered open to look around him and then closed again. *Too difficult.*

When he awoke again, he was able to take in more of his surroundings. He had an IV in his left arm, and the other arm was in a cast. *Huh. Guess I did break a wrist, after all.*

Then he felt up to his face with the free hand, gasping when he realized the right half of his head was wrapped all around and covered with bandages. *Did I actually smash my face with my hand when the airbag hit? Or maybe it was something worse. Maybe Amy collided with me.*

He drifted off again despite the incessant beeping noise in his ears.

The sound of voices woke him. "How are you feeling, there, Connor?" He looked up to see a man in hospital scrubs peering at him, a familiar face. *A doctor? Amy's doctor — he must have still been at the hospital.*

He licked his lips and tried to speak, coughing a bit at first and then finding his voice. "Okay, I guess. What happened?"

"Well, it seems like your car went off the road, and you were pretty banged up. Do you remember it at all?"

He looked away. "No, uh, not really. Where is … where is Amy?" *Not my fault. I had to do it. She wanted me to.*

"I'm sorry, son. Your wife didn't make it."

Oh no. Oh Amy. I didn't mean it — I did mean it. But I'm so sorry.

Tears ran down his cheeks. Or, at least, the cheek that wasn't bandaged. He couldn't feel the other side, under the gauze.

The doctor squeezed his good hand. "Now, now. Try not to do that. We don't want to soak the bandage. Let's just try to believe that your poor wife is in a better place now, and out of pain."

He nodded and let his head drift away from the doctor.

Two days in intensive care, another three in the regular hospital wing, and a round of procedures left him more physically stable, but not fully recovered.

He had restless sleep even with the pain medication. Couldn't get comfortable because of the cast and the bandage that was still over his eye. And the headache. The medical staff bustled in and out at all hours.

So he wasn't really surprised when he woke in the middle of the night with someone in his room. His gaze was drawn to the light at the end of his bed. A man in a black robe and old-fashioned colonial wig sat at a raised desk, holding a gavel and staring down at him with red eyes. The man was lit from behind with a harsh glow so that Connor had trouble seeing his face.

"About time you woke up. I've been waiting," the man said.

What the hell? Connor flailed around in the bed a bit, then realized he wasn't going to be able to sit up on his own. "Why are you in my room? And where is that light coming from?" He looked at the base of the judge's bench and saw only swirling dark clouds outlined against a bright light.

"Why is anybody anywhere? That's the question. Why are *you* here and your wife isn't?"

Connor's hand went to his mouth. "The car. There was an accident, you see. She … she died."

The man nodded his head, frowning. "I see. That's your story?"

"Yes. Um, who are you, and why are you here? Are you with the medical staff?"

"I'm asking the questions here. So, you say your wife died."

Connor nodded. *What's going on? Is he really a judge?*

The man sat back and crossed his arms at the desk, looking down his nose at Connor. "I say she was killed. I say you killed your wife. Can you deny that?"

Connor gasped. "It was an accident, I swear! The car … the road … The car went off the road at the curve. I must've fallen asleep or something. Am I in court, or what?"

"Well, there will be a judgment here. That's for sure."

"I think you need to get out of my room. This is *my* hospital room, and I'm not supposed to have visitors. They'll throw you out when they find you here."

The judge leaned forward with a thin smile. "No worries. Nobody else can see me. Just you. So, tell me, what's your prognosis for recovery?"

Connor relaxed a bit. This was something he could answer, at least. "Well, they say that I'll be out within the week. My arm will be in the cast for at least another two months. Apparently, it was a pretty bad break."

"And your head? Your face? Have you seen it yet?"

"No. No, it's still bandaged, can't you tell? They did some sort of procedure."

Another nod from the judge. "Oh yes, I know. They haven't told you yet because they don't want to make you depressed. But one side of your face was smashed, and they won't be able to fix it well enough to look normal. Assuming you make it out of the hospital alive, you'll be deformed for life." He chuckled. "Just like your wife."

A dark shape started to form in the corner of the room, becoming a person in a hooded robe.

Connor gaped at the hooded form and then at the judge. He noticed vaguely that the beeping sounds from his hospital console were increasing in both urgency and speed, along with his heartbeat. "Deformed? What do you mean, deformed? And, of course I'll get out of here. They said I'm getting better."

He felt the gauze on his face with his good hand, noting how thickly he was bandaged. *Could this be true? I'll be as difficult for people to look at as Amy had been?* He slumped in the bed.

The judge leaned forward, pointing directly at Connor with a bony hand. His eyes flared an even brighter red as he thundered, "I am the one who decides if you get better or not. You're here to face judgment for what you did to your wife. You killed her. You know it, and I know it. The question is, why did you do it?"

Connor quailed before the verbal assault. "She begged me to. She felt awful that she was ruining my life, that I couldn't go anywhere, I mean, *we* couldn't go anywhere anymore without people staring, and pointing, and talking about us. I mean *her*. You don't understand. It was awful." He sobbed. "I've never felt so alone."

The hooded form took a step closer to the bed, a long-handled sickle appearing in its hand. Connor cringed away from it.

"And how do you think *she* felt?" the judge continued, raising his arms as he spoke. "She was in pain, with a degenerative sickness, yet she worried about how it was affecting *you*. Which is also the only thing you worried about. How it affected *you*. I say that you killed your wife just to be free of her and her illness. Her disfigurement. Her effect upon *your* perfect life."

The judge pointed straight at Connor, and thunder clapped around them as the glow behind him flashed like lightning at the last words. He gestured to the dark figure, who raised one arm toward the bed. The monitors began to signal even louder, faster, as Connor felt his heart race and pound in his chest.

He put his arm across his face and tried to block the words, but the noise was inside his head. "No, no. *No!* She wanted to die. She begged me to do it!"

"She wanted you to say it didn't matter. That you loved her, no matter what. But you proved that you cared more about yourself than making her last days better. Let me ask you this: why should *you* be allowed to remain alive?" The judge grew in size until he loomed over the end of Connor's bed, his frowning face terrible to behold.

"I'm sorry. I'm sorry!" Connor burst out crying. "It was just so awful! Everyone looked at me as if I were contagious, myself. None of our friends came over anymore. We couldn't go out and see anyone or go anywhere. It was awful."

The judge nodded and leaned back, crossing his arms. "Admitting it is the first step in redemption. That means I can let you live."

He flicked his hand at the robed figure, which disappeared. The monitor sounds went back to normal, and Connor could breathe again. Then the judge reverted to his original size and rubbed his chin. "Now the question is, what is going to happen to you going forward? What are you going to do with your time remaining?"

The sobbing man reached out his good hand toward the judge. "Thank you. Oh, thank you." He wiped his face as best he could. "Wait, what do you mean, what is going to happen to me in my time remaining? The doctors said I could go home in a few days."

"If I allow it, you can go home. But, as I said, it's important that you know that they will not be able to fix your face. People are going to stare and shy away from you for the rest of your life. But you do have an option where you don't have to be ugly and deformed forever. Do you want to hear about it?"

Connor nodded. "Yes, please. Sir."

"Here is my judgment. I offer you a deal. If you can learn to live with your disfigurement, to get past it—reach out and help other people in the world who have this kind of issue—you can atone for your selfish actions. You won't have to be ugly forever. Are you willing to do this in order to live and redeem yourself for the death of your wife?"

"You mean, help disfigured people feel more like part of society?"

"More like, help society deal better with those who don't look or function just like them. People are ignorant. You're going to have to help them learn to be more accepting."

After a long pause, Connor looked up at the judge. "I'll do my best. And in exchange, I'll live? And … I won't be ugly forever?"

"That's right. You won't be ugly. You'll be handsome forever. We have a deal."

The judge's eyes blazed red for a moment as he banged his gavel. The light behind him flared brightly, then began to dim and waver, as did the outline of the man himself.

As the judge faded away, Connor reached out his hand. "Wait! How will I know when I won't be ugly anymore?"

The voice came faintly. "First, you'll stop being ugly inside yourself. Killing will become abhorrent to you. Then you won't care about the outside. And eventually, you'll become beautiful on the outside as well, forever." With a last flash of light, the judge and his desk disappeared.

Connor fell into a heavy, dreamless sleep.

His first night at home, in the bed he and Amy had shared for so many years, was difficult. Connor was tormented by thoughts of their early days together in the city, when they had been the beautiful young society couple that everyone wanted to be around. He couldn't sleep.

But then he started thinking about the quiet moments they had had together, after she became more housebound. Sitting and reading. Singing along with the radio in the car. Planning the renovations to their country house.

The most important part was that they had been together. *Who cares what either of us looked like?*

He missed her.

He turned on the light and fingered the piece of paper the doctor had given him—the address of a rehabilitation clinic. *I can fix my arm, get stronger. Even if they can't fix my face all the way.*

When he had asked, the doctor said he could volunteer his time there and learn how to help other people who were in recovery.

It was the first step. One of many he would take over the years to become a better person.

Five decades later, Connor was again in the hospital, as an old man. This time he was in the wing that had been named after him, following so many years of working at the clinic he had founded to improve the quality of life of those who had the same disease as Amy. Major strides had been accomplished in making adaptations that allowed the disease sufferers more mobility and access to the same activities that others had.

Connor had leveraged his position in society and his own disfigurement to call attention to the situation. By going public and creating a series of events and educational opportunities, he used his influence to help normalize what many had felt to be abnormal. People with the ETR disease were no longer ostracized.

He had started a chain of vegan restaurants, as he could no longer stomach the idea of killing a living creature just so he could eat.

It had eventually been a good life, after Amy died. He liked to feel that she hadn't died in vain—that he had learned something from her passing and helped so many people. In fact, he told the story of the accident so often that he frequently forgot what had actually happened. He even forgot to keep looking for the return of the judge with his promise of eternal good looks.

Thus, when he opened his eyes in the middle of the night in the hospital room, a flood of memories came back to him when he saw the judge behind his desk at the foot of the bed. Same dark robes, same wig, same glowing light behind him.

Same judgmental face with fierce red eyes.

"Well, Connor. It looks like you actually held up your end of the bargain. Seems like you have really redeemed yourself, and made things better for those with that dreadful disease."

Connor smiled. "Yes, thank you. I've really worked hard. I've tried to make a difference for all of them."

"For *all* of them? What about Amy, your wife?" The judge waved his hand, and a life-sized figure of Amy on their wedding day appeared to one side of his bed, frozen in the act of holding out her hand to receive her wedding ring. The love on her beautiful young face was unmistakable.

My love! Connor's smile faltered as he glanced at her and then back at the judge. "Yes. I still miss her. I feel so bad that she wasn't able to enjoy this change in society's perspective."

The beeping of the hospital monitor grew slower. The dark-robed figure started to take form in the corner opposite where Amy stood unmoving.

"Frankly, Connor, she *could* have, if you had only done all of these same things for her while she was still alive, instead of worrying about your own self and how people looked at you. If you hadn't killed her."

Connor frowned. "Killing is wrong. I can't condone it and don't even eat meat anymore. I feel like I've learned a lot more about the value of life."

The judge snorted. "Killing is wrong? Fat lot of good that does Amy, right? But you've fulfilled your side of the agreement, and I did say you wouldn't be ugly and disfigured forever. You'll be handsome again, now." The hospital monitor started blinking red.

"Well, that would be nice, but it doesn't really matter to me anymore. Living a good life and helping other people is what's important."

"Hey man, a deal is a deal." The judge beckoned to the dark-robed figure in the corner.

The figure came forward and pulled back its hood, and Connor beheld the most handsome man he had ever seen, standing over him at the side of his bed.

"Who are you?" Connor stared, unable to look away from the perfect face. Dark brown eyes, rich and engaging. Lips, full and sensuous. Cheekbones, high and elegant.

The voice, when it came, was rich and sonorous. It rang in his head and his ears. "I am Death. I have come, now that it is time for you to leave this world."

Connor took a deep breath. "All right, then. I've had a good life. I'm ready to go."

The judge tapped on his desk with a bony fingertip. "Not so fast, Connor. Remember I said you would be handsome forever? You are indeed going to go. My friend Death here is ready to die and take your place. As you will take his."

Connor frowned. "What do you mean, take his place?"

"You are going to leave this world as you know it, but you'll travel all over the globe, taking the souls of people who are about to die. You'll be killing them all, one at a time. Of course, it won't be all bad because you won't be disfigured anymore." He chuckled. "You'll be wearing this handsome face. Until the end of time."

Connor opened his mouth to scream, but the figure of Death morphed into a stream of black vapor that was drawn into his lungs as he inhaled, disappearing in a moment.

The hospital console emitted a long, steady beep, and a straight line appeared on the monitor. Footsteps sounded in the hall as medical personnel started running toward the room.

A dark-robed shape started to re-form in the corner, as handsome as the previous one but with Connor's bright blue eyes. When it was fully assembled, the handsome figure shrank back from the unmoving body on the bed.

The judge chuckled. "Oh, no you don't. Time to get to work. Take that soul to Hell. Oh, and Connor?"

The dark figure looked up at the judge, his handsome face perfect and symmetrical, but his blue eyes wide. "Ye … Yes?"

The judge gestured at Amy.

She held out a sickle attached to a long black staff, with a smile. "You're going to need this."

Bram Stoker Award® winner Carol Gyzander writes/edits horror, weird fiction, and science fiction—with strong women in twisted tales that touch your heart. Carol co-edited/contributed to the Stoker-winning/World Fantasy Award-finalist anthology *Discontinue If Death Ensues: Tales from the Tipping Point* (Flame Tree Publishing), including her Rhysling Award-nominated poem, "Bobblehead." Author Carol Gyzander cared for both of her parents through Alzheimer's.

This story originally appeared in *The Devil's Due: Nothing is Ever as it Seems* by Valhalla Books in October 2020.

Number 4 and Number 12
Chris Bauer

Krystal in number sixteen smiled a mouthful of baby teeth, her front two missing. The newspaper was where she'd dropped it on the motel walkway, out of the sun and opened flat next to me in my lawn chair. Her hands and what was in them were behind her back. We could have done this without her hiding her hands, but she'd never caught on.

She rocked forward on her feet then backward, toes-heels, on the parking lot blacktop. She waited for my first guess. The little bugger was counting her chickens.

"Blueberry," I said, hopeful.

"Nope."

"Strawberry." It was June, the season for it. There should have been plenty of strawberry.

"No strawberry. Last guess, Binkman."

I want it to not be lemon. I couldn't stand their lemon. "Peach."

I closed my eyes and held out my good hand, opened it, and waited. She dropped the Tastykake pie into it. I opened my eyes, thinking they should put pictures on the packages for people like me.

"It's lemon," she said. "Lemon's all they had. The lady in front of me got the last strawberry." She threw a leg over the crossbar of her bike, a tag sale special with some rust on the rims and three missing spokes on the front wheel. Her words whistled through the space in her teeth. "I asked the lady to trade. She said nope, she hates their lemon. Sorry, Binkman." She put out her hand. "Eight-fifty, please."

I knew my numbers, I reminded her. Two coffees, a small pie and the newspaper, plus her errand fee, and everything doubled for not guessing right on the pie. Inflation in the nineties had you by the balls. Still worth it, to me anyway.

The Veranda Motor Court Hotel was a pickle-tickle highway stop on Route 309 that wouldn't keep food on the owner's table if it weren't for government housing supplements, day rates, disabilities, and a few folks who thought they had the inkblots figured out, plus other water-treaders like them. A diner on one side, Bert's Smoke Shop and Package Store on the other, a convenience store just past Bert's. Pretty much centrally located. I sipped my coffee and finished the pie. The newspaper was for Honor, in number four. The second coffee was, too, if she could keep it down. Krystal rode her bike around the parking lot. I tucked the newspaper under my arm, walked a few doors up and knocked. The wait was always difficult.

Honor said to come in; she winced while she pulled herself up in bed.

"Newspaper delivery," I prompted, a smile behind it. "Rise and shine."

She coughed a greeting that turned into a hand wave halfway through. Her eyes were more ghoulish, her roots darker. She looked worse in general, but I held my smile.

I stuffed some pillows behind her, between her back and the headboard screwed into the wall. Honor was twenty-four, half my age, but she looked much older. An age she'd never see. She'd often told me she was thankful for that small favor. A torn-up wisp of a woman, all except for her milkmaid boobs. Them boobs and her cute overbite nearly got me into trouble soon after I met her, but she never held a grudge. It was the Bushmills talking, I'd said by way of an apology. Yes, the Bushmills talking, that's what it was, had been her comment. Loudest liquor I know, I said, and don't I know most of them.

You should think about quitting, she said. I know, I said. We both dropped it.

Going through door number four, that first time — the jury's still out if it was a good thing or a bad thing, for me or for her.

Honor rubbed sleep out of her eyes.

Her husband kicked her out of their double-wide and never let her back in, not even for her AIDS meds. He'll deeply regret that, the holding onto her meds part, Honor had told me. When they came looking for him — and they would come looking, she emphasized — they'd use the AIDS meds against him, the pervert.

It was five months since their separation, her husband granted custody. She'd whored for a living before they met. She had one lapse afterward, except she was sure it was a set-up. Had to be, since her husband had video of it. A video the court now had. But he's a pedophile, she'd pleaded, something she didn't know until after her daughter was born. So where's the video of *that,* the court asked. It was in her head she told the judge. In there and she couldn't get it out. Him with her baby. Heard it all before, the judge said, a common allegation. He said, she said, blah, blah, blah. Custody to the father, visitation to the mother, case closed.

Honor had no one to do for her except me.

"How's Miss America today?" I asked.

"Fine," was her pat answer. We never discussed her sickness much. It was what it was, I'd tell myself, like the missing fingers on my left hand. A longshoreman's accident on one of the Philly piers. Part their fault, part my fault, part the Bushmills.

Honor walked out of her final foster home at fifteen, was on the street till nineteen, quit the whoring and the drugs by twenty-one. Got married, got pregnant, had the baby, thought her life had turned around. Got full-blown AIDS. She had her baby tested and learned the baby was HIV-positive. That was Honor's story.

Her story, my story, other motel residents' stories, we never went that deep into any of them, except Honor wasn't going to get better, and she wanted to be cremated. There were papers to make this happen, in a drawer in her nightstand. She had me check on them every day to make sure they were still there. Every day I'd say to her, where else would they go? Then I'd take them out and show them to her like she'd asked.

She sipped her coffee and ran her tongue over her upper lip. We both held our breath. She sipped again, more this time, nodded an okay. It was how we knew if it would be a good day, if she could drink her coffee without puking it back up. I joked with her about it, said if there was a Dunkin Donuts nearby she'd have better days and more of them. They made better coffee.

Honor reached for the newspaper on the nightstand. She raised her eyebrows playful-like and tilted her head. "So?" she said. She knew Krystal in number sixteen was where the newspaper came from.

"Lemon," I said. "Struck out again." This got a small grin out of her. The way I saw it, Krystal would get a new bike sooner. A girl's bike, one without a crossbar. I'd learned to like lemon pies. Deprived kids don't need to stick out.

Honor had visitation with her baby daughter twice a week, half days, unsupervised. She fed the baby her bottles, changed her diapers, cuddled and talked to her like moms do. When she got tired she'd call my place and I'd watch the little darling for a bit so Honor could nap. I'd wake her up in time for the pick-up. Except they knew. The husband, the court, the social worker, they all knew how weak Honor was. That's why the visits were being terminated. It would have been bad for the baby if Honor died during one of them, the court had decided. I told the social worker I stopped in every day while she had the baby, explained to her it would never go down like that. Who the hell are you, the social worker said. Number twelve, I'd said. The social worker ignored me.

The last of the visits were scheduled to terminate in a week. If her sickness didn't take her by then, she'd go soon after, when the visits stopped. That I could guarantee.

She unfolded the newspaper. "Headlines or sports page?" she said.

The Pope's picture was on the front page. I wanted to know what was up.

"Headlines first," I said.

The Pope was sick. Gas prices were up. I listened as I grabbed a tall glass for her from the drying rack and turned on the kitchenette spigot.

"First the white bottle," she said. "A teaspoon."

More news. A White House intern went down on the president. There was a shooting at nearby Maxie's Tavern last night. AIDS was killing people. I put a teaspoon of her prescription into the glass. A few stirs turned the water a milky white.

A rock and a hard place was how Honor had explained it. It had never been much of a life for her, the abuse she'd suffered, and it went on in more than one of the homes where the courts put her. There were fates worse than death and that was one of them, she believed; far worse. A real sticking point with her, that for some, the sooner the passage into the next life, no matter the age, the better. A mother, had there been one for her, would have known this, Honor said. Would have known the misery Honor had lived, and the misery Honor was living now. A good mother would have done something about it. Whatever it took to get in front of the suffering.

Honor said a good mother made the tough decisions.

The happiest day of her life was the day her daughter was born. She finally had the world by the ass and was set to give it a good shake, was how she put it. They both would, she and her daughter. Then everything went to hell. Soon as she and the baby came home. Now her husband had the baby and there wasn't much she could do about it, considering her condition. Nothing different than what she was already doing.

A rock and a hard place. Frying pans and fires. Honor was now trying to be the good mother she'd never had.

"Square blue bottle, orange stripe. A teaspoon." The chalky water turned orange.

She turned to the sports page. The Phillies were hanging onto first place in their division by a thread.

Honor always harped about what should happen when the day came. The mortician would get the legal papers, her belongings needed to be burned. Everything, she'd said. Don't keep anything, you hear me, Binkman? Nothing to charity, nothing recycled. Burn it all and forget about me. I care for you a great deal, Binkman, she'd said, and I'm grateful our paths crossed, grateful you knocked on my door. You've got the rest of your life and you need to live it. Promise me you will do these things, Binkman, she'd said; please promise. So I promised.

"Two white pills, three red pills," she said.

I knew the doses, I told her, and I shook them out. I was always good at numbers. Reading words, not so much.

I reached for a smoky-brown jar with a wide mouth that contained a special mix of powders, the dose, according to Honor, whatever she wanted it to be. To rid her of the pain. She watched me stir in a few pinches, had me add a few more, the jar nearly empty, no expression on her face. She gave me a weak smile when I was finished. She nagged me until I washed my hands, had me wash them a second time. In case you're, you know, allergic or something, she said. She told me again how lucky she was to have me living eight doors away and doing for her. I'm taking advantage of you, she said, and I feel terrible about it. No, you're not, I said. She opened her mouth, wanted to say more, drew in air and held it. Wanted me to know but didn't want me to know. Wanted me to understand, to agree to something unsaid, was afraid I wouldn't, was maybe more afraid I would. All this from one breath, one look.

I didn't give her a chance to explain her intentions. "How about the travel section?" I asked. "Anything good?"

She exhaled, lifted the newspaper, and read to me about Alaska. Land of the midnight sun. I could never handle Alaska. I'd always been a morning person.

She finished taking her meds and wanted to use the toilet. I carried her there, then carried her back. She asked me to mix up some powdered baby formula for when her daughter arrived. We went through the same routine. A spoonful of this, a few pinches of that. Vitamins in powdered form, according to Honor, but some of it didn't look any different than her pain medication.

Her need to confess something to me froze her again. I coaxed her into reading from the personals instead.

She again had me wash my hands.

Honor was a good mother. One of the best.

The phone rang. I handed it to her and listened. It was her husband.

Her daughter couldn't keep anything in her, was vomiting, had diarrhea, was maybe dehydrating. What have you done to her, he said. No, what have *you* done to her, she said. He took a few more verbal shots at Honor. She handed the phone back to me. No baby visit today.

Honor started nodding off after a decent cry, and she fought sleep as she went over things with me again, me sitting next to her and holding her hand. My papers go to the mortician, she said, my stuff gets burned. Everything. No mementos, leave nothing behind in here, no traces outside of what was in that perverted bastard's trailer.

Like what she'd left in the back of his medicine cabinet, her husband there to take the blame. This, she didn't say to me. Had she tried, I'd have made her read the paper's comics to me.

Please, please, please don't forget all these things, she said. You agreed, Binkman, remember how you agreed? You're my Binkman. My dear, sweet friend Binkman.

She fell asleep, and I saw the comfort a morning nap could bring, the slight rise and fall of her chest, her breathing slow, calm, restful, through her nose and through her mouth. I leaned in close and kissed her on the forehead.

I whispered yes, I did still agree. To all of it.

Chris Bauer writes thrillers; his 10th is out now. He's a subject matter expert in none of the following, although his fictional characters are: firearms, crime scene cleaning, Hawaiian mobsters, law enforcement, fugitive recovery, NASA, or the Supreme Court, nor does he have six fingers on either hand. You can find out more about him at chrisbauerauthor.net.

This story originally appeared in *crappy shorts: number two* in 2012.

Alchemy
Ann Stolinsky

The unlocked wooden door creaked as I pushed it open and entered the hovel. Closing the door quickly, the package shifted in my arms. Master Fermon did not like sunlight illuminating his concoctions. He sat, bent over the table in the middle of the room, engrossed. He did not acknowledge my entry, nor my presence as I walked toward him.

"Master." No answer. "Master!"

My master usually ignored me when focused upon mixing a recipe, but the intensity of my plea for his attention gave him pause. He turned ever so slightly from the scattered ingredients on his table to shoot me a sideways glance.

"Yes, Teraken? What is so urgent that makes you disturb my experiment?" Fermon growled at me.

My voice remained steady.

"My apologies, Master Fermon. But I have the Stone."

His attention turned fully to me as he jumped from his chair, almost knocking over the table. His eyes shone, ablaze with desire.

"The Stone? *The Philosopher's Stone*? You, a nothing, a peon, not even a low-order wizard, *you* have the Stone?"

"I do, Master."

His rarely used smile was crooked; I had never seen it before. He held out his wrinkled, age-spotted hand, palm up, gnarled fingers waving at me. "Give it to me!"

Whispered chatter heard on previous visits to a village tavern told of an unnamed thief who tried to steal a Philosopher's Stone from a likewise unnamed wizard. The mumblings contained a few hints of who had found the secret mixture of chemicals to create such wonder, such power. My master was intent on obtaining the Stone, wishing greedily for its gift of transmuting base metal into gold. As he aged, he also fervently wished to discover the secret of immortality. To that end, as the sun began its descent, I placed myself strategically close to the drunken man I deduced as the object of the whispers, without appearing to be eavesdropping. Not sure if I had been provided the ramblings of a drunk or a genuine tip, I determined to find the truth.

The sot left the tavern with a young lad, tall and slender; his appearance indicated he was no more than fifteen years of age, just entering manhood. I followed, my shadow disappearing in concert with the sun, as I slithered against the wall several yards behind the duo. My master taught me sparingly, not wanting me to learn enough so that I might challenge his mastery or steal his customers. I knew only a few rudimentary spells, like the one I cast that night. Had the day's full light shone on us, the pair would not have seen me. The only concern I still had about detection was sound. I hadn't learned a noise-canceling spell as yet.

My master was a minor wizard, well above my own station in life, but not as revered as Merlin centuries before. His clients were also minor in station – craftsmen who couldn't afford a more skilled wizard; women and their husbands who served the nobility; and servants themselves. His spells cured warts, enhanced the crafting of swords so the blades were cutting-sharp, gave barren wives hope for a pregnancy, gave pregnant women hopes for a healthy offspring and their husbands hope for an heir. Fermon's aura glowed faintly, unlike the master wizards whose bright nimbuses surrounded their heads.

Fermon was, and always had been, a mistrusting and jealous man. Why he took me on as an apprentice for a contract of ten years is a mystery he shall carry to his death. His furtive endeavors to glean information from a peer's scrolls, whenever he encountered a rival engaged in wizardry, usually ended with him no wiser than before. His overt efforts at stealing both scrolls and rare herbs occasionally caused him to spend a night or two on a hard cot inside a cold prison cell.

Fermon's passion, his obsession, was with the Philosopher's Stone.

Arrogant, he believed himself to be the only wizard who could wield it. Jealous, he shared what little details he had gathered with no one. Passionate only for one item, he led a life of celibacy. His skills lacking, his only search was for the Stone, not for knowledge.

It was easy to follow the drunk. The smell of whiskey and piss clung to him. He leaned on the lad, using him as a crutch. The lad, in all probability, was getting tipsy from the proximity of his companion.

Their relationship puzzled me. A son was my first guess, yet the drunk's meager wisps of hair were flaming red, standing straight up on his balding pate, while the lad had a thick black mane, tied in the back with a leather thong. Their features, when I had studied them in the smoke-filled tavern, didn't strike me as similar. A servant, perhaps? This drunkard was of an upper class, and could afford a servant? Or was the drunk a skilled craftsman and the lad like me, an apprentice? No matter, I followed.

We walked for close to an hour, wending our way through narrow cobblestone streets. Mediocre surroundings gave way to more lush and wealthy environs, beggars and pickpockets left behind as we neared the better part of town. In the distance I saw the golden spire atop a church. The man seemed to straighten as he ambled, his back no longer bent, his grip on the lad eased. They glanced behind them furtively as the journey continued. Who were they afraid shadowed their trail?

A white-washed home fronted by a well-tended garden appeared to be their destination. The sot looked around one last time, then climbed the red wooden steps to the matching door. He brought a brass key from his pocket and, inserting it carefully, opened the door. The lad stepped inside first, the elder man close behind.

I reconnoitered the house, stealthily walking from side to back to side to front. The windows were shut. I presumed the back door opened into the kitchen, as was common in such construction. I saw nothing out of the ordinary for the home of a wealthy man.

I left the house, determined to return on the morrow's eve, desirous of using darkness and spells to hide my presence. The drunk had seemed familiar to the barkeep. I hoped he frequented it every eve and would not be in the house when I returned.

The wooden door opened quietly, allowing me to slip back into Master Fermon's home unnoticed. I slept fitfully, my plan to enter the wealthy man's home occupying my dreams.

Master Fermon shook me awake a few hours after my head hit the cot. He kept me busy and required my services far longer into the evening than usual. Did he suspect my anticipated nocturnal activity? I thought not. The darkness was total when he finally dismissed me, the hour close to midnight.

I slipped into the tavern quietly and walked to the bar nonchalantly. The scene was the same as I last saw it, the man and his lad seated at a table, conversing. Their utterances drifted to my eager ears. The words spoken by the man weren't slurred, his speech was crisp and clear. I surmised he wasn't drunk yet and would probably stay there for a bit. I had time to venture to his home and put into motion my plan.

As the door closed behind me, I stumbled, pretending to have imbibed too much of the tavern's offering. No one in that area of town paid attention to the whiskey-besotted so late at night. As I neared the better part of town, I became as gentrified as the architecture, my hat and cloak hiding my face, my bearing straight and tall. To conserve energy, I didn't surround myself with an invisibility spell until I was within a mile of the dwelling I sought.

The church spire loomed. My heart raced.

I faced my destination. My head swiveled right and left, as I peered up and down the street before slinking to the back of the house. My plan was to enter from the back. A creak startled me as the door slowly opened at my gentle touch. The darkness outside aided my eyes' adjustment to the darkness within. I whispered a few words of magic to become visible, and a few more to create a flame, no larger than my thumb, inside my open palm.

My presumption confirmed, the back door did indeed open into the kitchen. I momentarily thought about grabbing a knife in case the master of the house returned before I completed my quest. I shook my head. If he had found the right mixture of ingredients, had the ability to combine that with sufficient power to create the Philosopher's Stone, he could more than match my meager talents, and pluck the knife easily from my grasp. The kitchen appeared larger than the dimensions outside indicated. Walking straight through it, I came to another door. My ear against the wood, I listened for voices, for any trace of inhabitants, but heard nothing. I opened the door a tad, peeking my head through. I saw no one, so I continued with the rest of my body. This appeared to be a drawing room, a piano in one corner, a mahogany desk with matching upholstered chair on the opposite wall, and a settee in the middle. Wall sconces were unlit. The room contained four bookcases; their shelves crammed with tomes whose titles I could not read with the limited light I possessed. I salivated; my master would be extremely grateful should I present him with a rival's secrets, but I reminded myself I had another purpose for this illicit visit. Perhaps … if I should return one day …

An open door beckoned to me. I tiptoed to it, to find a set of stairs descending to what I presumed would be a cellar. The welcoming fragrance of fresh-cut herbs reached my nostrils and I inhaled deeply. I believed the cellar held what I sought – the mage's laboratory.

My feet skimmed the cold stone steps. Cautious, I peered into the gloom before lowering to the next step. I reached the bottom and realized I had been holding my breath. As I exhaled, I heard one word spoken aloud, in a language I did not understand. The candles in the wall sconces flared. The drunk and his lad sat on mahogany chairs, twins to those upstairs, in front of a table filled with fresh and dried herbs, and various implements, not unlike those used by my master in his experiments.

"Welcome, Teraken. We've been waiting for you. My name is Orske. My assistant is Lersart."

Frozen in place at the bottom of the steps, my hand, unbidden, flew to cover my open mouth. I glanced about. Orske's aura glowed golden about his head, Lersart's aura paler, the same as I imagined mine. Neither had shone yesterday. I was in the presence of a master wizard.

A nod of his head directed me to sit in the chair opposite him. The scent of the herbs mixed with the metallic taste of the iron and copper on the table. Was this it? Was I to witness the birth of a Philosopher's Stone?

"How did you get here so quickly? I left you at the tavern."

Orske smiled. "Ah, dear Teraken, you will soon learn the ways of master mages. We begin your education tonight."

Sweat dripped into my eyes as fear gripped me. Memories of Fermon's violent reception whenever I had arrived late ran through my mind. "I must take my leave. Master Fermon will wonder where I am." My words spilled out in a jumble, and I trembled, from fear, and excitement.

"Teraken, you may leave whene'er you wish. You are not now, and never shall be, a prisoner in my home. Please come back tonight, after Fermon has released you."

My cloak billowed about me as I ran up the steps. "I shall try."

I hastened to return to Master Fermon. I felt puzzled. Why would a master wizard take an interest in a stranger, in me? How did he know my name? Why would Orske tempt me with promises of an education in the mystic arts, one denied to me by my own master?

The door to Fermon's home creaked as I flung it open and stumbled in, lost in thought. Startled, I noticed Fermon stood at the table, his hands working upon powder in a bowl. I abruptly stopped my forward movement.

"Master, you are awake." Bowing my head, I removed my cloak, placing it on a peg near the door.

"I am, Teraken." Fermon turned toward me. "I called your name, and you did not answer. I rose and resolved to work until you showed your face. Where have you been?"

His calm demeanor didn't fool me. I knew from experience his anger would escalate, no matter my answer. I decided to be partially truthful.

"I was at the tavern, Master. My thirst for mead and company was strong."

"Ha! Drinking again!" His open hand shot up from the table, reaching my face before I could move. My cheek stung from the force of his slap. As I backed away from his shaking fist, I wondered again why he took me on as his apprentice.

Fermon reached for a broom and beat me about my arms, my legs, my torso, shouting as he did so, telling me I should not drink while in his employ. I put my arms above my head, my hands protecting my dome. When I was sufficiently bruised, his rage spent, Fermon dropped into a chair, laid his head on the table, eyelids drooping, and snored.

Blood dripped on the floor as I staggered to my cot, to tend to my bruises. I thought that I should not go to Master Orske that evening. I was not certain I could travel that distance while injured thus.

That afternoon Fermon demanded I deliver a potion to the smithy. I kept my face down, my hood tightly over my head, my cloak securely about my neck. A loud meow reached my ears. I stopped abruptly so as not to step on a hissing black cat. The cat stared at me while darting around my feet. My eyes still on the animal, not seeing where I was going, I bumped into Master Orske, causing him to drop his packages.

"Sorry, sir. Won't happen again, sir."

"Teraken, no need for apologies. How can you see when you're bundled up so? Hiding welts, eh? Fermon did this to you, did he not? Despicable behavior. I apologize to you if my keeping you last eve caused you pain."

Orske gently placed his hand on my arm. "Please, Teraken, come to my abode this evening. I promise not to keep you long past the midnight hour. Lersart and I care not for your appearance. We care for your mind and your ability."

"I'll try," I muttered, walking away to find the smithy.

The walk to Master Orske's was a complicated torture for me. I debated the wisdom of my journey, almost turning back several times, knowing that if I were to return late to Master Fermon, I would endure another beating. The desire to gain wisdom and learn magic encouraged me to continue. My footfalls lightened as I neared Master Orske's spacious home.

Standing at the closed door I halted, door knocker in hand. If I stepped within, I would begin a journey down a road from which I could not retreat. Once knowledge is gained, it cannot be unknown. I knocked.

Orske opened the door, smiling.

"Teraken, come with me to the cellar. I shall give you your first true lesson in wizardry."

We descended to find Lersart at work, muddling colorful ingredients with a mortar and pestle. Lersart looked up at me, and grinned.

I quivered, thinking of the lashing I would receive when I returned to Fermon. Orske noticed my dismay and drew me closer to him.

"Teraken, how large is this room?"

I turned slowly, north to south to north again. Moving along the north wall, I passed the table where Lersart worked. I paced for several minutes, stymied that the length of the room was far larger than the house. I headed east, and still walked for several minutes. Orske chuckled, as I returned to him.

"How is this possible? How can the room inside be greater than the house outside?"

"In time, dear Teraken, in time."

My fists clenched. White-knuckled, I seethed inside. Orske is the same as Fermon, withholding information from me. I thought back to when I began my apprenticeship.

"Master Fermon, thank you for taking me on as an apprentice."

"You sleep there, Teraken, on that cot." He pointed to a dark corner of the room. "We eat whenever I've finished for the day. You will do as I say, and I shall answer your questions as we go. You will learn to prepare mixtures as I do."

"Thank you again, Master."

Fermon turned his back to me, as if satisfied these were all the instructions I needed. I placed my few belongings next to the cot. Fermon handed me a thin blanket. Excitement filled me, yet I succumbed to exhaustion instead, and I lay down to sleep.

Fermon awoke me at dawn.

"Teraken, go to the village. Fetch me a stone bowl."

I rubbed my eyes and stood.

"Yes, Master," I drew closer to the table with its myriad herbs and spices, "but what are you working on now?"

"Insolent apprentice! Do as I say!"

A red mark appeared where his open hand met my cheek. Rubbing the affected bruise, I wondered how many smacks I would endure by his hand during my apprenticeship. Head down, I left for the village.

Frustration and fright boiled inside my body when Orske withheld the answer.

"You're just like Fermon!" My hands trembled as I turned to the stairs. Orske touched my back. I spun to peer into his eyes.

"Please, Teraken, stay a little longer." Orske's tone softened. "Your master once was an apprentice; did you know this?"

I shook my head.

Orske chuckled.

"He was my apprentice."

My eyebrows shot up. Surprise registered on my face without my consent.

"He was my apprentice when he was but a youth, a few years older than Lersart."

I stumbled to the chair I had vacated last eve.

"Fermon was an adequate apprentice, but not special. He could cure warts, but not true ills. Yet he believed himself to have the ability to be a grand wizard. Fermon grew jealous of the spells I could recite from memory, his facility to remember slower than mine. Fermon determined his station in life to be equal to mine without putting in years of study, so he began to experiment on his own. When Fermon learned of the existence of the Philosopher's Stone, he plummeted into a single-minded passion. His obsession grew with time, as did his temper."

I nodded. Orske's description of Fermon's current state was on point.

"When Fermon learned I had constructed a Stone, he demanded to know the secrets. Fermon was no longer my apprentice at that time; I had released him from his contract prior to my achievement. Yet he felt I owed him the secrets he sought, due to his years working for me. My beliefs did not match his.

"Last I saw Fermon, he was leaving my home after inflicting the same sting on me that he has inflicted upon you."

My ears caught the words "constructed a Stone" and my heart raced again. When Orske completed his monologue, I questioned him.

"Master Orske, what do you mean by 'constructed a Stone'?"

Orske walked to Lersart, ignoring my query. He leaned over the boy, guiding his hands as he prepared a concoction, of what I had no idea.

I fidgeted, as quiet as a lion stalking its prey. The boy's brew overran the stone bowl, smoke billowing into the room. Orske smiled, his hand on his apprentice's shoulder, murmuring words of encouragement, telling the lad he would be successful on his next attempt.

My head spun, both from the heady aroma of herbs, and with knowledge. I had but one more question that needed answering prior to taking my leave that evening.

"Master Orske, why did you choose to educate *me*?"

"Ah, Teraken, you are a dedicated and intelligent student. Have you not discerned the reason as yet?"

I shook my head.

"Teraken, when Lersart and I noticed you in the tavern, your aura blinded us. You, yes you, don't look so astonished, *you* were born to be a master mage."

Dumbfounded, I took my leave, promising to return on the morrow.

I returned to Master Orske each evening after my duties for Master Fermon were complete. I had always kept my own counsel, not sharing any thoughts with Fermon, lest his temper be aroused. The difficulty in working for him increased as I seethed. He knew that with knowledge and practice, I would grow to be a master mage. He kept my talent grounded in shackles while it could have soared.

Two months after our first meeting, the secret of the Stone was mine, to share as I chose. Orske was indeed a master teacher. Daily, I eagerly awaited for night to fall, for Master Orske to instruct Lersart and me. I grew to appreciate the kindness of a knowledgeable wizard, and to further resent the treatment I received from Fermon. A plan grew in my thoughts.

Fermon repeated his demand. His smile faded; his wrinkled hand remained outstretched. "Give it to me!"

Under Fermon's gaze, I unwrapped the parcel I held. His eyes sparkled with anticipation, believing his hands would soon be holding the object he had sought for so long, hands that I knew would misuse the Stone's power.

The cloth slipped and revealed a hint of a red Stone. He caught his breath. Red. A white Stone meant silver riches, a red Stone meant gold. He laughed, giddy with desire.

I held my arm straight, my hand palm up. "One moment, Fermon. I not only have the Philosopher's Stone, but I know its secrets. I can show you how to use the golden touch. Riches beyond wonder will be yours. I also hold the secret to immortality. You must promise to share your riches with me, or I shall withhold the Philosopher's Stone from you and keep it for myself."

"Nonsense, Teraken, I will make no such promise to an insolent apprentice. The Stone is mine. Give it to me!"

I replaced the cloth over the Stone and turned to the door. Fermon grabbed my arm.

"All right, Teraken. I agree. Now give me the Stone!"

"As you wish, Master Fermon." I had no blind belief he would follow through on his promise, nor, if my plan worked, would he have cause.

I withdrew the Stone fully from underneath the plain cotton cloth. Fermon was entranced. He didn't notice as I brought another cloth from my cloak, one that contained a bit of the Stone, ground finely. I disbursed this into his mead.

"A toast, Master. You have been given your heart's desire."

Fermon raised his cup and drank.

"What is this? What have you placed in my mead?!" Fermon shouted. His hand dropped his cup, spilling the last of the drink on the table. He clutched his heart.

"I have bestowed upon you the gift of eternal life, Fermon. You drank a bit of the Stone in your mead. You will live forever."

"Why are you smirking, Teraken? What magery are you hiding?"

"Ah, Fermon, I told you I had the secret to using the Philosopher's Stone."

I intoned the words needed to turn base metal into gold. Fermon had swallowed his mead, into which I had placed a base metal, mercury, and shavings of the Stone. He had consumed part of the Stone.

Fermon was rooted in place. The transformation started with his feet, dingy leather sandals turning into gold, tendrils of gold reaching up his legs.

Fermon screamed and pleaded with me to end his metamorphosis. "Ungrateful cur! I took you into my home, made you my apprentice, taught you magic. How could you repay me this way?"

"Fermon, my eyes have been opened. You took me on as an apprentice to prevent me from realizing my full potential. My aura is strong, much stronger than yours. You withheld knowledge. You deserve this fate." My smile grew.

"You will live eternally, Master," I spat out the last word, "as a statue. You will see all that goes on around you, yet you will be unable to move, to speak, to intone any spells. You now have all you desired, riches beyond imagination. For all eternity, you will be gold, and enslaved."

I retrieved my clothing from the corner of the room. Sunlight entered the window, engulfing Fermon in golden light. Looking back hurt my eyes. I turned, and, beaming, walked out the door.

Ann's short stories have appeared in 30+ anthologies. But her most phenomenal publishing credit is that two anthologies in which her stories appear have landed on the moon.
See *Writers on the Moon,*
https://www.writersonthemoon.com/how-it-works).

Ann Stolinsky is a partner in Gemini Wordsmiths LLC, an editing company, geminiwordsmiths.com, and Celestial Echo Press, celestialechopress.com.

This story was originally published in *Witch Wizard Warlock,* 2023.

How Not to Swallow a Dragon
Marisca Pichette

Silverfish had a dragon caught in her throat. It got there while she was sitting at breakfast, eating toast with peanut butter. One moment she was chewing, the next a sharp jab in the back of her throat. Scratching every time she swallowed.

"What's wrong?" Jasper asked, setting her own toast down on the counter. Jasper's kitchen was warm with morning sun. Fallen crumbs cast little shadows on the granite countertop.

Swallowing, Silverfish rubbed her throat and winced. *Scratch. Scratch.*

"Something's stuck. I think it's a piece of seed, or something."

She swallowed a mouthful of coffee. Jasper made coffee stronger than Silverfish liked, and she forced the bitterness down her throat—but the sharp sensation remained. She flexed her tongue, sending saliva and phlegm forward, then back. She swallowed again. *Scratch.*

"Let me see." Jasper took Silverfish's half-finished toast and set it on the counter next to her own before peering into her mouth.

As Jasper leaned forward, a bright warmth danced across Silverfish's tongue. Jasper jerked her head out of the way just in time. A tiny flame shot out of Silverfish's mouth and broke against the kitchen window.

"Babe, that's not a seed." Jasper couldn't stop smiling, sun catching her brown eyes and turning them copper. "It's a little green dragon."

There's only one rule when it comes to dragons: let them be.

Dragons liked to live where people did. Silverfish had seen them make nests out of hair and ride around on heads, take up residence in dishwashers so the owners had to wash everything by hand, and build little houses on top of mailboxes out of disposable straws and sticks.

Jasper had three dragons. One lived in the upstairs bathroom of her house, on a bed of shredded toilet paper. One sat next to a succulent in its pot on the porch. The third lived in an old birdhouse in the backyard.

"In my *throat*, of all places!" Silverfish ranted, small flames bubbling between her lips as she paced in Jasper's living room. This weekend they had been planning to move in together. Totes overflowing with Silverfish's clothes leaned against the wall, speckled with burn marks.

Jasper sat on the couch, a sympathetic smile on her face. She hadn't brushed her hair this morning, and it refused to lie flat, short strands sticking every which way so she looked like a pubescent lion.

"I don't know what to tell you. Does it hurt?" she asked. Silverfish stopped pacing, exhaling smoke.

"The fire doesn't burn," she admitted. Something about symbiosis, she supposed. Dragons took care of their homes—or hosts. After finding the dragon unwilling to relinquish its spot at the back of her throat, she and Jasper spent the morning Googling similar cases. It seemed that the dragon would stay for a few hours at most, maybe overnight. Soon, the articles assured her, it would find her to be an unsuitable place for a nest, and leave her alone.

Soon was far too vague an assurance. Silverfish swallowed, grimacing. "His claws poke me every time I swallow, and he stole bites of my lunch." She could still taste the rice they'd had in the flames the dragon burped into her mouth.

"He, she, they—you don't know their pronouns," Jasper said. She leaned back into the couch cushions, nudging an empty cardboard box with her foot. "I call all three of mine Loafer."

Silverfish glared at her girlfriend. The dragon in her throat squirmed. "Loafer? What, like Loafer 1, Loafer 2, Loafer 3?"

Jasper shrugged. "They're all living here rent-free, so I don't really care which is which."

"You make them sound like shoes."

"That opens it up for some jokes about how you've got a foot in your mouth."

Silverfish coughed up a lunch-flavored flame. Jasper watched it dissipate, then scrambled up from the couch, eyes shining. "Hang on, I have a great idea." She jumped over the cardboard box and started up the stairs, her grin telling Silverfish all she needed to know even before Jasper gave voice to her plan.

"Hold that fire ready—I'm getting the bong."

The dragon didn't leave that day, or the next. Reading articles about how to extricate dragons and then what foods they preferred, Silverfish found herself getting used to the scratching in her throat and the creepy, deep-throat sensation every time the dragon turned around or resettled itself. At night she stood in front of the bathroom mirror with her mouth wide open.

Her dragon's skin was Playdough green. Its two bulbous black eyes reminded her of the deer mice she kept as pets as a child. It was simultaneously cute and off-putting, like a miniature, slimy Furby. As she watched, it closed its eyes and appeared to doze off.

She closed her mouth carefully and looked down at the shimmering moonstone dragon on Jasper's bathroom tile. Silverfish had decided this was Loafer 2.

Loafer 2 was about the size of a chipmunk, and just as fat. Silverfish wondered if it ate moths or hair from the drains. Then again, Loafer 2 was nestled in its toilet paper nest at the base of the toilet…Silverfish decided to stop wondering how it stayed fat.

As far as she could tell, Loafer 2 didn't breathe fire. Maybe it spat water instead, or Febreeze. Jasper's bathroom *did* always smell fresh.

Silverfish turned back to the mirror and opened her mouth again. Her dragon blinked back at her over her scratched tongue.

When she'd been first saddled with it, the dragon had been a baby, no bigger than a peanut without its shell. Jasper speculated it had probably been clinging to the toast and was tossed back into her throat when she took a bite. Jasper said she could just have easily killed the poor thing.

Some nights, when she awoke with her mouth scratched and bleeding and Jasper swearing as she splashed saline on a smoldering pillowcase, Silverfish wished she had.

Despite the dragon in her throat, Silverfish finished moving from her apartment into Jasper's house one week later, adding herself and another dragon to Jasper's collection.

On her first morning as an official resident of the house, Silverfish brought her dragon on a tour. She opened her mouth so her dragon could see its fellow loafers.

The one next to the succulent was brick red and had little bat-like wings. Silverfish called that one Loafer 1, and the birdhouse dragon—which flew around at night catching mosquitos—Loafer 3. They were certainly pretty to look at and seemed less slimy than her dragon. Then again, they weren't constantly coated in spit.

Jasper asked her what she was going to call her dragon.

"I'm not calling it Loafer 4, if that's what you want to know."

Jasper grinned around a mouthful of peas and rice at dinner. Silverfish had discovered that her dragon was partial to rice, and curry especially.

"Well, come on then. It's gonna be with us for a while. Might as well make it part of the family."

Silverfish rubbed her thumb along the back of her spoon. She knew that Jasper wanted kids, eventually. She just hoped she didn't decide to call them all by the same name.

"Okay. Bone."

Jasper raised an eyebrow. Her short hair was backlit by the setting sun, a golden fringe that reminded Silverfish for some reason of a hill covered in dying grass. "Bone?"

Silverfish shoved a spoonful of rice into her mouth. Bone snatched their portion as she swallowed. "Yeah," she said, wishing her throat didn't hurt so damn much.

"Seems a gloomy name for such a cute dragon, but who am I to judge? I'm just your landlord."

Silverfish rolled her eyes. Bone squirmed, and she tried not to gag. "We're dividing the mortgage. Because of me, this place costs you less."

Jasper stood, collecting her plate and Silverfish's. "Well, the landlord needs her pay." She set the plates in the sink, glancing over her shoulder. "I take cash, check, credit card, or .... something more fun, also beginning with c?"

Jasper winked and Bone burped. Silverfish spat out a flame.

Silverfish woke up unable to breathe. She rolled over, clawing at Jasper's still sleeping form.

"Whu…" Jasper's eyes widened to reflect Silverfish's panic. She hauled Silverfish upright, covers tangling around them as Jasper pounded her back with the heel of her hand. Silverfish gasped once before her airway was blocked again.

"Stupid. Fucking. Pest." Jasper grunted the words in between smacks. Every strike made Silverfish's chest reverberate with hope and panic. Jasper crawled behind her and gave her an imperfect Heimlich.

Something shot from Silverfish's mouth and bounced across the bed, rolling into a trench formed by the rumpled comforter. Silverfish drew a wild breath, feeling the surge of life. She sagged against Jasper, gasping and heaving in the early morning light.

Jasper dropped her head on Silverfish's shoulder, breathing heavily along with her. "What happened?"

Silverfish drew a few more breaths before opening her mouth for Jasper to peer inside. She stayed some distance away, out of experience. More than once she'd had an eyebrow singed.

Silverfish waited, breathing, tears of fear drying on her cheeks.

"Holy shit."

Jasper sat back, hand over her mouth. Silverfish closed her mouth, rubbing her throat. Unease crept up her esophagus. "What? What is it?" Her voice was scratchy, thin.

Jasper turned away, hunting through the covers until she found the object that had been blocking Silverfish's airway. She held it up, pinched between her fingers.

At first Silverfish thought it was a bead. She didn't recognize it and couldn't imagine how it had gotten into her throat. Then the sun slipped between the curtains, shining through the little ball, partially squished in Jasper's grip.

It shone pink, translucent like a pearl of popping boba. Or a fish egg.

"Bone has laid eggs in you," Jasper said, her tone soft with wonder.

Silverfish suppressed the sudden urge to cough. Bile stung her throat. "Eggs? What happens when they hatch? *When* will they hatch? Can I eat? Will they fly out or…"

Jasper looked at her, eyes catching the sun. "I don't know. I've never seen them have babies before."

Bone had laid her eggs in a layer at the top of Silverfish's throat.

Jasper drove her to the doctor's office, though they agreed afterward that maybe a veterinarian would have been a better choice.

Doctor Haley peered into Silverfish's mouth. "Dragons hatch in a week or less. I can have them removed, if you want."

"You can?" Silverfish's hopes soared. Haley nodded.

"With a serum to dissolve them, they'll detach and you'll have no problem at all."

"Wait." Jasper held up her hand, leaving a cold spot where it had been resting on Silverfish's thigh. "Dissolve them? You mean kill all the babies?"

Haley nodded. Behind her left shoulder, a cabinet stood ajar, wedged open by a dragon's nest of nitrile gloves and tongue depressors. Silverfish could just see the tip of a bubblegum-pink tail, flicking every few seconds.

She swallowed, causing Bone to shift. "What about the mother?"

"She should live. Once her eggs are lost, I don't think she'd be very interested in staying," Haley said, folding her arms. She looked between Jasper and Silverfish. Jasper was shaking her head.

"No. You can't kill them. It's…it's not right!"

"I can't see any way of removing them without the serum that would be risk-free," Haley said. Her tone was so bland, so reasonable. Silverfish winced as Bone's claws poked her.

"How long did you say, until they hatch?"

"A few days," Haley said.

Silverfish looked at Jasper. "What do you think?"

Days.

Silverfish ate no solid food. She could tell by Bone's stillness that the dragon didn't eat anything at all. Too busy caring for the eggs, Silverfish guessed.

It was a strange sensation, being a surrogate to a dragon's offspring. She felt some motherly instinct taking over, spreading down her trachea and into her lungs. Each breath was more than her own.

On the third day Silverfish sat on the couch with a cup of tea cooling in her hands. She couldn't drink it when it was very hot, for fear of killing Bone's eggs. She let the steam dampen her face, closing her eyes.

Jasper came downstairs, toweling her head after a shower. She sat next to Silverfish on the couch, skin tacky with moisture. She smelled of Old Spice. "How are you feeling?"

Silverfish opened her mouth to reply, and choked.

Her mouth filled with tingling, a million little twitches moving forward from her throat to her lips. Tears streamed from her eyes as she tried to suppress the coughing fit her body wanted her to have. She could breathe, but she couldn't talk to let Jasper know what was happening. She just stared, mouth gaping.

"Shit. Fuck. Shit shit fucker."

Jasper pulled the mug from Silverfish's hands and tossed the towel onto her lap. She put her hands on Silverfish's cheeks, fragrant and still slippery with the lotion she'd just applied. "Babe, you got this. Just wait. They know what to do. I read online they can walk as soon as they hatch, be self-sufficient and shit. Just wait and *oh fuck what the hell shit goddamn!*"

Dragons were pouring out of Silverfish's mouth. They dropped in bunches onto the towel, stuck together like dandelion seeds. Tiny legs grabbed at the air, at each other, at the towel. Jasper sat back, frantically counting aloud.

"…twenty-four, twenty-five, thirty? Oh, god."

The tingling moved from Silverfish's throat to her tongue. Her nose was running, snot mixing with saliva and dragons. Spit slid back down her throat, and she hoped it didn't take any dragons with it.

"They're almost out, I think. Babe, holy *fuck*."

Jasper was dividing her attention between the now squirming towel and Silverfish's mouth. Silverfish's jaw hurt and her tongue felt horribly alive. She closed her eyes, willing herself to stay still.

When the tingling had reached the tip of her tongue, something shifted back in her throat. She couldn't stop the cough then, her eyes flicking open. Jasper jerked back as she was sprayed with spit. Tiny dragons speckled her cheeks and she wiped them off as quickly and carefully as she could, dumping them onto the towel with a slur of breathless obscenities.

Bone moved again and Silverfish gagged. Jasper pulled the towel back, baby dragons sprawling in the pink cloth in sticky bunches. Silverfish's jaw trembled. She could feel Bone climbing forward from her throat. Needle claws pricked her tongue and clicked against her teeth. All at once, the dragon spilled out, a smooth green salamander with sharp yellow claws.

Bone landed among their progeny and was immediately swamped, tiny dragons running up their legs and settling along their back. Jasper scooted the stragglers toward Bone, peeling them apart from one another and guiding them up the slimy back. Silverfish saw that she was crying.

"Oh my god," Jasper's voice dropped to a whisper. She seemed at a loss for swears, her eyes sparkling in wonder. "Look at them."

Silverfish swallowed. No scratching, no choking. She could breathe clear for the first time in weeks.

Bone lay on the damp pink towel, crowded by tiny dragons, each no larger than a grain of bright green rice. Silverfish stared, wiping her mouth and feeling like she'd been scrubbed clean from the inside out.

"There must be a hundred or more," Jasper said. She reached out and touched a clump of babies, sticky and squirming, by Bone's back leg. Silverfish swallowed again, looking from the dragons she'd carried to Jasper, the other side of the towel draped over her knees. Her hair was half-dried, fanned across her head in sharp orange spikes. Sitting across from her, Silverfish had the feeling there was nothing more beautiful in the world than the contents of the towel, and Jasper's eyes.

She reached out, lifting Jasper's hand from the tiny dragons. When Jasper looked at her, Silverfish beamed.

"What are we going to call them?"

Marisca Pichette is a queer author based in Massachusetts. More of her work appears in *Strange Horizons, Clarkesworld, Fantasy Magazine, Asimov's,* and others. Her poetry collection, *Rivers in Your Skin, Sirens in Your Hair,* was a finalist for the Bram Stoker and Elgin Awards. Her eco-horror novella, *Every Dark Cloud,* is out now from Ghost Orchid Press.

The Strangeness of the Story
Joanne McLaughlin

First one into the office every morning, last one out every night: Those were the terms of Miranda's imprisonment. Corporately incarcerated near-robot that she was, however, she could still recognize when she hit the wall. When the garbage flowing into her brain no longer flowed out transformed, somehow, into this quarter's groundbreaking marketing campaign. Another fourteen-hour day registered, she slammed her laptop shut and jammed it into her designer briefcase. She slung it over her shoulder, hit the light switch, and navigated to the elevator.

Down, down, down to the lobby. Doors opening and closing at every floor. Twenty-six floors. Express cars stopped operating at 7 p.m. Trivial details she was certain she would still rattle off if dementia claimed her.

The job might kill her long before that, assuming she didn't beat someone to death first with a thigh-high boot. Brent topped her victims list. One-time lover, real-time boss, full-time asshole. She liked to think her mere presence tormented his conscience; what else explained the beaucoup bucks he paid her and the stupidly lavish corner office in which he situated her? Or maybe their relationship was always transactional, with those years of happiness and good sex just part of a deal that had since expired. She was still creative director of Brent's oh-so-hot firm, which for him effectively translated to: "I know you're the genius of this operation, Miranda. Figure out how to keep the clients smiling."

Did *she* remember how to smile—sincerely, that is, not just to win over a client?

"Jesus, I've got to get out."

Miranda sprinted from the elevator, hurrying across the lobby. She pushed her way through the revolving door to the sidewalk. And froze there, the weight of the job immobilizing her.

Why should she even bother going home? She'd never sleep, dwelling instead on the mess that was her current project. Another one ill-conceived by her own personal Satan, who had tasked her with devising a marketing campaign that, she so itched to tell the client, lacked viability because there was no discernable strategy, or persuasive message, or actual audience to direct a message to. She wasted hours today talking to Gen Z influencers about antacids. Their blank stares gave her indigestion, though that might have been because she never actually got to eat the lunch that accompanied their lunchtime meeting, yet she drank at least two glasses of wine. Could sentient human beings under thirty imagine heartburn as a byproduct of all-hours partying in skintight clothing? She couldn't, and she was only thirty-three. Lack of imagination wasn't her problem. Or was it?

Icy drops chilled her back to reality — she had left her coat upstairs. The street facing the downtown office tower glistened as raindrops beat down and floated on a sheen of motor oil and who knew what else. Most sane people had escaped this part of the city hours ago. No one accused Miranda of being sane. Certainly not recently.

"I am so screwed. Plus exhausted, cold, and hungry."

She turned to reenter the lobby.

"It's just a revolving door, Miranda, nothing to be afraid of."

Every year at Christmas, when they traveled downtown to the big department stores to see Santa, the whirling copper doors intimidated Miranda. Was she supposed to push? Was she supposed to wait until someone else did?

Every year, she balked.

"I don't like these doors, Mommy. Is there a secret word that will let me pass through?"

"The secret word is courage, sweetheart. Be brave and push. It's only when you hesitate that you get stuck."

She could hear Mom's voice, feel the love in it. Wanted to call her now. Wished they were cycling through this door together, St. Nick waiting for them on the other side.

A wise woman, her mother, though she probably never pondered the physics of how to circle in an earlyish twentieth-century door with a twenty-first-century MacBook Pro hanging in a large briefcase from one's shoulder. A currently wedged briefcase. Miranda's dilemma: how to solve for x, the number of attempts needed to clear the door without losing an arm.

"Courage, goddamn it," Miranda repeated each time the briefcase hindered forward motion. "Take your time."

There was no one behind her to trap, or to trap her, within the door's glass-and-metal embrace. When she at last managed to maneuver the briefcase from side to front, from hip level to chest level, she wielded it like a shield and shoved back into the building. And why? To fetch a coat she would get soaked wearing anyway? Just the thought of another twenty-six elevator stops…

Loud music blasted across the lobby. "It's All Over Now" by the Rolling Stones, which meant the pub's dinner crowd had thinned to nothing and Frank, the bartender, had reset the playlist to classic rock.

The pub served marginal food until 10 o'clock and weak drinks until whenever last call was on a given weeknight. It was 9 o'clock now. Decision made.

Miranda caught Frank's eye, and the volume projecting Mick, Keith, and the rest of the Stones diminished. She scooched up onto a barstool, setting her briefcase on the vacant seat to her left, so she could see both it and the entrance. Unlikely a hit man was coming after her, but still.

"Let him take his best shot," she muttered and rotated, repositioning the briefcase to the stool on her right.

"Quite the moving target, aren't you? Trouble making up your mind tonight?"

She shrieked, startled. The barstool wobbled under her. A long arm in a blue pinstriped sleeve reached out to steady it.

"I was going to walk farther down the bar, but I think I'd better stick close, to protect you," a deep, rich voice said. "No telling what damage you might do to person and property."

Mortified, Miranda forced herself to look straight ahead, into the mirror behind the bar. Frank approached, reading her mind for all she knew.

"Doesn't feel like a margarita night, does it, Ms. P.? Let's call it vodka and tonic. Lime, no lemon, two olives?"

Her new guardian leaned over her right shoulder. "I'll have the same. She's buying."

"One tab, got it," Frank said and slipped away to busy himself with glassware and bottles.

Thus abandoned by the man she knew, Miranda could choose to make eye contact with the unknown owner of that smooth, maybe Irish, maybe Scottish, accent or instead pluck a paper menu from the stack resting under a container of plastic swizzle sticks.

She plucked. Metal stool legs scraped against wood two spaces away. She contemplated sodium- and fat-rich dinner options.

"Anything good here?" the voice wondered.

"Depends on your definition of good, I suppose. Tasty enough, but will too much of it kill you? Without a doubt."

She glanced at the mirror again and saw her bar buddy struggling to keep a straight face. A very handsome straight face. This guy, whoever he was, seemed by far the most delicious thing in the pub.

"I'm from Glasgow," he said. "Clogged arteries and a bad liver are probably built into my DNA. Talking to strangers definitely is. So, you see, you must take pity."

Frank set down their drinks and took the stranger's side. "He did save your life, Ms. P. It's only fair."

"Men always stick together. So much for your tip," she said, and lowered her briefcase to the floor. Mr. Scotland took the hint and the barstool beside her and put out his hand.

"James Fraser. Jamie."

She knew that name.

"Wait, like the character in *Outlander*?" She tilted her head and squinted at him through the low light. Mr. Fraser was very broad and, judging by the length of his legs, rather tall. Your typical romance-novel cover dude, minus the kilt.

"I get that question a lot, because of the TV program, you see. But I swear I've not traveled from the eighteenth century. Want to see my passport?"

He produced a small book whose cover declared it to be from the United Kingdom of Great Britain and Northern Ireland and whose interior contained the name and a photo of one James F. Fraser.

"What does the F stand for?"

"Ferdinand," he replied. "Don't ask."

"Okay, I won't."

Miranda debated whether to give this man *her* name mere minutes after meeting him in an underpopulated bar.

Gorgeous trumped good judgment.

"Miranda," she said. When he offered his hand again, she shook it and noted the absence of a wedding ring. Which signified nothing definitive.

"Miranda." His larger hand engulfed hers. "The bartender called you 'Ms. P.' Can it be your last name is Prospero?"

A blush warmed her face, and she eased her hand free. "You guessed it. Mom majored in English in college. When she married my father and gave birth to a daughter, my fate was sealed."

Frank picked that moment to appear and regale them with an often-told tale—much too gleefully, in Miranda's opinion.

"Ms. P.'s boss—okay, Brent used to be her boyfriend—well, he donated a copy of *The Tempest* for our bookshelf over there, just to tease Her Literaryness." Frank pointed to the shelf, which was filled with more dusty volumes than Miranda believed a food establishment should be permitted. "After a few rounds, if we get lucky, she might act out a scene or two."

"Not on your life, buster." She pinned Frank with a "Definitely forget about that tip" glare.

He pointed to his wristwatch. "So, you two want to order food? Kitchen's shutting down soon."

"Hummus platter," she replied. "And Mr. Fraser will have the black bean burger with sweet potato fries. Let's give the first-time customer something the kitchen *actually* makes well."

"Good selection. Also a good thing the cook didn't hear you say that." Sweeping the menu back under the swizzle sticks, Frank ordered them to pick a table. "I line the glasses up along the length of the bar after I wash them, they dry faster. So scoot over there please."

Mr. Fraser stood and stretched, filling out that blue suit better than Miranda could have imagined. "Thank God," he said. "My knees are bruised from banging against the bar."

A problem Miranda didn't have. She hoisted her briefcase onto her shoulder, grabbed her drink, and selected the brightest spot in the empty restaurant.

"The better to see you, my dear," she admitted, and took a seat visible from both bar and kitchen.

Mr. F. groaned and took the other chair. "Not one for romantic comedy meet-cutes, are you? If you were, you'd know the Big Bad Wolf is never the new guy. He's always the ex."

"Very funny."

She sipped her drink and inwardly scripted the scene. *A hunk walks into a bar, curious if not outright interested in Miranda. She hems and haws.*

Could he tell, she wondered, that she was the reigning queen of playing it safe?

Chance encounters, Miranda seldom had these days. You needed to get out into the world to meet other inhabitants of it. And online dating sucked, of course. Quick meet-ups with men who at first glance seemed promising, her Apple watch at the ready to call 911, plus pepper spray to fight with if needed. Occasionally, quick sex followed, sometimes followed by second or third dates but more often followed by no further communication. She had slept with more ghosts-to-be than she could count, and had been that ghost herself.

Only that Shakespeare-gifting boss Frank referred to never disappeared from her life, an eternal emotional specter. At least Brent knew better than to revisit the physical aspects of their relationship.

She chose to join Brent's company when he started it, lovestruck fool that she was. She chose to stay with Brent's company after their break-up, idiot that she was. If she were being honest with herself, she'd acknowledge that she let Brent talk her into it. She deserved what she got, she supposed: an indefinite sentence of soul-sucking bullshit. When she finished this ridiculous marketing campaign, she vowed, she would hand in her resignation and rejoin the living.

Only gradually did she become aware that her dinner companion had retrieved *The Tempest* from the pub's bookshelf.

"Do you intend to read that now?" she asked.

"You seemed lost in thought, so I decided to impress you by quoting the Bard. Have to reacquaint myself with the play first."

"You want to impress me?"

"Naturally, milady." His eyes twinkled in the dimness of the dining area.

She fished the lime wedge out of her drink, squeezing the juice out of it, biting into it aggressively. "This lady has worked ten fourteen-hour days this month. Maybe I wasn't so much lost in thought as dozing off in this chair until you started flipping pages."

He massaged the reddish stubble shading his jaws. "I'm so tired, I might believe you if you claimed you were raised on a faraway island by a sorcerer. I flew here from New York, after a horrendously long journey that started days ago in Cape Town. I barely know which continent I'm on, let alone which time zone this is."

She couldn't top that.

"To quote that other Miranda, the one on Prospero's mystical isle, 'The strangeness of your story put heaviness in me.'"

He swirled the ice cubes in his glass, watching them swim through the clear liquid.

"Not at all what I want for either of us, milady."

What did that mean? Miranda bit the insides of her cheeks, barricading the question within.

Jamie shifted his blue gaze up to her green one. "The strangeness of my story is that it isn't strange at all, is it? Sounds remarkably similar to yours so far. What if there were a way to rewrite *this* tempest? Relocate it to a city while keeping the part where a shipwrecked soul named Ferdinand discovers a lovely woman named Miranda. What would happen next, do you suppose?"

Possibilities floated unspoken between them when a server approached from the kitchen. As if sensing he had crossed a magnetic field, the server delivered their platters and fled. Miranda removed her black jacket, stood, and hung it from her chair. She rolled the sleeves of her white blouse halfway to her elbows.

She felt Jamie's perusal. A charged silence lingered, and she knew she would have to be the one to break it.

"I have an amazing affinity for landing my wrists in whatever I'm eating. Club soda and dish detergent are part of my office-supplies inventory." Before sitting again, Miranda smoothed nonexistent wrinkles from her black pencil skirt. She unfurled a paper napkin and lay it on her lap, where it absorbed some residual dampness from the rain.

"A busy businesswoman must be prepared. That explains the short haircut too, I'm guessing."

He understood, which simultaneously gratified and unnerved Miranda. She tucked a stray brown wave behind her right ear. "Much easier to stick my head under the faucet and blow it dry before an early morning meeting."

"And the black-and-white clothing is interchangeable. Intentionally so, yes?"

Miranda eyed his outfit. "Dark blue suit, light blue shirt, small-print tie. How many of those did you pack for this trip?"

"Touché," Jamie said. He finished his vodka and tonic and signaled Frank at the bar. "Two more of these please."

She dipped pita slices into her hummus. Jamie worked his way through his burger.

Quite the pair, voyagers adrift in high seas — Miranda was pretty sure a line in *The Tempest* covered that. Certainly, she carried enough baggage for an around-the-world trip. She could blame Brent, but why delude herself?

What, or who, pursued Jamie Fraser from port to port, she wondered but did not ask. Asking questions might get you the answers you wanted, she had learned, but the important details often emerged unsummoned.

They ate as though famine chased them through entrée, dessert, and coffee. When the kitchen cut them off, they talked as if they craved conversational nourishment even more.

Like two people who had known each other forever, Miranda imagined, though they had only just met.

Two more vodka and tonics for her, several shots of a single-malt Scotch Jamie pronounced surprisingly good, and Miranda found herself once again leaving the pub at closing time.

Frank winked as he handed her the tab. "Good to see you tonight, Ms. P."

Jamie snatched the check. "I'll get this. Meeting you has been my special treat this evening."

"No, I can't let you pay for me—"

"Say yes, Miranda," he insisted. "If you're like me, you say it all the time, for all the wrong reasons."

How often did she tell herself that very thing?

Before Frank could hurry them out, Miranda stopped at the restroom. When she emerged, she saw Jamie through the pub's door, standing in the building lobby.

The clock over the reception desk read 2 a.m. She had an 8:30 a.m. staff meeting, but she needed to get away from this place, if only for a few hours. She pulled out her phone, opened her ride-share app, and arranged for a pick-up. Eight minutes, the app responded. Not soon enough.

"You don't want to know how many nights I've slept upstairs in my office since the beginning of the year. It's a beautifully decorated office, but still. How's that for a pathetic confession?"

"I travel constantly," Jamie said. "I left commodities market research, a fine, boring desk job, for a consulting gig based out of London. Day after tomorrow, I join a conference of chief financial officers from agribusiness and food multinationals to network for my current employer, but also to see who else might want what I have to offer."

"And so for what's left of tomorrow, you'll do room service and bad TV? Hope you're staying somewhere with lots of pillows and a decent mattress. Goldilocks-worthy, not too soft, not too hard."

"The Four Seasons, just a few blocks away. So I'll wait with you until your car comes. Mustn't shirk my protector duties." He pretended to doff a hat and bow to her.

Surely, he had someone to protect, somewhere. "No wife to call? No kids to video-kiss trans-Atlantically over breakfast?"

Miranda thought she detected a flicker of regret, quickly disguised with a yawn—a trick she recognized because she used it often.

"Divorced after five years, the last three of which we mostly argued," he said. "No kids, for which I'm grateful, given how bad a match we turned out to be."

She and Brent had been together since grad school, and they talked for a while of marriage and a family. Relinquishing that dream had been hard. Relinquishing Brent—or, rather, the shining, successful Miranda she had become with him—proved harder.

Jamie yawned again, a genuine-seeming fatigue Miranda also felt.

"You're jet-lagged, Mr. Fraser, whereas I leave here at all hours, all the time. No need for you to stay and be my guardian. The security staff here, the guards and the guys who monitor the cameras overnight, watch out for me."

"I'm glad someone does."

Jamie put his arms around her and kissed the top of her head. Miranda sank into him, wishing she could stay there. But eventually, she backed away.

"Give me your hand," he said. Onto her right palm, he wrote a phone number. "I'm here for a week, Miranda. I'd love to see you again."

Her phone chirped with a notification: Her ride had arrived. Miranda blew Jamie a kiss and pushed her way effortlessly through the revolving door to a black SUV at the curb. From the back seat, she watched as the door propelled him onto the sidewalk. He turned in the same direction the car headed.

At the first red light, Miranda tapped into a navigation app. "Can you take me to this address?" She dictated a destination. The driver agreed.

Miranda looked at the number on her right hand and at the phone in her left. She sent two texts.

"I quit," the first began. "Accept it."

"Walk faster," the second began. "Say yes."

Joanne McLaughlin writes sharp mysteries and sexy vampire tales, including *A Poetic Puzzle, Chasing Ashes, Never Before Noon, Never Until Now,* and *Never More Human.* A longtime editor for newspapers and public media, her recent short fiction appeared in *Ruth and Ann's Guide to Time Travel, Volume 1,* and *mysterytribune.com.* She can be found at joannemclaughlin.net.

The Ladies and the Tiger
Susan Shwartz

The King had set spies upon his daughter Althaia. His mistrust, though justified, had broken her heart. She would never, never forgive him. King Lars had distrusted her when all she had done was to love honorably a man as noble as he was poor. That was the first heartbreak.

Her second came when he sentenced Sethre, whose only crime was to dare to love her, to judgment. It was public and it was quick. He must walk across the sands of the arena, salute the king he feared and the princess he loved, face the two doors of judgment, and open one of them. Waiting behind it might be a lady who matched him in fairness and heritage. The other door concealed the most ferocious tiger King Lars's beast masters could procure.

Althaia's cunning and her gold won for her the name of the lady behind that door. Althaia hated Lady Tanaquil with all her heart. She had dared to glance adoringly at Sethre. Althaia would never forgive him for glancing back.

Let Lady Tanaquil pray and tremble behind the left door. Althaia sat to her father's right in a chair only slightly less than carved and gilded than his throne. As his heir, she shone in crimson and purple and gems, stately as one of the statues that graced the arena's colonnades.

Genial and flush-faced, King Lars sat drinking wine from the south as Sethre was released. His spear of office, a leaf-shaped bronze blade, leaned against his chair.

Sethre, tall and fair-haired, his face pale, he marched through the arena's mysterious cloisters onto the sands. He saluted the king, then Princess Althaia. Their eyes met. Her hand, clenching the armrest of her chair, twisted slightly to the right.

Sethre flushed. He walked to the right-hand door and, without hesitation, flung it open.

The tiger, longer than a tall man was tall, sprang at this new prey. It flung him to the ground, thrust its fangs into his throat, and then it fed while blood stained the stands. Sethre had no time even for a death scream.

Iron bells clanged out. Hired mourners lined the arena and wailed. Their lamentations muffled the growling and snapping of the tiger as it fed. A chorus sang its lament. Servants flung black silk drapes over the marble statues guarding the colonnade.

Was it still consolation to Althaia that Tanaquil did not have him? She would not hear the growls of the tiger or the sobs of the people. By now, she must have realized that Sethre had chosen the tiger, not the lady. She would probably be weeping. Her sort always wept. That frailty made people want to protect them, to ease their way while Althaia must remain strong.

Even when King Lars, genial at the success of his scheme in proving her lover's guilt, leaned over to ask whether she had learned her lesson, she did not flinch. She inclined her head in a gesture he could take for humility. Usually, he was not that stupid, but he loved getting his own way even more than he loved her.

The beast masters emerged from the depths of the arena with nets and knives to force the tiger back into its cage. *What a pity it did not attack them too, but it was sated, sleepy.*

The people poured out of the amphitheater. Once they all were gone, King Lars and Princess Althaia retreated from the royal box into the long corridor that led between the amphitheater and the palace. Torches lit the way. They cast only the pallid flames, like the luminescence of decayed trees, that the city reserved for plague or death by tiger.

Guards escorted Althaia back to her rooms. Her father still did not wholly trust her. Nor should he. Some of those guards had taken her gold, and she had made her own plans.

She could not evade eating and drinking with her maids. They were avid to discuss every minute of Sethre's noble bearing, his death, and how Althaia had shown herself to be a true princess. The youngest ventured a word of how the lady behind the other door must be grieving. She was sent from the room.

Althaia made herself smile. She thrilled them by pouring wine for them herself. In it was a strong sleeping draught. She pretended to drink, yawned hugely, dismissed her maids, and locked herself in her room. Yes, the walls probably held spy holes. She turned her face toward the one large stained-glass window.

Now she could let her tears flow, if only in silence. She had killed Sethre as surely as that tiger. But could she have borne to see him embrace Tanaquil, to walk off with her down a path strewn with flowers while children sang and flutes played? Could she bear to imagine him entwined with her on a bed fragrant with flower petals and fine oils?

Her heart had been broken so often that she wondered if she shed tears, not blood.

When she finally ceased weeping, she dressed without help in gray almost the color of the corpse light of the torches. She tucked jewelry and gold pieces into sleeves and pouches, securing them with firm knots. She strapped a sword, forged from precious iron, to her back and sheathed a dagger at her belt. It was leather, not her usual gem-studded silk. It would serve. *It must serve.*

When she slipped from her rooms, her maids still slept their drugged sleep. She passed guards, one or two of whom had served her well in discovering where the tiger had been kept. She entered the corridor that led to the amphitheater and walked between rows of ghostly torches, out into the royal box where she had caused her lover's death. The black-draped statues looked like the spirits of dead kings.

She climbed down the stairs and rows of benches, carved out of the living rock, into the arena. The beast masters and cleaners had already strewn it with fresh sand, hiding the blood, the splintered bones, and the scraps of flesh that the tiger might have left behind. Light glinted in the sand, and Althaia bent to retrieve a ring she knew well. She had given it to Sethre herself.

She clutched it in her fist until it stung her palm. Striding over to the twin doors that held judgment, she flung the left-hand door open. The tiger had emerged last time from the right, and she knew her father shifted lady and tiger from room to room.

The tiger owed her a life. She would kill it if she could. No tiger sprang from the opened door. Instead, Althaia heard the sound of hopeless weeping. More gently than she had intended, she entered the room. Peering into the half-light, she saw the Lady Tanaquil curled up on a rainbow of brocade pillows. Weeping openly in what had become her cell and mourning ground, weeping as Althaia had not dared.

A breeze swept in. As if alerted by the change in the air, Tanaquil flung herself off her couch and onto her feet. Seeing Althaia, she gasped. She would have flung herself down in prostration, but the princess caught her.

"Have you come to feed me to the tiger as you did Sethre?" No man would have understood the choice Althaia had made, or even that she had seized the power to make one. Any woman would have known it in an instant.

No tiger would touch feeble prey like you, Althaia wanted to say. But the fury in the lady's blue eyes flashed like gems from the Land of Lions and silenced the spiteful, unworthy words. Grief-stricken Tanaquil might be, but for what Althaia had considered a weak, pallid creature, she had courage.

"How could you watch him killed?" Tanaquil demanded. "Would it have been so terrible if you had let him live, live and be happy? Was I so hateful?"

Only that morning, Althaia's answer would have been "yes." But looking at the distraught lady, strong even as she surrendered to tears before the woman who was her mortal enemy, her heart changed.

For one mad instant, Althaia had the impulse to fling her arms about the only other person to whom Sethre's death might have meant as much as it did to her.

Then, she cleared her throat. "I was hoping," she said, "to meet the tiger."

"Why would you wish to die? You have everything – or you had." Those last two words stung.

"Must you be as foolish as I wanted to think you?" Althaia demanded. "That beast owes me a life."

The younger, smaller woman raised her head. Her chin was stronger than the princess had realized. "You owe yourself a life. And me, too. I loved him too, Highness," she said. "Had *I* been on your throne, *I* would have let him live."

She met Alathaia's eyes without flinching. The princess felt herself flush in the presence of such restraint, such self-sacrifice. She could not have endured seeing Sethre happy with someone who was not she herself. Tanaquil could. What was more, she could go on living thereafter, while Alathaia was not sure what lay next for her. She lowered her head, unable to meet those candid blue eyes. Then, memory of who she was, whom she had loved, and her need for a future made her stare Tanaquil down.

Lady Tanaquil seemed to understand. "How will you live now?" she asked. Althaia could almost believe she cared.

Althaia pointed to the door. "Give me your cloak," she ordered. "I will leave through the door. They may think I am you for just long enough to flee."

Tanaquil bowed, not the ironically abject prostration this time but a bow between ladies who understood each other. Althaia reached her hand out, the hand that held Sethre's ring, which had once been hers. Tanaquil held out her own hand to receive it.

"My father gave it to me. I gave it to..." her voice failed for a moment, and then she commanded herself again. "It is yours now."

Althaia had a future and ideas about how to achieve it. Tanaquil, with her gentleness, her tears, and her soft voice did not. And men preferred ladies such as she, not seeing the iron that lay behind the ready tears and the flawless skin and form.

Seeing that she had a future would be the last thing Althaia could do for Sethre.

"After I leave, wait until dawn. Then, show this ring to my father."

King Lars might welcome a daughter more biddable than Althaia. Or even a new wife he would not have to spy upon – although, undoubtedly, he would.

So, she had done what she could. She snatched up Tanaquil's cape, the color of a mourning dove, and wrapped it about her. It would serve to conceal her and her station as she left the city to seek her own future.

She had her jewels. She had her sword. She had skills painstakingly acquired when a deceptively indulgent father let her learn to ride and fight as well as the womanly arts. How else had she met Sethre but on the practice grounds?

She slipped out of the door, stooping and adopting a maidenly gait, not her usual firm stride. Let watchers think she was Tanaquil returning to her father's house. Walking like this took forever. She quickened her short steps, as if fearing to be alone here. Then, she reached the two doors at the far side of the arena's heavy wall. One door opened into the city. The other led to a stone passage that wound into the space between the city's inner and outer walls. It was a killing zone for enemies and a way out for fugitives if the city were overrun.

A narrow gate was hidden behind a corner. Her father had taken her to see it when she came of age, then never spoke of it again. She slipped out of the city, out of her old life, and toward a field where she could steal a mount. She could ride without saddle, like the warriors who fought bare and barebacked in the craggy lands across the narrow sea. Her horse galloped toward the new life she vowed to make in the south where lay the great city that had given her father his deadly notions of empire and amphitheater.

Five years after leaving the city of her birth, Althaia rode back beside the southern general Aquila, freed from his duties in his own city to lead his army. Following the army was its train of grooms, smiths, camp followers, merchants, and the nomadic small town that kept it fed.

Like her consort the general, Althaia wore a cuirass. On it was emblazoned a Greek letter. Alpha for Aquila. Alpha for Althaia, too, who rode and ruled alongside him. When she fled her own city, she had shrewdly deployed her jewels to bring her to the general's attention. Her wit, strength, and beauty had kept her at his side. They looked more like brother and sister than consorts: both tall, both dark of hair, tanned of skin, piercing of dark eyes.

They were warriors together, fierce with the desire of people who have a life to win, a need to prove themselves, and love for the consorts who guarded their backs. They understood each other well. Their alliance possessed everything that Althaia needed, even if it lacked the cleanly, innocent passion she and her dead lover had felt.

Ironically, it was precisely what her father might have wished for her.

Ironically, his daughter and her consort marched on his city. The army bore their standards and banners, black and crimson, high. Behind them rumbled the siege engines that made the southern kingdom such a fearsome enemy.

The walls of Althaia's former home reared up, taller than she remembered, ornate with carvings. Aquila flung up a hand. Behind them, the army halted, grounding spears and standards. The siege engines rumbled to a stop. Camp followers clustered until officers, riding down the crowd, shouted them into ranks of their own.

"They build well," Aquila remarked.

"My father's added to it," Althaia told him. "He's improved the roads..."

"He will regret that..."

Althaia nodded. "We cannot underestimate him."

I will not make that mistake again.

She rose in her stirrups, trying to see the tiny gate by which she had exiled herself. It was covered by new construction.

Aquila's face hardened. "You may have to search out that gate yourself," he told her. "Your report of the killing ground between the walls — they cost more lives than I want to pay."

She nodded. "Siege first?"

"We will soften them up. Maybe King Lars will seek terms."

King Lars would not negotiate, especially not with a daughter at the head of an opposing army.

Not long thereafter, men were digging trenches and building fortifications for a proper camp. The followers would sprawl out around it, although sergeants would ensure they had proper latrines, did not foul the water, and paid for what food they took.

The army would create a wilderness. As its sappers redirected the courses of rivers and streams and engineers studied the ramparts to place moving towers, the city would come under attack without a drop of blood being spilled.

Yet.

By birth or by conquest, she was determined to rule. Aquila would sit at her side. That was their wedding bargain.

Every day, the sun's chariot rose higher in the sky. The air trembled with the summer heat. Siege did not mean that the army sat waiting to starve the city into surrender. Engineers studied the walls. Shielded by a tortoise of fighters, they went up to the very stones to measure them. Sometimes Althaia accompanied them, seeking the hidden gate, until she found it, covered by a tomb whose rocks were treated to look ancient. She told only Aquila.

Aquila's officers commanded the troops on raids, daily drills, and camp maintenance. Field doctors prowled the camp and the followers for signs of illness that could weaken the army.

Rations were sparse, but still enough for all. Inside the city, Althaia knew how well-supplied it was, with flocks, granaries, and cisterns full of water. Her father understood his work. Sometimes King Lars would appear on the battlements, fully armed. He looked older. He used his spear of office like a cane.

The fighting began. As the siege engines barraged the walls, soldiers manning them fell. The missiles that landed therein destroyed houses and shops and the people within them. The king had to retaliate. If he ordered fire arrows shot from the walls, Aquila ordered the siege engines covered with skins drenched in vinegar. If sorties erupted from the gates at foot soldiers, they lowered long lances to spit men and horses alike.

The city's casualties mounted. Each day, armed parties rode out to bury the dead. The days grew hotter. Water in the cisterns might be running short. One day, the main gates opened. As the army prepared to launch an attack, Althaia whispered urgently to her consort.

"Hold!" Aquila shouted. His voice carried much more effectively than hers.

City guards drove a throng of people out the walls: the elderly, some pushed in chairs or carried on wagons; beggars; women and children with no protectors; people of no respectability at all. They could be spared and must be sacrificed. Althaia scanned the crowd. Perhaps the begging, weeping crowd included some court ladies. Gods knew, they were practically useless.

She dismissed that thought as unworthy of a general and ordered soldiers to find them some sort of shelter. If they fell ill and died, camp and army too might fall ill. Besides, a show of mercy might weaken King Lars's hold on his people.

"Too many diversions," Aquila muttered to her one night after their staff meeting. It had been very divisive. "We are at risk."

Althaia nodded. "It may be time for a strike force to enter the city..."

Aquila shook his head. She had found the entrance, but Aquila still protested her leading the attack. Her consort did not often show such concern for her.

"I know every stone between those walls," she argued. "It is worth the risk. The man speaks, not the general," she said. "Remember our bargain."

Uncharacteristically, he swore. He drained the skin of watered wine. He slept much of the day, a startling breach of his usual control. The next night, he helped her arm herself for a mission that would either win them a city or lose Althaia her life.

The night was moonless as Althaia led a handpicked force, their armor and weapons blackened for the greatest secrecy, toward the gate concealed within the tomb. She refused to see that as an omen. Her men knew that the gate might be guarded. Archers might line the walls, or an armed force might rush toward them. It was what she would do. No one said she was foolish.

Her father's men were indeed waiting for them. Her father retained his old cleverness. He allowed her to lead her people between the walls. Then, his guards struck hard and fast. Althaia met the eyes of her officer: no time to warn Aquila, and she could not spare a fighter. She dodged, heading for the second gate, the one that led into the amphitheater.

The passage was dark. Armed with her knowledge of the place, they slunk through the darkness, through the intricacies of the corridors, and toward the rooms that held the secret: the lady or the tiger?

She would have to bet. She laid her hand upon the doorplate. Her officer pushed her away and flung wide the door. The tiger sprang, but Althaia's spearsmen were swift. She herself pulled the dying beast off the man – not as badly injured as he might be. She herself put the beast out of its misery. Would that she could have done that for the entire city.

Emerging from the tiger's lair, she and her surviving soldiers stood on the sands of the arena. She gestured for one man to take the officer into the room reserved for the lady in her father's little contests, and see to his wounds. They protested.

"Would you object to Aquila?" she demanded.

She thought not.

"Once again, you bend a beast to your will," came King Lars's voice from the royal box. Althaia remembered the seat from which she had watched Sethre die. "You are less merciful to men."

"You showed no mercy to me," Althaia snapped. He was goading her.

She glanced up at her father. Florid – too ruddy by half – he half-lay, half-sat on his throne. Lady Tanaquil stood beside him, a cuirass incongruous on her slender frame, one hand on her father's shoulder.

"Sir and Father," Althaia greeted King Lars respectfully. "I have returned."

"As an enemy," he remarked. "Not my heir."

Had he and Tanaquil had children? Tanaquil would not have failed in her duty.

"You taught me how the city is supplied. Even after you exiled so many people, how long can you hold out?"

"Long enough," said King Lars.

He clutched the spear and forced himself back onto his feet. Tanaquil supporting him (weeping again), he made his way down onto the sand. He threw his spear onto the sand before Althaia and drew his sword.

"Will you kill your own father? I am fresh out of tigers."

He advanced upon Althaia. Hesitant for the first time since she had exiled herself, she drew her own weapon. Her hand shook, and he laughed, raising his blade to strike at her neck. She forced herself to parry his stroke. He was older than she, fatter, and far slower. But he was her father and he had been her king.

Then the arrow came, swift and deadly, an eagle stooping on prey. King Lars clutched at his eye, screamed, and fell. Blood stained the sand. Tanaquil screamed.

Aquila cast down his bow and strode forward.

"You," he demanded of Tanaquil. "Are you consort here?"

Tanaquil forced herself to stand as tall as she could. Her tears dried up in a way Althaia understood.

"Have I half-brothers or sisters?" she asked.

The other woman crumpled onto the bloody sand.

"I promise you their safety. Stay or go as you choose," Althaia said. "But you must surrender the city, and you must do it now."

In the end, things worked as they must. Tanaquil surrendered. Althaia and Aquila would rule, at least long enough to yield the city to Aquila's commander. It was victory. It was vengeance. It was even freedom of a sort. Aquila draped an arm around her shoulders. They both wore scarlet capes that signified victory.

Nevertheless, Althaia shuddered. What she and her consort had won must be enough now. Victor as she was, she would never again have the innocent joy of her first love. She told herself it no longer mattered. Aquila at her side, Queen Althaia seated herself upon her throne.

For Frank R. Stockton

Susan Shwartz is an internationally published author of around 30 books, more than 100 pieces of short fiction, and articles in *The New York Times*, *Vogue*, *The Wall Street Journal*, and *Amazing*.

The Girl Who Loved the Stars
L. H. Phillips

Carly pressed her nose to the grimy living room window.

"What are you looking at, sweetie?" asked her mom from the kitchen.

"There's a big meteor shower tonight," said Carly. "The biggest one of the year. The Perseid shower."

"Oh, no luck looking out there," her dad said from the sofa. He was watching the late news on TV. "Too much ground light here in the city. Shooting stars will be too faint to see. Even if we were in the suburbs, we probably couldn't see'um."

"But there'll be so many, sixty or more an hour! Maybe some will be bright enough to see, even here," Carly persisted. Her dad's attention had drifted back to the TV and her mom was loading the dishwasher, and neither one replied. Carly turned from the window with a sigh.

Later, when everyone was in bed and it was totally dark and still, Carly slipped from the bedroom she shared with her little sister, Sarah. She padded as quietly as she could back into the living room. It was the only place in the little apartment that had decent-sized windows. Carly took a cushion from the sofa and put it on the floor beneath the front window and pulled the drapes as far open as possible. She laid down on the musty carpet and adjusted her cushion so she could watch a little patch of sky in relative comfort. Surely if she looked long enough, at least one shooting star would appear. That seemed a fair reward for patience. Carly's ambition was to become an astronomer. She loved the precise language of mathematics and the incalculable expanse of space in equal measure. Most of the grownups around her seemed to think her math skills would be better applied to a business degree. Carly found this idea horrifying, if practical.

"I just need one," Carly whispered into the deep night. It would be a sign that she was on the right track for her future.

She woke to a clatter in the kitchen. Harsh August sunlight was pouring through the window. Carly sat up with a wince. Her makeshift bed on the floor had left her with a crick in her neck. Her eyes were gritty from staying awake most of the night.

"Goodness, Carly," her mom said. "Why were you sleeping out here?" Her mom smiled. "Star-gazing?"

"Yeah, and I didn't see anything," Carly said. She felt the sting of tears in her tired eyes and a heaviness that started in her chest and spread through her whole body.

"Come have some breakfast, then." Carly swiped her eyes and sat down with her mom at the table. It didn't seem right that the pleasure of seeing shooting stars was denied to her just because she lived in the middle of a big city. A thing like that was for everybody, she thought. Everyone should own the sky.

Carly slowly got through her Saturday chores, listless from her lack of sleep. After lunch, she asked her mom if she could go to the comic book store. She had a little birthday money left and hoped she could find something she hadn't read yet. She set out, relieved to be out of the cramped apartment for a while.

The summer heat added to her doldrums. School would be starting soon. Carly mostly liked it. She was looking forward to having access to the school library again, but Carly couldn't shake the feeling that summer had slipped away with nothing to show for it. Just one hot, monotonous day after another. She wished she could have gotten a job and earned a little money, but at thirteen she was still too young. Anyway, her folks expected her to look after Sarah while school was out.

Even the short walk to the store left her sweaty. With relief, she slipped into the air-conditioned comics shop. Tom, the owner, acknowledged her with a slight lift of his eyebrows and then went back to reading behind the check-out counter.

Carly thumbed through her favorite comics section without really reading the titles, the bright, busy covers all seeming to run together today. In the middle of this garish mob, a stark black and white pamphlet caught her eye. *The Elysian Labyrinth*, the title read, followed by, *Open today only. Walk the Labyrinth and discover your gift.* A stylized graphic of a maze was centered on the cover, and below this was written, *In the midst of Summer, look to the Winter Road.* There were only five or so pages of text, and no illustrations beyond the cover design.

"The Winter Road," Carly whispered. The phrase seemed familiar to her somehow, but she couldn't place it.

"Hey, Tom," Carly said, walking up to the register. "What is the deal with this?" She held up the thin pages. Tom took it from her and frowned as he flipped through it.

"Somebody must have stuck it in the stack," he said. "It's not anything for sale. It looks like an advertisement to me. Maybe for a new video game." He handed it back to Carly.

"Can I have it?" Carly asked.

Tom shrugged. "Sure, take it. Let me know if it's anything interesting."

Carly walked out of the store. She was intrigued by the weird flyer, or whatever it was. She opened it and on the first page she read: *Follow these directions exactly and receive something to your benefit.* That was all. On the next page were the directions, which consisted of walking this way and that a certain number of steps, probably ending up at a dumpster in a back alley. Carly wondered if it was a set-up for a silly social media prank—The Gullible Dumbass Challenge, say. Still, it promised a gift of some kind. Maybe Tom was right and it was a promotion for a new game or movie. Maybe she could score a cool T-shirt, or a cute toy for Sarah. It wasn't like she had anything else to do.

So Carly went twelve steps up the street—which surprisingly did take her to an intersection—and twenty steps to the right, and back fifteen steps down the next street, and so on until she found herself facing a chain-link fence surrounding an abandoned lot. *Close your eyes and turn widdershins three times,* the last line of the instructions read. Carly had read enough fantasy books to know "widdershins" meant counterclockwise. She felt as though she was caught up in someone's D&D quest.

"Sure, why not," she muttered. Feeling foolish, Carly slowly turned three times and opened her eyes, expecting a random guy with a phone to appear, immortalizing her dopiness on the internet. What *had* appeared made her jaw drop. The chain-link was gone, replaced by a massive red brick wall. There was an ornate black iron gate in its center, with a little silver bell affixed to it. Carly looked wildly around. The rest of the street seemed quite unchanged, right down to the trash-strewn sidewalk. Carly hesitantly touched the brick. It was solid and hot from the sunlight. Had the chain-link fence and weedy field been some kind of projection? This wasn't an idle prank; this was next-level trickery. Something impressive, something powerful, was behind it. Carly felt both freaked out and excited.

Carly looked through the bars of the gate. A gravel path led away from it, into a maze of high hedges. The hedges had tiny pink flowers blooming on them, the evident source of the delicate fragrance that wafted over Carly's face on an errant breeze. Carly gave the gate an experimental shake, but it was locked.

Carly looked down at the pamphlet. The directions to the gate had been on the last page, she was certain, but now there was an additional page at the back. *You have reached the Elysian Labyrinth,* it said. *Ring the bell for admittance.* Carly stood still in the hot sun, considering. Whatever this was, it was not part of the ordinary flow of things. There was a kind of fairy-tale playfulness to the whole set-up. But she didn't believe in magic, did she? Her life's goal was to become a *scientist.* Maybe this new page had just been stuck to the previous one. Maybe this was all a ruse by kidnappers or cultists to lure dumb kids in. Carly looked into the dark, fragrant maze and somehow couldn't believe it was a ruse or a joke. She had no idea what it was, but she wanted to find out. She had spent all morning resenting the horrible monotony of her life, and here was something decidedly different. She couldn't turn away.

In for a penny, Carly thought, and gave the bell a firm pull. With a quiet chime, the gate swung open.

Carly took a cautious step forward onto the gravel. It felt much cooler in the hedges than on the sidewalk, and it smelled much better, too. Carly walked until she reached the first branch in the path, then paused to consult her paper oracle again. *The Labyrinth is a meditative walk, not a puzzle. You cannot get lost. Think on what is closest to your heart and proceed to the center.* Closest to my heart, Carly thought, and with each step her mantra became *the stars, the stars, the stars.*

True enough, there didn't seem to be any dead ends, no matter which direction she chose at each fork in the path. Carly found she was enjoying herself, despite the strangeness of it all. Her headache had lifted in the cool, sweet air, and so had her spirits. The light in the maze had a pleasant green quality filtered through the hedges, which seemed to be growing taller the deeper into the maze she went.

In a fairly short time, she reached the center. It was a circle of lush grass, with a gray stone plinth rising up in its middle. The light, which had been subtly fading as she walked, was now so dim as to approximate twilight. Carly sat down on the grass to await developments. She didn't have to wait long, as the light now vanished completely, leaving Carly in a darkness blacker than any night she had ever experienced in the city.

Carly sat very still, feeling real fear for the first time. She was considering blundering her way back down the path, no matter how dark it was, when a soft glow in the sky caught her attention. A vast, diffuse ribbon of light was forming right above her. Carly lost her breath in astonishment. It was the Winter Road of Norway (of course! her mind leapt in recognition), the Backbone of Night of the Kalahari, *the Milky Way*. She had never seen it before, except in photos. Carly fell back on the grass and stared at her home galaxy in wonder, fear forgotten. And if this glory were not enough, other marvels began appearing.

A bright star winked into existence off to the right, and as Carly watched, four pinpricks of light arrayed themselves around its middle—Jupiter and its Galilean moons. Off to the left, a tiny crystal whirlpool formed—the Andromeda galaxy, unimaginably far away. Red Mars, glowing like a coal, now strode onto the black velvet stage next to Jupiter. Venus rose in a matter of seconds, challenging Jupiter in brilliance.

The rest of the summer stars sprang into view all at once, hardly twinkling in the clear, still air. Carly lay gazing at the luminous sky, trying to fix it in her memory forever. It was more beautiful than she had dreamed.

She saw a bright streak flash out of the corner of her eye, then another. In a moment, the sky was filled with shooting stars, a silver rain that never reached the ground.

"Thank you," Carly whispered. The meteor shower slowed, then stopped. The sky began to brighten gradually, the stars fading, diamond-bright Jupiter and Venus the last to leave.

Carly stood and brushed off her shorts, a little dazed. She picked up the little book, which had been lying forgotten on the ground. She turned toward the gravel path to find it no longer existed. A solid wall of hedges now surrounded her. Carly pushed tentatively at the hedge and then drew back with a short curse. Bright beads of blood bloomed across the back of her hand. The hedge was equipped with sharp thorns in addition to the pretty pink flowers, it seemed. She hadn't noticed them before.

She looked anxiously at the newest last page of the book and read: *Sights beyond your imagination are yours if you choose to dwell in the maze. If you wish to return to your old life, place the book on the pedestal. Your choice is final.*

Carly looked up. The hedges seemed much closer, somehow. The circle of grass she stood in was shrinking. Apparently, her choice was not only final, but needed to be made quickly.

She thought of everything she had witnessed. She had no doubt that if she remained, endless wonders awaited her in the everlasting night of the Labyrinth. A voyage through Saturn's rings. A trip to the Pillars of Creation. A view of galaxies that had died before the Milky Way was born. She, Carly, a poor girl, a nobody, would see things not yet seen by the most sophisticated telescopes.

Hard on the heels of these visions came others: her mom, exhausted at the end of a twelve-hour shift. Her dad, working two jobs so that she and Sarah could have a few little luxuries. Sarah, sweet-natured and filled with hero-worship for her big sister. What would her family think if she stayed here? That she had been swallowed up by the violence of the city, that she had run away? That she cared so little for them that she hadn't even left a goodbye note? Carly couldn't bear the thought of their sorrow.

Her family would help her realize her dreams any way they could, she knew, even if they didn't fully understand them. The things the Labyrinth had shown her weren't fantasies. They were absolutely real. She could still have them in the real world, maybe, with a lot of work and a little luck. Harder than just lying back in the grass, but that was the way it needed to be. Carly realized it was no decision at all. The endless worlds of the cosmos were beautiful, but so was the little world that existed in her family's apartment. The stars weren't the only things she loved.

She closed the book and smoothed its cover wistfully, gratefully. She cast a nervous eye back at the encroaching hedge, and placed the book on the pedestal.

Carly jumped at the sound of strident honking. She was standing outside of the chain-link fence. The sun was a little lower in the sky than she remembered, the smell of car exhaust a little stronger. She leaned against the fence for a moment to collect her thoughts. She looked up at the bright, hazy sky. Her stars were still there, just a little hard to see. Carly couldn't decide if the Labyrinth was an inspiration to follow your dreams, or a trap allowing you to sink mindlessly into them. Like most things, she supposed it was all in how you took it. Carly turned toward home, the glow of ancient starlight in her eyes.

L. H. Phillips is a retired molecular biologist with a life-long love of speculative fiction. Previous stories have appeared in *Aphelion*, *The Nameless Songs of Zadok Allen* (anthology), *Road Kill vol.9*, and *Mysterion*. She lives in San Antonio, TX with her husband and cat.

Taxi
Carson Buckingham and Philip St. James

"It was rainin' hard in 'Frisco. I needed one more fare to make my night. The lady..."

"Jesus, *again*?!" The driver snapped off the radio. The song had been out for over a year and still played constantly. Cabbies hated that mawkish Harry Chapin tune like bar bands hated the interminable requests for Billy Joel's latest, "Piano Man."

He motored through the rain-drenched darkness in silence, alone with his thoughts, and wishing that his heater worked. The end of October in the Northeast was not the time for it to quit.

Emil Haydn stared out his fifth-floor apartment window to the empty street below.

He did that almost every night, afflicted as he was with insomnia. He could never sleep during the night—the quiet was deafening, and his mind played back his life and how badly he'd managed it, on an endless loop until he thought that just opening his window and jumping might be preferable to going through the damning movies his mind chose to run night after night, when there were no distractions... when his attention was undivided... when death or alcohol were the only escapes.

He chose alcohol.

"*Verdamnt!* Glass empty again." He rose slowly and stepped painfully from his post at the window; his 52-year-old body riddled with arthritis as a result of genetics and many sub-freezing winters. He fetched the bottle of cherry brandy and brought it back to his post, pouring himself another four fingers. He'd be numb by six and be able to pass out in bed for a few hours' sleep, with the early morning noises of the city for company.

At three in the morning, there was no company.

He sat back down and stared out the window again—an unknown sentinel keeping watch over an uncaring city.

"Ah, here is something different," he muttered as the yellow cab pulled up at the curb in front of his building. "Whoever called a cab at this ungodly hour? Three a.m.? Someone must be leaving an assignation." He was glad for the diversion.

The cabbie idled at the curb far longer than any driver Emil had ever heard of, waiting for the passenger—had to be about twenty minutes—before it pulled away and drove off.

"Huhm," Emil snorted, taking another long swallow and resuming his staring into the featureless night. "Must have decided to stay the night."

He'd taken this apartment because there were other people from Bavaria who lived in the building, and he thought it would be nice to have some friends from the old country. And things worked out well in that area for a while. But then he felt, inexplicably, that he must back away from contact with others, and so let the promising friendships lapse; though Albert Katz, from the third-floor rear did come up to play cards with him a couple of times a month, but that was getting rather old too—Katz always won. And nobody else in the building had any better luck—Katz kept to a schedule and played cards with each tenant twice a month. He was conversant with every card game there was, and he was adept at them all. He belonged in Vegas, that one.

And Emil was perfectly content with his own company anyway. As long as he had his *Kirschwasser*, he was about as happy as he was going to be. He read, of course. He didn't spend his entire life looking out the window. He'd tried to write his memoirs, but after a point, he had to put the pen down—it was too unbearable—both his arthritis and his story. He'd thought of getting a dog—a little dachshund—but when he inquired, he discovered that there was a building regulation against pets... so the bottle was his *schatzi*.

He sorely missed Bavaria and thought of returning many times; but there was really nothing left for him to go back to. His wife, his entire family, both immediate and peripheral, were long dead. He had watched a mass murderer dispatch each of them in a hail of bullets as they knelt for Holy Communion.

He had done nothing to stop him.

It was a truly terrible thing to be so alone in the world; but he knew he deserved it and so sat at his window and waited for God... or whomever.

The next night, right at three on the dot, the cab hove into view again, but this time, Eva Huber—at least, he thought it was Eva—stepped out from under the lobby awning and made a beeline to the vehicle.

The rear door opened, though Eva hadn't touched it; but she got in and the cab drove away.

He'd have to go down and see Eva tomorrow and find out what that cab was all about. He'd always had a knack for getting people to talk to him. Maybe he'd just watch for her to come back and drop in on her right when she arrived.

His plan went awry when he nodded off in his chair after his fifth snifter of brandy.

Waking up late the next morning was not a pleasant event. The sugar in the brandy left him with a colossal hangover, and he wished that someone would come along and saw off his leg to distract him from the pain in his head.

"Water. Need water," he muttered, levering himself up from the chair. The crick in his neck made him absolutely certain that someone had tried, and failed, to hang him during the early morning hours.

He shuffled to the tiny kitchenette and drew a tall glass of water, guzzled it, drew another, and emptied that one as well, just managing to stave off the nausea that would have resulted in some difficult time in the bathroom. As much brandy as he drank, Emil knew by now exactly how to handle the morning after and what would work the best. Water always did it... to start with. It didn't get rid of the headache, but it stopped the nausea and dizziness.

Feeling a bit more human, Emil swallowed some ibuprofen and set about frying up some sausage for breakfast, though he'd have to press every bit of grease off it. He added a couple of hardboiled eggs and a banana to the plate, too. This formula, along with coffee, got him over his morning affliction in an hour or so.

It was hard to get the first bite in, but afterward, the cure went down smoothly. "After this, I shall get dressed and pay a visit to Eva on the second floor."

He stood at her door and knocked, but he didn't hear anyone moving about inside, and he knew that Eva was always up and around early in the morning.

He rapped louder and longer this time, then put his ear to the door.

Still nothing.

Karl Kraus from across the hall opened his door to see what all the ruckus was about. "I don't imagine she's home, unless she has suddenly gone deaf. You are disturbing the people at the end of the block with that pounding."

"But there is a cemetery at the end of the block."

"Exactly," Kraus said. "Have you tried the door? Perhaps something has happened to her. Perhaps she is ill and needs assistance."

Oh, this was way more involved than Emil wanted to get, but he dropped his hand to the knob.

It *was* open.

"Well, come then, Karl. If I am going to trespass, I will want a witness to attest that I did not steal or damage anything."

"For Eva, I do this, not for you."

They entered the apartment... which was completely empty... of everything... right down to bare walls.

The men gazed at the vacant room in stunned silence, which Karl finally broke.

"But how did this happen? I am right across the hall. This is impossible—I would have heard it if she was moving out. And we are friends. She would not have left without letting me know where she was going."

"Have you been at home for the past couple of days?"

Karl palmed his forehead. "*Nein*. I only returned this morning from a journey across the state to hear the Philharmonic."

"Oh, yes? And what did they play?"

"Beethoven's 9th. It wasn't von Karajan, may he rest in peace, but it wasn't bad. And it was late afterward so I remained overnight. I have difficulty driving in darkness—my cataracts, you know."

"Of course. Returning to the subject, I saw Eva get into a cab this morning at three."

"Still haunting the fifth floor all night long?"

"I suppose, since I am the only tenant up there. You are aware of my insomnia."

"Ah, yes. I had forgotten. But where could she have been going at three a.m.?"

"The taxi was a yellow cab and I believe that they are all registered. Perhaps if we telephone the company, they can tell us where they went after she was picked up."

"*Was für eine hervorragendee Idee*! Come in—my telephone is closer."

Karl looked up the number and his call was answered on the first ring. "Hello, Yellow Cab."

"Good morning, *Fräulein*. I am interested in tracing the route of one of your cabs that picked up a fare at 453 Stanyon Street last night. It seems she... erm... did not make it home, and she was expected for... an important meeting this morning. We are most worried that something may have happened to her."

"Oh, gosh. Okay, let me check that address. What time was that pick-up—do you know?"

"Right around three in the morning."

"Okay, please hold." After a wonderful evening of Beethoven, Karl was forced to listen to the Muzak version of "Midnight Train to Georgia" and was halfway through "Higher Ground" when the young woman came back on the line. "I'm sorry, sir. I checked all our cabs' trip sheets, and according to our records, there was no pick-up anywhere near that address this morning. Are you sure it's correct?"

"Quite sure. Please check again, if you please."

"Yes, sir." Muzak again, playing "Half-Breed" this time. She came back on the line on the final note. "No, still nothing, sir. I'm so sorry. I hope you find her."

"Thank you. Goodbye."

"So?" Emil asked.

"It is a mystery—no yellow cab made a pick-up here this morning."

"But I saw it! It was here the night before too. It waited twenty minutes, then left without picking anyone up."

"Perhaps if it comes back, you might go down and speak to the driver, or at least get a license number—that would help."

"Why me?"

"Because I am not up at that hour, you are."

"All right. I will keep watch, then... as I always do."

"Meanwhile, I shall speak to the building superintendent about this," Karl said, indicating the empty apartment.

"Fine. We can compare notes tomorrow morning."

"Not too early, mind. About ten o'clock would suit me."

Though he had many failings, Bavarian cookery was not one of them. After a supper of *Leberkäse* (a meatloaf made from lean pork, pork belly and bacon), a side of *Kartoffelpuffer*, (German potato pancakes), and a stein of *Krombacher,* he took up his post at the window. He may have been a curmudgeon and a recluse, but he ate well.

He brought a glass and a fresh bottle of *Kirschwasser* with him to while away the time until three a.m.

That was, if the cab even showed up.

He was dozing lightly in his chair, but fortunately, had left the window open, so the approaching vehicle woke him.

He glanced at his wristwatch. The time was three on the dot, and there it was. He rose from his chair as fast as his creaky, throbbing joints would allow; but before he could even turn around, someone walked out of the downstairs lobby and got into the cab.

It was Karl Kraus!

"That is fine. I can barely walk at the best of times. Karl will find out what happened to Eva and we shall discuss it in the morning."

He spent the balance of the night sipping his cherry brandy and finally went to bed and passed out at first light.

Another day, another hangover, so Emil hoisted himself out of bed, took his morning cure, then showered, shaved, and felt a bit more human.

"Now to see Karl," he said, locking his apartment and shambling down the hall to the elevator. The arthritis was bad that day—he had to use his cane.

A few moments later, he was outside Karl's door. It was well after ten, so he would have no complaints about being disturbed. Emil knocked.

Nothing.

He used his cane to pound on the door.

Again, nothing.

His heart quaking, he turned the knob and opened the door.

Karl's apartment was in the same condition as Eva's—completely cleared out.

So what the hell was going on here?

Oh, he was going to get some damned answers—oh, yes, he was! The first thing he was going to do was speak to the building superintendent. He limped into Karl Kraus' apartment, hoping that the phone was still connected, but it was not, so he turned around...

... and then a horrible thought struck him.

How long has this been going on?

He stepped into the elevator, but instead of pressing '5', he opted for 'Lobby.'

The elevator opened right across the hall from the super's office, a small mercy that he didn't have far to walk. He knocked on the door.

Nothing.

Oh, please, please.

He rapped louder; then, without waiting, he turned the knob and opened the door onto a furnished, but vacant office.

Emil shuffled in. There was a large note pinned to the back of the desk chair, which read, "TAKE THIS JOB AND SHOVE IT! THIS PLACE CAN KISS MY ASS!"

It would appear that we no longer have a superintendent. I wonder how long he's been gone. He moved closer to the desk and took up the Rolodex thereon, rifling through it for the main number of the property management company. When he found it, he picked up the desk phone and dialed.

It rang and rang. Nobody picked up.

He hung up, glancing at the desk calendar. *But it's Tuesday. There ought to be somebody in attendance.*

He tried again.

Same result—and he'd let it ring at least fifty times.

"Apparently, we are on our own. Time to take inventory," he muttered, walking back to the elevator. He pushed '1' and away he went.

First floor—Josef Fischer, Maria Schmitt, Hans Wagner, and Georg Weber.

He knocked, he turned the doorknobs, he entered bare-to-the-walls apartments.

He must have nodded off at three o'clock more often than he thought.

He had the same result on the second, third, and fourth floors.

By the time he reached his apartment on the fifth, his arthritis was screaming and he realized that he was the only one left in the building.

He ate a light meal of *Radi*, beer, and a soft pretzel, and waited until three a.m.

The cab pulled up and idled at the curb.

Fortified with his *Kirschwasser,* he bestirred himself and took the elevator to the Lobby.

Emil shuffled out to the cab and tried the back door, but it wouldn't open, so he tapped on the window.

The cabbie rolled it down.

"You're not my fare."

"Well, who is? There is nobody left in the building but me. Who called you?" He tried to open the back door, but it wouldn't budge.

"You are not my fare," the driver said again, pulling away from the curb.

The next night, the cab pulled up in front of the building again, and this time, Emil felt inexplicably drawn to the Lobby, so he left his apartment and went downstairs.

He tapped on the cab window, and the back door opened.

"So why are you letting me in tonight?"

"Because I wasn't sure before. But you are my fare tonight."

Emil shrugged and got into the cab.

I'm glad I have my wallet with me in my pants so I can pay the cabbie.

After a few minutes, he noticed that there were no interior door handles. He couldn't open the door from the inside.

"I understand that police cars do not have a way for the back passenger to exit the vehicle, but why is it the case with a cab?"

"Oh, they're all that way now—keeps people from getting a ride, and then running away before they pay for it. I have to let my fares in and out. If they don't have money at the end of the ride, I drive them to the police station."

"*Ja*, I see."

They drove for a time, and then pulled up in front of an all-night *Biergarten* that Emil didn't know about. "Oh, this is wonderful. I will get out here. What is the charge?"

"Nazi war criminal," the driver said as the partition slid upward, and the back seat filled with Zyklon B gas.

Albert Katz drove up in his KATZ MOVERS van to find Joshua Goldberg's yellow cab parked at the curb waiting for him. Even though it was the end of October, it was hot as hell out and he wore a T-shirt.

"Everything's cleared out... including the vermin," Katz said.

"Good. Did you find any original art or antiques?"

"No original art this time, but a couple of nice-looking antique pieces of furniture. Don't know what they're worth— you're the furniture expert, not me."

"Okay, well, just take it down to the warehouse then, and I'll go through it. If there's any Nazi loot there, I'll notify my people at the Jewish Digital Cultural Recovery Project. They can put it on their database and try to locate the people the items belong to. Anything else, any furniture, lamps, and electronics, you can have—cash included—to keep or to sell, as our way of repaying you for all your help."

"Don't the people at JDCRP want to know how we came by all this stuff? I mean, last week alone I cleared out two Monets, a Matisse, three Picassos and a Reubens."

"They don't ask a lot of questions. They just want to get these things back to their rightful owners."

A little girl carrying a stuffed sock monkey walked up to Albert and pointed to his left arm. "Where'd you get that, Mister?"

"Auschwitz, honey."

Professionally, Carson Buckingham has made her way in life doing all manner of things, most of which involve ukuleles. She has been writing horror since Christ left Chicago, and loves reading, cooking, and gardening, but not at the same time. She lives in Kentucky, though originally from Connecticut—and Connecticut is glad to be rid of her!

Philip St. James's abilities include proofreading, editing, generating amazing story ideas, woodworking, baking bread, and cooking big dinners. He spends his spare time searching through ancient spell books to find effective curses to keep the grass from growing. Phil is originally from Connecticut, but lives in Kentucky now, desperately trying to find out what the plural of "y'all" is.

Home Is Where the Haunt Is
Christopher D. Ochs

Ralph stared at the pair of matching Victorian houses separated by a driveway for several minutes before he recognized the buildings.

"This is…" he said with a sudden tightness in his voice, "where I grew up?" The moment he spoke, he realized he had no recollection of how he had gotten there.

"Last thing I remember," he mused aloud, "I was driving my Porsche along Route 1, and then some headlights came out of nowhere…" He shook his head, rattling away images that made no sense.

Shielding his eyes against the setting sun, he surveyed the neighborhood. Gone were the soybean fields that had surrounded the two houses, now replaced by rows of cookie-cutter duplexes. The two original buildings had changed as well — one for the better, the other not so much. His old home, the northern half of the pair, presented a study in color fit for a painting. A stained-glass oval depicting a welcoming pastoral scene graced the front door, protected by an electronic keypad lock and camera. The first floor's brick had been sandblasted clean, and the upper floors sported well-maintained clapboard. The third-floor turret and gables stood tall and proud. Every window had sturdy shutters, with matching window boxes overflowing with perennials. The house's lawn and sidewalk were perfectly manicured. All in all, a cheerful Painted Lady.

The southern building looked like it hadn't been touched since his youth. Its brick, stained brown with grime, had patches of moss fed by decades of rainfall. The clapboard had lost a few tiles, with cracked shutters covered with peeling sun-bleached paint. Curtains in the windows were ragged and torn. The storm door seemed ready to fall off its hinges with the next strong breeze, and the crabgrass, dandelions, and clover outnumbered the half-foot high ryegrass. Add a thunderstorm, and it would be a perfect setting for a Halloween movie.

Curious to see what the owners had done with their backyards, Ralph ambled the length of the sidewalk. His head smacked against something at the northern property line. It warbled like he had head-butted a rubber drumhead. Testing with an outstretched hand, Ralph encountered an invisible surface. Humming louder as he pressed, it yielded barely an inch.

Ralph rubbed his eyes. Everything past the wall of force was out of focus, like glass smeared with Vaseline. Hurrying past the southern Victorian, his hands quickly found a similar boundary.

"What the hell is going on here?"

A trifling sting zapped the tip of his tongue, and he spat, trying to clear whatever it was. Nothing.

He squinted, trying to make out a small brown creature scurrying toward him on all fours along the sidewalk. Once it passed through the barrier without effort, it stood, walking on its hindquarters. Ralph thrust his hand down, searching for the timber wolf toy he carried since he was a kid. That stupid plastic trinket always reassured him, long after his father, in a drunken fit, had thrown away the rest of the cheesy Noah's Ark collection mom had given him one birthday. But now, Ralph couldn't find his lucky charm — he couldn't even locate a pocket.

The critter, a river otter, waddled up to a pace away.

Ralph took a step back, drawing his arms close.

"Welcome to your new home, Ralph," it said, extending its right forepaw.

Ralph gasped, blinking in disbelief at the talking animal. "Who—or what—are you?"

"I should have expected that you wouldn't recognize me." The animal lowered its paw, and its whiskers drooped in disappointment. "I am Nanuq, your spirit guide."

Ralph sputtered out a raspberry. "I must be dreaming. Well, then—don't I rate a guardian angel? Shouldn't be surprised, though I expected my spirit animal would be a wolf. Or that I'd be reincarnated as one." His smirk faded when he groped again for the toy that wasn't there.

"Sorry to disappoint," said the otter, "but I'm not the one with a spirit aptitude of two out of ten. That's what happens when you mix and match belief systems like an à la carte menu and ignore your moral code whenever convenient. If you had a decent rating, you'd be well on your way to your final reward, not stuck here as a wraith on the earthly plane." He shot Ralph a disdainful glance. "Wolf, indeed."

Nanuq gestured toward the houses. "Your abysmal score is also why you're offered a limited selection of locations to haunt. Be glad your rating isn't zero." A shudder like a wave of fur ran up its sleek back.

Ralph folded his arms. "Don't give me your sanctimonious horse—" A somewhat sharper sting on his tongue kept him from completing his sentence. He spat again, but still nothing. "You don't know me. Despite all the garbage dealt me over the years, I lived a good life."

"Oh, really? Is that why you always cheated at Monopoly as a kid, taking money from the bank when your friends got a snack or went to the bathroom? Or how you overcharged every delivery customer and never told Mr. Keims, the first person to give you a job in your teens, while you pocketed the difference? Or how you sapped funds out of charities for which you 'volunteered?' Not to mention how you embezzled a cool million from your last employer."

Ralph's stance deflated, and he faced the creature directly. "How did you —?"

"And let us not forget your adulterous relations with your friends' wives. But that is an entirely different can of worms. Suffice it to say that your avarice and covetousness were symptoms of a larger problem — namely, self-centeredness taken to the extreme. Frankly, I am amazed that you managed a rating as high as two."

"Enough with the psychoanalysis. If you know so much, then you know my dad's to blame." He glanced at his past and possible future home, then shook his head to stop unwanted vignettes of the past from flooding back in. "You really mean it — I'm *dead*?"

Ralph raised his hands to his face. His limbs held their familiar form but were a featureless white from which swaying sheets of translucent gauze hung. "Oh, shit — *Ouch!*" His tongue smarted from a sizable jolt.

"Apologies for not forewarning you earlier. Please monitor your language if you wish to preserve what's left of your rating."

Ralph swallowed with an audible gulp. "How did I die? Last thing I remember, headlights —"

Nanuq looked to the side. "Does it matter? At least you weren't in the middle of something hideously cruel. Otherwise, we wouldn't even be having this conversation."

Ralph tested the rippling boundary again. It resisted his touch with a happy trilling. "Why here, of all places? I don't have the fondest memories of this place. My dad was a real son-of-a —" Once again, a sting tripped up his tongue.

"Yes, we know."

"Did I leave important business from my childhood unfinished? Do I have something to avenge? What am I expected to do here?"

Nanuq planted its paws on what could have been hips. "As I already mentioned, you must select which of these two domiciles to inhabit."

"Forever?"

"That's up to you. Depending on your actions, you could improve your rating and eventually move on. In your case," said Nanuq with a click of its tongue, "that could be a considerable amount of time. I strongly suggest you don't backslide." Another shiver made its fur bristle.

"And here I thought spirit animals were supposed to be *helpful*." Ralph eyed the structures with a raised eyebrow. "Who lives there now? The people living in my childhood home look well-off."

"No idea. But you must make your decision before sunrise."

"What if I don't choose?"

Nanuq's whiskers bristled. "I would advise against that."

Ralph gave a shrug that was more like a twitch. "I've pretty much made up my mind already, but I suppose I should test-drive them before I choose."

"That is the first wise thing you've said today."

Ralph approached the northern house's opulent door and attempted to open it. He chided himself when his hand passed through the brass handle. Holding his breath — or what passed for it — he stepped through.

The ground floor's layout bore little resemblance to his old home. The living room overflowed with splendor. The fireplace had been replaced with one fit for a lord's manor. Above and on either side of its mantle hung stupendous works of art. The plush seating and modern accents would feel right at home in an issue of Architectural Digest. A new wall separated the front room from what had been yesteryear's dingy open dining room. From the divider hung a massive flatscreen surrounded by a high-end sound system. In place of the rickety bare wood staircase to the second floor rose a carpeted flight of stairs with a palatial handrail boasting a mahogany horse's head on the newel post.

The dining area was equally sumptuous, backed by a kitchen with every modern convenience.

"I'm gonna fit right in."

Returning to the front room, Ralph gave a start when he discovered a teenager playing a video game on the enormous television.

"Where did you come from?" said Ralph out loud. The lad ignored him, weaving back and forth in his seat, controller in hand. Ralph waved his gossamer arm in front of the teen, then screamed "Hello!" into his ear. The boy still paid him no heed.

Something else was different—the sun had somehow set unexpectedly early. The windows revealed evening's dusk lit by a rising full moon.

A clatter rose from the kitchen, and Ralph was drawn to investigate. A man and woman busied themselves preparing a meal for three, between frequent hugs and kisses. Ralph inhaled deeply. The air was devoid of any savory aromas. "Well, *that's* disappointing," he groused.

Like their son, the couple remained oblivious to their visitor.

Gliding past the kid, Ralph ascended the staircase and explored the second floor. The rooms' layouts were similar to what he recalled from his youth, except one bedroom had been converted to an office, neat and ordered to an almost compulsive degree. He finished his inspection at the stairs leading to the third floor.

Unwanted memories banged on the upper landing's door. The darkest image in Ralph's mind pounded the loudest, demanding to be released. Steeling himself against his misgivings, he glided up the staircase.

The attic felt cramped. Scratches marking where old furniture and rumpled packages had been moved were muted under layers of dust. Ralph circled the room, passing through its obstacles with ease and leaving no footprints. He lurched to a halt when he bumped into a battered rocking chair at the center of the turret dormer.

Tentatively, he touched the rocker's top rail. It creaked as it swayed back and forth.

Ralph gasped with recognition. The dark memories flooded back—how he huddled himself between the chair's arms, his hand clutching his small plastic wolf; how he hoped it would keep his dread at bay; hoped his father and his fists wouldn't find him; prayed that a beating was the least of the things that bastard would do.

Testing every movement, he carefully lowered himself into the chair. With a single groan of wood, it angled backward. It felt as comforting as it did when it served as his childhood refuge. He tried to scoot the rocker forward to get a better look out the three windows of the Victorian tower, but the chair wouldn't budge. It simply wobbled in place. With a sigh, Ralph peered through the dingy windows and their sheer curtains as best he could—the leftmost viewed a quaint park directly across the street, the center angled down the road, while the rightmost pointed straight into the southern house's ramshackle matching dormer.

He did a double-take as he spotted the moon already high above the house's roof. "What the…?" Force of habit made Ralph check his diamond Rolex that wasn't there.

"Time doesn't move quite the same for us." Nanuq's

voice emanated from the front window, as loud as if he were in the room. "It jumps ahead unpredictably as you move around."

Ralph jumped to his feet and searched for the voice. Sure enough, there stood the otter on the sidewalk far below, regarding him with a tilt to its head.

"That makes it all the easier for me to decide to stay here," said Ralph.

"You'd abandon the other house, its contents sight unseen?"

"Spend eternity in *that* dump?"

A flicker in a window in the forlorn house's second floor caught Ralph's attention.

A column of light spread across a darkened room's floor, illuminating a threadbare pink rug and running up the side of a small bed, revealing covers faded as chalk dust. A burly figure stood in the doorway. He cast a shadow across a child with flowing brown hair.

The little girl huddled herself into a ball. Tightly crossed arms smothered a plush toy against her chest.

"She's not even seven years old," whispered Ralph. "Eight, tops."

The man, in boxer shorts and a ratty T-shirt smeared with stains, closed the door behind him. Circling around the bed, he approached the window, peering outward.

By the room's feeble nightlight, the man's grin reflected nothing remotely close to parental affection.

Garish shadows streaked the man's face. His expression transformed into something Ralph was all too familiar with. He gasped at how that lustful smirk resembled his own father's.

The man pulled the window's lower half-curtains closed. That might have kept prying eyes of the perfect family next door from watching, but Ralph could still observe from his vantage point.

The man's sneer disappeared, replaced with one of feigned warmth. He folded back the corner of the bed's covers and sat next to the girl. She scooted away, scrunching herself tighter into a quivering fetal position. The man raised one leg onto the bed, snaking it under the covers. He spoke to her softly.

Ralph twitched all over. "Don't you dare."

The brute caressed the girl's shoulder. At his touch, the girl swatted at his arm. His face flashed a scowl. He brusquely spun her over, raising his hand to strike.

Like a switch being thrown, Ralph found himself in their room, standing at the foot of the girl's bed. The window's curtains unfurled from a sudden gust.

The girl emitted a smothered peep, squeezing herself so tight that she left herself no room to inhale. With a start, the fiend lowered his hand and swung his legs onto the floor. He approached the window uncertainly, pushing aside a kid-sized wooden chair with blue flowers and "Holly" painted on its back. Sweeping the half-curtains aside, he tested the closed pane. A subdued curse erased the consternation written across his face. His leering smile reappeared. He closed the lower curtains again, along with the raggedy uppers for good measure.

The mattress sighed under the man's weight.

"Get away from her!" Ralph cried, his hands curled into spectral fists. His voice died away without a single echo. He repeated his command, screaming with every fiber of his spirit. It, too, faded into nothingness.

The door swung open. The bare bulb in the hall cast another harsh shadow across the bed. A woman tottered into the room, her hand jumping to her mouth and the wedding ring on her finger glinting. She lunged at her husband. Her fingernails reached to tear at his face.

The bastard grabbed her wrists, wrestling her away from the bed. Ralph threw a punch at the cretin as the pair approached. His blow passed through the man effortlessly. Dragging his wife with malicious ease into the hall, the man slammed the door shut behind him.

The little girl whimpered, curling the covers over herself. She shuddered with every blow thudding behind the door.

Ralph stood impotent. Wanting to cry, shout, scream, he paced a tight loop at the foot of the bed. "I can't watch this! What am I supposed to do?" He swiped at the curtains, hoping to see the street below and glower at Nanuq. They hung undisturbed.

He returned to policing the pink rug, shouting at the ceiling. "Spend God-knows-how-long watching this pervert hurt his daughter? If I could only—" Ralph froze in his tracks to gawk at the girl.

She had poked her head above the covers, watching him wide-eyed as he paraded around her room.

"Y-you," he stammered. "You can... *see* me?"

She replied with a timorous nod.

"And you can *hear* me?" he asked, scarcely above a whisper.

She nodded twice. Her eyes were no longer fearful but beamed with wonder.

"What's your name? Is it Holly?"

She lowered her head without answering.

"That's okay. You don't know me from Adam," he said gently, managing a smile for her. "My name's Ralph."

"Wolf?" Her face warmed with the hint of a guarded smile.

"No, just plain Ralph." He knew it couldn't be possible, but his hearing thrummed with the rapid beating of a heart. Perhaps it was Holly's? "Has your dad done this before?"

She silently nodded, raising a single finger from her sheet's frayed binding. A tear brimming in one eye and her frown tore at the fabric of Ralph's spirit.

"I feel your pain." Ralph held his hand against his forehead, realizing how callous that sounded the moment he had said it. He knelt by her bed. Holly turned, following his movements.

"I'm sorry, that was a stupid thing to say. I—" Ralph tried to ignore the constriction that clawed at his throat, the grief-driven straining of jaw muscles that couldn't possibly be there. "My dad was just as bad to me as a kid. I wished I could make him stop for the longest time." He laid his hands on the edge of the bed. "I wish I could make your dad stop, too."

"*Your* daddy, too, Wolfie?"

He chuckled with a shake of his head. "Just Ralph. Not the most imposing name for a ghost, is it?"

"No," she said, reaching for a lump under the covers. With a snap, she shoved her wolf plushie at him. "Wolfie!"

He reached for the stuffed animal. Out of the nothingness of Ralph's palm tumbled his miniature plastic timber wolf.

Holly snatched it up and held both her prizes up to him. "See? You're Wolfie!"

The door to her room swung open again. Her father plodded into the room, any pretense of kindness gone from his manner. His face was a blank slate, devoid of emotion.

Ralph trembled. But not from fear. He leapt up to face the bastard, his hands balling into fists again.

"Now, Holly, where were we?" growled her father.

Years of pain, anguish, and shame boiled up within

Ralph. "You son of a bitch," he roared, ignoring the sting on his tongue. A feral snarl roiled within his ears.

Ralph grabbed at him, bunching the father's T-shirt in one hand. It shredded apart, leaving a gaping hole. Encouraged, he clamped his other hand around the cretin's throat. With his will hammered into an iron desire to do violence, Ralph rammed the man against the nearest wall. The door rattled in its frame.

The man slumped into a huddle, his rear end plopping on the floor with a resounding thump. His eyes goggled up at Ralph, wide with terror. His hand flashed to his neck. He gagged harshly, and rivulets of blood scored his fingers.

Ralph gaped at the man's throat. Trickles of blood wept from both sides of his neck, oozing from two V-shaped rows of… *teeth marks*. He glanced down at his translucent hands. They shook—clenched, but free of red. Ralph tasted blood in his mouth.

Tasted?

He spat out a mouthful, and a red splotch joined the other stains on the man's shirt.

With a gurgling cry, the wretch scrambled out of the room on all fours. Ralph slammed the door, silencing the echoes of the father's whimpers receding down the hall.

Ralph wheeled around and dove to kneel again at the bed. Holly quaked under her covers. He nudged her with her wolf plush toy's paws. Inch by tentative inch, she drew the cover back. She lobbed Ralph's old plastic wolf in his direction. The toy bounced once on the bed, and Holly disappeared under her blanket once more. Ralph tried to pick it up, only for his hand to pass through it. A desperate need to console Holly rose within him, but he knew a stranger's touch was the last thing she needed. He clutched Holly's toy and pressed its soft nose against her side. Again, this time, adding his best imitation of a puppy's whine. Once more for good luck.

"I don't understand how all this works, Holly, but…" In his phantom grasp, he still managed to manipulate the furry toy into a playful position and wag its tail. "…I *want* to help you."

She crawled from underneath her sanctuary and snatched her plushie away from him. Indecision harrowed her eyes.

"It's time," came Nanuq's voice from the window.

Ralph found himself transported to the sidewalk between the houses. The moon hung low, racing away from the growing light of dawn.

"What? No!" Ralph exclaimed, spinning around. "Put me back, Holly needs me. That bastard of a father might come back any minute." He sputtered a cough in the direction of a red fox. It paced around him on its hindquarters, its white-tipped tail whipping back and forth.

"Where's Nanuq?" said Ralph.

"I am before you," replied the fox. "It seems there have been a few developments." It inspected its black forepaws with raised eyebrows. "I am pleased, though a little surprised. It seems your aptitude has crept up a notch in the space of a single night."

"I guess that's why you've changed, too."

"As a result, you have earned a third choice of domiciles which to inhabit. There's just enough time to visit—"

"No," said Ralph. "I'm staying here. With Holly."

The new Nanuq folded its forelegs over its chest. "You are sure?"

Ralph whooshed out a determined sigh. "I am."

"So be it. Until we meet again."

In the space of a heartbeat, Ralph returned to Holly's room. She sat in her bed, her back propped against her pillow and the headboard behind it. She rocked back and forth, her arms hugging her knees under the covers. She stared intently at her blue-flowered chair. Placed by the side of her bed, it faced the door of her room. The plushie wolf had been planted in its seat, its glass eyes patiently watching the door.

With his resolve unsteady, Ralph ventured, "I'm back, Holly. Are you okay?"

Her eyes flashed wide. She sat erect, and her smile lit up the room. "Wolfie!"

He returned her smile. Placing the stuffed wolf at his feet, he sat in the dainty chair. It shifted but did not groan from any weight. "You can sleep now. I'll take care of things."

Though Holly nodded off with a peaceful grin snuggled between her cheeks, troubled thoughts dogged Ralph. What would happen to him as Holly grew up? What would he do if she no longer saw him? How long would he be able to protect her? What about when she was old enough to strike out on her own?

"First things first," he murmured. Ralph chuckled at the phantasms of his paws dangling over the seat. He stared at the door and licked his canines, ready.

Forever, if need be.

Ochs writes scifi, horror, and fantasy: *Pindlebryth of Lenland* and *If I Can't Sleep, You Can't Sleep* were followed by *My Friend Jackson*, Finalist in Indies Today's Best Books 2020. His latest novel, *Eldritch, Inc.* is Runner-Up in Indies Today's Best Books 2024. His short stories are published in several award-winning anthologies.

The Illusionist's Daughter
Wen Wen Yang

Nearly all the secrets of Riverview Academy for Young Ladies passed through my infirmary. If my patients were not looking for healing powders or bandages, they were quietly paying for beauty illusions. I craft smoother skin or flowing hair that could fool the closest inspection. I also know how to hide a growing belly until the winter break when a student would visit an aunt in the country and return to her studies the next year.

I kept all their secrets as if they were my own, though they never knew mine. They never saw my mother's ghost haunting the halls.

The university's medical office smelled faintly of ginseng and herbs. I poured the powder onto the three-beam scale. The powder had no smell, but the woman standing in front of my desk seemed to have stopped breathing. Her hands were clasped, holding herself together.

"Do you have someone who will stay with you this time?" I asked.

It wasn't the first time Ursula Zheng, the chancellor's maid, had asked for something to return her menses, or something to fight an infection. She wasn't even the first person to storm into my office cursing the chancellor. However, it was the first time Ursula had seemed so weary, dark bags under her eyes, dry cracked lips.

Get out, Mama hissed in the far corner. She looked like she wanted to hug Ursula, and to shake her until her teeth rattled. I had many years of practice ignoring her while others were around.

"You could spend the night here." I tapped the movable mass for a hundredth of a gram. "When you're ready to take it." I scooped a small amount back into the brown jar.

Ursula wore a speckled smock over her dowdy plaid dress. Her pursed lips gave the impression she was already drinking the bitter concoction. Her straight black hair was braided then coiled at the base of her neck.

"Yes, thank you." She sounded younger than the students but was actually in her mid-twenties. Her younger sister was a senior at the Academy whose most serious complaint was a sprained ankle from soccer practice.

I drew out a sheet of paper and poured the measured powder onto the sheet. My fingers folded the paper into an envelope, my thumbnail sharpening the creases.

"Could you cast an illusion over me as well, Nurse Diao?" She pointed at her face. "I've heard students talk about your illusions. They say it rivals even the Academy-trained illusionists. Could you make me ugly?"

My mother clicked her tongue. *The chancellor hunts close to home, no matter your looks.*

I passed the powder-filled envelope across the desk.

The previous nurse had warned me when I was hired five years ago, not knowing the stories my mother told me before her death. At functions, several women made sure the chancellor was never left alone with a woman.

Mama had shoved her ghostly form through the chancellor as if he was a doorway. *Meet me in hell, you coward.* He turned slightly green, nauseous, but that was the extent of her influence.

Whenever his gaze turned to me, I made myself exceptionally dull and disengaging, an unlikely target of his unwanted attention. A nurse who can cast small illusions was quaint compared to the Professor of Illusionary Arts' new year's fireworks and glittering phoenix.

It was amazing the chancellor did not recognize my mother in my eyes, but my thick-rimmed spectacles were enough of a disguise.

Mama hated that I was diminishing myself in front of the Academy.

"Would you like to find a new position outside the university?" I suggested to Ursula, not for the first time.

This time, Ursula brightened. "Maybe I could work for a widow? The cook has taught me twenty recipes."

I nodded. Her sister would soon no longer need discounted tuition.

"I'll write to my friends. Now, let me see your face." I brushed my fingers over her brow then cheek. I tapped and crumpled magic from the ether. On one corner of her mouth, I built yellow pustules, ringed with red blotches. It felt strange anchoring the uneven illusion wires to her cheek, when usually I knitted the wires together to cover blemishes.

Mama did not comment on my work, having taught me the moment I showed illusionary talent.

Ursula caught her reflection in a glass cabinet and grimaced. For a moment, I thought she could see Mama but her fingers slid over the new imperfections. "It looks so real. I've never had an illusion on my face before."

"Try not to touch it," I said. "The illusion may last only a couple days without my redoing the work. I made the illusion wires softer than usual because it has to move with your expressions."

She opened her mouth slightly to tug at the wires. "It's as soft as silk."

I smiled at the compliment. "Could you come back Friday night?"

I spent the next two days furiously writing to friends in nearby towns. I had hoped to have good news by the time Ursula returned to the infirmary.

Mama spent both days whispering in my ear. One afternoon, she ran her ethereal fingers along the unmarked bottles containing lethal amounts of caffeine and nicotine. *Ursula could poison his last meal.* The powders would have mimicked the signs of a heart attack or food poisoning.

I shook my head, as my staff was helping patients in the office.

On Friday afternoon, my mailbox was still empty. I hoped messages were delayed due to the thunderstorm.

There was no laughter, no chatter in the hall. The thunder rattled the windows in the infirmary behind me. All afternoon classes were canceled due to the weather. I had sent my staff home after lunch.

I flipped through my address book, wondering who would receive my next batch of letters.

"Who was that man and his partner, the dancers?" I asked my mother. Before she could answer, the health office door swung open with a bang.

"Nurse Diao," Ursula trembled in the doorway. "Please, help me." She fell into my arms. She was soaked through, hair plastered to her scalp.

Mama rushed to help me but caught herself at the last moment. The chill of her fingers brushed my arm.

I led Ursula to the door behind my desk, opening to a large infirmary with six empty hospital beds. Ursula collapsed onto the closest bed.

"I've done something awful." She clutched her side. Her teeth were chattering. I made soothing sounds and brushed back her damp bangs. Her skin was burning.

"I had taken your medication to come here. Castro, Chancellor Castro, he tried to come after me. He-he-." Her eyes were wide, darting back to the door as if the chancellor was going to barge in. Mama even looked over her shoulder to make sure. I would be surprised if he knew where the medical office was.

I locked the door from the inside.

"It's all right, you're safe now." I couldn't send her back after the weekend. I knelt to open the heating vents at the baseboards around the room. The warmth drifted upward.

"Let's get you out of those wet clothes." I opened cabinets to pull out supplies.

Ursula unzipped the soaked dress and peeled it off her shoulders. Blood was smeared down her thighs. She stepped out of her bloody underwear.

"Is that where he hurt you?" I tossed Ursula a few clean towels, a set of clean underwear and a package of sanitary pads.

"No, no." She started wiping down her clammy skin.

I hung her dress on a drying rack by the heater and kicked the underwear aside.

"I--I struck him." Ursula bit her lip as she wrapped another towel around her body. Her eyes were pleading, desperate. "In the head. He's dead, in his library."

My heart twisted and my mouth went dry. I steeled myself not to look at Mama for her reaction but she was transfixed.

Dead, finally.

"Is anyone else there?" My voice was a croak.

Ursula shook her head, pale as the gown in my hands. "The cook comes in the morning. They'll hang me for murder."

They should give her a medal. Mama beamed at the woman more courageous than her daughter. More murderous.

I helped Ursula toward the communal showers at the end of the infirmary.

"I'm going to hang," she whimpered.

"You're going to get clean and warm, then rest."

While she showered, I filled a hot water bottle, retrieved her keys from her dress's pocket and pulled on my raincoat.

What are you doing? Mama swirled around me.

Under my breath, I asked, "Did you know?"

Of course not, she sneered. *Do you know every new student who enters campus? I wonder which hell they sent him to.*

Ursula finished her shower and returned to the beds draped in the hospital gown. Color had returned to her face, though she still chewed on her bottom lip.

"Ursula, when did it happen?" Sweat beaded on my brow.

She looked at her watch. "I ran right over. Around five o'clock."

"When was the last time someone saw you, other than the chancellor?" I was going to evoke his name, daring his ghost to materialize. Mama stood guard, nostrils flaring.

Ursula flinched. "Noon, I think. The cook wanted to get home before the storm."

"If anyone asks, tell them you came here right after lunch."

Ursula slid onto the hospital bed, wrapping her arms around herself. "I'm going to hang."

"I won't let that happen. When the police come, I'll tell them you were here." I draped blankets over her, pulling them up to her chin. Ursula's teeth no longer chattered and she curled on her side.

"Is there someone else who would want to hurt him?"

Mama snorted. *Every woman in the university.*

"I didn't want to hurt him. I had to stop him before he hurt her." Ursula clasped her hand over her mouth, her tears rolling down to the blanket.

"Hurt who? Is there someone else there?" I pressed handkerchiefs into her hands.

"No, my sister visited a couple weeks ago." She wiped her eyes, sniffling. "Then when I told him I wasn't feeling well, because of the medication to return my menses, he said maybe my sister could work for him instead. I couldn't stand it." She shook with rage, face reddening. "Even if the next maid isn't my sister, he can't do this to another woman." She clutched her side, moaning through the cramps.

Mama nodded her head. *And he won't.*

"I understand." I set a bucket beside her bed. "I'll be right back." I locked the infirmary door.

Don't rush. Mama passed through the door. *Fingerprints.*

In the office, I pulled on two sets of rubber gloves. I flexed my fingers above my head and cast an illusion down to my shoes. Instead of Nurse Viola Diao, I now looked like a man about the chancellor's height but with a wide brim hat and upturned collar, prepared for the cold rain. The world looked dimmer from behind the illusion's veil. I could barely see Mama.

After locking my office door, I started toward the chancellor's residence. It was just half a mile away from campus, but the rain made the journey feel more treacherous. Rivers ran down the streets. There was no one else enduring the torrential downpour. The wind drove the rain in a nearly horizontal assault.

I slipped once, but caught myself on my hands and knees.

Careful, Mama chided in my ear.

If anyone had seen me fall, they would have thought a tall man suddenly had another pair of hands at waist level as they passed through the illusion.

The residence was a three-story townhome, dark on the inside. I circled it to the service entrance by the kitchen, opened it with Ursula's keys. When my eyes adjusted to the darkness, I crept upstairs, remembering the end of semester parties he would throw at his residence.

Before my first faculty party, the previous nurse had warned me to watch my drink. I created illusions to distract him or cause a scene. A mouse or a roach. Once, a phantom call of his name because I could replicate vocal cords with fragments of illusion wires. My mother taught me that. Then, when everyone's attention was focused on the commotion, I poured the drinks into his precious orchids or simply knocked the glass over. I could not fix his crooked tenure system, couldn't argue for fair salaries, but I could waste his expensive alcohol and kill his precious plants.

In the library, the chancellor lay in a crumpled heap by the door. The fire poker was beside him, pointing to the sticky pool of blood. He was in his dressing gown, a burgundy that contrasted his pale skin. His urine and shit stained the expensive rug under him. His mouth was slightly agape, no longer curved into his usual smirk.

Mama stood over the body, then tried to spit on him. Then tried to kick him.

From the liquor cabinet, I selected three glasses and gave each a bit of brandy before pouring it into a potted plant. I left the glasses in front of his desk as if he had welcomed and was entertaining two visitors.

Perhaps he was drinking with an impressionable professor and a gifted, attention-starved student. Perhaps he reminisced about his years as Professor of Illusionary Arts, when my mother was his prize pupil. Certainly, she was his prize.

I pushed all the papers on his desk onto the floor. I yanked all the drawers open. There was a small roll of cash. I stashed it in my pocket, a much-delayed allowance.

Take the rings and watch. Mama pointed.

"It's too recognizable to pawn."

Just do it!

His hands were cool to the touch as I removed them.

I wiped illusion wires across the shelves and knocked every book onto the floor. Papers fluttered down like giant snowflakes. A flurry of photographs erupted out of one, or maybe it was hidden behind a book.

Mama floated over to the photographs. *You pervert!* She returned to kicking him, her ghost foot sailing through his body.

I returned downstairs to unlock the front door, a point of escape for the would-be murderers.

Beside the kitchen, I found a tiny room with a narrow bed. It might have originally been built as a second pantry. From the clothes in the wardrobe, it was obviously Ursula's room. I pulled on Ursula's raincoat on top of my own and grabbed her half-packed bag of toiletries that she would have brought to the infirmary.

I locked the kitchen entrance as I left. This time, I covered myself in the gray-green mist of the unending rain.

Instead of returning to the university, I first went to the river to throw in the chancellor's ring and watch. I had not inherited his need to keep mementos.

It was only midnight when I made it back to the health office, with a shadow draped over my features, drenched in Ursula's raincoat.

Hang it up so it'll be dry by morning. Mama flitted around the office. I obeyed and I tossed the gloves into the trash with the other used gloves.

Ursula hobbled to me when I unlocked the infirmary door. "What do I do now? The cook will discover him dead when she comes in with his breakfast."

I nodded and handed her the toiletries bag. "Will the cook notice you're missing?"

"She knows I wasn't feeling well. She'll tell the police I'm here." Her stomach growled.

"I'm sorry, where are my manners?" I rummaged through my desk for a tin of week-old mooncakes and held them out to Ursula. Next came my jar of jasmine tea leaves and a kettle. I turned on a Bunsen burner.

"How are you feeling?" I asked as I waited for the water to warm up.

"I think I've passed the worst of it." Her eyes were half closed as she chewed on a red bean mooncake. We drank our tea in silence before Ursula made her way back to the bed.

I settled onto the open bed across from her and fell into an exhausted, dreamless sleep. A sharp knocking on the office door woke me a little before 9 a.m.

I slipped from the bed and out of the infirmary. I did not cast illusions to hide my exhaustion. Bleary eyed, I opened the office door. A tall man with dark skin tipped his hat to me. The bright orange police armband was wrapped around his left bicep on top of his raincoat.

"Hello, I'm Officer Yaro." He held up his identification.

I squinted at the card then at his face.

Where were the police when he cornered a student or staff member? Mama scowled, her phantom finger passing through his ID.

"Nurse Viola Diao." I covered my yawn, steadying my shaky hand against my cheek. "Sorry. How can I help you?" I pointed at the visitor chair.

He settled into the seat, his eyes wandering over my many glass-paneled cabinets and brown bottles. I remained standing between him and the infirmary door.

"We're looking for Ursula Zheng."

"She's here. She's feeling poorly." I gestured at the door behind me. "I'd rather not wake her right now. We've just barely slept." I rubbed my eyes, adjusted my glasses.

"How long has she been here?" Officer Yaro pulled out a notepad and pen.

Mama read over his shoulder. *Pfft, nothing about the crime scene.*

"Since yesterday, a little after lunch. Two days ago, I had given Ursula medication for her sick stomach. She felt so sick after eating that she came again, drenched from the rain." I pointed at the dry raincoat. "It was--uh, personal women's problems." I wrung my hands, letting some of my anxiety leak out.

Officer Yaro waved his hand, dismissing the information. "And she was here the whole time with you?" He glanced at the two doors.

"Yes, I locked ourselves in the infirmary. Besides, we barely slept, with the thunder and her nausea. Is someone looking for her? She told the chancellor she was coming here when she wasn't feeling well."

"The chancellor died last night."

"What?" My voice was a touch too loud. "No." I blinked the tiredness out of my eyes. "But he was just at the Mid-Autumn Festival!" I leaned heavily against my desk.

"He was attacked in his home last night."

I dropped into my chair, my hand over my heart.

Don't be so dramatic, Mama tsked.

"Did you know the chancellor, Nurse Diao?"

More than I wanted to, I thought bitterly.

I shook my head. "Enough to say hello in the hallway, at the school events. Staff and students come to see me but the chancellor has his own physician."

"Could I speak to Ursula?" Officer Yaro nodded to the infirmary.

"Let me see if she's awake."

I opened the infirmary door. Ursula nodded from her hospital bed.

While the policeman interviewed Ursula with Mama eavesdropping, I tidied the medical office. After the officer left, I returned to the infirmary. Mama wasn't there, but I ignored her absence. Perhaps she went to follow the policeman.

"Do you have somewhere to stay outside of the chancellor's residence?"

Ursula shook her head.

"You can stay here while the police are in the residence. In a few days, you can ask to retrieve your things, if you still wish to leave."

Ursula shook her head. "The devil is gone from that house. I will stay."

Then I realized the truth of Mama's absence. The devil was gone, and so was she.

I hid my tears from Ursula. She stayed in the infirmary for the weekend, with visits from her sister.

On Monday morning, the hallways thrummed with whispers. At the end of the week, newspaper articles revealed the truth of the chancellor's character. Some said the revelations tarnished a defenseless man's name. Others were finally safe to speak about his roaming hands and unwanted attention.

The semester ended with the appointment of the Academy's first woman chancellor and the chancellor's murder still unsolved.

I burned the newspapers, hopeful that my mother would read them in the afterlife.

Wen Wen Yang is a Chinese American from the Bronx, New York. She graduated from Barnard College of Columbia University with a degree in English and creative writing. She often writes about people watching out for each other. A full bibliography is on wenwenwrites.com.

This story originally appeared in *Luna Station Quarterly*, March 2024.

To Maeve
Annie ZH Sun

Dear Maeve,

They showed up at your funeral, the men with greed tucked beneath velvet suits, and the women who hid the stench of coin rust behind their lilac-sweet smiles. They have come to support our parents as good friends, as sympathetic colleagues and amiable, respectful acquaintances. But I know the truth.

Your funeral is a social gathering for them. An empty casket, five years too late. Those who aren't carrying hopes to seal business deals with dad have come to make connections with the first female mayor of town.

The sky erodes into pearly grey by the time they lower what should've contained your body into the freshly dug earth. The crowd is one massive cast of marionettes with tear ducts for strings. All it takes is one pull—a bright-eyed swallow from mum, and the whole crowd catches grief like a respiratory disease. At the first salty drop that dollops down dad's chin, they break into sniffles and crocodile sorrows.

That's when I see you.

You look not a hair older than the day you went missing, your body in a skin-tight dress and your hair in the same luscious locks. Your presence should have turned all heads, but you are merely a flimsy shadow of bone and flesh. I stand perfectly still as you make your way to me. I've trained myself to not flinch when you edge close enough for me to smell the sour sweetness of your breath. You motion me to follow, and obedience is an unbreakable habit no matter how long you've been gone. Together, we loop aimless circles in the square cemetery. The guests sing your praise in torment and poetry. You sneer at them, pulling your mouth from east to west, until daylight shines on your discoloured gums. I watch, and listen, and say nothing. For a long moment, everything feels like how it used to be. Except, all the gazes were on me this time.

Five feet away from your casket, a tall man snuffs out his cigarette with the heel of his polished leather shoe, and croaks out, "That pudgy one's the younger McLeod. Estelle, I think." He stares at me some more and mutters, "Genetics' a bitch."

His description of me is carrying, and more eyes turn to me. Under their gaze, I feel the weight of stubborn fat and acne scars and hear your laugh, a mocking, silent victory. Even after all these years, after puberty, mum's strict diet, and the most extensive make-up tutorials, nothing's changed. Blood rushes hot into my fists, to the surface of my face. I clutch the daisies closer to my chest and search for escape. My eyes catch the baby-green mosses crawling out of the names of the tombstones around me. I wish the moss could continue crawling, over bodies and memories, until the world could forget that the Frankenstein monster once had a fairy Princess for a sibling — without the contrast, maybe it'd make me less of a disappointment.

But I've never stood a chance.

The first few weeks after you went missing Maeve, the police combed through the entire town. There were flyers of your face stuck on the chipped lamp posts and at every twist of the rundown streets. When the weeks trickled into months, and they still couldn't find you, mum's eyes became a permanent, red-rimmed state, like ripe pomegranate seeds. Dad chugged down sleeping pills as if they were orange-flavoured Tic Tacs. I hated how your absence inside the house was even louder than your living presence. I hate that, still.

"Pity," a squat man with perhaps the biggest pot-belly at the funeral shakes his head. "My kid knew the older one from school. They'd be the same age by now."

The smoke-snuffer rolls out another cigarette between tapered fingers. "What does it matter? It's not like they could've been friends. Bunch of vipers, the McLeods." He juts his chin towards mum, who's navigating her way around guests with a polished face and business brisk. "Pretty convenient to hold a funeral so close to the election, isn't it? Especially when they haven't found the body. It's as good as pronouncing the missing girl dead."

"Maybe they need closure." The chubby man scratched through his rust-coloured curls. "I heard they were pretty close."

I fiddle with the daisies. I cannot look at you. I don't want you to know that it is your absence that finally unites us.

Shortly after you were gone, mum cleaned your portraits and pageants trophies off the mantlepiece, which led to one of our parents' abuse-hurling-roof-shaking fights. But after that, she dug out my SpellBee Prize and dad's twenty-year-old wrestling medal alongside a single framed photo of you. For the first time there was space for all of us in the household. Things finally seemed fair.

It doesn't change the fact that you'll always be her favourite.

She still talks about your glory and feats with a smile I could never put on her face. You were best friends who whispered all the time. She chose you to keep her secrets while I eavesdropped like a starved pigeon, pecking for specks of leftover affection. It didn't help that you were her exact replica; hollow-boned and silver-tongued, with hair the colour of dry sandcastles. I was all dad; I got his beaky nose, his large frame and his freakishly strong grip. Even though people knew there was a three-year age difference between the McLeod sisters, no one could tell that I was supposed to be younger.

"Did you know Estelle McLeod was the last person who saw her sister?" The tall man murmurs. The sharpness of my name on his tongue turns me queasy. But his whispers catch my ears like an infection, and I can't stop listening. "I've got an uncle who works at the police department. Apparently they parted right outside Mary's confectionery."

"What are you trying to say?"

"There's no camera around that area and with the woods starting so near, too. All very…unfortunate."

I twist around and the man meets my eyes, so cool and composed that sweat breaks inside my palms.

Ten minutes. All it takes is a ten-minute walk for the real world to tip into an alternate universe, where crunchy brown leaves bury the gravel road, and the sun trickles through the gaps of ruby-veined trees the same way the soil particles are currently dripping on top of your empty coffin. Back then, when I could catch you in a good mood, the woods were my favourite place on Earth. We'd snack on candy, play tag, and pretend to be runaway princesses. But in one wrong move, you'd fling both stones and words at me, and I could never tell which hurt more.

I still dream about that day, Maeve; the heavy press of air as the clouds blackened over the sun and the sting of sour candies in my mouth. The wind knifed across our skin, but our brown candy bag was still full as we, high on sugar, continued to whirl like two drunk fairies. Only, I could never fit into a fairytale. And you, snatching the bag from me with a mouth full of taunts and a jeering laugh just like our mother's, weren't much of a fairy, either. But I continued to trail behind you, because you were so determined to get to our secret hideout, and I was so eager to do whatever pleased you. Despite all the cruelty making up your bones, you were the only one who noticed me.

Together, we trekked off the marked path, deeper and deeper into shadowy trees, until we both half-turned into shadows ourselves. We brushed our sticky fingers across bark after bark and did not stop until the trees spaced out. And there it was, the spot under a rough oak you beheld as your throne and a silent lake that you claimed as your own.

You tumbled onto your knees and took a long drink from the cold water. Then, against all my warnings, you leaned over the edge. You stared at your own reflection, and I admired with you, gelatinized honey for hair and opalescent moon for skin. Eyes the colour of northern lights. You lifted your head and directed your signature smile towards me, a smile as sweet as the sugar granules I had licked away from the corners of my mouth only seconds ago. I came willingly and peered over your shoulder. When the distorted images of our faces appeared next to each other, you pointed at my face in the glimmering waters and called out, "Frankenstein."

You didn't even know enough of Frankenstein to articulate a proper taunt, but it hurt, Maeve.

"Frankenstein." You laughed. It was a cackling laugh that haunted me in the strangest moments. I heard it during the police interrogations. I heard it every time I passed by your empty room. Even as I stand now, amongst strangers at your funeral, your sharp cackles continue into my ear and go on until my blood vessels threaten to burst at my temples.

I stumble towards them, open my mouth to say something, anything, so they could stop staring and you could stop laughing. Nothing comes out. My nails bite so hard into the daisy stalks that the chlorophyll stains my palms a strange yellow-green. The dried blotches look just like the bruise marks your fingers imprinted on my wrists as you thrashed beneath me.

Maeve, of all the mean, despicable people who had called me names, none of them could ever hurt me as much as you did. And I wasn't a monster. If I were truly evil, I would've knocked you into the pond just to watch you flail and sink. But I didn't. I kept you anchored safely on shore with my weight. When I straddled onto your back, threaded my hands through your hair and shoved your head into the freezing water, I just wanted you to stop laughing, stop hurting me.

In between the breaths bubbling out of your mouth, you had ceased to be my sister. You were the worst of the fairytale creatures. I hated you for the ability to silence a room with your looks and then charm it back to life with nothing but a smile. You flourished under the spotlight like a preening peacock while I was driven to become a permanent dweller in your shadows. I hated you, Maeve.

I hated that I wasn't you.

And now, gone as you are, I still find myself moving the way you'd move, smiling the way you used to. My best attempt at eloquence and charm is a pale, laughable imitation of what you could do. I try anyway but it's hard to determine the right amount of grief to pepper a funeral. I don't want to be a sobbing mess, all blotchy and hideous like dad. There are cameras around; we will appear in the town's newspaper tomorrow.

I make my way towards mum, who is securing connections for the next election in between the exchange of condolences. As I pass by the two gossipy dolts, their voices drop even lower but I hear them anyway. "The police didn't find anything in the woods or through town," said the round man. "Wasn't the younger one like eleven at that time? How do you reckon a kid got rid of an entire body and left no evidence?"

"Mary did lose her shovel around that time. She left it standing outside the shed by her confectionery, and then it was gone," said the tall man. "Also, it rained that day."

The pot-belly man stared blankly. "Did it?"

It did rain, very hard. Lightning had split the sky apart as I held you down, Maeve. By the time you'd stopped struggling, the first beads of rain hammered down with a blinding intensity. I dragged your limp body out of the water and tried to rouse you from your stillness. But even though your eyes were wide open, you didn't move.

"Hold up. Are you really saying that an eleven-year-old had the strength to dig up an entire grave on her own and bury a body perfectly?"

My heart pounds in my throat. It wasn't me, Maeve, but even if you were here, truly here, you would've never guessed who it was.

Maeve, you refused to wake up, and I was scared. So, I left you by your oak throne and dashed for help. I slipped and skidded through the endless rotten leaves and churning mud. I didn't stop until I held the corners of her shirt beneath my trembling fists. Blubbering and sobbing, I choked out that you were in trouble.

I led her to you, Maeve. I thought she'd know how to help. In semi-darkness, mum trudged towards the human-shaped lump that was you, and against the slick rain, shone the torchlight onto your face. The next few moments were absolutely terrible. She let out a scream, and flung herself at your direction, frantic, hysteric attempts to force air into your unmoving lungs. Her moans were closer to a wounded animal. When she finally accepted that you'd never move again, she pushed back your wet hair and examined every inch of you.

Then, her eyes paused on me, on the bruises on my wrists, and she dragged me to you. I thought of lying, Maeve. But under the blinding torchlight, she matched the shape of your fingers to the prints on my skin.

Something changed in her. When she instructed me to stay and wait by your body, her tone was devoid of all emotion.

I held your hand the same way I'm holding this bunch of daisies—numb and limp. And when mum returned with a shovel, we buried you together. Throughout the whole thing, she moved as if she were a wind-up clockwork toy. With the same mechanical motions, she wiped the shovel clean and tossed it into the bottom of the lake.

At home, we scrubbed ourselves clean with scalding water and shoved all our clothes into the fireplace. As the fabrics incinerated into ashes, mum looked at me in pure disgust. "No one must ever find out, do you understand? I'm this town's first female mayor. I can't let this scandal ruin the family. Do you understand, Estelle?"

Outside, a yellow beam swept through the window and the sound of dad's car thundering to a stop was evident despite the rain. Mum shook me and repeated, more frantic this time. "Do you understand?"

When I nodded, she let out a sigh, picked up the phone, and dialed 911. Minutes before the flashing sirens wailed into our front yard, she took me aside, fussed with the long sleeves of my shirt and whispered, "You can do this. You're my daughter, after all."

And Maeve, I am. I was her daughter just as much as you were. But it was the first time she'd acknowledged me.

In the centre of the cemetery, people continue tossing handfuls of dirt onto your empty casket. I drop the dying daisies onto your casket. The night after my first police interrogation, I locked myself into your bedroom, rolled up my black sleeves, and stroked the blue-black bruises you tattooed onto my skin. I feared that they'd stay forever. But they slowly blossomed into yellows and greens and faded out as if they never existed.

All I felt was hollowness.

I miss you, Maeve. You've always been the sister who I wanted to hug and throttle to death at the same time. That has never changed. And Maeve, I don't regret it because you've never truly been gone.

This morning when I came to see you, sweet petaled daisies crowned above the spot you've been buried in. I know it's you, bits of you. It's your flesh that nourishes the soil and your bones that will become the minerals that glide in the green stalks in the future daisies that I cut. But for now, we'll both have to make do with the small amount of you that I managed to bring back.

Mum and dad find their way to my side as the undertakers refill the hole. Amongst the people who swarm around your shiny casket are the two gossipers from earlier. Gone are the malicious speculations. All they murmur is, "I'm sorry for your loss." I want to snip back, but under mum's narrowed eyes, I accept with grace. We line ourselves by your side, a picture-perfect family in grief. The ghost of you no longer tries to catch mum's attention. Instead, you go to dad, but you should know by now that he is stupid and blind—and currently extremely ugly from all that crying. Even though he loves you, he's too naive to be your ally, Maeve.

So you watch him curve his arm tight around me, your eyes hawk sharp but mouth dead-silent. Mum is barely able to touch me but it doesn't matter. For once, I meet the ghost of your gaze, hold it and smile. Even though this is your funeral, it's no longer all about you.

You've had fourteen years of spotlight, Maeve. It's my turn to live.

Annie ZH Sun is a Chinese writer who grew up in Malta. She graduated from the MSc Creative Writing programme at the University of Edinburgh. Her work has been published in *Hex*, IHRAM Press, Bag of Bones Press *This is Tense* anthology and others. She is the winner of the Horror Competition in Edinburgh Writer's Club.

A Divine Comedy
Kay Hanifen

Business has been rough for children's entertainers in the past couple of years. Especially for clowns. Don't laugh. I'm being serious here.

I graduated from Bobo's School of Clowning in 2015. Again, don't laugh. Less than a year later, there was that creepy clown epidemic. Then, the next year, the first *It* movie came out. And I get it. I saw it opening weekend in my civilian clothes, and it's a damn good, scary movie. But man, the clown slander in it is just painful. I look nothing like Pennywise in my costume, but kids and adults alike started calling me that. It lasted two painful years before the second movie came out. Being weaker than the first and the duology now completed, some of the Pennywise craze died down.

And then the pandemic hit.

Do you have any idea how hard it was to be a party entertainer when no one's having parties? It sucked.

Even though lockdown was now over, business was still slow. I'd been training with Clowns Without Borders, a group that brings entertainment to refugees and impoverished towns, and occasionally visiting children's hospitals, but that doesn't pay the bills.

I'm not scary or evil. All I've ever wanted was to perform magic tricks, create balloon animals, bring joy, and make children laugh. If there's one thing in this world that I'm serious about, it's clowning.

So, when I received a call hiring me for a child's sixth birthday party in the richest part of town, I was shocked, but jumped at the chance. It was strange that it was in the evening—most parties are around noon—but I figured that one or both of the parents worked, and this was the best they could do. They offered me double pay, which wasn't necessary, because I was glad to do it. That doesn't mean I said no, though. Man cannot live on dropped banana peels and whipped cream pies alone.

Before leaving my apartment, I began my pre-gig ritual. I donned my patchwork dress and slipped into my big shoes before sitting in front of my old-fashioned vanity like those that used to be found in theater green rooms. It was something I found at a thrift store and painstakingly restored as a graduation gift to myself.

As I applied the white base coat, I could feel myself slipping into GoGo's character like a favorite old T-shirt. I call GoGo a character because that's the best way I can describe her without getting odd looks, but GoGo is more than that. She's an inseparable part of me, like the three dotted side of a dice cube. She's my best, most joyful, most outgoing self. If I'm being totally honest, she saved my life more than once. Putting on her makeup is like throwing up a shield against the world. GoGo is never hurt or afraid. She faces every challenge with a clever quip and a magic trick.

No, I haven't gone to therapy. Do you think I can afford it on a child entertainer's salary?

Putting on the wig completed the transformation. I smiled at my reflection in the mirror, and she grinned back at me. "Let's do this," I said, grabbed my bag of tricks, and flounced out of the apartment and into my beat-up, ancient van.

It looked out of place in a neighborhood full of luxury vehicles, but GoGo wasn't self-conscious. Some people had more than others, and just because I had less, it didn't mean I was less of a person.

Shouldering the bag, I rang the doorbell. The house was strangely dark and quiet, especially for a child's birthday party. I felt compelled to check the address again to make sure I was at the right place. It was the address that they gave me.

I may be a children's entertainer, but I'm not a child. I know just how dangerous it can be to come into a stranger's home and perform a show for them. Usually, the kids are fine. Sure, you might have a hitter, a biter, or a heckler, but those are easily dealt with. It's the adults you have to look out for. I've lost count of the number of handsy, drunk dads and uncles who seem to think that it's okay to try to squeeze my lapel flower, if you catch my drift.

I was about to call the number they gave me when the door opened. A pretty woman in a high ponytail and slinky cocktail dress stood smiling, though it didn't seem to meet her eyes. "Oh, you must be GoGo. I'm Clarice."

"It's a pleasure to meet you, ma'am. May I have a few minutes to set up?"

She waved a dismissive hand. "No need for that. Little Delilah can't wait to see you. And what she wants, she gets."

The house was enormous. The kitchen alone probably had the same square footage as my apartment. Adults milled about, but there were no children playing like there should be. "Delilah is turning six, right?"

Clarice nodded, her smile looking as painted on as mine. "She's six and already such a little hellion. But we love her dearly." She cupped a hand to her mouth and shouted, "Delilah! Your clown is here!"

The little girl who came bounding up was perhaps the most darling child I had ever seen, like if they put Shirley Temple in a blender with Little Orphan Annie. She was smiling, but when she saw me, her brows furrowed in confusion. "I thought clowns were supposed to be scary."

I shook my head and sank to a knee, partly to get down to her level, and partly to prep the first of my magic tricks.

"Those scary clowns are from movies and TV. Real clowns have a code of ethics. Do you know what that is?"

She shook her head.

"It's a set of rules that we all have to listen to. One of those rules is that we aren't allowed to be scary on purpose. Our job is to be funny, and —" I pulled a quarter from her ear. "To do magic."

She giggled. "That's not real magic. It's just an illusion."

I winked. "And I'm just a girl under some makeup. Magic is what we make it."

"Mom says I'm not allowed to do magic. I'm not ready yet."

"I can teach you a few tricks if you want."

Crossing her arms, she furrowed her brows with a frown. "I thought magicians weren't supposed to reveal their secrets."

I made a coin disappear in my hand and then reappear in the other one. "I won't tell if you won't."

She stared at me, her gaze appraising and calculating beyond her years. It made me feel like I was back in high school trying to make friends only to be rejected at every turn. "I asked for a scary clown," she finally said. "But you're nice. You should go."

A part of me wanted to get out, to flee this creepy house and creepy party. The hairs on the back of my neck prickled as I felt eyes on me, but glancing around, everyone else was wrapped in their own conversations. And she seemed to be the only kid at her own birthday party. I know what it's like to be alone in a crowd. If there ever was a kid who needed a clown, it was Delilah. "But if I go, who will play with you on your birthday?"

For a moment, she looked like she was going to protest, but then she stared past me. And the expression on her face almost looked like fear. I followed her gaze and met the eyes of Delilah's mother. Surreptitiously, I gave Delilah a once-over, checking for obvious bruises. This may turn into a situation where I have to call CPS. I'd only ever done that once with the parents of a kid, and I had no regrets.

I scanned for a place that was private enough that we could talk undisturbed while still in full view of the parents to prevent any concerns of impropriety. Not that they seemed to care. They didn't even bother to invite kids to their daughter's birthday party. "Come on, let's go to the living room. I can show you all kinds of magic tricks and balloon animals. Since you're my only audience member, I can give you a rare, behind the scenes peek at what it means to be a clown."

With a final glance in her mom's direction, she smiled and took me by the hand, leading me into the living room. I sat her on the couch. "First, I'll show you the performance. Then, I'll teach you how to do it." It was a bit harder to do my act with one kid, but I quickly fell into the groove.

"So, for my first trick, I'm going to—ah, ah, achoo!" I grabbed a handkerchief and faked a sneeze, sending confetti flying. "Sorry, I'm allergic to boring adult stuff. And that seems to be the only thing going on at this party. So, let's have fun. You're not allergic to fun, are you?"

She giggled. "Achoo!" The party of one may have been awkward, but at least she was engaged.

"Bless you!" I exclaimed, offering her my handkerchief. She flinched at my words, and as she took it, and the next one tied to it, and the one after that, and the one after that, I felt the air around me grow frigid. The conversation had died like I'd yelled a nasty word at Delilah. "Did I do something wrong?" I stage-whispered.

"We don't say words like b-l-e-s-s you," she whispered back.

It seemed like a weird rule, but I wasn't here to offend anyone. "Sorry, I didn't know."

"It's okay," she said with a shrug. And then, she glared at the rest of the group. "Right?"

All looked to Clarice, whose smile became forced. "Of course."

Maybe I'd misjudged the situation. Delilah seemed to have command of the room, something I never would have expected from a six-year-old. I gave Clarice an awkward wave. "Still, I'm sorry. It won't happen again."

"Just as long as Delilah's having fun," she said, and the party resumed.

Once that weird moment had passed, I completed the rest of my routine. I performed a few more magic tricks, made some balloon animals, and even juggled. Once I was done, I showed Delilah how to perform some coin tricks and the secrets to my more elaborate ones.

"Do you have a destiny?" she asked suddenly as we made balloon dogs together.

I winked. "I think I was always destined to become a clown. It makes me happy, and when I'm happy, I can make others happy too."

"What if your mom and dad's idea of your destiny is different than what you want?" Strange, I didn't remember her or Clarice ever mentioning a dad. I'd assumed that he was either dead or absentee, but maybe not.

"Can I tell you a secret?" I asked. She leaned in, and I whispered. "My parents wanted me to be an accountant." She giggled, and I threw my head back, gagging. "Can you imagine me as an accountant? Blech!"

She worried the balloon in her hands, twisting it out of shape. "Were they mad at you when you told them you wanted to be someone else?"

I shrugged. "For a bit. They told me that it would be hard and that I wouldn't be good at it, but I did it anyway. And eventually, they saw how happy being a clown made me and decided that me being poor but happy was better than me having money but being miserable."

The little girl sighed. "I don't think my mom and dad would ever understand."

"I got lucky." Well, mostly. If anyone asks my parents what I do for a living, they'll say I'm something more respectable, like a stripper. "And I don't say this often, but sometimes, parents are wrong, and don't know what's best for you. You should still listen to them, because there are things that you might not want to do that are still good for you like getting shots and eating your veggies, but sometimes, adults want you to do things that don't feel right. If you feel in your soul what the right thing to do is, you need to do it, even if adults tell you that you're wrong."

"Delilah, it's time to cut the cake," Clarice said from the kitchen. She held up a professional looking three-tiered cake with six candles on each level.

"No, I don't want to," she said, crossing her arms, and, for the first time, actually acting like a six-year-old having too much fun.

Her mom set it on the counter. "You can't do magic until you cut into it."

"But I'm doing magic now, and it's better than yours."

Her mom's expression grew tight. "Delilah. Now."

"No! You always do what you want to do and don't care about me at all," she shouted, getting to her feet.

One of the adult men put a hand on her shoulder. "Delilah, you should—"

"Don't touch me!" she screamed. It was not in the voice of a little girl. The deep baritone reverberated through the room, creating a shockwave that sent him flying into a window. The glass shattered around him, embedding itself into his neck. The room fell dead silent, amplifying the sound of shifting glass and the gurgle coming from his throat as blood pooled out of his wound. Funny. The red against his increasingly pale skin reminded me of my own makeup.

For a moment, I forgot myself, and the clown code of conduct when it comes to using adult language. I jumped to my feet and yelled, "What the fuck?"

I'm sure that the Clowns of America International will forgive me, considering the circumstances.

Delilah turned back to me, her eyes wide. "Please don't be scared of me, GoGo, I—"

"I'm sorry, Delilah, but I have to go." Grateful for the acrobatic courses I took at Bobo's School of Clowning, I nimbly jumped over the couch and made a beeline for the door.

A wall of partygoers blocked my path. I turned toward the backdoor, but that was blocked too. I was surrounded, and they were slowly closing in. Grabbing my bag, I searched for something, anything, that would help me escape.

And then I found my old glitter bombs.

I'd bought them online. Biodegradable seaweed glitter meant to be used outdoors because of the mess. Once a kid got into my bag, stole one, and opened it in the house. Luckily, the parents didn't stick me with the cleaning bill.

I guess I never really got the chance to clean them out of my bag. I popped one in some faces of the partygoers and used the distraction to run. But I didn't get far. By the time I reached the kitchen, they had me cornered again. I pressed my back to the wall.

Something cold and metal dug into it. A door handle. It was probably just for the pantry, but it, at least, gave me a door between them and me. The small barrier would have to do.

When I opened the door, though, I realized that it wasn't to the pantry. It was to a staircase of unfinished wood that sank down into the dark depths of the basement. I'd seen enough horror movies to know where this was going. I would either have to deal with the telekinetic kid and her cult or go down into the creepy basement. Both options led to almost certain death, but if I braced the door properly, I might be able to buy myself enough time to escape.

I slipped inside just as someone grabbed for me, pulling off my wig as I slammed the door shut. The cultists tried to yank it open, but I held firm.

"GoGo!" Delilah yelled from the kitchen. She sounded on the verge of tears. "GoGo, I'm sorry! I don't want to hurt you. They're making me."

"It's the only way," Clarice said. "GoGo, you're about to become the sacrifice that fully awakens the powers of the antichrist. Think of this as a blessing. Instead of a sad, miserable existence as a third-rate entertainer in a dying industry, you'll make something of your useless life. You'll be one of the few truly significant people in the history of the Earth."

"I think I'll pass," I said, still bracing the door shut. "And have you ever considered what Delilah wanted? Because I don't think it's this." What would GoGo do? Something clever and brave. She was always the best part of me.

I grabbed my extra-long handkerchief and tied the handle to the top of the railing to make it harder for them to open the door from the other side. Then, I set some small balls at the top of the steps as tripping hazards for the first few who managed to break through.

Times like this, I really wished I was a sword swallower. Then, I would at least have a useful weapon. But I did take a lot of improv courses. They made me quick on my feet and creative with props. If I played my cards right, I could "yes, and" my way out of this.

I dug my phone from my bag. It shouldn't have been a shock that there was no signal. These people were rich enough to be able to buy one of those jammers that blocked cell phones. But it wasn't dead, so I could still use the flashlight function. With the light on, I carefully made my way downstairs.

The basement was just as dark as the staircase. I found a light switch at the bottom and flicked it on.

Only to immediately wish that I hadn't. They weren't kidding about thinking that Delilah was the antichrist. The entire basement looked like a twisted version of a chapel. An altar sat on one side with a massive pentagram behind it and a humanoid lump stretched across it. Lit, half-melted candles surrounded it and a statue of Baphomet lurked in the opposite corner. But the worst part was the smell. Old blood and rotting meat. Animal carcasses hung from the ceiling, the fresh ones still dripping their blood and entrails.

I ventured closer to the altar. In the center lay a dried husk of a human being. Whoever it was, they had been dead for a very long time. Their eyes were nothing but empty sockets, and the skin of their lips had rotted away, leaving them bearing a rictus grin. It had to have been lying there for at least several months to be in this stage of decay.

Bile rose in my throat, and I doubled over, vomiting on the floor.

"Poor kid," I muttered. I may have watched her kill a man with her mind, but anyone raised in a place like this would be incredibly messed up.

I don't believe that people are born bad. Sure, some people are born with less natural empathy or with a tendency toward impulsive acts, and all people are capable of evil. But just because you naturally have these certain traits, it doesn't make you a bad person. Evil is as much a choice as good. But if you grow up being worshipped in a murderous satanic cult, you're bound to be screwed up. Delilah was just a kid, one who seemed to be interested in learning right from wrong despite the cult's influence. So, yeah, even in this horrific situation where I might not survive the next hour, let alone the night, I felt bad for the kid. She didn't have any choice in this.

Above, the door burst open. I yelped and hid behind the altar. It wouldn't buy me much time, but it would have to do. Bodies tumbled down the stairs, and above, a little girl laughed at the slapstick display.

I dug through my bag, searching for anything that might be useful. My long handkerchief was gone, as were several balls and glitter bombs. The most important tool in a magician's belt, though, is misdirection. I didn't see any exits from this creepy basement, which meant that the only way out was up the stairs. I needed to draw them away from the staircase.

"Roger's dead!" someone shouted. He must have snapped his neck when he tripped down the stairs. I couldn't bring myself to feel guilty about it.

The body on the altar looked important. They wouldn't have left it here for so long if it wasn't. And it was dry kindling. All it would take was a little nudge of one of the lit candles, and—

I ran as soon as the flames ignited the papery skin, taking cover behind the statue of Baphomet, which stood closer to the staircase.

And then the body sat up and shrieked.

"Master!" Clarice cried. "Someone get water! Our Dark Lord is burning!"

In the panic and confusion, I kicked off my oversized shoes and sprinted on socked feet to the staircase. No one seemed to notice as I climbed the stairs, closing the door and bracing it behind me with one of the kitchen chairs. They'd realize soon enough.

"Mom's gonna be mad," Delilah said. She sat at the kitchen counter nibbling on her chocolate cake. Devil's food cake. Ha. Ha. "Dad too. He was looking forward to using your body to sustain him here for another year. I was supposed to be the one doing the sacrificing this time. It would let me access my full power or whatever."

"You're not going to kill me, are you?" I asked.

She shook her head, poking at the cake with her fork. "I don't want to kill anyone, especially not someone kind. This was the best birthday I ever had. All because of you."

I grabbed her by the shoulders, turning her to meet my desperate gaze. "Delilah, come with me. I-I can take you away from here and away from human sacrifice and murder and demons. We could be safe."

She gave me a smile far older and sadder than her six years. "No, we can't. They'll never stop looking for us. You told me that if I feel in my soul what the right thing to do is, I have to do it, even if all the adults around me tell me that I can't. I know what I have to do. But you need to go before I can do it."

"Do what?" I asked, flinching at the pounding against the basement door.

"Delilah! Delilah, open this door!" Clarice shouted.

The little girl jumped down from her seat and wrapped her arms around my waist. "The fire is spreading, and soon the floor will collapse. Come on." She took me by the hand and guided me to the front door.

"Don't," I choked, tears streaming down my cheeks. She stood on her tiptoes and brushed them away.

"You are a normal girl under there," she said, "I'm sorry about this." And she pushed me out the door with her mind like she did to the man she killed. I landed in a thorny bush as the door slammed shut.

"Delilah!" I shouted, banging on the door. But the flames were already too high. The Earth shook as the floor collapsed. She was gone.

I don't remember driving home. I don't remember climbing the stairs to the apartment. I don't remember going inside and sitting in front of the vanity.

But there I sat, staring at the canyons my tears carved into my makeup—my wig gone, my costume tattered.

GoGo was gone. She died with the others in the fire. Now, there was only me.

Kay Hanifen's work has appeared in over one hundred anthologies and magazines. Her first anthology as an editor, *Till the Yule Log Burns Out*, was published in 2024. Her first novel, *The Last Ballard*, debuted in 2025. You can find her with her black cats or at kayhanifenauthor.wordpress.com.

This Time, I Did
Marie-Hélène Lebeault

Nico Alvarez didn't see the sky change.

He was too busy pacing his office, thumb grinding against the side of his phone like it owed him an apology. Their conversations, initially focused on dinner and a new dumpling place Suzie wanted to try, changed tone by the third time they spoke. Not angry. Just tired.

"Can we just talk later?" he said, already wincing as he said it. "I've got this fire to put out with the Fremont proposal and—"

"I'm not trying to start a fight," she said. "I just want five minutes where I feel like I matter more than your inbox."

Nico hesitated. Guilt rose like heat behind his eyes. He opened his mouth—a dozen half-apologies crowding his throat—then closed it again.

"I know," he muttered. "We'll talk tomorrow, okay?"

A pause. Then: "Sure. Tomorrow."

The way she said it—it wasn't sharp, but it wasn't soft either. Like a window sliding shut.

The line went dead. He remained motionless, gazing at the unlit screen; its warmth lingered from their conversation. The room buzzed faintly—air vents, copier hum, the stale neon buzz of the office staying late without him. Outside, the light had dipped into amber, the kind that tricks your brain into thinking the world's about to forgive you for something.

Nico grabbed his coat and laptop bag, shaking off the residual guilt like dust. Lately, even apologies felt as futile as rearranging furniture in a burning house. Except the part of him that kept count—the one she couldn't see—was wondering if those makeups were losing their shape. Suzie was good at understanding. Patient to a fault. Maybe too patient.

He took the elevator down, trying not to think about how silence filled the space where her laughter usually lived.

The lobby was mostly empty, just a security guard scrolling his phone and a couple of stragglers from another floor. Nico nodded a quick goodbye and pushed through the revolving door with practiced ease.

He stepped outside into the golden hour and the faint smell of roasted peanuts from the cart across the street.

And froze.

Suzie was there.

Standing just off the curb, holding a brown paper bag, her hair pulled up in a loose knot. She looked soft, tired, and unmistakably lovely, and it made something shift in his chest. She saw him—raised a hand to wave.

His stomach dropped.

He started to shout, then a horn blared.

A screech.

A blur of motion.

A car ran the light.

Suzie turned toward the sound—

Too late.

The impact wasn't loud, but the silence after it was deafening.

Nico couldn't move.

A bystander screamed. A man sprinted forward. Someone dropped their coffee.

And all Nico could do was stare at the space where she had been standing a moment before. The brown bag crumpled on the asphalt.

His legs moved before his mind caught up. He staggered backward—toward the building, toward anything, anywhere that wasn't this moment. His breath came fast, shallow. The edges of his vision curled in like burning paper.

He stumbled back through the revolving door. He wanted to scream, to undo the moment with his own hands, but there was no grip strong enough to hold back time.

And the world—

Flickered.

There was a sound, like metal flexing under pressure. The door warped strangely, softly, as if twisting multiple times simultaneously.

Then darkness. Like a hand over his eyes.

The first thing Nico noticed was the quiet.

More than silence, a stillness. A too-clean hum under the surface.

He sat up in bed, blinking hard. Light streamed through the slats of his blinds, warm and familiar. His room looked normal—exactly as he'd left it. His sneakers by the dresser, yesterday's coffee mug on the desk, phone charging on the nightstand. He reached for it.

7:08 a.m.

One notification: Suzie Chen, 11:49 p.m.

Can we try again tomorrow? I don't want to end the night like that.

His breath caught. He stared at the screen. This was the exact message she'd sent yesterday. Word for word.

No.

He rubbed his face, stood, and walked to the kitchen in a haze. The noodles hadn't moved. The banana leaned closer to ruin. It was as if the day had… reset. But that made little sense. None of it made sense.

On autopilot, he dressed, grabbed his messenger bag, and walked toward the subway. At the corner, the coffee cart guy fumbled a cup—identical spill, identical curse. Like déjà vu. A woman bumped into him hard enough to knock the earbuds from his pocket. "Sorry!" she called, already rushing away. Nico didn't reply.

His heart beat faster—something between hope and horror. Like being given a second chance by mistake and not knowing how to hold it without breaking it.

He surfaced at his office plaza just after eight. Across the street, the traffic light blinked red. A cyclist zipped past. Someone yelled about lunch orders on speakerphone. And there, standing near the fountain, was Suzie.

Alive!

Real.

Laughing at something on her phone.

For a second, Nico couldn't move. It was like watching a video you'd already seen, but hoping the ending could still change. He walked toward her, almost unsure of his own body.

She looked up as he crossed. Her eyes lit up. "Hey! You're early."

"I—" He stopped. Swallowed. "I needed to see you."

Smiling, she tilted her head, her quiet concern evident as she anticipated his facade of normalcy. "Everything okay?" Instead of answering, he pulled her into a hug.

She went still, surprised, then melted into him with a soft exhale. "Well, hello."

He held on a second too long, face buried in her hair. She smelled like the coconut shampoo she favored. She was warm, solid, and impossibly alive. His throat closed with the ache of it.

When he finally let go, her expression had shifted. Still kind but searching.

"Nico, are you okay?"

He nodded, even though he wasn't. "Yeah, I just … didn't sleep well."

She gave him a look that said that's not all, but didn't push—yet.

"You don't have to tell me everything," she said. "But don't assume I wouldn't understand. Let me decide that. I brought you breakfast. Your tofu wrap. I figured you'd forget again."

She held up the brown paper bag—the same one she'd been carrying when—

No. He wouldn't think about that. Not here. Not with her standing in front of him.

"Come with me," he blurted.

Suzie blinked. "Where?"

"I don't care. Anywhere. I don't want to go to work today."

That earned a grin. "Wow. Either you hit your head or I'm dreaming."

She stepped closer, tucking the bag under her arm. "You ever feel like time's punishing you for being stubborn? Like it won't let you move on until you finally say the thing you're avoiding?"

Nico gave a short breath of a laugh. "All the time."

He took her hand. "Let's just go."

And to his amazement, she didn't argue. She tucked her bag under her arm and walked beside him, step for step, like it was the most natural thing in the world.

They spent the morning wandering the neighborhood. They got second coffees, walked through the farmers' market that opened on Tuesdays, browsed books they wouldn't buy. Nico clung to every moment like it might dissolve.

She teased him gently about his existential mood. "You're like a sad poet who works in spreadsheets."

She paused, watching him sip his coffee. "You never talk like this," she said softly. "It's like you're trying to say goodbye without saying it. Or maybe finally saying something you've swallowed for too long."

Nico looked down.

"I don't want to guess what you're feeling," she added. "I want you to tell me. Not just today."

He laughed. Actually laughed. "That's painfully accurate."

When she reached for his arm crossing a side street, he tensed—but nothing happened. No cars. No screech of brakes.

They made it to a bench outside a quiet café; the paper bag now folded between them.

Suzie bumped his shoulder with hers. "Are you going to tell me what's actually going on? Or should I guess until I land on alien abduction?"

Nico looked at her, unsure what to say. She was here. Safe. And he didn't know how long that would last.

"I just wanted today to be different," he said. "That's all."

She studied him; long enough that he felt a little exposed. Then nodded.

"Okay," she said. "Different it is."

And she leaned her head on his shoulder, like she had no idea the world had ended yesterday.

Because for her, it hadn't. Not yet.

It should have worked.

Nico had accounted for everything—every variable, every vulnerable moment. He made sure they didn't cross the same street. Didn't leave at the same time. Didn't even go near the plaza.

He kept Suzie close all day, like proximity could defy fate. She humored him, mostly. Thought he was being overly sweet, maybe a little clingy. But she let him hold her hand as they walked through the art district. Let him ramble about a coffee table book on brutalist design. Let him change the subject every time she brought up how distant he'd seemed lately.

She didn't push. She rarely did.

They ended the afternoon tucked into a quiet sidewalk café, Suzie sipping a ginger lemonade and humming along to the faint music overhead. Her laugh came easy. Her body angled toward him, open, trusting. He couldn't stop staring. He knew this wasn't how yesterday had gone.

This time, he'd done it right.

He glanced at the clock on his phone. It was past five. The light was golden again. The time when it had happened — would have happened — was passing them by without incident.

Relief flooded him. Sharp and dizzying. He had done it.

Suzie stood and stretched, pressing a hand to her lower back with a groan. "Okay, spreadsheet poet, what's next on the itinerary?"

"Just… walk with me a little longer?" he asked.

"Sure." She looped her arm through his. "But only if there's ice cream at the end."

They walked slowly, meandering through the quieter blocks, until they reached a narrow side street flanked by trees and delivery trucks. It felt removed from everything — no honking horns, no rush-hour shuffle. Just birds, faint jazz from a record store, and the soft shuffle of her shoes beside his.

Nico felt it building in his chest, the words he hadn't said. The ones he wanted to give her — You died yesterday. I watched it happen. And now I don't know what's real, but I would trade every deadline, every ounce of control, just to make you laugh one more time.

He opened his mouth.

And the cyclist came out of nowhere.

A flash of motion. The sound of tires skidding against pavement.

Suzie turned a second too late.

The messenger swerved hard—barely missed a parked car—and clipped her shoulder with his bag. She spun, stumbled off the curb, and crumpled onto the asphalt.

Her head struck the edge of the sidewalk.

Nico screamed her name.

She didn't move.

Everything snapped quiet; the world narrowed to the space between her stillness and his breath. Voices spiked around them, sharp as broken glass. The cyclist looped back, words tumbling from his mouth. Nico dropped to his knees, hands hovering over her face, afraid to touch her.

Blood. Not much, but enough.

"Suzie. Suzie—please."

She blinked, dazed. Tried to sit up and winced. "Ow. What…?"

"Don't move." He was already fumbling for his phone, calling an ambulance with fingers that barely worked. "You're okay. You're going to be okay."

She looked up at him, confused. "Why are you crying?"

He only noticed when a tear hit her sleeve.

The waiting room smelled like antiseptic and vending machine coffee. Nico sat alone, hands clenched between his knees, staring at a poster that warned about dehydration by using a cartoon cactus.

The nurse said she'd be fine. A mild concussion, bruised shoulder, a few stitches.

But she hadn't remembered what street they were on. Didn't know why they were there. And for a moment, he thought: maybe it's better this way. Maybe forgetting is mercy. Then hated himself for thinking it.

She kept asking, "Did we have a fight? I feel like we fought. I don't remember."

Nico had nodded and said, "Not really."

He didn't want to explain that in another version of today, she died. That despite every effort, every calculated change, he still failed to save her.

The city was quieter as he walked back toward his building. Dusk had settled in, casting everything in soft pink and orange. It looked peaceful. Undeservedly so.

He stood in front of the revolving door, watching the glass glint with his reflection.

He had thought if he did everything right, he could fix it. Like solving for an equation. Like love could be reverse-engineered. But this wasn't about logistics. It never was.

He stepped forward and pushed through the door.

The world bent.

Not violently—just enough to make his stomach lurch and the light pulse oddly in his vision. The air felt thick, like syrup. As the door turned, a low hum vibrated in his chest.

And then—

Nothing.

Darkness. Silence.

Not like sleep.

More like surrender.

Nico came to mid-spin, already halfway through the revolving door.

His bag slipped off his shoulder and thumped against the glass. He staggered forward, catching himself on the railing just past the lobby. The air felt sharp, buzzing faintly in his ears. Like a speaker turned on with no music playing.

He blinked. The receptionist looked up from her desk. "Morning, Mr. Alvarez. Running early today?"

Nico didn't answer. He turned slowly, his pulse rising like it recognised the day before he did.

Same lobby. Same elevator. Same too-loud hum from the soda machine.

He checked his phone.

7:52 a.m.

Tuesday. Again.

The text was there.

Suzie Chen: *Can we try again tomorrow? I don't want to end the night like that.*

His stomach dropped.

Another loop.

But something was off.

When he reached the street, it was like watching a glitchy video on repeat. A man at the hot dog cart dropped the tongs. A bird flew past, circled, then flew past again. Twice. A child pointed up at nothing. "Mom, look! It's doing it again!"

Time was stuttering.

Reality — not quite stable.

Nico stumbled through the day like an actor without a script. The office didn't see him. Suzie didn't hear from him. He had no idea what version of her this was — how close she stood to that intersection, how far they were from the next reset.

He went home, shut the blinds, and tried to wait it out. But the world didn't care what he did. Time folded anyway.

He woke the next day to the wrong version of his apartment—slightly off. The furniture in different places. A photo on the fridge he didn't remember taking. Suzie's handwriting on a sticky note he'd never seen before: Stop waiting for a disaster to make you show up.

That time, he tried telling her everything.

He met her early, held her hands, and spilled it all: how she'd been hurt, more than once. How he'd watched it happen. How he was trapped in a loop he couldn't break. And how, deep down, he wasn't sure he deserved to.

She looked at him like she was bracing for the fall. But something sharper flared behind her eyes—hurt, yes, but also disbelief. "Is this your way of breaking up with me gently? Because if it is, it's a hell of a performance." She paused for breath. "You disappear emotionally for weeks, then show up talking like we're in a novel. You think I haven't noticed something's wrong? That I didn't *want* to say something? But I kept making space, hoping you'd step into it."

"No," he said, voice cracking. "It's my way of telling you I've already lost you—more times than I can count—and it kills me every time."

She stepped back. "You haven't."

Her jaw set like she wanted to say more, to push—but something held her back. A flicker of distance passed through her eyes. Then—

Then the ambulance sirens started.

He ran—toward the only thing he knew to do. The revolving door spun.

Nico didn't try to explain this time.

No dramatic gestures. No sidelong glances at traffic signals. Just coffee, laughter, a quiet bench in the park.

Suzie read aloud from a poetry book they found in a secondhand shop, laughing at how terrible it was.

"We should write our own version," she said. "'Ode to Unclaimed Sandwiches.'"

For a moment, it felt like life—not a do-over, not a test. Just them. When the sun dipped low, he walked her home. Held her hand the whole way.

No car. No bike. No fracture in time.

Just a sunset.

And the haunting thought: what if *this* was the version he never saw again?

Another loop.

This time, he avoided her completely.

He ghosted the day. Took the subway to nowhere, rode it in circles. Thought maybe if she never saw him, she'd be safe.

But when he came home, there was a voicemail from her sister.

Suzie's in the hospital. Bike accident. Shoulder's fractured. Said she was distracted, looking for you.

The universe wasn't letting him opt out.

The loop wasn't about the event.

It was about him.

The next time, he didn't fight it.

He went straight to the office, stood in front of the revolving door, and said aloud, "What do you want from me?"

No answer.

So he stepped through.

Again.

Time fractured further.

Conversations overlapped, then looped. A pigeon touched down on a parked car and flickered, as if the air around it had glitched. Nico's own voice echoed back to him, delayed by five seconds, like the world was playing catch-up.

He saw Suzie across the street once, laughing — then flickering like a VHS on pause.

In one version, they were already broken up. She didn't look at him when she passed.

In another, they were engaged.

He couldn't tell which version hurt more.

He stopped trying to control it.

He started remembering.

Not just what happened — but what didn't.

Their last real conversation. The one before the loop started.

She'd made them dinner — spicy noodles and soft-boiled eggs — and asked him, gently, if he was happy.

He'd said, "Of course," and reached for his laptop.

She didn't argue. She just sighed and said, "I wish you'd reach for me like that."

Even so, he hadn't moved. As if staying still would make the moment last. But the stillness became the silence that buried them both. He hadn't replied. Not then. Not the next day. And then — she was gone.

And now he was spinning in place, trying to fix a moment he'd refused to inhabit. The door would keep turning until he stopped trying to fix time and started telling the truth.

Maybe it wasn't time breaking — it was him. The loop wasn't punishment. It was permission. One more chance, again and again, to finally show up.

This time, Nico didn't rush.

He didn't check the clock. Didn't change his route. The weather, the curb, the angle of the sunlight—he let it all be. And then he walked out of the building like it was any ordinary day.

Because maybe it was.

The plaza buzzed around him—low chatter, soft horns, someone selling iced tea from a cart. Everything looked the same. Nothing shimmered.

The revolving door spun once behind him, smooth and silent.

And then there she was.

Suzie stood near the bench by the fountain, arms folded, watching the world with that half-smile she wore when she was trying not to think too hard.

Nico felt his chest tighten. Not with fear. With clarity.

He walked toward her slowly. She spotted him and waved, a little hesitantly.

"You look like you've been arguing with a metaphor and lost."

He gave a breath of a laugh. "You have no idea."

Suzie tilted her head. "What's going on, Nico?"

He opened his mouth to lie. To say something soothing. Something controlled.

But he didn't.

Instead, he said the thing that lived just under his ribs. The thing that kept rewinding the world.

"I've been afraid," he said. "Not of being with you. Of needing you so much that I'd rather control the world than risk you seeing how small and scared I really am."

Suzie blinked. "Where is this coming from?"

He smiled. "I missed too many chances."

She softened, the tension around her shoulders easing as she stepped closer.

"You could've told me that anytime."

"I know," he said. "But I kept thinking I could fix everything without being honest. Like if I just got the timing right, or made the perfect plan…"

She reached up and touched his cheek. "I never wanted a perfect version of you."

He closed his eyes briefly at her touch.

"I just want the one who shows up."

Nico nodded, tears prickling at the corners of his eyes. "I'm here," he said. Not a promise, but a fact. His hand in hers, solid. Present.

For a long moment, they didn't move. The city kept going around them—honking, clinking, the rustle of trees—but it all felt distant.

Just noise, finally, instead of warning.

When she reached for his hand, he took it.

They started walking toward the intersection.

He didn't stop her.

They crossed the street together.

And nothing happened.

No screech of tires. No time warp. Just the soft click of a crosswalk signal and a breeze that lifted a napkin from the curb.

When they reached the other side, Suzie turned to him. "That's it? No existential confession? No dramatic chase through traffic?"

"I think I used all my drama up before this loop," he said.

She raised an eyebrow. "What loop?"

He smiled. "Never mind."

They walked on. Their hands still linked.

When they reached the bookstore, she liked—the one with the crooked floors and the good chai—he paused. Looked back across the street. The revolving door to his building spun once for someone else.

Then stopped.

The glass gleamed. Nothing warped. No flicker of light. No hum. No catch in the air.

Just a door.

Just today. Finally.

Suzie tugged his sleeve. "Come on. You owe me a pastry."

"Only if I get to choose it."

She gave him a look. "You'd pick something with raisins."

He grinned. "Exactly."

They disappeared into the shop, laughing.

And the world kept turning.

No reset.

Just onward.

Marie-Hélène Lebeault is a Canadian speculative fiction author of over thirty titles, from YA quests and time-bending adventures to adult fantasy and sci-fi. A retired educator, she blends magic, mystery, and emotional depth in stories rooted in courage, identity, and hope. She lives in Quebec, hiking, dreaming, and sharing books with her grown children.

Ere the Bat Hath Flown
Irene Liang

Mom always leaves the porch light on for me. It stutters slightly with every step I take. Feels kind of like I'm an old lost cat, errant and coming back home—like the one we used to have. Got him for my eighth birthday, named him Noodle. He died a long time ago, but at least he kept Mom company for a good few years.

The door is closed. I used to knock, but it's the middle of the night, and Mom is old enough that it takes her more than a few minutes to hobble over. Before I do anything, I check myself—wipe any stray blood off my chin, adjust my clothes, run my tongue over my teeth. When it brushes over my canines, I push up until the teeth puncture the soft skin. The pain is bloodless and wooden, as removed as a horror movie, a vivisection on anesthesia.

And then, I mist, skin turning into particles of something not-quite-shadow, and slip through the crack under the doorframe. Coalesce, once I'm back inside, into a humanoid body.

Flick on the lights. They brighten to reveal a messy room, newspapers piled on the low coffee table, empty mugs strewn about the counters. She might've painted the wall while I was gone, from one shade of white to another, but I'm not sure. I pause to check the calendar tacked to the wall. *Seventeenth of May.* It's only been a month since the last time I came back.

Sometimes, it's hard to keep track of time, and I'm gone for weeks, months, even years. Worst of it was a decade ago, when I left in January and came back in October—six years later.

The porch light was still on, though. She was still waiting.

I flit through the living room and down the side hallway that leads to her bedroom. The door is cracked open. Inside, her shape is dim and lumped upon the bed, curled under a blanket. Reminds me of a mole, or maybe a small shrew, hidden from Father Winter. Or maybe a termite queen, winged and plump. When I'm feeling peckish, I'll dig into anthills, place handfuls upon my tongue and pop them, let the bitterness wash the taste of copper from my mouth.

"Mom," I say, and she sits up immediately, throwing the blanket off. Blinks once, confused, before her gaze focuses on me, and an emotion I can't read crosses it.

"Lucy, oh! You're back."

I pad closer, and for a moment, I feel like I'm eight—*actually* eight—years old, trying to find comfort after a nightmare. And then, I notice that Mom is eighty, not thirty, and my skin is cold and it's been so long since then.

Still, I crawl onto the bed, settle down near her. Tentatively, she places a hand upon mine. You never realize how warm skin is until you're *cold*. I can feel every beat of her heart, every contraction of her veins. It's comforting. Like a lullaby.

Good thing I just ate.

"Have you done your homework?" she asks softly. I look at her askance.

"What homework?" There *is* still homework in my room, I'm sure, the remains of arithmetic or long division or whatever I was doing in third grade, but not anything I've worried about since I was mortal.

She blinks once. "Oh. I'm sorry, Lucy."

Forgetting is something that happens with old age too. I still haven't gotten used to it; and by the time I *have* acclimated, I don't think she'll still be...

"How many was it?" she asks. For a moment, I still think she's talking about homework, and I stare at her blankly, until she continues, "In a month. How many?"

"...Three," I say eventually. A waiter throwing out the night's food, alone in an empty alleyway. A teen smoking behind a convenience store, concentrated on the cigarette instead of the shadows. A woman I lured out of her house by crying *help me!*

"Three," she repeats dully. Slowly, her hand comes up to stroke through my hair. "I guess you're hungry."

"Yeah."

She should know this. It's why I had to leave home. I stayed here for three years after turning, but eventually, the missing people in our neighborhood — and even in our county, in our city, grew too many.

That's not all of it, of course. I think, by the end, she couldn't really stand having me around anymore. Three birthdays with cake that I didn't eat, no change in my appearance. No longer going to school, not after what happened to Ms. Holloway. Spending my days glooming around the house, or getting too bored, too hungry, to do anything but stand by the door and wait for night to fall so I could go out and hunt. Near the end, whenever I walked out of a dark hallway, or smiled at her, there'd be just a little bit of fear in her eyes.

One time during those last few weeks, I was playing with Noodle in my bedroom — cradling him in my arms, scratching his head. She walked in and saw me holding him, screamed something along the lines of *what have you done?*

Shocked him so badly that he leapt, scratched a nasty line down my forearm.

She got all teary and worried and apologetic after that, of course, tried to get me to sit down at the dining table. Brought over Neosporin and a band aid, but when she turned my arm over, we both watched as the bloodless scratch sealed up on its own. Then she went to her room and locked the door and threw up in the toilet, and I just sat at the dining table alone, trying not to feel hungry.

It sucked. So I left. Better for both of us, to only return every so often.

Who she wants me to be, what persona I put on, changes each time I come back—sometimes we're distant, and she's unable to look me in the eyes, sitting on opposite ends of the wide dining table. No conversation to break the silence, hands tucked primly in my lap, nails of the right digging thin pockmarks into the wrist of the left.

Sometimes I'm the rebel, and she'll demand I stay at home, and I'll yell that I *have to leave*! Eventually, I'll depart dramatically, all door-slamming and stomping, because I know that she doesn't actually want me to stay.

I'll always come back, though. Because I have nowhere else to come back to.

Tonight, judging by the hand in my hair and the way she's looking at me, the light of nostalgia in her eyes, I think she wants me to be the child she lost. So, I snuggle into her side, curling my legs up to my chest, and let her continue the babying.

"I worry about you," she says, hand still running through my hair, "so much. So, so much, Lucy."

"What?" I ask, pitching my voice higher. It's settled out of the timbre of an eight-year-old girl, but I can draw that tone back easily. I get enough practice. Nothing like a little girl crying to get good Samaritans into dark alleyways. Bad people fall for it too, luckily enough.

"When you're gone. I think it's the motherly thing to do."

"I'm fine," I say, "I'm strong." Stronger than she could imagine. Strong enough to break a grown man in two, strong enough to live until the end of time or the end of a stake, whichever comes first.

"I know," she says, and her hand comes down a little harder on my head, "but when you leave for... for such long times, I worry. I start looking at crime reports. Missing people. Trying to track where you are. I miss..."

She misses who I used to be, the child that had this body before the night took it, and all the memories I have are just things I stole from a living little girl. She knows that and keeps letting me come back anyway.

"I miss it too," I say, and some of it isn't even a lie. It would be nice to be sixty and have a job and a spine that aches when I stand, to walk around in the sun and know the difference between days and years.

But of course, to have that, I'd have to give up the night and the moon and the richness of blood. And be able to turn back time. I don't think either of those are possible.

She doesn't respond, simply sighs. We sit upon the bed in silence for a long moment before, suddenly, she removes her hand from my scalp and sits up straighter. "It's late, Lucy. You should be getting to bed."

I know what she wants me to do. With the best false-protest I can muster, I plead first not to make me sleep, then ask if I can sleep in her bed and then, finally, ask if she can tuck me in.

"Okay," she agrees, reluctantly acquiescing to the request, and we're both play-acting at a normal life, even as she slowly swings out of bed, stands with the help of the walker beside it. Progress is slow, one hobbling step and then another, but I pretend like it's normal, walk behind her with small, shuffling movements.

She opens the door to my room to reveal another darkened den, curtains drawn across the windows. There, in the corner, is my old dollhouse, the dolls still stiffly shoved into afternoon tea. Math homework on the desk, pencil placed haphazardly beside it, doodles in the margins. Paper yellowed, thin as old skin.

"Go on," she says, and I crawl into bed, trying to ignore the dust caking the sheets, the small spider that is making its way across the blanket.

"Goodnight," I say, because the way she's looking at me makes it clear that she wants me to say it first, wants my confirmation. "Love you."

"I love you too," she returns. She doesn't bend to kiss my forehead like she used to. Small reminder that, despite all this pretending, she still cannot bear to touch my forehead with her lips, cannot bear to fake a gesture so tender as that.

Once she's gone, the room is empty and quiet again. Creatures like me don't sleep, so I simply lay there for a few hours, staring at the ceiling and feeling the stillness in my chest. In the other room, I can hear her heart beating first quickly, then slowly. Then the sound of breathing, which swiftly becomes the sound of crying, before hitching sobs slowly transform back to the intake of breath once again.

Eventually, once I'm sure she's solidly asleep, I crawl out of the bed. Become mist again, seeping through the cracks in the closed window, rematerialize and let the night breeze brush cobwebs from my hair.

It's a while before I think about returning. I'm not sure how long. The moon rises and sets more times than I can count, and the ads on the billboards change, and snow comes and then leaves and then comes again a few more times, and then I'm walking down that quiet street again. Wiping blood from my chin, adjusting the clothes that I stole from the Lost and Found at the library.

I can't find the house, and it takes a few turns up-and-down the street to realize why.

The porchlight is off.

I don't go in.

Irene Liang hails from Texas, where she studies engineering in college by day, and moonlights as an author by night. During the rare snatches of time when she's doing neither, she's an avid reader of fantasy, horror, and weird lit. Her work has also appeared in *The Future Fire Magazine*.

Jasmine's Quantum Quandary
Angelique Fawns

Jasmine pulled the sleeve down over the ugly red scars on the crook of her elbow even as she balanced on the barrier of the bridge. They were her personal map to Hell, each track mark leading to this cold, windy moment overlooking the river.

A shiver ran up and down her spine. Dancers' bodies are ill-equipped for damp night air. Her gelled nails scraped across the metal support strut, the pole the only thing keeping her from plunging into the dark abyss below. The sound was worse than fingernails on a chalkboard, and she cringed, wishing her palms weren't so sweaty.

Why were these little things bothering her now? She was seconds from oblivion.

This was the last dirty pole she'd ever hold on to. Jasmine shuddered, remembering the dirt caked onto her belly from the bills shoved there by leering patrons last week. Worse was how she didn't even care. All she could think about was buying a tab of Oxy, a few bills slipping from her trembling hand as she met her dealer in the back alley. The cycle was never ending. Even though she'd been clean for seven days, she knew the shame of stripping would have her seeking oblivion again.

These last few seconds were agony. She'd made the decision to try her luck on the other side of the roiling waves. Whatever waited for her beneath the surface had to be better than what her life was now.

An old-fashioned cruise ship, red water wheel spraying up a mist, meandered down the river. The soundtrack from the musical *Oklahoma!* – played by a live band – offended her with its cheeriness. Jitter-bugging retirees and champagne-sipping tourists were oblivious to her misery. Jasmine willed the ship to float faster. She was hovering between two worlds, the living and the dead. She'd made a lot of poor decisions in her life, but she wanted to do this one final thing correctly: without splattering herself across a deck and traumatizing all the passengers.

Her hand slipped a bit on the pole. It was taking an eternity for the vessel to pass under the bridge.

"Ma'am? You're not thinking of jumping, are you? That would be a waste of a good soul."

A deep, resonant voice startled Jasmine; her plastic high heel slipped on the mist-slick surface. A firm hand steadied and drew her back from the edge. Irritation warred with relief as Jasmine whirled, shaking his hold loose.

The smell of smoke, expensive cologne, and car polish tickled her nose as she checked out the interloper. His handsome face was carved with austere wrinkles, his brows drawn together in concern. A top hat perched on thick black hair, as dark as her own. He was dressed like the old American presidents she'd seen in history books. Before she dropped out in grade ten.

Curiosity percolated beneath her despair. His clothes weren't even the strangest thing about him. A raven perched on his shoulder, silent and huge.

Jasmine blinked, wondering if she was hallucinating through her tears. "This isn't your business, sir. Just leave me, please."

He held his hands up and stepped back. The raven flapped and kept its balance. "Surely, whatever you plan to do can be done after you have a drink with me? I'm Lesley. The owner of the Steamhouse Pub. Best in the vicinity."

The raven cawed in agreement, bobbing its sleek head.

Fury, red and hot, washed over Jasmine. Men were forever trying to pick her up. Couldn't a lady even off herself without being propositioned? Her cheeks burned red, noticing how much of her skin was exposed. She should have at least changed out of her dancing outfit before heading to this bridge. The memory of the last client of the day clung to her like cheap perfume. His requests were the straw that broke the dancer's back. No matter how thin the line between stripping and hooking, she wasn't a hooker. She'd charged out of the club and right to this spot, not even bothering to go home and change out of her tight red sheath.

She clenched her teeth. "I'm a bit busy. I'm sure you can find more pleasant companionship on Main Street. Or anywhere."

He held out his hand again, the one that had pulled her back from the brink moments ago. A goat's head cufflink adorned his wrist. "The Steamhouse is just on the other side of the bridge. Try my new shooters for me. You'd be surprised how transforming a good drink can be."

The raven threw back its head and gurgled.

Jasmine flinched when her hazel eyes met the man's black ones. They had a glittery intensity. Hypnotic. As deep as the river she was waiting to dive into. She saw the riverboat had paused, the passengers gathering to admire the city's biggest cathedral. In the moonlight, the stained-glass windows were ethereal.

Until the riverboat was well clear of the bridge, she wasn't going to jump. The man was eccentric and strange. But she was thirsty. Plus, she'd dealt with worse every shift she worked.

She shrugged. "Okay then. One drink."

He opened the passenger side door of a nearby Rolls and nodded to the empty seat. The smell of Cuban cigars,

Canadian Rye whiskey, and old leather promised decadence and danger.

Jasmine's self-preservation flared. "I don't get into cars with strangers."

Lesley's eyebrows shot up, and she understood the irony. Hadn't he just delayed her from hurtling herself off a bridge? Jasmine glared back stubbornly. She wanted to leave this world on her own terms, not subject to the whims of a madman or serial killer.

A laugh burbled out of him. "You are wise for one so young and sad. Make your own choice. The Steamhouse is just on the other side of the bridge. I hope to see you there. Sometimes, one drink can change your life." With that, he rolled his top hat off his head with a flourish, bowed, and got back into his vintage vehicle. The raven settled on the dashboard.

Jasmine bit her lip as the Silver Cloud chugged away from her. The riverboat was still anchored under the bridge. Should she go for just one drink?

Three tiny shooters sat in a row on the old mahogany bar in front of Jasmine. Dry ice, or some sort of steam, wafted from the cocktails towards the wood ceiling. Each one swirled with viscous multi-coloured fluids. All different colours. One was more red, one green, the third blueish.

Lesley wasn't in the pub when she'd opened the door into the gothic, Irish-looking bar. In fact, there were no clients at all, just the large black bird she'd seen earlier roosting on the back of a booth. The place smelt like stale beer, mint, and old man. A middle-aged woman, statuesque and ebony-skinned, gestured at the burgundy bar stools.

Her smile was brilliant. "I'm Morag, your bartender for the evening. Lesley gave me your order."

Jasmine's cheeks burned as she tugged on the short hem of her cheap dress. The bartender was dressed in an elegant Celtic gown. Glittery love knots and symbols decorated ankle-length green velvet.

Jasmine looked at the three shooters, a dubious frown creasing her face. "I was thinking of maybe a draft beer. Or a Guinness?"

A corner of Morag's lip lifted and her voice softened to a silky purr. "I suggest you try one of these. Do you want to change your life?"

Jasmine tilted her head. "What do you mean? Most alcohol has changed my life for the worse."

The bartender lowered her voice even more. "What is your deepest dream? How do you wish your life had turned out?"

Jasmine pulled on one of her long dark curls. "I always wanted to be a famous dancer. Or even a cruise ship dancer. See the world while entertaining travelers."

Morag raised her dagger eyebrows and nodded to the first shot in the flight.

Jasmine's throat dried and a thirst like she'd never experienced made her shudder.

The raven rumbled deep in its throat.

The lights in the dark bar flickered.

She picked up the red drink on the bar and tossed it back.

The taste was orgasmic. Red velvet chocolate, ripe raspberries, and the finest of Irish creams filled her mouth. She shut her eyes to savour the taste –

Her entire world spun. Or the world spun around her. For a moment, she was convinced she was blown into a million different particles and then zapped back together.

Jasmine was herself...but different.

She felt sleek, layered with muscle like a thoroughbred. She was also sweating like a racehorse, the heat around her oppressive. Beads of perspiration dripped as if she'd just finished the Preakness or some other top-level stakes race. It reminded her of the one vacation her parents ever took her on: a cruise ship from Florida to New Orleans in August when she was sixteen. The recreation director had seen her dancing and offered her a job. If she'd only taken that offer...

The air felt the same as it had on that cruise. Sultry. Thick. Deep southern heat.

Pulsing music, a combination of Gregorian Chant and Opera, vibrated her ribs. The pressure of a strap around her head alerted her to the presence of heavy goggles on her face. Her eyelashes fluttered open behind their glass shields.

It took her brain a moment to grasp her situation. Intricately carved black bars marred her view of a Faustian brothel. She grabbed the bars of her cage, taking in the ugly, grotesque faces of ancient customers ogling beautiful dancers in torturous costumes. The captives danced, gyrating and twerking to the strange music.

Clients surrounded each cage, their tortured faces rapt with hunger. Corruption gleamed in soulless eyes. Their sweat smelt like the corpses of a thousand long-dead skunks.

She felt a sharp pain in her own nipples. Her toned, scarred body was bound with black leather, chains, and clamps. Her cage hung in the middle of the enormous pit of decadence. This was Hell's nightclub, and she was the star attraction.

A familiar man in a red leather suit carrying an evil-looking trident poked the bottom of her cage. Lesley. His eyes glowed red. "Dance Jasmine. This is your destiny, isn't it?"

Jasmine frantically searched for a way out. This would not, *could not*, be her destiny.

She drank that shooter and ended up here. She poked a finger down her throat and vomited an iridescent red liquid all over Lesley's upturned face.

And the world spun again.

Jasmine steadied herself on the bar, accepting the napkin Morag gave her to wipe her mouth. She noted she was back in her cheap red dress.

"That was clever," the bartender said, as an expression of respect flitted across her face. "No one has ever thought to purge the drink from their system before becoming firmly established in the other."

"The other?" Jasmine stuttered.

"Dimension. They're many," Morag said cryptically. "Lesley never lets anyone leave until he is finished with them."

Jasmine winced, remembering the glowing red eyes and trident. "Lesley is –"

Morag interrupted, pushing the greenish swirling drink towards her. "Lesley is the King of the Underworld."

A violent shiver ran down her spine. "So, I'm in Hell." Jasmine looked around the bar frantically. One small blessing: the devil wasn't there. The place was empty except for the raven.

Morag's eyes flashed a warning and she spoke quickly, "You are still alive. Your soul is one of those rare, unclassified ones. Your life to this point has been equally evil and good. Lesley is giving you the chance to try different lives in alternate dimensions, hoping you tilt the needle to dark." Morag tilted her chin at the shooter again, the steam making a haze between them. "Drink."

Jasmine tightened her jaw. "I'd have to be crazy to drink another. I'm leaving." She hopped off her stool but froze when she saw the raven launch itself off the bench.

The black creature stretched its wings wide and then, in a grotesque series of bubbling jerks, turned into a tall, muscle-bound thug. Stark naked, and coated in oily sweat, the man blocked the door.

Jasmine gasped and rubbed her eyes. He snarled at her, snapping his teeth.

Morag grabbed her arm and gently guided her back to her bar stool. "I'm afraid you aren't going anywhere. Please take your next drink." She pushed her mouth close to Jasmine's ear. "Beware of your intention, your soul literally depends upon it."

Jasmine met her intense gaze and gave an almost imperceptible nod.

Morag drew back and spoke with ordinary volume, "How do you wish your life had turned out?"

Jasmine bit her lip and then spoke clearly, "I wish I'd dedicated my life to helping others."

She tossed back the green shooter. The flavour of lime, melon, and truffle coated her tongue as the world spun again.

Jasmine's ears rang with the song of hundreds of birds, and though it was warm, it was nothing like the heat of the last dimension. This time when she opened her eyes, she was in a glorious forest. A thick bough of green hovered overhead, streams of sun catching pollen, and the branches burdened with rows and rows of birds. Little birds, songbirds, birds of paradise, every kind of bird you could imagine. Except ravens.

An elfin elderly woman with long silver hair materialized from behind one of the enormous trees.

"Greetings, I'm Adrasteia. What brings you to our sanctuary? You are our first human visitor..." Though her voice was angelic and her green eyes kind, Adrasteia gripped her flowing white dress with tight fists.

Jasmine put her hands up in the sign of universal supplication. "I came here to help any way I can. I'm Jasmine."

Belying her age, Adrasteia moved with unbelievable swiftness and hooked an arm around Jasmine's waist. "Walk with me. How did you get here? This is a protected dimension." Her voice cracked with concern.

Jasmine allowed herself to be hustled down a twisty path through the forest, the birds twittering and flying in circles behind them. Jasmine's heart caught in her throat. Had she made the wrong wish again?

She tried a light-hearted laugh. "It's the most ridiculous story; I was in a pub called the Steamhouse owned by Lesley–"

Adrasteia pushed her cool palm against Jasmine's mouth and said, "Do not say his name!"

The sky darkened, and leaves flew as a strong wind descended on the forest. A tree, just inches from them, cracked and fell to the ground. The birds flapped into the sky, their bodies tossed in all directions as the torrent engulfed them. It was as if a tornado had hit with no warning.

With a loud crack and flash of lightning, Lesley appeared. He was in the same guise as the first time Jasmine met him. Top hat, elegant long-tailed suit, human eyes.

He pointed at Jasmine. "You are proving to be a tricky conquest. But thank you for leading me here. I wondered who was collecting my lost souls."

Jasmine's mouth flooded with saliva and panic. She looked over at Adrasteia who had picked up a fallen branch.

The elderly woman shone with a silver outrage. "Where did you think those dancers you were tired of went? You turned them into birds and set them loose in the world. They've found refuge with me. Leave us!"

Lesley's eyes flared with anger, actual flames dancing out of his eyes. Then, he shrugged. "Your fate is in the hands of Jasmine. If she leaves with me, I'll forget you and your forest of pathetic ex-burlesque performers. Plenty more lost souls where they came from."

Jasmine's knees went weak, and she grabbed Adrasteia's hand to keep herself upright. "I don't understand. I thought I was exploring alternate realities? Choosing a different future?" The woman gave her hand a reassuring squeeze and then released her fingers.

Her birds, the ones that hadn't been tossed by the tornado, landed behind her, shielding themselves behind her skirts.

Lesley tipped his sharp chin back and laughed. "Your choices follow you wherever you go. You can't live a new reality; you can only move on from where you've been. No matter how many alternate dimensions you visit."

Jasmine paled. "What was this about then?"

He shrugged. "I just wanted you as a dancer in my club. Corrupt souls become immune to an infinity of flames and torture. So I throw in a bit of entertainment. You are something special. An exotic dancer in every sense of the word."

Jasmine stuttered, "I am just a stripper."

Lesley's nostrils flared. "You are the sum of your choices. So many souls never reach their full potential."

Adrasteia stomped her bare foot. "These poor souls get caught between Heaven and Hell. Once you cage their souls, they have nowhere to go. It's dancing in that infernal club or being cast out as a bird!"

Lesley pinched his lips together, entertained by the elfin woman's fury.

The hundreds of birds behind Adrasteia flapped up into the trees, alighting on the branches like a grim row of miniature jurors.

Jasmine felt a slow burn of anger travelling up her chest. "So, it was all a ruse? I never had a chance to redeem myself?"

Adrasteia said, "As long as you are alive, you can save yourself."

Lesley spoke at the same time, "You were lost when you stepped into my bar." He gave a short bark of laughter, smoke swirling out of his nose. "I gotta tell you though, you are the first person to taste the second cocktail. Most drink the first shooter and end up dancing."

Jasmine looked between the two of them. Kindness and hope radiated off Adrasteia. Lesley looked like a fat cat after a good meal. She'd seen so many men, and some women, with the exact same look when she was stripping. They thought they were so superior to her.

She cocked her hip and propositioned Lesley. "Aren't you curious as to what happens with the third shot?"

A tiny smile tickled the edge of Adrasteia's lips.

Lesley looked stunned for a moment. "Pardon?"

Jasmine let her voice drop a register into her sexy slur, "Tell you what. You leave these birds and their caregiver alone and I will come back to the bar and try that third shot. I will have that drink with you. That is, if the offer is still open--"

Lesley paused ...

The birds set up a raucous cawing, daring him to accept.

He gave a snort. "These birds are giving me a headache. Why not? I'll follow you to your next reality, and then you will dance for me for the rest of eternity. My biggest cage is still empty."

With a flourish of his hand, the world spun.

Jasmine winked at the astonished expression on Morag's face when she landed back on her Steamhouse stool. Lesley appeared beside her and slammed his hand on the bar.

He pointed one long claw-like finger at his bartender. "You are going for some safe-serve training after this."

Morag paled and nodded. Then she pulled the third bluish shooter out of a tiny bar fridge. "Here you go, Jasmine. Good luck."

Jasmine smacked her lips and said, "I wish I was back on the bridge and never came to the Steamhouse Pub in the first place!"

Lesley roared, and the raven flapped towards the bar, but Jasmine picked up the drink and shot it back.

The drink tasted like blueberries, blue freezie, and bananas. Lesley grabbed her arm, but the world was already spinning –

Jasmine was back on the bridge. This time, she didn't bother to pull her sleeve down over the red scars. She had made some bad choices in the past, but it was time to move on. The wind picked up and she teetered on the brink. She now knew that whatever waited for her beneath the surface of the dark river was better than spending eternity dancing for the devil.

The old-fashioned cruise ship was just passing under the bridge, the band playing a jaunty, and only slightly butchered version of "Grease." She bit her lip, she still didn't want to traumatize the tourists, but she could hear the roar of the Rolls Royce starting up the bridge.

Lesley was coming for her. No time to wait.

She launched herself off the bridge, hoping she'd achieved the right angle to avoid hitting the boat. The free fall was exhilarating. This time, she felt no fear or regret. There were other dimensions and possibilities out there. If there was a Hell, there must be a Heaven. She hoped by leading the devil away from the bird sanctuary, she had tipped the scales in her favour.

The water rushed up faster than she thought possible. Her heart stuttered in her chest as the unbelievable cold engulfed her. She closed her eyes and let the black waves –

"Get her in here! Someone get a blanket!" a firm voice ordered.

She was being dragged up the ladder of a ship, her face sprayed by the mist from the red water wheel. Warm hands laid her in a deck chair.

"I'm okay, just let me be," she murmured.

A woman dressed in a nautical uniform handed her a warm cup of tea. "I'm Captain Stella. Here. Sip this. What were you doing?"

Jasmine noticed the retirees and tourists surrounding her, their eyes filled with concern. Someone had put a blanket around her shoulders.

She forced a fake laugh. "I was trying to take a selfie with your boat in the background by moonlight, and I must have slipped!"

The look of concern on the captain's face transitioned to aggravation and relief. "You sure you weren't jumping?"

Jasmine put a bright smile on her face. "So sorry! No, I wasn't jumping." Her eyes flicked up to the bridge; Lesley was there, leaning over the rail, smoke curling out of his ears. She rushed on, "I've always dreamed of working on a boat like yours. That was careless of me."

Captain Stella put a hand to her chin. "Funny you say that. I do have a position available in our entertainment division."

Hope warmed Jasmine more than the now damp blanket. "Really? I'm an excellent dancer. Experienced. I'm happy to clean, cook, sing, whatever you need!"

The captain helped Jasmine stand, "Let me show you to the staff quarters. This isn't how I normally conduct my interviews, but I was moaning just this morning about how hard it was to find good help, and you literally fell out of the sky!"

Jasmine smiled, not believing her luck.

Captain Stella was acting like she'd also won the lottery. "Consider this a trial. But if you work out, we have cruises scheduled for all over the continent. Dry clothes is the first order of business."

Jasmine did a little dance step as she followed her new boss into the galley. "I just left my previous employment tonight, so I promise you, I will make it work."

Those devil shooters did give her a chance at a second life. This time, when she was offered a job on a cruise boat, she was taking it. If she'd learned anything tonight, it was that you couldn't run from your problems, nor start over. But you could make better decisions going forward.

There was a reason she was hauled out of the river.

She would choose to be a good person and a good dancer. No one was going to put Jasmine in a cage for eternity.

In any dimension.

Angelique Fawns is a journalist and speculative fiction writer. She began her career writing articles about naked cave dwellers in Tenerife, Canary Islands. After selling her first story to *EQMM*, she fell in love with weird fiction, which is ACTUALLY stranger than non-fiction. You can find her lurking at @angeliquefawns on X, blogging about upcoming calls at https://angeliquemfawns.substack.com, or gazing into the abyss hoping it stares back at her. Over 100 of her stories have been published. Find some in *Mystery Tribune*, *Amazing Stories*, and *Space & Time*.

This story originally appeared in *The Dance*, April 2024.

An Obligation of Obols
Lorina Stephens

In his last will and testament Pasion, the trapezite, left instructions he was to be buried, not cremated, and all his wealth laid with him like the pharaohs of Egypt. It had been his living wish to be assured of coin to pay Kharon, that he might cross the rivers Styx and Acheron, and thereby reside in peace and luxury under the rule of Hades. That his wealth had accumulated on the backs of his fellow citizens, whether in pocket or not, didn't signify. He'd operated his business in the shadow of Athena Nike. Wisdom prevailed.

But such is the wish of the living.

He'd arrived before Kharon's ferry in a rattling, jingling clatter, hauling coffers and sacks upon a karótsi. His noise was at odds with what he found, and he shrank into himself for the first time in his life — well, afterlife, he amended. Not an auspicious start.

As he eased the handles of the karótsi to the ground, he watched the press of spirits upon the shingle, some as solid as himself while others ranged through degrees of substance until finally there were those drifting, silent souls like fog rising from the water.

Not an auspicious start at all. Was it possible so many of the dead had been unable to cobble together but a single obol? Could, or would not their families, their friends, have even offered one single coin? It seemed ludicrous. What was an obol?

It was movement, and not sound, which drew his attention to the shore, and it came as a further surprise to Pasion there was also no sound when Kharon beached his ferry. For that matter, there was now a noticeable lack of sound from the river, and the land. All was hushed, as though making way for the eddying spirits around him. Pasion realized he'd been like a braying ass in this marketplace of the dead.

He turned his attention away from the procession of death to Kharon and quailed beneath that glare. Pasion sensed the potential for violence, for harm beyond what he knew. The living had always spoken of the ferryman as a large and fierce man-almost-beast, but that gossip did nothing to give reality to what stood in the stern of the boat, resting easily upon his oar, studying Pasion. He wondered if this was how his own clients had felt in the market, measured and quantified like coin in the balance.

Ludicrously, Pasion thought it a wonder the ferry didn't sink under Kharon's bulk.

"You have coin?" Kharon asked.

Pasion nodded, gestured to the cart. This was something he understood.

Kharon snorted a laugh. "I need only one obol."

"Which you will have." And Pasion leaned out, obol between his fingers to offer as payment. Which Kharon apparently refused as the ferryman made no move to accept the coin, instead gesturing to the karótsi.

"I'm not taking that."

"But this is all my life's work!"

"Not much to show for a life."

To which Pasion sputtered in indignation, flinging the coin at the ferryman.

Kharon glanced at the coin in the bottom of his boat, then gestured with his chin toward the nearest wandering spirit. "That would buy him passage."

"And why should I pay his passage? Plainly he's wandering this shore because he has no coin, which likely means he was a shiftless vagrant all his life. There's work if one's willing."

"Not when you've lost everything." Kharon looked at the spirit and nodded toward Pasion. "Tell him."

"Tell me what?"

"That I'm here because of you," the spirit said.

So they did speak, these wandering spirits.

"Outrageous," Pasion said. "These beggars will say anything to cheat their way into coin."

"You loaned me coin because I needed to repair my boat, and without my boat I couldn't fish, and without fish I couldn't support my family. But the interest kept mounting, and the fishing failing, so you took my boat, my house and all." He gestured behind him. "My wife, my daughter, my sons, all of us starved. Because of you."

"If you'd hired yourselves out for any kind of labour, even indentured, this wouldn't have happened, and I wouldn't have been forced to collect on my debt."

"And we did, which kept us barely alive, until it didn't."

"So, what, I should now increase that bad investment by paying your passage?"

"Seems reasonable to me," said Kharon.

"You cannot mean that!"

"My ferry. My terms."

The audacity! But when Pasion found Kharon was unmoveable, he grudgingly plucked an obol from his purse and made to hand the sum to Kharon. Which again the ferryman refused, saying, "You must pay the man. And don't fling it. Place what you owe him in his hand."

The effrontery was not to be borne, but Pasion could see no way around this, and so, chewing on his anger he placed the coins into the fisherman's hand, who in turn gave each of his family their passage as they stepped into the ferry, climbing in last himself.

Kharon nodded his satisfaction, and poled the ferry out into the dark, turgid waters of the Styx.

"Where are you going?" shrieked Pasion.

"I'll be back. In the meantime, you'd best talk to the others here and find out why they're stranded. If they borrowed any coin from you, then you will pay their way before you set foot upon my ferry." When Pasion made move to protest again, Kharon simply called over the water, "My ferry. My terms."

Pasion sank to the shingle, his back to the wheel of his karótsi, and glared at the wandering spirits. This wasn't how he'd thought his afterlife would turn out. He'd worked hard, he told himself. It wasn't easy to assess whether an investment was worth pursuing or not, whether to gamble on the loan for this merchant's kerkouros to expand trade across the sea, or an olive grower who wanted to increase his grove and press his own harvest. Or even as simple as a few drachma or obol to bridge a labourer's expenses.

And as he watched the shifting, drifting indigent spirits, he wondered how many of them were here because he'd had to make the difficult decision to foreclose. How many wandered here with no ease for the lives they'd lived? Was he responsible?

He stood and gestured to a woman who ventured near, her attention a little more focused than some who shambled on the shore. She seemed familiar, and when she stood before him, he could see this was Elini, wife of Loxias the baker.

"But why?" he found himself saying, unable to reconcile why she was here when he knew she'd carried on the bakery and paid out the loan Loxias had undertaken to refurbish the ovens. But as he now learned once the debt had been paid, there was nothing left to buy flour, and patrons were unwilling to bring Elini their custom now she no longer had the protection of a husband. Didn't matter that she'd been the baker, and Loxias the bluff and bantering face behind their market stall. Life was like that. And then it wasn't, and left you without coin so you could pass over and rest at last.

He hadn't known.

He glanced at the wealth he'd brought with him, back to Elini whom he remembered as hard-working and kind, a sensible woman. Now the weight of the karótsi seemed immense.

"How came you to be here?" he asked at length.

"I was robbed. I don't think they meant me harm. They were just hungry, is all."

He took a coin from his purse and pressed it into her hand, gesturing to Kharon's wharf.

"At what terms?" she asked.

"No terms."

She closed her fingers over the silver coin, nodded once, and turned toward the others who queued to take passage with the ferryman.

Pasion listened to the story of the child who came next — a runner who had lost his parents after they'd died because of Pasion's collectors — and the apothecary, and the basileus, the potter and the judge. People whose lives he'd touched and tipped into ruin, and now, on the shore which might see them at rest, he pressed coin they had surrendered to him back into their own hands. The task felt immense. He found himself cowed, beaten, bruised with knowledge of a life misspent not as a libertine, but through deleteriousness.

The queue formed. The queue dissolved. And Kharon poled his ferry out into the dark waters again and again, carrying the souls Pasion now released from indemnity. It was enough to crush a man. It was enough to render him dedicated to redress, so that when at last there were no longer spirits here because of his actions, he gave what he had left to those who had need until at last Kharon gestured to him to board.

But Pasion found he'd emptied his last purse. The coffers stood open and devoid of silver. He spread his hands, looking up at that ferocious face aboard the ferry.

"I have nothing."

"And thus is justice meted out." Kharon gestured to Pasion's karótsi, which was again full of coin. For a moment Pasion felt hope, and relief, and grabbed up coin to pay his way. But once again the ferryman declined Pasion's payment, only indicating another drift of impoverished souls waiting on the shore.

Lorina Stephens is a writer, editor, and artist, currently editing and reviewing for *On Spec Magazine*. She co-edited *Tesseracts Twenty-Two: Alchemy and Artifacts*, and is a juror for the 2025 Sunburst Award. Lorina has four novels, two collections of short fiction, and three non-fiction books in publication. You can find her at fiveriverspublishing.com.

Deeper You Go
Kemal Onor

Our mother was asleep, so we met outside. Like thieves shrouded in darkness we crouched in the dying light. A warm, sickly-sweet night. The crickets chirped on, and the frogs peeped in the hidden bog land. I watched Carmen as she came down the hill from our house, the light in her eyes fierce with excitement. It was the time we both knew that had finally arrived. An eagerness hidden in the folds of darkness, excitement charred into our bellies. We were children then, and Carmen and I were both frantic and eager to get the summer started the best way we knew how.

We scuffled along, bent low to the ground. Running like convicts trying to duck under the watchful eye of a searchlight, swinging back and forth like a lantern held at the end of a withered, gnarled hand. Our laughter in our throats, but we didn't dare let a sound escape our mouths. Not until we were safely tucked in the woods, and the house disappeared behind weaves of branches. Even then, I always felt something watching us. Something that always eluded us, like the temperature rose a degree because something had stood there only a moment before. A strange smell, like old perfume hung in that lucid heat, it wafted like a bat at your nose. Still the excitement was too much, and we were both unafraid.

Now and then I spotted Carmen, her glinting blonde hair shining like a ghostly wig as she appeared between dark stands of tree and brush. We both knew what was at stake. We ran through the trees, breaking branches that reached out to touch our faces, pawed numbly at our clothes. Now and then one stung my arm like wasps' stings, but there was no stopping either one of us.

Then we stood before the spot. The hidden desire of our child hearts. Smooth gray stone glinted in the evening. Large faces of clean rock polished by rain and sun. I remember it like a mouth. I came from the trees, and my heart sank. Carmen had beaten me. She was laughing and dancing in the evening air. Already she positioned herself near the diving spot. I watched my feet as I approached the rim of the water. I pressed my toes into the stone so hard my sneakers bent back, and I could see a point where the seams might split. I heard her strike the water. I knew it would be a moment before she came back up for air. The water was deep, and the best treasures lay at the bottom.

I picked up my head and tried to make out Carmen's form in the water. The brightness of her hair always gave her away. When she was midway down, or coming back up, she looked like a pearl, full of moonlight. I saw her making her way for the surface. She swam with one arm. The other clutched what I could only guess to be her prize for winning the race to the water. Then she brought her head above the surface, gasping for the sickly warm air. She puffed and took in a breath, water streamed down her nose and in her eyes, but she was all smiles. Awkwardly holding her haul from below, she kicked her way to the shore.

I slid down the face of an angled rock and reached out to help her to land.

"What'd you find?" I asked. She did not respond. She tried to place as much as she could onto the shore. Together, we managed to get everything up and out of the water. We sat back from the stone edge and looked at the haul Carmen managed to retrieve. I looked at the trinkets on the ground between us. The air stirred overhead as if conducted by an invisible hand. As if pulled along by a string. I blinked hard and tried to examine the expression on Carmen's face. We never really knew what it was that we pulled from the water, but it always held some reverie, a touch of mysticism, like holy relics pulled from the ground. I wanted to say something, but silence muzzled me, and I could not speak.

Carmen was better at the discovery part than me. I remember her on all fours, hair matted to her forehead and face. She bent low, examining the trinkets like they were fossils not to be touched, until they could be properly examined. She looked like a hound dog tracking a scent. Her face bent so low to the objects. Sometimes, we pulled chests up from the water, but mostly, it was small pieces. Fragments of something greater. We never knew what we would find.

"Teeth," said Carmen. In her hand she held a perfect pair of canines. Their shapes extended like they had grown too large for a mouth.

"Must be a dog," I said. I gaped, feeling a pinch in my stomach, like I could feel those large canine teeth – fangs – clamping down on me. She set the teeth to the side and continued examining her treasure. There was a silver locket, a stalk of petrified broccoli, and an empty glass vial. There were also several small pieces of brown pottery. I reached out and attempted to match the edges together, thinking they might fit back like puzzle pieces. Some things we pulled from the water were easier to decipher than others. Carmen made her thinking face. A look that our mother always told her was most un-lady like. Carmen never cared for being a lady, she always preferred to be herself. Perhaps that's what I liked most about her. She was honest, pure, unwilling to hide what she was. I managed to set the pieces into a kind of plate, but the breaks were not quite right.

"Want to do another dive?" I asked.

"We don't have time," said Carmen. Her voice sounded like sand being scraped over ice. Being stamped into the glass surface by heavy boots. I knew she was right. We marveled a moment more, but already we could hear the rumblings of a coming storm. Today we were both ten years old. It was an age more significant than all the rest.

Carmen still had water dripping from her long locks. She grabbed at the teeth, the broccoli, the silver locket, the empty vial. Each she retrieved and bundled in her shirt. From the driveway, I caught the sound of a truck engine. We didn't have much time left. We scrambled to get to the edge of the pool. We tumbled like so many rocks sliding down a cliff face. Then Carmen flipped her shirt over. The teeth, the silver locket, the pottery pieces, all disappeared into a shallow hole.

We both ran our hands, our fingers raking the earth, quickly covering the hole with dirt. We buried our found treasure. Over the years, the pile had grown. Neither one of us knew how deep the hole went. There was never enough time. We managed to get the last of the items covered with dirt when we heard the first call from the direction of the house.

"Kids, children, come home." We climbed up the bank and washed our hands in the pool. It felt bitter cold to the touch now, and my body filled with so much ice creeping up my veins. It was like a poison making its way through the bloodstream. Then there came a stomping through the trees, a breaking of branches. Like some giant creature chewing on bones.

"Children, your mother wants to see you."

We both slowly stood. The ice was now in my throat. This was how it always was. On the edge of the clearing stood our father. His dark figure seemed to blend in with the spindly trees. We knew our day of freedom was over. Carmen took my hand, and we both walked with our eyes at our feet. Shuffling as though walking in a dream. This single hour was ours, but all the rest were spoken for. All the seconds, and minutes. All the moons, stars, the years that stretched themselves like skirts being pulled; they were not ours.

We walked past our father. He said nothing as we marched back toward the house at the top of the hill. The lights inside had been turned on, and I could already taste the faint hint of ash on my tongue. The countless years that lay caked. The moon was a yellow cheese, like a terrible eye, it looked down on the house. This was how it always was. The ice turned to a fist in my throat. I looked up to those windows with the jack-o-lantern light spilling out. The curtains had not been drawn yet.

Carmen gave me a squeeze of her hand, and I knew without looking she had also looked up to see the house. Our father continued to creep behind us, like a wall slowly following, urging us forward. Moving us in a forced migration as the tides rise. We were being driven without force, without words, toward that terrible house. Toward the terrible stove.

"Hello, children, happy birthday," said our mother. She sat out on the porch knitting fresh baby garments. Her straight hair, like straw stuffed under a pointed hat, stuck out in all directions. Her toothy smile worn deep with uncounted centuries. I blinked, trying to commit the scene to memory. This time I did not want to forget. I did not want to keep sensing the memories like a ghostly fog. We had been living in a dream for so long, but what could we do?

Carmen had not let go, and this time I squeezed her hand. We moved inside the home. On one side of the wall was a massive stove. The front grate reminded me of a smile made up entirely of iron bars. Like a castle gate. It drove a lance into my chest every time I saw it. Every time we were ordered to climb inside.

"Come along, children, come along," said our mother. The sound of her voice practiced over the years, the centuries, the millenniums. How many times had we trusted her? How many times had we relived this exact scene? Once, a hundred? A thousand? There was no knowing for sure. It had been only recently that some of our memories started to remain intact. Like the letters were not quite so faded. Each time, we grew steadily more aware of what nightmarish trap we had been placed in.

Carmen squeezed my hand so tightly as we moved toward the stove, that I thought my bones might break. Our mother whispered softly to us, told us lies. Said no harm would come to us. We were told to climb inside the iron maw. We did as we were told. No protesting. It was important to keep everything hidden.

Then we climbed inside. The black ash soot disappeared into the darkness as mother closed the door. We sat with our legs folded under us, breathing in the dark. Inhaling the intoxicating smells of burning, of blood boiling, dissipating to nothing. We had still not let go of each other. Carmen started to take short breaths, and my heart thundered in my chest, rising like a fire consuming all. Inside, it was quiet, silence stuffed around us. Only our mouths drawing in short, shallow breaths made any noise. We quivered in that silence. We knew death was present. Any moment, it would knock on the grate and peer inside at us.

The temperature rose a minuscule amount at first. A third of a degree, a quarter, then half, then five. The darkness was swept away by the red glow of the walls. All at once, the silence was sucked out, all at once, the humming of wires coming alive, carrying heat, electricity back and forth. The temperature rose even more. We sweated. We were frogs being boiled alive. The temperature became too much for us, and we screamed. The sound of fire rose all around us. Then there was nothing. It lasted just a moment, a blinking of a tired eye, exaggerated. I no longer felt Carmen at my side. I no longer felt anything.

We had both been swept away from thought. Our old selves, our ten-year-old bodies were no more. Like reaching for the surface of a sunlit lake, we were drawn back into the world. We were delicately taken from that oven, with its grim iron smile. At first, my head swam like my brain was not yet solidified. It was like it was all just an unformed mess of tissue and guts. But, this time I remembered a little more. I remembered the sting of the heat on my arms, I remembered how tightly Carmen had held my hand. It was like looking out into the world when you know it is not real. Your brain slowly clicking on, deciphering the falsehood of the dream, the nightmare.

I could not speak, as my mother cradled me and Carmen in her arms. There was new youth in her cheeks, and a glowing aura surrounded her. I blinked and let my head roll back.

The years crept by, and still we only remembered through strange dreams. The way the wind knocked branches together was the sounds of the oven igniting. The starter clicking on. Those early years we were helpless to our mother and father's care. Unable to speak. Unable to act. Yet our nightmares were filled with visions of the grinning stove. The darkness that lingered in its terrible maw. We continued to grow as ordinary children. But steadily we felt ancient memories stir in our minds. Everything felt sealed away in a tomb.

How many times had we grown up? How many times were we forced to relive adolescence? Never to escape the bonds of being ten years old? Forever we had lived those same years over and over, never reaching eleven. If we could reach eleven, it would be significant, somehow.

Time would continue to loop around and around like a terrible cyclone. Like wheat that grows only to be cut down. Only to start over again and again. On the eve of our seventh birthday, it was like a curtain was suddenly drawn. All at once memories rushed at us like speeding cars in the night.

The water, the hole with buried treasures. It poked in on our dreams. It consumed our talk. Another year went by and we were both eight. More memories appeared like ghosts in fog, faint, but present. Trying to make themselves known. Then we were nine. We could talk. We could see, and we could explore, but only under the watchful eye of our mother and father. They convinced us that the forest was off limits. They told us stories about the monsters that lived in the trees. About the terrible things that inhabited the outside world. We were both nine, so we believed them.

Then one night I had a terrible nightmare. I dreamed I sat in absolute darkness, crying. I dreamed I was alone. I went outside and walked down the hill. It was early spring, and the grass was bitter cold on my feet. Still, I felt some strange presence. Something called my name. I stood near the bottom of the hill, looking up to our house. I could not make out the memory that pressed its face against the glass, breathed its hot breath behind the frosted window. I knew there was some presence, but it felt faint like a voice at a great distance. The moon was bright, and for a while I looked at the shadows cast by its glow. I turned and faced the trees. I marched toward them. There must be something there.

I went slow, walking as though still in a dream, but it all felt familiar too, like pulling a time capsule from the earth. The things you buried once significant now eaten away by time. You just can't quite remember why you selected to place it in the ground in the first place. Something you once cherished now forgotten. I passed between trees and lances of moonlight.

There was no voice calling to me, but I went because something dormant in my mind urged me forward. It spoke without speaking. Beyond the ring of trees and brush I came to a clearing. My heart was in my chest. There were no monsters here. I felt a hand brush the frosted window, and I blinked, transfixed by the pool of water, the glazed, weathered stone that stuck out like bad teeth in a mouth.

I wondered if this place was calling to me. I wondered if I had stood there before. Trapped in the same pale moonlight reflecting off the stone and water. I stood near the edge of the stone, and pressed my foot against the rock. I sat on the ground, hugging my knees. There was something sacred about this spot, but I could not remember fully. From then on my mind was plagued by the pool of water tucked away in the trees. There were no monsters here. Our parents had told us those stories to keep us close, to keep us from wandering. Both my mother and father had started to show more gray in their hair, and my father's beard was all but snow clinging to the front of his face.

I spoke to Carmen, and she told me of her own strange dreams. Only after mother was asleep and father away, were we able to go and sit, looking at the pool of still water. We explored it, but the memories were so faint that we were grabbing at shadows in an unlit closet. In hushed voices we sat just beyond the terrible eye of our childhood home. The tremor of fear that we could only gape at. Never speaking its name. Time continued its dreadful march, and each day that passed we felt the slow churning of death lumbering through the world. Dragging behind it a tide of ghastly spirits. We felt helpless to time, the approach of the next season. Were we just trees forced to bear the seasons? Time and time again to drop our heads, lose our leaves in the winter? To die only to return in springtime? There was some unspeakable fear that had been pinned in our chests. I could see the way each night, as we returned to the home, that Carmen squeezed my hand a little harder as we returned to our beds.

The iron maw smile of the stove was ever-present. Sometimes I thought the grinning smile to be clicking, flicking its tongue against its teeth like the ticking of a horrible clock, counting down. Each night mother and father returned home they looked weary and more worn out, like too little snow trying to cover the world. Patches of sunlight burning holes into the gray pall of an autumn sky.

They now watched us more closely when they were around. They eyed us as though we were livestock that had grown fat over the years. Like pigs we had gorged and grown. I remember one evening, sitting by the mysterious pool of water, sitting in the twilight, listening to the wind, looking up into the dark clouds that filled the sky.

"I'm not starting over," said Carmen. A few days ago, we had discovered a buried trove of treasure beside the pool. Our fingers had pulled at the earth, brushed away the dirt. While we were reset every ten years, the items we buried had remained. The treasures we pulled from the bottom of the pool, things lost to our memories, lost in past versions of ourselves. Each one held some significance. Our memories came back. Carmen held a silver locket between her fingers. "I'm not afraid of growing old. How long have we been forced to live like this?" She did not pick her eyes up from the locket in her hands. She turned the polished silver in her fingers, trying to guess at its mysteries.

A cold wind blew about us, and Carmen's hair snapped in the breeze. I could smell the hint of rain, of thunder, a coming storm in the air. I was reminded of the terror of the darkness inside the stove with its iron smile. I wasn't sure in that moment what it would mean if we did reach eleven. I thought about all the terrible stories our mother and father had told us to keep us from wandering.

The years had been unkind to our mother and father, and each night they appeared thinner, like they were ghosts melting before the approach of dawn. I did not speak then. Carmen's defiance provoked some thought in me, and I wondered intently what would happen if we managed to escape this nightmarish cycle. We would soon be turning ten once more, and it put a stone in my stomach. I could no longer sleep. Almost every night, I would leave my bed and stand in the kitchen looking at that terrible stove. I would rest my hands on the iron bars. I would close my eyes and imagine, trying to conjure the memories from the many past lives we'd lived.

It might go on like this forever, I thought.

Kemal Onor is a neurodivergent author. He has an MFA in Creative writing from the Solstice MFA in Creative Writing Program at Pine Manor College. His work has been featured in *Tales from the Moonlit Path*, *The Dark Void*, *The Creepy Podcast*, and more. He has twice received the JSC/VSC Fellowship award. His novella *Curse of the Black Horn* is available on Amazon. He lives in Michigan.

A Witch's Lament
Sylvia Heike

As I stand in the kitchen, stirring a pot of nettle soup, it's too quiet. It seems the house that usually creaks on every step has not a single opinion today. It makes the small sounds — the clatter of my spoon, the shiver of my skirts — that much louder, while the cotton-like silence suffocates me.

All my life, the prophecy of my ancestors, the Blackoak witches, has shadowed my life and darkened my future — any child of mine would be born a monster with a giant's lust for flesh and blood. And so I vowed not to bear any, and have spent the last century making peace with that. Renovating my cottage, practising rune magic, learning the language of the birds and trees. A good life in a good realm, for anyone. After all, can you really miss what you never had? Have nostalgia for something that never was? Grieve what was never yours?

I shred more stinging nettles into the pot, toss in a handful of unlucky clovers, and stir. Who knows if I could even bear children anymore? Thanks to my elixirs, I may appear youthful as a water nymph, but inside, I might be like the honeysuckles by the brook that blossom despite root rot.

I imagine my children, my beautiful children, playing around me. Their toenails scraping against the floorboards, their little claws leaving stains of gooseberry jam and dirt and chicken blood on the kitchen cabinets. Their snorts and shrieks as they chase each other through ferns and brambles and my vegetable garden. Their snarls and hisses and glowing eyes, the soft breathing from the crib, the sleep-barks, the howls and cries as the youngest calls for mama in the middle of the night.

Yes, I miss them. My beautiful little monsters who cannot be. In their bloodlust, they would suck the marrow of all living creatures as easily as a babe sucking milk from a teat.

As the years passed by, I might have forgotten about my wants, had the house not kept whispering and wanting too. *Let us have just one,* it sighed. *Let us love and keep it safe, shape it to fit into this world. Have you looked outside? Read the newspapers? So many monsters already roam this world, wearing human faces. A child, loved and nurtured by us, surely could not be the worst of them. The room in the southwest corner would make such a wonderful nursery —*

"No!" I snapped, as much to myself as the cottage. I couldn't afford to torture myself with any kind of false hope. It was already hard enough to live with my decision while the world carried on with no knowledge of my sacrifice. I jumped on my old red bicycle and rode to the nearest village, coming back with tools and paint cans and iron nails. Turned the empty rooms into libraries, herbariums, broom closets, cat rooms, dusty tombs of forgotten things. But I couldn't actually stomach getting any cats — I'd had dozens and outlived every one of them.

I remodeled the kitchen and mixed rejuvenating potions and carved new runes into my skin; translated and re-translated the original scroll, finding no loopholes; learned to speak with the ravens, the bees, the spiders. But most such things only speak when spoken to, sing when sung to, if then, and I'd been living alone so long I could barely hold a conversation with a bedbug. Sometimes I caught myself humming tunes that could be lullabies but never gave them words.

There were days when even the house stopped answering. I curled up in my green velvet armchair with a thousand-page book on my lap, and just sat, and everything was silent, padded, and soft like moss on a rock.

I didn't know how much longer I could take it. Every

day was the same and nothing changed. My whole existence felt like a wordless prayer.

One night, I heard a thud on the roof, a whisper from the hearth. *May I come in?* Yes, I thought, and there he was already, the Nephilim, standing between me and the blazing fire. The first I'd ever encountered, with his stark figure, obsidian wings, and heavenly features. His voice hummed like ancient oaks inside my head. *Your loneliness is a scream. You nearly deafened me as I flew above, and I came to see if I could help.*

I had so few words left in me, I didn't know what to say to my visitor. I didn't need to. He pressed his lovely finger to my lips. *Let your pain speak, Isadora. I am here to listen.*

I don't know how well he could hear me, exactly, but that night, I let it all out into his silky robes and warm skin and soft feathers. The tears and the pain, the grief and the longing and the need. Never in my long life have I felt as comforted and understood as in the Nephilim's arms, his giant wings wrapped around me, his lips and fingers softly brushing against rune-carved skin, lost on a plane of tenderness.

At first, he only wished to console me. But as he drank my secrets, he also divulged his own and more. Upon his touch, I saw grand visions of heaven's gates, of winged creatures like him falling down to Earth; I saw the child-shaped yearning in his heart, as deep as my own. I saw myself the next morning, sweeping feathers; I saw myself several months later, painting the nursery a soft sunflower yellow and my belly growing.

Had I been a fool for fighting the prophecy this long? Inevitable was written all over it. Yet it was one thing to believe an age-old prophecy and fear the worst, and a whole 'nother to glimpse the best of it with my own eyes.

The time had come to own my fate.

My vision.
My child.
My prophecy.
I wouldn't let anyone take it away from me.

I tiptoe to the sunny nursery, where in a crib, my sweet boy lies. Such pink cheeks he has, and lips, such lovely white tusks pressing at the corners of them. I stroke his milk-filled belly, his downy wing-nubs, and it's not a monster I see.

I will raise him in secret, in safety, douse his prophesied bloodlust with love. The coven won't have to know. The house will make sure the ravens won't gossip. His father can visit anytime he wants.

One day my boy will be tall and strong like his winged father. He will bring chaos to this realm, set the sky ablaze, weep in my arms, curse at me, scorch the Earth he walks on. Someday. At two, thirteen, seventeen—at a thousand-years old.

But before that, he will call me mother, and I will call him my sweet, sweet angel. I cannot determine or change who he becomes, only try. And until he brings the end of days, he shall brighten mine.

Sylvia Heike is a writer from Finland. Her short fiction has appeared in *Flash Fiction Online*, *PodCastle*, and *Nature Futures*. Her work has been nominated for Best of the Net and the Pushcart Prize and been longlisted for the BSFA Award for Best Short Fiction. When not writing, she enjoys knitting, gardening, and watching birds.

A Locked-room Murder
Scott MacPherson

Groggy and stiff, Penny slowly lifted her head and groaned. The room was unfamiliar, as was the soft, comfortable armchair beneath her.

"Good morning, sunshine," said a man's voice from above.

She leaned forward, blinking and pushing her hair out of her face. Her head ached, making it hard to think. What happened? Where was she? She squinted around the dimly lit room.

There wasn't much to see. Just a thick, worn area rug on the floor, bordered by well-used mid-century modern furniture. On one side of her armchair was a love seat, on the other an old wooden console TV. Directly across from her was a matching couch.

Sprawled across the couch was an unconscious man in his underwear.

Startled, she staggered to her feet and realized two things. First, she was only wearing the short, black nightie that she kept special for her stolen evenings with Eddie. Second, Eddie was the man on the couch.

She took three long, barefoot strides and knelt beside him.

"Eddie," she said, whispering and lightly smacking his face. "Eddie!"

Eddie mumbled something, snorted, and turned away.

Penny shook him again. Nothing.

"I'm sure he'll wake up soon, Penny, but I dosed him after I dosed you."

She was awake enough this time to follow the tinny voice upwards. It was coming from speakers mounted in each corner of the room.

The man's voice sounded familiar, but the distortion and flat affect kept her from recognizing it.

"Who are you?" she said to the air. "Where am I?"

No response.

The last thing Penny remembered was locking up the front door of the Anderson house. Nice split-level. Walking distance to an elementary school. She wasn't going to have to bother with the Open House she had booked for Saturday. There would be an offer by tomorrow latest.

Unless it was already tomorrow.

She didn't know if it was day or night. There were no windows in the room, no clocks, no phone. Her cell was gone with her clothes, and she didn't see any of Eddie's belongings, either.

No way to tell how long she had been unconscious. She wasn't hungry, but with her throbbing headache, that didn't mean much.

On the couch, Eddie's mouth fell open and he started to snore.

Where am I? What the fuck happened?

The walls around her were bare and grey. No photographs, no paintings, no art or detail of any kind. Nothing but two identical-looking doors, metal and rounded at the top, on two opposite walls. Each door had a valve wheel in the centre. She tried to turn the one closer to her, but it didn't move at all.

Penny rested her hand flat against the wall. The surface was rough and cold. Not drywall. Concrete. A basement wall.

A basement with no windows? And sealed doors, like a submarine?

"Hello?" she called. "Is anyone there? Can you hear me?"

There was a soft, almost inaudible electric buzz from above, but no other response.

"What do you want?" she said softly, tears and panic welling up. At least her headache was starting to subside. Whatever her kidnapper had dosed her with was finally wearing off.

Kidnapper.

She tried to twist the wheel on the door again and then sprinted to its twin on the other side of the room. Neither budged a millimeter.

"Listen, I don't know what's happening, but if you let me go, I'll do whatever you want," Penny said, looking up at one of the speakers. "I have some money in the bank. If you have my purse, I'll go to an ATM right now."

Penny glanced down at her revealing, satin nightie. Money was probably not the solution, but she didn't want to think about the alternatives.

Eddie snored loudly from the couch.

Eddie.

The nightie, from the back of her drawer.

The familiar voice from above.

"Oh my God," she whispered. Then, louder, "Patrick?"

"I knew you'd get there eventually," her husband said through the speakers.

"Patrick, what is this?"

After another electric pause, Patrick said, "I followed you, Penny. I know."

"I don't know what you mean," she said lamely, unsure of where to look while she spoke. "Why don't you let me out of here and we can talk about it?"

"No. There's nothing to talk about. You made a choice. You've been fucking this idiot behind my back. Maybe that makes me the idiot. I don't know."

His voice was still so flat and strange she almost couldn't reconcile it with her husband of five years. She couldn't even picture his face as he spoke.

"Patrick," she said, heart racing. "Patrick, let me out of here."

"Not concerned about your boyfriend? That's disappointing."

"Let me out of here right fucking now!" she screamed, shrill and panicked.

For a second there was nothing at all. Then Patrick's disaffected voice returned.

"You made a choice, Penny. You made a choice about our marriage, about our future. About *my* future."

She sat down heavily, tears running down her cheeks against her will. Eddie was still blissfully unconscious. Unaware.

"Patrick, I'm sorry, I didn't want to hurt you."

Nothing.

"I just—I don't know. We got into a rut, and you didn't want to talk about it. Eddie was fun and new, and interested in me—"

Patrick laughed through the speakers, a hard bark. "Yeah, I bet he was. You never wore that thing for me."

She jumped back to her feet.

"This is crazy. Where am I? What do you want?"

"I wanted a wife that wasn't a slut. It doesn't matter what I want anymore. What do *you* want?"

"I want out."

"Fine. Then you just need to make one more choice. There are two doors in this room. One door leads to the stairs."

"What about the other door?"

"It… doesn't."

Penny waited for him to explain. He didn't.

Try something else. "Both doors are locked, Patrick. I checked."

There was a loud click from one side of the room, followed by another from the opposite.

"Not anymore. Pick a door, any door. You've got a 50/50 chance of being right."

"What if I don't?"

"You do. Two doors, one of them leads to safety."

"No, I mean, what if I don't pick a door?"

An audible sigh from the speakers. "Well, then you have a one hundred percent chance of starving to death down there."

Penny thought for a second. This was crazy. Patrick wasn't a violent man. He had never hit her, had barely even raised his voice when they argued. Finding out about her affair had completely short-circuited something in his brain.

He'd definitely lost the thread, but she was still alive. Maybe there was a way out.

If he wanted to kill her (or Eddie), he could have done it while they were unconscious. It would have been easier than stripping off their clothes and dumping them in this homemade escape room.

She wasn't going to die down here.

"What's behind the wrong door, Patrick?"

"Only one way to find out, sunshine. See you when you decide." There was a fuzzy, electronic click.

"Patrick? Patrick!"

No response.

Alone with her thoughts (and Eddie's soft snoring), Penny paced the room.

It was small and square, about twenty feet by twenty feet. A little chilly in her current wardrobe but not freezing. There was a vent near the ceiling, but much too small for a *Die Hard*-style escape, even if she figured out a way to get up there.

Her last impression was the same as her first impression. Clean, spare, and solid. Concrete walls, floor, and ceiling (as far as she could tell). No windows, no other doors, no cracks.

Penny returned to her chair and perched on the edge, staring at the blank screen of the old TV. She ignored the faint, curved reflection of Eddie's bare legs in the glass. It was the bright orange pattern of the rug that drew her eye.

The rug.

Grunting with effort, Penny shoved the chair, love seat, and TV back, freeing three sides of the thick area rug. Filled with hopeful certainty, she curled the far edge onto itself and duck-walked the roll to the edge of the couch.

Dropping to her bare knees on the concrete, sweating despite the cold, she looked back to see what she had uncovered.

Absolutely nothing.

No pull-ring in the floor, no trap door, no grate she could pry open to escape. It was just more flat, clean concrete.

"Fuck," she said, shoving Eddie's feet out of the way so she could sit. She kicked the rug with her heel and watched as it flapped back into place.

Two doors. No other options.

"Fuck!" Her scream echoed around the sparse furniture, just as trapped as she was.

"Can you keep it down, babe? My head really hurts," said Eddie, wincing as he propped himself up on one elbow. Blinking, he looked around the room. "Hey, where are we?"

After a couple of attempts to explain the situation to a very confused Eddie, he got up and started his own investigation of the room. Running his hand along the wall, he came to the first door.

"So, your husband is a nutjob," he said, squeezing his aching head and staring at the metal wheel on the door. "Is he rich?"

"What do you mean?"

"I mean, is he rich? He finds out about us. Instead of just getting a divorce, he builds this fucking death bunker? Why didn't he just shoot us or stab us or something?"

"No," Penny said absently, looking around the room at the old furniture. The old TV. "No, he's not rich." Eddie was still talking, but she wasn't listening.

She knew where they were.

Patrick's mother lived alone on a small farm just outside of the city. It was really just a couple of acres, left to her by her father. The first time Patrick brought Penny home, he took her on the ten-cent tour of the property.

Reaching the windbreak of trees at the western edge, Penny noticed two rusty metal doors mounted in the ground. "Storm cellar?" she asked.

"Nope. Back in the '60s, during the Cuban Missile Crisis, Grandpa decided that the end was nigh and sunk some cash into a fallout shelter."

"Seriously? I've never seen one. Can we have a look?"

"I don't think so. Nobody's been down there since I was a kid. Not even sure where the key is." Penny never bothered to ask about it again.

She looked up at the ceiling.

"Eddie. He didn't build a bunker. He didn't have to. It's an old fallout shelter."

Eddie stopped pacing.

"There's a bomb shelter on my mother-in-law's acreage. This has to be it. Patrick just added some speakers. Probably a camera."

Eddie looked back at the door closer to him. "What about the door? Do you really think it's booby-trapped? A stick of dynamite? A hungry tiger?"

"I don't know, Eddie." She was exhausted. "His voice was so strange, I barely recognized it. He already did this to us," she said, waving her arms vaguely at the bunker and their partially unclothed state. "I don't know what he did or didn't do."

Penny went back to the couch, quietly sobbing.

Eddie stood up straight. It was difficult to look brave and dignified in your Fruit of the Looms, but he wasn't going to wait around until this joker shot a can of poison gas or something through the vent.

"So, if he's telling the truth, we have a 50/50 chance of getting out of here."

Penny sniffed. "Yes."

"And there's no visible difference between these two doors."

"Not unless you see something I don't."

"Okay. Okay." Eddie strode back and forth between the two doors, examining them, and ended up beside the door where he started. "Fuck it," he whispered, spinning the unlocked wheel and grabbing the dull, metal handle.

"No!" Penny screamed, leaping to her feet. There was a loud, echoing *clack* and Eddie started shaking violently, frozen in place, helplessly gripping the handle as thousands of volts flooded his nervous system.

Every muscle in his mostly nude body was clenched and taut, all spasming at once. There was a rapid sequence of terrible, bone-cracking pops from his jaw. His teeth were explosively destroying each other under the implacable pressure.

Another *clack.* Eddie stopped shaking and dropped, but his hand was cooked to the handle, unable to let go. Acrid smoke curled up from his hair and eyes. Piss puddled on the cement around his collapsed knees.

He was dead.

Penny stood there, numb. None of this could be real. The kidnapping, the bunker, the murder. It was madness. Things like this didn't happen.

She turned and walked to the other door.

"You win, Patrick. It's over. Eddie's dead," she said, not looking up. She spun the wheel and grabbed the handle. There was a spark, painful enough to make her flinch, but she didn't let go.

It was just static electricity.

She pulled the door open and stepped through.

No sunlight. No fresh air. Just a small, dark landing that led to a small, dark staircase.

Barefoot, Penny slowly trudged up the cold steps, swiftly reaching the top. The same metal doors that she had seen once from the other side lay nearly flat across the entrance, the final barrier to her freedom.

A push knob protruded downwards, similar to the kind on the inside of a walk-in freezer. Gripping the cold metal, heart racing, she shoved it with every ounce of strength she could muster.

No click.

No light.

No other latches or handles.

"Patrick, you goddamn liar!" she screamed. There was no way out. There never was. Penny sat and put her face in her hands.

She was going to die down here, but not quickly, like Eddie. Would she starve? Would she resort to cannibalism, just to survive a little longer? Would she find a way to kill herself, just to escape?

It didn't matter. Nothing mattered. She might die today or in a week, but her life was over. She was never going to have kids. She would never see her parents again. Or her sister. Or the sky.

This old bomb shelter was her space-age sarcophagus,

Gripping the railing, Penny stumbled back down the stairs. The burnt pork smell of her dead lover grew stronger with every step.

Patrick dumped the last load of dirt from his wheelbarrow onto the rusted, metal doors, using a rake to smooth out the surface. Whistling a quiet, indistinct tune, he unrolled fresh sod over the dirt. It only took four and a half pieces. Hardly anything.

He lay down on the grass, pressing his ear tight to the fresh green surface. Silent as a grave. His quick landscaping was a bit steep for a random little hill in the yard, but nothing that would draw attention.

"Patrick? Are you all done out there?"

"Yeah, Mom, just a minute while I water this new sod down. All patched up over here."

"What?" The house was too far away for her to hear what he was saying.

"I'll be right there, Mom!"

"Okay, dinner is on the table."

"Fantastic, I'm starving."

He started spraying the grass and resumed whistling that same nameless tune.

Scott MacPherson lives and writes in Calgary, in the shadow of the Canadian Rockies. He is a husband, father, and grandfather, and probably looks like your dad. Sometimes, you can find him making lame jokes on Instagram (@sonoftheparson). This story marks his debut appearance in an anthology.

Under the Pale Mother Moon
Garick Cooke

Dower had not expected to make it back alive, and now that he had, he did not know what to do. Death had followed him home, and he stood before the bay window, waiting.

He'd gone for a walk on the muddy game trail overlooking the bayou, a place he thought he knew well. The morning was swathed in a steaming mist, and he couldn't see ten feet in any direction. He had the sense of walking alone in his own world. But he was not alone.

He found the print pressed into the muddy floor of the trail: clear and fresh, with tiny puddles in the bottom of the pug marks. He knelt in the muck and covered it with his hand and found that his splayed fingers would not quite span its length or breadth. He stood up and looked about himself, suddenly aware that the mist might hide many things.

"You're a big one, aren't you?" he said softly.

He hadn't expected to be answered. The voice that came back to him was a tiny, mewling cry on the threshold of hearing. He hesitated, turned back around. The call came again: the low moan of someone in pain. He knew that sound too well. He was about to go searching into the mist—expecting, perhaps, to find an injured jogger on the trail—when the voice changed and took on a bestial edge, like the keen of a hunting dog straining at the leash—

Old Father was proud. He'd taken a risk in bringing his pack from its northern homeland into this unknown hunting ground, but the risk had proved itself. Here the prey teemed and thrived, and the pack thrived in turn.

Theirs was a small family but a strong one, with the big names already filled: Old Father and his mate Old Dam; his sons, the strong Clincher and the brave Climber with his clever paws; his swift daughter Chaser; and the youngest male, the nameless yearling who showed promise of being the next Tracker.

They ranged far and wide in this vast new city, but they encountered no other packs. The great wealth of prey remained theirs to claim.

The human outcasts of this place slept under the bridges and overpasses, huddling under roofs of cold concrete, and here the pack did its work, carrying off those who would not be missed.

Old Father taught his family well. The cubs learned reverence for the prey who gave them life. They learned to judge a likely victim, to cull the ones who were ready to give themselves to the pack — and after every feast they learned the secret songs of the wolven that must never be sung in the hearing of men, for the prey slept, and the hearing of the songs might awaken them from their dreams. Men were creatures of strong habits and weak senses, but sometimes, rarely, they might find one who was awake.

They had found this one by accident. The yearling had been practicing the cry by which they sometimes toled their prey. But the yearling's call was as yet imperfect, and the man fled at the last moment. He had the manner of one who was awake.

It was fitting that the prey was sometimes dangerous, for how else could the wolven prove themselves? It had always been so.

Dower lived alone in a Depression-era bungalow, the last house on a dead-end spur of blacktop overlooking the bayou. His one neighbor to the north had learned to respect his space. On the other two sides of the house, and across the street, a jungle of undergrowth encroached on his property.

He turned away from the window, kicked off his muddy boots, and went into the bedroom. The mattress on the floor was surrounded by stacks of books, pillowed in dog-eared paperback histories by Tuchman and Shirer and von Clausewitz. A collection of Hemingway stories lay open on his nightstand, and he picked it up and read the first sentence over again: "Certainly there is no hunting like the hunting of man and those who have hunted armed men long enough and liked it, never really care for anything else thereafter."

Dower liked Hemingway. The man had seen war and known it and wrote the truth about it. Sometimes reading calmed the distant recesses of his mind where his memories echoed and burned. Sometimes he could read himself to sleep at night.

Later he put the book down and returned to the window overlooking the driveway and the old GMC Sprint parked under the twisted oak. Thus far the winter had been mild; it was ten o'clock, and the mid-morning sun had already burned away the mist. By the light of day, the footmark in the mud seemed distant and fanciful, as if the mist and the things in it had really been dreams. He knew something about wolves in Texas. He knew that no wolf lived anywhere near this city, unless it was in a zoo. Besides, something had been wrong with that footprint—

He held out his hand and looked at his splayed fingers for a long time.

Old Father crept away from the house and into the hollow in the brush where the rest of his family awaited him. The man—the awake one—was still inside. The pack had taken turns watching the house, but the man hadn't come outside all day. Now it was dusk, and the man's scent said he was sleeping.

The pack watched Old Father expectantly. He tasted anxiety in their scents, but he pretended not to notice. He was not Old Father for nothing. He knew the man would have to come outside sometime.

He growled deep in his chest, expressing strength, and went to each of the pack members with his tail held high. They understood him.

Climber and Clincher slipped away. They would take positions outside the house and wait. When the Moon was high, Old Father and Old Dam would replace them. He sensed a restlessness in the prey, and he thought the man would try to escape in the middle of the night.

Darkness fell, and Old Father led the pack in silent prayer. They raised their faces to Great Mother Moon, the giver of all. Night was their element and the Moon their guide. It was given to the pack to know the prey, man, but it was not given to man to know the hunter. Their existence must remain a secret. That was the law.

The banshee wail of a bottle rocket going off woke Dower from an uneasy doze. It was followed by the staccato crackle of a string of firecrackers. Neighbors up the street had been setting off fireworks at odd intervals since noon.

Dower had almost convinced himself that he hadn't seen what he thought he'd seen down by the bayou. He spent the afternoon packing a duffel bag anyway, and slipped off in front of the TV while Cronkite reported on President Carter's visit to Poland.

Now he couldn't go back to sleep. He decided that he wanted to go out.

It was the chance of a car on the road that saved his life, for it was already dark, and the car's headlights picked out the eyeshine of something in the branches of the old oak tree. Dower had one foot on the porch when he saw it, and he stepped back into the house and let the screen door slam shut. It might have been a 'possum or a 'coon, but he thought he'd seen the silhouette of something big hugging the trunk of the tree. He picked up the shotgun behind the door and racked it; he'd loaded it with #000 buck earlier in the afternoon. He stepped back out onto the porch, raising the gun to his shoulder as he moved, and fired. The report echoed over the water beyond the tree line. Something heavy hit the turf below the oak. The old tree shivered, shedding twigs and tattered leaves.

He stepped off the porch to check under the Sprint: clear. As he straightened up he saw the second one coming down the driveway, and the shock of seeing it so big and close almost undid him; his foot slipped as he pivoted, but he went down on one knee and fired when it was still ten or twelve feet away. At that range, the tightly grouped load of pellets hit the thing like a giant fist and punched it over backward. It rolled twice and lay still.

Someone emptied a pistol in the middle distance, probably in answer to the blast of the shotgun. It sounded like a .38.

He went back into the house and replaced the shotgun behind the door and picked up the .45 he'd left on the coffee table. He hefted the duffel bag he'd packed earlier and went to the car and got in. He laid the .45 on the seat beside him.

At the entrance to the subdivision, between the two brick columns that said Pineview Place, he paused and looked both ways down Harrisburg Boulevard. To the east he could see the stacks of the Chevron plant belching smoke that glowed pink in the last rays of the sun over the Pasadena skyline; to the west Harrisburg seemed to terminate at the foot of the tall white spire that was One Shell Plaza.

He turned left and put his foot on the gas. He would drive through downtown, in and out of a hundred other cars, and then south to the outskirts of the city. He wouldn't visit his own brand of bad luck on his neighbors.

Old Father howled his rage at the sky. To make himself known in this manner was forbidden, but he didn't care. His sons were gone—both slain by the man—and he knew that it was his own fault. He'd guessed that the man would move in the deep of night, and he'd been wrong.

The pack dragged the bodies of their dead into the underbrush. Later they would return to consume them. But just now they must hunt.

The man had fled in a car, thinking that the wolven could not follow him. But the man was wrong.

To travel under the harsh artificial lights in the heart of the city was dangerous, but Mother Moon looked down on the pack and smiled. The night was their friend, the shadows were their friends, the dull senses of the prey were their friends …

The man thought he had won. But he had not won yet.

The motel was a slovenly building at the end of a crumbling asphalt driveway, a row of peeling front doors under flickering neon. Dower parked the Sprint and stuck the .45 in the waistband of his pants and went to the door marked Office.

The inside was stale and yellowed by decades of cigarette smoke. An old man sat behind the counter and a young woman in pink gym shorts sat on the threadbare couch opposite.

"Help ya?" said the old man.

"I need a room."

The girl smiled when Dower looked over at her.

"Don't mind Casey," said the old man. "Pretend she's part of the furniture. Twenty for the night." He took a key from the rack on the wall behind the register and handed it to Dower. He looked at Dower's ODs, tattered and faded by sun and too many washings. "You a vet?"

"What's it to ya?"

The old man held up his hands. "Nothing but respect here, son."

Dower nodded and went back outside, heard the door creak open behind him, and turned back around, reaching for the .45.

It was the girl in the shorts, still smiling. "You lonely, G.I.? Need some company?"

Dower let his hand fall away from the butt of the gun and shook his head.

"Nah. Just passing through."

"Well, that's not a problem," said the girl, coming close enough that he could smell her: sweat and cigarettes and some candy-flavored mouthwash.

"Some other time," said Dower. He turned away.

"I'll be up front if you change your mind," said the girl to his back.

In the room he laid the heavy nylon bag on the foot of the bed and unzipped it, removed the contents carefully, piece by piece, and laid them out on the bedspread: steel helmet; heavy ceramic body armor, its nylon carrier musty with old sweat; Ka-Bar knife in its shiny leather scabbard; olive-painted steel egg of a fragmentation grenade. He shrugged out of his windbreaker and strapped on the armor and then pulled the windbreaker back on and zipped it up to his neck. He stuck the knife in the top of his boot and set the steel helmet on his head and sat down on the end of the bed. He picked up the grenade and bounced it once in the palm of his hand.

He thought about the girl and her legs below the pink shorts, but he'd come here to get away from people.

The old aluminum window in the bathroom squealed when he opened it. He pulled the pin out of the grenade, squeezing the arming lever tight, and laid it in the groove of the windowsill then jammed the sash down on top of it. Then he left the bathroom, closing the door behind him, set the .45 on the nightstand and lay down on the bed. He hadn't realized how tired he was until that moment, and there wasn't even a book in sight.

The blast of the grenade picked Dower up and threw him off the bed. He landed on the floor with his face jammed into shag carpet that smelled like an old gym locker, his ears ringing. He got to his hands and knees and coughed. The air in the motel room was full of smoke and drywall dust, and he was covered in pulverized gypsum and wood splinters. The corner of the room where the bathroom had been was a smoking ruin. He coughed again and went to the door.

When he stepped out from under the eave of the motel roof, something descended on his shoulders, taking him off his feet and sending him face-first into the gravel of the parking lot. He felt a vast weight on his back. He could hear the ceramic plates of the body armor creaking as they ground together. The M1 was still on his head; it had been shoved back when he hit the ground, and he could feel the steel rim digging into the base of his neck—

Old Father tore at the killer with tooth and claw, but the man would not die.

The covering that all men wore over their tender, hairless skins came away in ribbons, but beneath that was something else, something hard and unyielding. Old Father's talons scraped and squealed and found no purchase.

Enraged, he seized the man by the shoulder and picked him up and shook him. He felt a tooth snap off on the man's hard shell, and then a sudden pain in his side—

The beast howled, and Dower felt the life go out of it in that cry.

The hilt of the Ka-Bar was hot and slimy in his hand. The weight of the thing was killing him, like a car parked on his chest. It slumped over to one side and Dower dropped the knife and pushed it the rest of the way off with his right hand. His left arm hung useless. The beast had picked him up and turned him—to get at his throat, Dower thought—and something had popped in his shoulder then.

He looked up and saw another one on the roof, knew it was already too late. The thing was crouching into a leap that would knock him down again and this time he wouldn't be so lucky. He reached for the bloody Ka-Bar anyway—

From his left and behind came the blast of a shotgun. The thing on the roof was gone. The motel's proprietor had a shotgun half-lowered from his shoulder, both barrels dripping smoke. He was dressed in pajamas and a faded red smoking jacket.

"You all right? Any of that blood yours?"

Dower shook his head. His ears were still ringing. "Don't know. Don't think so."

He wobbled to his feet and drew a long, careful breath: no ribs broken. He ripped open the Velcro straps of the body armor and let it fall.

"Chicken plate," said the old man. "Could've used that on Omaha Beach." He broke open the shotgun and reloaded, fishing shells from the breast pocket of his pajama top.

"Hey," said Dower. "Thanks."

"Aw, shucks, private. It was a slow night, anyway."

"Private? How d'you know I'm not a full-bird colonel?"

The old man bared a mouthful of stained teeth. "Son, an *officer* wouldn't be caught dead in this shithole." He stepped forward and toed the body of the beast. He was wearing big fuzzy slippers. "What the hell is that thing, anyway?"

Dower shook his head. Even in death, the beast had a face too keen to belong to any animal. Its long body possessed the spare, polished symmetry of an ax-helve—

"Anyway, sorry for the delay. I usually keep this loaded with rock salt. Had to think where I left the buck. Hazards of old age."

"You hit the one on the roof?"

"Both barrels! Ran off like it was nothing." The old man glanced at his watch. "By the way, Happy New Year."

The two men looked at each other and laughed.

In the brush behind the motel, Old Dam exhaled a last rattling breath and died. The yearling huddled beside her body in silence. He was alone and young and afraid, but he knew what he must do. He was a wolven, and the wolven were hunters.

And patience was the first quality of the hunt.

Garick Cooke is a hobbyist writer of speculative fiction. In 2021, his first published story, "Moon-Eye," appeared in the e-zine *Zooscape*. A three-time contributor to *Horror Library*, he has also had stories appear in a variety of genre publications, including *Neon Dystopia*, *Dirty Magick*, and *Go West: Frontier Adventures*. This story originally appeared in *Horror Library, Volume 8*, in July 2023.

House Rules
Zelda Knapp

I brought the child into my home. It wasn't quite like the story people told years later. There was no tower. No lock. No climbing her hair to reach her seclusion. But there were always rules. At night she could run through the garden, could dance under the moon, could sing to the stars. My evening bloom, my Jasmine. Her hair grew long, and longer. We braided it back, so it wouldn't catch on the spines in the succulent garden. I raised her kindly. Loved her even, which I had not foreseen. A child I had taken to save a life. My pride and my shame. A bargain I would not have struck had I not been as bound to the rules of the house as any who cross the paving path. She knew how she came to live with me, I who was not her true mother. Weeping and somber, her true mothers had brought their miracle birth to me as reparation after their transgression, and did not return to plead for her. But I could ever feel the ache of their wound across town, as surely as I had felt the blood gouting in my garden the night they stole from me. There are no clean hands in a bargain struck at the house.

Jasmine knew some of the stories about me and my garden, just as she knew the stories of the Guardians of the Creek, who witness all and have a memory longer than water. Jasmine knew the stories about me, but she laughed them off. Who could be scared of old Mam, Mam who needs help braiding her own hair, who goes out to sit on the porch when people come politely calling? Jasmine would listen at the window but knew not to come out. I wondered later if she had been seen anyway, if that was how he found her. Or if he perhaps always knew this would be the bargain struck that night, her life to save theirs. Perhaps he knew the rules of the house, of its garden. That any theft must be paid with that which they prized most. The witch at the south bend in the creek, for sure, he sent her mothers here that night with promises of fertility and healing in exchange for only a little taking. A flower blooms in order to be plucked, he had told them, he who grew no garden of his own. So perhaps he knew, and he merely waited for her to grow into readiness.

It's an ugly story. He came to her in beauty and I did not see, at first. By day he never came to the house, but he would stand across the street to find her in the window. She stayed for hours looking. By night he came to sing with her. And I did not hear, at first. It had been so long since I had seen the witch, and never had I seen him in his beauty. But he came for her. And she wanted him, to leave with him.

What bargain could I strike, to keep her? To keep her locked, I would lose her love. To give her up, I would lose her to whatever purpose he had. And what would it do to the house, to have her break the bargain she had not known she made?

In the end, he took, as men will, with no chance for bargaining. He took her, though the plants tore at his arms, his face, to keep him back. He took her and knocked three times on the newel post as he left. The garden was a ruin. The pear tree was split. And Jasmine was gone.

That was what was underneath the story people would tell later. Under the trappings of prince and curses, thorns and tower. And they would tell it as a daring escape, not as an old woman bound to a house and a bleeding garden, not as an abduction by a witch of waxed veneer and smirking song. That morning, I knelt at the pear tree. I packed its wound with sap. I bound it closed with jasmine vines. I wept over it, and hoped my tears might seal the scar. Some stories speak of healing tears. *Just in case.* I replanted and repaired, my knees creaking as I knelt, my neck as hooded as a buzzard's. As Jasmine's mothers' had been that day. With my nails baked in soil, my hair wisping from its braid, I looked like a wild old witch. I worked all day, thinking quietly. As twilight descended, I sat against the tree and watched the moon, waiting for reply. When night hit full, I took up my stick and began to walk.

They were not pleased to see me, the two women, their hearts shattering over again across their faces. But there are rules and there are stories, and they had enough wine to pour me a cup when I sat down.

"She's been taken. By him, he who sent you. Our bargain is breached." They listened but did not speak. "There is a price." There is always a price.

The dark-haired mother looked down at her clenched hands and whispered, "What more can you take from us?"

I looked at my own hands, the nails still dirty with the day's work. There were no clean hands in a bargain struck at the house. "I have no further demands on you, who fulfilled already the payment fourteen years ago. But I may ask, and you may refuse. He cannot mean her well, and I would bring her home. With your help, if you will give it. To yours or mine, I do not care, but—I would bring her home."

They did not understand at first. There are different ways of being what I am, what we are. I am like the Guardians of the Creek. I would be left alone to tend my garden, I speak to those who approach kindly, I advise but I do not invite. I tend to the house, and the house tends to me. There are rules that must be followed, and sometimes stories are told.

This witch chooses a parasite's path, one which gives him beauty but which takes and takes without satiation. He will take and he will not care. In a bargain with him there is always a loser and that loser is never him. I told the women, we do not go to bargain. He came to the house and he took what was not his to take. There is and must always be a price.

I do not make the rules.

But I do choose the execution.

And so the three of us left for the house at the south bend in the creek to take her back. I walked evenly, my thoughts turning over the problem. The price the house demands from those who take. The thing they prize most. For the women, it had been their child, not yet born. For him — was it his beauty? Easily marred, easily mended, for such as he. His power? Not given with an open hand. His life? He must have several to spare. And he cannot keep Jasmine's.

"If we do this," the fair-haired mother spoke as we arrived at the gate, "if we win her back. She comes home with us. That is the new bargain."

A curtain at the front window stirred — Jasmine's face, peering at the three of us. I felt the wall of the witch's spell, a dense choking screen holding us back.

"That is the new bargain," I agreed. I turned to grasp her hand, her wife's hand too, holding her gaze a full ten seconds, then the other's. Sealing the contract. "Wait here."

I walked alone to the creek, bowing my head in acknowledgement of the Guardians. I knew he would come to me; he could not resist a gloat.

"It really is a shame," came a murmuring voice, over-sticky with a honey charm, "how the only use you found for her was to let her sing in that foolish garden. Such a waste."

"She is not a tool, nor a toy. I saved three lives when I took her in, as you would know if you knew the value of a good garden."

He snorted delicately. "But so fragile, so easily mussed. And all that time in the dirt."

"An injured garden is readily tended, with enough respect for the dirt."

"In any event, was her life ever yours to save? I say it was always mine."

I held still, turning my head just slightly to eye him. "Yours then? Is that the bargain you struck with them?"

Another snort. "A gardener such as you knows all that grows must have a seed. Of course I took her. She was always mine to take."

"A gardener such as I knows a seed is sterile without the nurture. And that which sheds a seed and vanishes is no such nurture, and has no such rights. She is not your bloom."

"Ah, but you bargain differently than I, old woman. I lent those fools my most valuable gift, but I did not say they could keep it. She is but a debt collected. And my use of her is not for your care."

"You would use your own child this way."

"My child!" A harsh laugh. "She deserves no such honor. She is the seed grown, the harvest to be reaped."

He did not say but I began to hear. The thing he valued most: his seed. I could wish he would be less predictably male, but then—

"You have taken from my garden that which was not yours," I spoke slowly, the magic of the house's rules a thick smoke to carry the words. "That which *the house* recognizes was not yours. You have taken." Within the cloak of the house's rules, I saw the shimmering silver bond of the mothers' loves, a final trade offered in our contract.

"She was ever more mine than yours," he sneered, but his words had no weight, no air within the building power of my magic, not against the honest witness of the Guardians of the Creek.

"You have taken, and you will return, but that will not be the end. Your seed is gone and shall not flower again. You can no longer reap from these or any others."

"Ridicul—" he tried to say, but choked on the air as he felt the bargain take hold.

"I will not take your life, for what value is that to me? But I have taken your life-giver. What you do from here matters less than a dust mote. The Guardians have witnessed."

I returned to the mothers through the house, Jasmine with me. The spell he'd woven was now easily enough turned to scattering sand, with both her mothers standing at the gate. Perhaps they did not know the magic inherent even in that, but it was they who turned the bolt in the door. And though she'd had but days with them, she knew her mothers and ran to them, the three weeping. Four weeping, if we must be honest, and we must.

She hesitated once, my Jasmine—my Jasmine for a few breaths longer—to look back at me. She took a step back, even as they held her. I shook my head, once. "A bargain struck, a bargain ended. Perhaps you were no more mine to keep than his." Eight more steps she took, a kiss blessed on my cheek, and then the three were gone.

I have heard whispers of other stories since that time, of one of the fair folk come down from the river source to empty he who lived by the south bend until he was a husk, splintered and peeling in his dryness. I have heard of a great battle where the Guardians of the Creek struck down an ogre who stole a damsel of the village. A beautiful prince dissolved into mud when he disdained a sorceress in disguise. A dragon beheaded. Sometimes even I hear whispers that I, the garden witch who stays by her porch, had witnessed the battle, and perhaps I could be persuaded to tell them the story, if they could but find the right question to ask. So they call on me, knocking three times on the newel post. Some of them even note that a young woman with long hair visits often without bringing her own questions, but just to sit, and they wonder. Wonder, but do not ask.

People want to believe in the stories, want to believe that they are not just stories. And they have sense enough to tread as if they *might* be true. *Just in case.* So they don't throw things into the creek. They don't pick pears after twilight. They always save enough wine to fill one more cup, for the unexpected visitor. And when they pay a call to me, they walk up the paving path and don't touch the succulent garden. They knock three times on the newel post of the porch, and they wait. *Just in case.*

For if the stories could be true, then all the cannot-bes of the world could suddenly turn possible.

And perhaps they can be.

I don't make the rules.

Zelda Knapp writes fiction, poetry, plays, theater reviews, and academic articles. In addition to her collection, *This Is What They Made It Out Of: tales from the end of the world*, she's published with a variety of journals and books, and has produced four of her plays in NYC. She can be found at www.zeldaknapp.com.

Mixed Emotions
Jacinta Palmer

Marron hurried along the dusty walkway, hugging the wall as much for shade as for anonymity. It was not yet ten in the morning, but the heat of the city dampened her hair at the nape of her neck. Her nose was assaulted with smells as trade awoke, roasting coffee from restaurants and cafes, earthy and sharp aromas of the fruit and vegetables in the covered market layered with the cloying, yeasty smell that cloaked the breweries. The streets were not yet bustling with the smart people, but for the minions who oiled the wheels of this world, the working day was well underway.

She turned down a side street, burrowing deeper into the poorer district, where odors from bad drains and burnt tyres provided the top notes, so Marron tried breathing through her mouth. To reassure herself she patted the breast pocket of her coveralls. The shape of the small vials she carried lent her comfort, alongside a stab of anxiety, which she tried to quell.

The people in this district did not move with purpose. Instead, the adults, mostly men, loitered with expressionless faces, their body language telegraphing hopelessness and despair. Time hung heavy on their hands, without work to give them purpose and self-respect. The children here were scrawny and dirty, but they scraped together games to play. Marron observed a handful of them crouched in the gutter, watching beetles race, their small faces avid with concentration. As she turned down another grim alley, she heard a girl's whoop of triumph behind her and smiled; her beetle must've won.

She saw the doorway up ahead, perhaps originally blue, but now its paint was peeled and faded to almost the same shade of grey as the weathered wood it once protected. When she pushed at the door, the bell sounded as exhausted as the man it summoned.

"Collection or deposit?" he asked, ready to scribe it.

"Collection," she responded tightly, fingering the credits in her pocket.

He handed her a perspex sheet, inscribed with a list of options for her to peruse, but Marron had done her research and already knew what she wanted. The question was, did she have enough credits?

She scanned the list, unsurprised to see emotions that any person, rich or poor, might experience required few credits. In this insalubrious place, she couldn't even give away common emotions such as uncertainty, embarrassment, or anxiety. Likewise, many negative emotions, sadness, frustration, despair, resentment, and disgust were not sought after. It was a matter of supply and demand, especially on the black market.

She chinked the credits in her pocket, knew they were not enough for invigorate, and optimism was priced out of her league. Marron's shoulders drooped with disappointment, but the carefully wrapped packet of vials waited in her pocket-if she only had the confidence to offer them.

The man behind the counter flicked an irritated glance her way. He didn't have all day; it was written loud and clear on his gaunt face.

Marron shuffled her feet and cleared her throat, uneasy about breaking the law. She knew it had to be here. She couldn't make this transaction at a government-controlled emotion dispensing clinic. And it had to be now; the current trajectory of sickness was rapidly diminishing her window of opportunity.

"Before I collect, I have a deposit," Marron said in a rush.

She stood, armpits pricking with sweat following her announcement, but it was just another routine for the man. He muttered under his breath but placed two sterilized vials and stoppers on the counter.

He passed her another perspex tariff, which showed lower rates than if she was purchasing. She pushed the tariff back at him.

"This is new," she said, her voice softened with caution, but she pressed on. "I've found a way to mix emotions and create a spin-off."

The man said nothing, but Marron knew she had his full attention. She dipped her hand into her pocket and produced two pipettes with clear fluid in each.

"This is crush," she indicated the one with a green band around it. "It's aimed at businessmen making deals, students taking exams, people going for interviews, or wanting to make a stellar first impression. I've blended three emotions: focus, ambition, and tenacity."

The merchant had 'poker face' down to a fine art.

"Do you want to try it?" Marron held her breath.

He beckoned her to join him on the other side of the counter, then ushered her into a pokey room, lined with numbered cubby holes. She presumed it was the filing system, for their bottled stock of emotions. He pressed a buzzer and waited.

Soon they were joined by a stick-thin youth in his early twenties. His face was bland and slack, a sure sign he'd been selling his emotions. He'd never get them back, or the memories associated with them, but he could possibly experience them again if he didn't drain his well too deep.

"I need you to try an emotion," his employer told him gruffly.

The youth nodded and opened his mouth, putting out his tongue. Marron let one drop of crush fall on the glistening pink of its surface.

The effect was instantaneous. The youth's body language altered, he stood tall with shoulders back and his expression sharpened with intent.

"How'd you feel?" The merchant asked suspiciously.

"I feel great-sharp as a tack, really motivated. Boss, I have an idea I've been meaning to share, a new place to seek donations and …"

The merchant cut him off with a raised hand. "Later Effrin, back to work. We'll talk after I serve this gal."

"I'd like to stay and watch, Kruup, I reckon I could learn to take donations, and today's as good as any to start."

The merchant gave him a withering stare, but turned to Marron with more interest than previously.

"How much do you have of crush?" he asked.

"Ten mil," she replied.

"What's in the other pipette?" Kruup asked.

"I call that flare," she explained.

"What does that do?" Effrin stepped closer.

The fluid looked the same as the other vial, but the pipette had a yellow band around it.

"Do you want to try it?" Marron asked Kruup. "It's too soon for Effrin to absorb another emotion," she cautioned.

Effrin looked as if he could take on the world, but that was part of the blended emotion's effect. The merchant gave Marron an assessing look and pressed the buzzer again. An old woman soon shuffled into the room.

"I need you to try an emotion, Zorelle," Kruup raised his voice, from which Marron guessed Zorelle was a little deaf.

Zorelle opened her mouth, as Effrin had done, and Marron released one drop, to splash onto the older woman's tongue. The transformation happened in moments. A smile split Zorelle's lined face and she appeared younger and more carefree. She looked around at her companions, as if waking from a pleasant dream.

"What was that dear?" she inquired of Marron. "I feel boosted, like I could fly or dance; I want to do something fun!"

"I've blended joy with a small portion of agitation. Unlike the synthetic joy the government sells, but only to those who fit their criteria, a person experiences bliss, minus any lethargy.

"Taking flare makes you feel euphoric but still motivated." Marron enunciated the last part loudly, for the old woman to hear.

"Exactly," trilled Zorelle, flouncing about like a girl with dreams of being a ballerina.

"How much of that have you brought?"

Effrin prepared to calculate the profit that could be made. When Marron supplied her answer, his fingers flew over the keys of the adding device, Kruup looking over his shoulder with keen interest.

"We could offer you –"

But Marron held up her hand to Kruup, pausing the negotiations.

"I don't want credits, I want a vial of optimism and one of invigorate."

That stopped the merchant in his tracks. Optimism was a gold-tier emotion, but both were rare and costly. He sucked his teeth while he considered, then Effrin pulled him into a huddle and they spoke in murmurs.

"How long does this last?" Zorelle asked Marron, ignoring the men and their deliberations.

"About two hours," Marron held up two fingers, to be sure Zorelle understood.

"I'm off to have a good time," Zorelle announced to no one in particular, before she left the shop.

"Can you make more?" Effrin asked.

"Maybe." Marron had planned this as a one-time deal, but of course they were greedy for more.

Kruup clasped Marron's hand to shake, and with the deal sealed, she passed over the precious pipettes. She watched as he stored them carefully, in a dark, padded box, and wrote their names on each. Then he reached down two similar boxes, from which he dispensed just a droplet of each emotion into travel vials for Marron.

When she moved to take the rare liquid, he noticed the bar code tattooed on her wrist and paused. His face became guarded.

"You work for the authorities?"

Effrin looked nervous.

"The children's hospital," she explained, and the men relaxed again.

"Come back soon," Kruup told her.

Marron left the shop, making the bell ring dully.

She hurried along the weed-infested pavements, passing more broken men with the same vacant expressions she had observed earlier. In them, she recognized the look of people who'd sold too many emotions and hollowed themselves out.

On the street corner she saw the children again. They were playing some kind of tag game and Zorelle had joined them. Her face was transformed by the simple pleasure of relaxed human interaction, and Marron felt true joy to see it.

In a few more twists and turns Marron was back on the main drag where the city had come to life. The sky trains shuttled overhead and people went about their daily business. Marron took the familiar route to the hospital, where she stowed her coverall in a locker.

She showered and put on fresh scrubs; routines which kept the transference of germs to a minimum. Then she walked to Fleek's ward.

Marron had a smile or a kind word for all her patients, but Fleek was special, he'd managed to touch her heart. He appeared tiny and frail in the clinical surroundings, his bed crowded with medical equipment.

Today she was bringing him hope, literally. She had it in liquid form in her pocket.

Marron drew the curtains around his bed, then slipped one of the two vials from her pocket. She'd picked up a mini cupcake from the nurse's station, and with sleight of hand, she put a drop of the precious essence onto the cake's icing.

"Dig in little man, it's your birthday treat."

Marron watched with trepidation as the sickly boy bit into the cake. He didn't usually have much appetite, and it hurt to think he was eating to please her. As Fleek chewed slowly, her heart went into her mouth: Would the emotions work? Was Kruup a good source? Had she left it too late for the emotions to be of help?

Fleek's face began to change, initially with a grin through the chocolate frosting smeared over his lips.

"This is good cake Nurse Marron!" he affirmed, in his soft voice.

"Have some more." She smiled.

"I think I will," he declared excitedly.

Taking another bite he chewed, then pushed himself up to sitting. "Is the sun shining today, Nurse Marron?"

"It is, Fleek," she was already encouraged by the colour in his cheeks.

"Could we go for a walk? I'd like to see the birds on the lake."

"Sure," she smiled, blinking, "I'll wrap you up, and push you outside. Let me fetch a wheelchair," and she ducked out of his cubicle.

She hurried out of the Oncology ward, back to the locker rooms. Taking a moment to ensure she was alone, Marron located a clean vial, which she pressed to her eye to catch her precious tears of joy.

Jacinta Palmer writes fantasy fiction that blends the speculative, the magical, and the romantic, sometimes influenced by folklore or the supernatural. Her work spans from lighthearted, cozy tales to darker narratives with menace, always with a focus on transporting readers into immersive worlds and unforgettable adventures.

Broken River Cantina I
Desmond Astaire

I'm drunk but not drunk enough. It don't count until the aching's gone, that's for goddamn sure. So, I tell the Bartender to turn that Three Wisemen into a Nine Wisemen. That's multiplication. It's science. I gulp down my whiskey in one big chug, and the burning hits hard like a drink's supposed to. *Ugh.* Maybe too hard. I stifle a sloshing from my stomach, wave down the Bartender for a pint of beer, and fiddle with the silver dollar I found outside while I wait.

I'd pulled my truck off of Highway 32 to take a piss by the privacy of the trees by the river. It was every bit of a record-setting, frozen December in Michigan and there was probably a warm bar a few miles ahead, but you know what they say about when nature calls. I would've finished and left, but while I was lighting a smoke I saw a shiny little something sparkling in the dirt. Sure as shit, it was an 1893 Morgan silver dollar—100 years old—with a slick, old art deco ad sticker on it that read "Broken River Cantina."

"Where'm the fuck issat?" I asked myself. I didn't have the answer, which was unusual. I may have only been twenty-five, but you'd better believe Joey Bridges was either a V.I.P. regular or banned at every bar in the tri-county area—and I'd never heard of the Broken River Cantina. An overhead light popped on over to my right that answered my question, though. I turned around and, sure enough, there was a dive bar staring right at me that most certainly had not been there a hot minute before. I knew I was tanked but not tanked enough to have missed an entire building, I don't think. And yet, there it was, and the sign above the entrance read "Broken River Cantina." It looked as good as any other joint to continue my bar crawl, so of course I walked in.

I'd never seen a bar like this before. The interior was all warm wood and old, orange light, like a log cabin-turned-dive bar. And it's warm. Not like the heat was turned on, but like it was a summer evening. All across the room, there were names and dates written or carved on the log walls and joists. Dozens, maybe a hundred. But tonight the crowd was about as sparse as you'd imagine for a Tuesday, with certainly no outstanding selection of women to go home with and no dudes looking like they were asking for a fight. That was okay; I'd just have a few drinks and be on my way to mosey to the next stop on my nightly adventure.

"You're supposed to be here, kid?" the Bartender asks. He looks around mid-forties, slight build, dark hair over his ears, with a thick mustache over a scruffy face. I could take him. Fighting words with the staff was not how I wanted to start any visit, but nobody ever talks down to me. And if they do, I make sure we tangle over it so they don't forget their mistake.

"Who says'm not, dude? 'Sup?" I ask.

"You misheard me, friend," the Bartender says. "That was a statement, not a question. You're supposed to be here. Welcome." He nods at my hand, where I am still holding the stickered silver dollar. "That there's your token to get in. Can I see it?"

I accept the miscommunication, mosey up to the wood bar, and slide the coin on the countertop.

"Oooh, an 1893 Morgan," the Bartender says, examining it close in his hand. "She's been out traveling for a while. Thanks for bringing it back. What can I get you?"

"Can you do, um… a Three Wise'im?" I ask.

"Jack, Jim, and Johnnie?"

"Yah, that'um," I say. "Make 'er a triple."

"You got it."

The drinks are good and strong—I can taste that much—but the more time I spend in the bar, the less drunk I feel. My head gets clearer and more level as time goes on, and I don't like it. That's not what I'm here for. But I don't want to start no trouble about it, so I give the cantina one more chance with a double shot of silver tequila and a menthol cigarette chaser.

"Cool if I smoke in here?" I ask the Bartender.

"Depends," he says. "What year is it?"

I laugh and the cig almost falls from my lips. "It's 1993, jackass."

"Oh yeah, 1993's all good," the Bartender says.

"You've got a weird sense of humor, man," I say while lighting the cigarette, and we laugh about it.

"Ahhh, you never know," the Bartender says. "Different rules for different years; 2010, very bad year for smoking inside."

"What the hell, man?" I don't get it.

"Doesn't matter in here anyway," the Bartender says, "but I always like to ask."

He says that last bit with such a straight face. If there's a joke or punchline or something in there, it's going way over my head. No, instead, there's an itch on the back of my neck telling me something's off about the whole place. And the more I look, the more I see. There's music coming from a jukebox—it's playing everything from Glenn Miller Band to Pearl Jam to some new stuff I've never even heard yet—but no TVs. And no windows. The clock on the wall don't have hour or minute hands. Just a second hand ticking and spinning around and around. The digital clock back behind the bar reads, "00:00," and it's not blinking like it's lost power or something.

Yeah. I've declined to barely tipsy now and fully weirded out, so I stand from my stool to leave.

I flip out a couple of ten-dollar bills onto the bar—should be plenty to cover my drinks and a tip—and leave the stickered dollar. But the Bartender puts down a firm grasp over my forearm.

"Why don't you hang out just a little bit longer?" he asks me. "Pick out an appetizer—on the house."

"I'm good; I can drive," I mumble.

"No, it's not that," the Bartender says. "It's *her*."

He nods toward the back of the bar, where a woman sits alone in the corner at one of the cocktail tables. She's watching us with steely blue eyes that just catch a twinkle of the track lights. She nervously brushes a wisp of hair out of her face when she realizes she's been noticed, and it's a lovely shade of gold blurring into platinum. She's gorgeous, for her age. I'll give him that. But she's maybe in her early 60s? My cutoff for picking up chicks is usually twice my age.

"I don't know who that is," I say.

"I know," the Bartender says. "You haven't met her yet, but she's known you for a very long time."

I yank my arm back and square off with the Bartender, my fist drawn back. "What the hell is this place, man? And who the hell are you?" I demand. "If this is one of those kidney-stealing operations, I swear to God--"

The Bartender puts his hand on my shoulder, and some calming power washes over me. It's warm, like a blanket. I can't even fight back. "Nothing like that at all, Joey. This place is a very special moment in the universe—where the equation meets the event horizon. And me? I'm just the guy serving the drinks." He raps his fingers across the wood bar and gives me a wink as if he's just revealed the secrets of the universe, and I remain frozen in my utter confusion. Calm but confused. The

Bartender takes the opportunity to step back from the bar with a reassuring smile, and then I realize the woman is now sitting next to me staring a hole into the side of my head.

Oh, what the hell. I give up, crank up the old Joe Bridges charm, and offer her a handshake and a smile. "Joey."

"Audrey." The woman takes my hand, and her voice sounds like Main Street on a summer Saturday night, when the amber lights shine down on the sidewalk and you're on top of the world. Her smile is just as exciting. Her touch on my hand feels electric and familiar, like something I've known forever, or been searching for just as long. I don't understand. She's magnetic, and I'm enchanted.

"Who are you, Audrey?"

She smiles inward, sheepish. Bashfulness is a sensation she's not used to, if I had to guess. But we're in some sort of unique situation here. "I, uh-- Well, I've worked in healthcare my whole life," she says. "Hospitals, intensive care, emergency department, stuff like that. I dunno. I think it's given me an eye for stories, and you just seem like you've got one."

I chuckle and take a sip of one of the two fresh draft beers that have appeared in front of us. "No story here, Audrey," I say. "I work second shift at the factory during the day and party at night. Wake up, rinse, and repeat."

Audrey's smile melts ever so slightly into a look of concern. "Do you enjoy it?"

"I *love* it," I say, punctuating the statement with a healthy gulp of beer. "Do whatever I want, whoever I want, whenever I want, seven days a week. What's not to enjoy?" I make it sound as glorious as I wish it were, but even I know I'm lying.

"What I mean is, did you ever dream of more?" Audrey asks.

"I dunno. No. Not really. Life's a game of poker, God's an asshole dealer, and I've been dealt a shit hand of cards my whole life. I'm just playing the cards I'm dealt. What can I say? That's my story."

"Can I tell you a story, then?" Audrey asks. Geeze, how can I say no to those hypnotic blue eyes? She takes my hand in hers like she's making sure I'm not going nowhere. "Twenty-four years ago, I was driving home from work. It was about 11:30 p.m., just after my shift at the hospital. I'll never forget how bitter and dark and cold it was that night. But I saw a man walking down the side of the road, out in the middle of nowhere. Not hitching or anything, just walking. It was *so* cold.

"So, I pulled over to offer the guy a ride into town. But he doesn't want it. He just stares at me and keeps walking, like he's invincible or has a death wish or something. He was clearly drunk, and I tried to talk to him a few more times, tried to talk him into going to the hospital with me, but he wasn't having it. Not a single word. So, I went ahead and kept going. I called the police when I got home to tell them what I saw, just to be safe.

"A few days later the newspaper did a story about how a local guy was found frozen to death along the river. All alone. They ran his name and photo. It was the same guy I saw. I know it was him. It absolutely broke my heart. I couldn't get him out of my head. I felt *drawn* to him. So, I started looking into him, who he was, all that. I researched the man, got to know him, learned just about everything about him. I could start to see who he was, who he could've been, what he might've done with his life. I can't explain why I got obsessed, but I thought about him all the time. I loved everything about him—the good, bad, and ugly. He was a beautiful soul. Broken, but beautiful. The world lost something when he died. Today would've been his fiftieth birthday. I've been out here dozens of times, I guess to feel close to him. This is where they found his truck. They figured it died here and he walked for help. That's when I saw him. I knew this guy for maybe ninety seconds, but he's been living in my head for the last two decades. How do you explain that?"

I sigh and clink my drink with Audrey's. "I'd say it's guilt. You think you could've done more, that his death is on you for not trying hard enough. But you work in healthcare, so you know that's not how it works. People live, and people die. You do your best to intervene, but sometimes it's just not in the cards. So, maybe there's something more to it. Maybe you were supposed to meet this guy, but the stars just didn't align quite right. Maybe he was your soulmate. Maybe something went wrong and he died too soon, but the cosmic connection or whatever between you two didn't, and you had to go on living feeling that. Maybe you got dealt a shit hand, too."

"Maybe we can stack the cards on the next hand," Audrey says.

"What?" I light another cigarette and offer one to Audrey.

She declines, with a polite smile. "Hardly anyone smokes anymore where I'm from," she says.

"No kidding. Where's that?" I ask.

"2017."

"'2017?' What, is that like a Canadian zip code or something?"

"No, Joey. The year 2017."

"I'm not following."

Audrey moves in close and takes my free hand in hers. "The guy I found on the side of the road, the guy who died?" she says. "His name was Joseph Allen Bridges. He died on December 11, 1993. He was just twenty-five."

My seat becomes an electric chair and the stool topples onto the floor when I jump off it. The woman has to be crazy, a total nutcase, maybe a stalker. That's the only way to explain it. I back away from her to make a run for the door. But the Bartender catches my eye first, and I'm paralyzed. He don't even have to say nothing. He just nods at me, and somehow my tank is filled up with just enough reassurance to hesitate.

"What *is* this place?" I demand again.

"Just a bar for people who need it, at the right place, at the right time," the Bartender says. He nods to Audrey. "She's the one you should really get to know."

Audrey meets me where I am. "I would've liked to meet you twenty-four years ago," she says. "Maybe given you a ride to the hospital? They had a pretty good alcohol recovery program there. Who knows what might've happened if you had a second chance."

What is that look in her eyes? Like they're begging me a question I'm supposed to answer. Maybe it's the booze wearing off. Maybe I'm just tired. I know I'm exhausted. But that's life. No, that look is projecting something to me. I barely recognize it. I've certainly never felt it before from another human being, not for as long as I can remember.

It's compassion.

A slinky country song heavy on the piano comes on the jukebox and Audrey puts her hands around the back of my neck. It's the kind of song you can't not slow-dance to, so I give in. I put my hands on her hips and we sway to the tune. It's methodical, rhythmic, like a lullaby. Between that and the dark ambiance of the bar, I finally start to relax and accept. It's a good feeling, relief. My entire upper body unclenches from the tension I didn't realize I was carrying, and Audrey pulls us in closer until her head is resting on my chest while we dance.

So, we sit, talk, drink, play pool, dance to the jukebox. I don't know how much time passes, if time even passes in this place. Hours and hours. Maybe the whole night. At one point, we brush too close to each other and our eyes get stuck. We kiss—gently, cautiously, at first. Then, like we've been looking for each other for years.

"Please take the ride," she begs me. "Check into the hospital. Get cleaned up. Then call me. I've never been so sure of anything in my life." Audrey takes a piece of paper and forces it into my hands. She tells me it's her phone number in 1993. "Promise me, Joey."

What can I possibly say? I don't promise her anything. I know the path I'm on is a roundabout to nowhere. I know I keep hitting the gas, seeing how fast I can go. I even know it's only a matter of time before I lose control and spin out. I'm not a complete idiot; I'm just playing the cards I've been dealt. I don't know how bad the crash will be, but of course, I know it's coming. Maybe I want it to happen. Maybe I want it to all be over. Maybe this is my path all along. But what was it that Audrey said earlier?

"Maybe we can stack the cards on the next hand."

"Just a bar for people who need it at the right place, at the right time."

Although there is no passage of time in the cantina, we both eventually feel when our moment together has come to an end. It's not the Bartender. There's no last call, no cut-off. It's just a sensation in our guts that it's time. I think it's the front door. It's calling out to me, drawing me closer and closer. Pulling me back.

"If I go back out there, the future's changed and you won't exist," I say. "What happens to you?"

Audrey stares at the front door for a few moments, and I think she's looking into her non-existent future. She wraps her fingers around mine and squeezes like she never wants to forget the sensation.

"I don't know what will happen when we walk out those doors," Audrey says. "But I have to take the risk. And I'm not leaving here without you." Audrey wraps her arm around mine and we walk each other to the exit.

"Have a good night, folks," the Bartender says. Or did he say *life*?

I open the door into the unknown and exit first. Audrey follows close behind, and then--

Nothing.

There's nothing surrounding me except the woodland forest by the riverside where I've pulled over for a bathroom break. No bar. No Audrey. I'm all alone in the quiet cold, just where I started. And the drunk is back, with a vengeance. The world is spinning around me like my head's on a swivel and my feet don't know which way's up.

How drunk am I? Did I blackout? Was the cantina a dream? The more I stand dumbfounded in the bitter winter, the more distant the place feels.

I am confused and disoriented, but it's too cold to figure it out here. I make my way back to my truck, but the battery is dead. I left the headlights on, and now the truck won't turn over. So, it looks like I'm hiking it to the next bar for a payphone. The temperature is nasty frigid; the kind of cold that makes it feel like your skin is peeling off in the wind. I don't have a coat or hat, just like I don't have a choice. I don't know where the next bar is, or how far away it is. So I pick a direction and start walking.

Solitude and physical discomfort are a recipe for introspection, depression, and pity. Enough time for me to think back to every mistake I've made, every hurt I've felt, every trauma I collected. All the way back to the beginning. All the things that made me who I am. All the things I try to drink away every night. And it works, for a while. Until it don't. But those are the cards I play.

I'm going to die.

Several miles in and I can't feel my fingers or toes no more. I haven't seen a single car pass by. Maybe this is how it's supposed to end: a pathetic drunk frozen to death on the side of the road. I don't deserve no better. I certainly wouldn't expect the universe to write me a check for nothing else. But screw the universe, I'll at least keep moving my legs left and right until I can't do that no more either, just out of defiance. That's who I am. A defiant son of a bitch.

Eventually, to my surprise, I see headlights coming from ahead in the distance. Finally.

The truck pulls over alongside me and the driver rolls down the window.

"Hey! You need a ride?"

Her voice is beautifully melodic and vibrant. I remember it. I think I remember it. It's the same voice that told me what was at the end of the road ahead of me. It's the same voice offering me the chance at respite now.

This is it. The final cards are dealt, no more draws, no more bets. It's time to show the table what I've got.

I've got nothing. Not even the high card. The dealer smirks. He's invincible; he don't give a shit what I have, because we're all just players on his table, and you know the saying—the house always wins.

But Joey Bridges doesn't go down without a fight. This time I smirk back at the dealer, stand up and leave the table. He's confused. I win, because I'm not going to lose anymore.

"You need a ride?" she asks again.

"Yes, please," I tell Audrey.

"Jump in," she says. "It's freezing!" Her truck is warm, like a blanket that beckons you right into the comfort of sleep. Her voice immediately wakes me back up. "Where are you heading?"

That's a powerful question. My go-to answer for that used to be, "Straight to hell if I don't change my ways." But now I don't feel it's right to say it, joke or not. My voice cracks under the weight of the emotion, and hot tears sting the frozen corners of my tired eyes. "Hosp'tl."

There's an ever-so-slight hesitation in Audrey's voice like she's beginning to understand a larger, unseen picture. "Are you okay?"

"Jus' drunk too much."

"No problem. You got it," Audrey says. She cranks up the heater and gives my knee a rub. "Hang in there. You're going to be all right."

I focus so hard to enunciate my next words. So they're heard. So they're understood.

"Thanks—for the ride."

Sometimes there's a dive bar nestled against the riverbank pine in Alpena, Michigan. The Broken River Cantina hides outside of time, serving the right guests at the right moments — the bartender, the photographer, our vigilante, a sinner and a saint, the counselor, an executive, and so on and so forth. It's said a stickered silver dollar is the token that gets you through the phantom bar's doors. But when you exit them, you'll find nothing around you but crickets and moonlit clouds. Eventually, you'll begin to wonder if you imagined the cabin tavern where the clock always reads 0:00 p.m. Rest assured, however. That which you need — what was found at the Broken River Cantina — will never fade away.

Desmond Astaire is an award-winning, best-selling science fiction and fantasy author from Central Illinois. He was first published in *Writers of the Future Vol. 38*, for which his short story "Gallows" received the L. Ron Hubbard Golden Pen Award.

We hope you enjoy reading this anthology as much as we enjoyed compiling it.

Our open submissions call was so successful that we decided to publish *Volume I* and *Volume II*, the same as we did for our last anthology, *Ruth and Ann's Guide to Time Travel*. *Volume II* will be released two to three months after *Volume I*. You can find out when it'll be published, and also information about other open submission calls, by visiting our website: celestialechopress.com, signing up for our periodic newsletter, and/or joining our Celestial Echo Press Facebook group.

About Celestial Echo Press

A few years ago, Gemini Wordsmiths LLC's partner, Ruth Littner, had a crazy idea to expand into publishing. That crazy idea became reality in June 2019 when we formed Celestial Echo Press. Our first anthology, *The Twofer Compendium*, contains 36 stories based on the theme of twins, penned by 34 international authors. *The Trench Coat Chronicles* was our second anthology. *Ruth and Ann's Guide to Time Travel Volume I* was our third, and *Volume II* our fourth.

We are deep in thought about where we go from here. …

Thanks for joining us in our adventure!

About Gemini Wordsmiths LLC

Gemini Wordsmiths, LLC, a woman-owned editing, copywriting, and proofreading business, was founded in 2011 in Abington, Pennsylvania. As karma would have it, Ruth, Ann, and Gemini Wordsmiths were all born under the astrological sign of Gemini.

Every project is given the same intense review, regardless of whether it is a one-page document or a 100,000-word novel. And instead of getting one editor for their dollars, our clients receive a second set of eyes at the same cost, as both editors review each project separately and then collaboratively. For more information visit geminiwordsmiths.com.

Other publications from Celestial Echo Press

A POETIC PUZZLE, A MYSTERY IN 32 PIECES

Internationally acclaimed poet Mary Irene Jones has vanished-calls and texts unacknowledged, bank accounts emptied, car abandoned. But before she disappeared, she mailed never-published manuscripts to a lesser-known namesake poet, M. Irene "Mimi" Jones. Are the manuscripts clues only Mimi can decipher? And what about the handsome Philadelphia cop assigned to the case? He seems as intrigued by Mimi as by the missing celebrity poet. Talk about a person of interest...

We had so many submissions for *Ruth and Ann's Guide to Time Travel*, that we decided to publish *Volume I* and *Volume II*.

Volume I contains stories written by 21 authors: Jonathan Maberry, James Ryan, Teel James Glenn, David C. Strickler, Phil Giunta, Joanne McLaughlin, Gordon Linzner, Judith Field, Carol Gyzander, Ken Altabef, Charles Barouch, Grigory Lukin, Gary Every, Ef Deal, Neal Wiser, Brenda W. Clough, Daniel Lumpkin, John Bukowski, Stephen W. Chappell, Karen Eisenbrey, and Jon McGoran.

Volume II contains stories written by 30 authors: Abigail Gervase, Andrew Majors, Brandon Barrows, CJ Erick, Darrell Schweitzer, David Partington, Elizabeth Davis, Garrett Rowlan, Gary Every, Gary Zenker, Heidi Voss, James Harper, James Pyles, Janet A. Hopkins, John Haas, Kara Race-Moore, Ken Altabef, Ken Goldman, Kerry Gans, L.N. Hunter, Lance Schonberg, Larry Hodges, Marisca Pichette, Michael A. Ventrella, Rik Hoskin, Sandra Skalski, Steve Davidson, Toni V. Sweeney, Trisha Ridinger McKee, and William R.D. Wood.

CHASING ASHES

In 1992, shortly before a tragic fire on their college campus, Laura Cunningham saw her best friend, Kate McDonald, for the last time. The fire's 20th anniversary elicits Laura's guilt and ignites her passion to learn what actually happened to Kate. Now a journalist, Laura teams up with her hot detective ex-husband to pursue cold leads in hopes of sparking interest in the decades-old mystery of what happened that day.

DRACULAND

A New York City real estate developer decides to buy Dracula's Castle in Romania and turn it into a theme park. Not her best idea.

TIME BLINKED

Just like Dorothy in the Wizard of Oz, college athlete Bobby spends his days with those he loves and stays close to home. But unlike Dorothy, when Bobby's "tornado" bushwhacks his world, it doesn't move him into a fantastical realm of color and delightful beasts. He is propelled into a complicated past, where his dreams come true through a somewhat mystifying, somewhat terrifying wrinkle.

THE TRENCH COAT CHRONICLES

This murder mystery anthology is dedicated to Sam Spade, Hercule Poirot, and Dick Tracy, as well as to all the writers of hard-boiled detective stories of years past, many of whom formed the basis for the crime mysteries we read today. Enjoy this wide variety of storylines, each of which includes criminals, victims – and trench coats.

THE TWOFER COMPENDIUM

"Twins are said to share special bonds, understand each other's unspoken communication, speak their own languages, even possess powers of ESP. Their doubleness continues to fascinate the rest of us. Adored or abhorred, sheltered or shunned, twins have universally and perpetually aroused attention and curiosity. It was that fascination that inspired this collection of twin-themed stories. In them, you'll find all matter of twins: the good, the bad, the fantastic, the fearsome, the magical, the envious, the secretive, the devious, and more. Being a twin. Fun, right? Think about it. *What could go wrong?"*

--From the Foreword by Merry Jones

All Celestial Echo Press publications are available at Barnes & Noble and other fine bookshops, and online at amazon.com.

www.ingramcontent.com/pod-product-compliance
Lightning Source LLC
Chambersburg PA
CBHW052025220726
48293CB00015B/280